TO LIVE ANOTHER DAY

A NOVEL

NEW JEWISH FICTION

ELIZABETH ROSENBERG

ISBN 9789493322066 (ebook)

ISBN 9789493322042 (paperback)

ISBN 9789493322059 (hardcover)

Publisher: Amsterdam Publishers, The Netherlands

info@amsterdampublishers.com

To Live Another Day is part of the series New Jewish Fiction

PROLOGUE

"Friendship is born at that moment when one person says to another,
"What! You too? I thought I was the only one."
—C.S. Lewis

In a makeshift playgroup, through signs posted in various synagogues and community centers in Brooklyn, three adorable little girls named Ray, May, and Fay met in September of 1978. When they found out that their names rhymed, the girls were elated and decided it was a sign that they were meant to be best friends. They attended different schools and colleges, but always stuck together. Where there was one, there was sure to be the other two. Though their families had nothing in common, nor did they live in walking distance to each other, the girls became close friends.

They varied in temperament. Ray was usually the ringleader, the one with the plan, while May was timid and the most reluctant to ever break the rules. Fay was the middleman and could be persuaded by either of the two. Often, she was the tiebreaker and endured alternating heaps of praise and curses from Ray and Fay.

Physically, the girls were also nothing alike. Ray possessed warm, olive-dark skin that tanned well, and was tall and lanky. She had dark eyes and straight, jet-black hair that reached the middle of her back.

As a teenager, she grew to five feet eight inches tall and 117 pounds, was lean and athletic, with little to no body fat to impede her natural tendency to jump, run, or climb, even when it wasn't necessary. Keeping up with Ray's energy level was often a daunting task. May complained about it bitterly at least three times a week to anyone who would listen. In response, Ray would smile and offer her a hug. Most of the time, that was enough to placate May.

Fay was the acknowledged beauty of the group. Almost as tall as Ray, with dark-brown, curly hair and obsidian eyes that sparkled. She was curvier and more feminine than Ray. Fay had an effortlessly innate sense of style and grace and was often compared to a young Elizabeth Taylor. She claimed her poise was a genetic gift from her impossibly sophisticated Hungarian grandmother, Ava, who was always elegantly clad. As a child, Fay loved playing dress-up in her grandmother's massive walk-in closet for hours on end. Every shoe, hat, scarf, dress, and suit seemed to have a story behind it, and she was always fascinated to hear Ava talk about her wardrobe.

May was the anomaly in the group. She was petite, barely five feet tall, had a heart-shaped face, tiny button nose, sky-blue eyes, and chin-length, light-blonde hair. Her sedentary lifestyle and lack of variety in her meals contributed to her slightly rounded tummy, hips, and thighs, which did not bother her at all. By nature, she was a calm person. Growing up as an only child only reinforced this. Often playing alone, she became creative and imaginative on her own. She would stage elaborate tea parties for her Barbie dolls. As she got closer to adolescence, she would endlessly watch episodes of her favorite TV shows and copy to a tee how Tooty, Natalie, Blair and Jo on *The Facts of Life* dealt with life. Like those tv characters, May learned that in the absence of caring parents, she could count on her best friends Ray and Fay. While neither friend was a perfect substitute for what was lacking in her family, Ray and Fay were the closest thing to sisters.

All three girls attended a different yeshiva system, a private Jewish day school. Each one had its own specific cultural orientation: from Fay's Orthodox to May's Conservative and Ray's Modern Orthodox school. While they also had other friends in their formative years, they gravitated towards each other and unconditionally supported one another. They got together every single Sunday and on national holidays. They met on Fridays at the library, and most Thursday nights throughout the winter season, they skated at Rockefeller Center or at SkyRink in Chelsea Piers in Manhattan. As they got older, their interests broadened. They enjoyed attending concerts together, having dinner, shopping, the theater, and occasionally going to museums when Fay's European-born grandmother Ava, insisted they acquire culture.

Because none of the girls felt a close connection to their own siblings, they chose instead to rely on their friendship to navigate their lives. It should have remained that way for them forever, sharing happy and hectic moments of life, whether it was the torment of adolescence and teen years, their trip to Poland, graduation from high school and college, weddings and anniversary celebrations, or the experience of motherhood and married life. However, it all almost ended. There was no going back, the lives of many people would be irrevocably changed when Fay after nearly twenty years of covering the truth, finally found the courage and filed a lawsuit, accusing Danny Salem, Ray's oldest brother and May's husband, of raping her on the night May gave birth to her first child.

1

"Our lives begin to end the day we are silent about what matters."
—Martin Luther King Jr.

1990

Ray had been unhappy for as long as she could remember. Beneath the surface of her pretty exterior, she was insecure, afraid and lonely. It was mostly because she felt like an outsider in her own home. May and Fay often straight-out told her they envied her status as the daughter of the distinguished plastic surgeons Isaac and Victoria Salem. For Ray, however, there was no joy in it. She chose her coordinated outfits with a personal shopper at Saks, worked out with her personal trainer in her designer leggings and hoodies at a private gym, and went to the synagogue on Saturdays, more to please her Egyptian- and Syrian-born, Sephardic grandparents and less because she wanted to pray or see the boys from the community.

Her parents were never home but always together. In their insular community in Brooklyn they were an anomaly. Both had the same drive and ambition and were determined to shed any semblance to their roots. That they were born in Aleppo in Syria and came to America as children must have affected their choices, of that Ray was sure. Instinctively, she understood early on that she was merely an

5

accessory for her parents. For one glorious moment, she remembered spending time with her mother as they appeared together in a mommy-and-me charity event held in Deal, New Jersey, where nearly all their neighbors summered in magnificent homes. For Ray, the day was magical until it wasn't—it was patently obvious to her that for the camera, her gorgeous, slim, and sophisticated mother was invested in hugging her and talking to her. The instant the videographer turned elsewhere, so did her mother.

Ray was a resilient child and soon got into a daily routine of hanging out in the kitchen and discussing her problems and fears with the live-in housekeeper Lucía, who was warm and affectionate. She was later replaced by a bona fide therapist when Ray turned 11 and appeared to be angry all the time, as well as socially withdrawn and anxious. Ray knew she was different, certainly different from her brothers.

She was grateful for her best friends. They were the sisters and cousins she never had, her dearest, most trustworthy friends whose support and tolerance of her moods made her life just that more tolerable. However, even to them she could never verbalize what was wrong with her life. She hid it from them as much as she hid it from herself.

Sometimes Ray wondered what was wrong with her. She had access to everything money could buy, but what she really craved was what she saw in the Zweig and Goldman homes. In Fay's house, family was the most important element on which everything pivoted. Ray loved going there for Shabbat, which Fay referred to as Shabbos, especially when Fay's aunts and uncles, cousins, and grandparents were there. There was something so incredibly satisfying about sitting there among a few generations, listening, and watching them interact, pretending that she was one of them. She even loved the Ashkenazic food the men ate so heartily, from the matriarch grandmother known as *Bobby* Ava whose stuffed cabbage, potato kugel, *kokosh* chocolate cake, and gefilte fish was all so different from the Sephardic *kibbeh*, *muffaletta*, Moroccan cigars, Hawaij-spiced chicken, platters of *mazza* and *madjari* rice that Lucía prepared every single week.

Everyone was always so animated at the Zweig table. It didn't matter if four or 14 extra people showed up for one of the elaborate Shabbos meals. In fact, Zak, Fay's father, had a propensity for doing just that. He would often spontaneously invite a few men for kiddush, which meant that at 11:45 on Shabbos morning, Suzi, Fay's mother, could expect any number of men ready to make a blessing and have a preview of her Shabbos meal. They would enjoy her sponge cake and Linzer torte cookies, then proceed to sample the *schmaltz* herring and *kichel* crackers. Zak only had to tell Suzi once that he poignantly remembered his own father bringing guests home from the shul, inviting them to sample his mother's simmering hot cholent: the hearty stew that was the mainstay of their lunch. Suzi never let him down. Although Zak never talked about his birth parents, she knew from her sisters-in-law that he and his brothers suffered enormously when their parents died in a tragic car accident. Suzi innately was drawn to her husband's tragedy, wanting to 'fix' him and somehow make up for his loss. This strong need to do something was a pattern of behavior that Suzi and her sisters were innately familiar with; an offshoot of feeling helpless as a function of living with parents who survived catastrophic events. To please her husband, Suzi got into a routine of preparing two large Crock-Pots on Friday afternoon, filled to the brim with pearled barley, beans, potatoes, succulent beef short ribs, onions and garlic, and huge marrow bones cut exactly to her specifications by her butcher. She would season it liberally with Hungarian smoked paprika. Overnight, it would morph into a fantastic stew—a cholent, like that eaten traditionally in Europe by thousands of observant Jews who did not cook on Shabbos.

When Suzi would see the men approaching her house, she would open her oven, take out the food, and set it all on the buffet table. All were welcome and there was always more than enough.

On Friday night, when welcoming Shabbos into the home, the table was beautifully set, with candles burning brightly. It didn't seem to matter to anyone that the flatware wasn't Buccellati, the stemware Waterford or the dishes Versace, nor did anyone seem to think it was necessary to banish the youngest children from the table. They were enthralled by the special treats, little gifts, books, and puzzles they always found at their seat. Not once did the children seem to be in the way. On the contrary, their presence was revered, especially when Bobby Ava and her husband, Imre, were there. She, a Holocaust survivor, would look around at all those gathered. The expression on her face was indescribable. In her thick Hungarian accent, she would say, "Never in my vildest dreams did I think I vould survive Auschwitz and live to see so many generations." Nearly everyone present would tear up. Suzi would solemnly say, *"Baruch Hashem* [praise God]." And everyone at the table would repeat it.

Even when it was just the immediate family of Fay and her siblings, it was wonderful and satisfying to Ray. In her mind, it was a glorious 24 hours. Being Shomer Shabbos, Sabbath observant, defined how Fay's family observed the Shabbat: there was no TV, going to the movies, going for a blowout or mani-pedi, no getting in a car or using electronic devices. Ray sat with a real family at a table where both parents actually talked to their daughters and instilled in them the traditions of their religion. After the meal, they would all play Rummy, Clue or Scrabble, and Suzi always had snacks prepared for them. It was very different from life in Ray's home. Her parents, while committed to their religion as Jews, simply followed traditional Sephardic customs which included a fierce devotion to the Rabbi and the community needs. For the most part, the Salems' life revolved around other priorities; work, vacation, or entertaining other doctors with whom they were conspiring to collaborate with. There was a typical Friday night Shabbat meal, but immediately thereafter everyone in the Salem home did their own thing. Although the Salems remained in the Sephardic community—and even that was subject to change—they had very little time for their children and no time whatsoever for extended family with whom they believed they no longer had anything in common. Instead, they provided their daughter and three sons with all the luxuries they themselves never had growing up. Later in life, Ray understood the desperation that drove her parents to such extreme behavior, but growing up, she resented them for never being present in her life and was jealous of her best friends. She was also terrified of her father's fist, which he routinely and often used on her brothers. She feared that she and her mother would be next if they ever stepped out of line.

It was virtually impossible for Ray to understand how Fay could be unhappy or why she ignored her younger sisters, Bethie and Deenie, who seemed so nice whenever she saw them. According to Fay, one of her biggest outrages was that her parents had very specific plans for her future,which college she would attend, and what type of boy she would be allowed to date and marry. The ultimate goal for her parents was for Fay to be married before her 19th birthday so that Bobby Ava would live to see this milestone. To Ray, these plans seemed ridiculously old-fashioned, like a page out of *Fiddler on the Roof*: the Yiddish writer Sholom Aleichem's depiction of Tevye the Dairyman's extreme efforts to make 'matches' for his daughters in the late 1800's in Russia. And yet, in spite of these archaic restrictions that Fay resented, Ray would have happily become Orthodox and anything else the Zweigs would have wanted her to be if she was their daughter, but alas she was not, except in her fantasies. There, she was a beloved, important daughter who was never lonely, unsure, or guilt-ridden about anything. More importantly, in those fantasies—many of which occupied her mind during class—she was wanted, loved and cherished, never belittled, humiliated, ignored or criticized.

In May's house, though the Goldmans were almost never home, Ray fantasized about the way in which the home was a backdrop for everyone's comfort. Every room was arranged with a La-Z-Boy chair right near the TV. The coffee table had nicks and scratches, the velvet sofas were worn, but everything was arranged in a convenient and cozy way. It was nothing like Ray's decorated home, which was replete with cold marble, custom bookcases of the finest burl wood, and other luxurious furniture, all exquisitely arranged but rarely used. That May was lonely or emotionally starving was something Ray never saw.

2

"I never lose. I either win or learn."
—Nelson Mandela

Fay turned the key and let herself into the small, semi-attached brick house that was her home ever since she could remember. Every room she passed on her way into the kitchen was beautifully decorated and immaculate. If the President of the United States or the long awaited Messiah would ever show up, her mother was fully prepared. Suzi spent her days food shopping, cooking, baking, cleaning, organizing, and rearranging every surface in their home: books, clothing, furniture, flowers, and odds and ends. In her own way, she was more like a mom depicted on *Ozzie and Harriet, Father Knows Best*, or *The Donna Reed Show*—television programs from the 1950s that glorified the average American stay at home mom—than she was a homemaker in the 1970s. Fay never thought twice about her mother's choices; in her mind, her mother represented all Orthodox Jewish-American housewives. Her mother was like her aunts and their closest friends, but infinitely different from Ray and May's moms, both of whom were never home.

Fay, wearing her navy-and-gray school uniform coordinated with navy opaque tights and navy suede loafers, found her way into the kitchen. It was a large room and the hub of the house. Suzi, like her mother Ava, had wonderful taste and enjoyed cooking. Limited to living on a budget, she used her creativity. Though often impatient, she waited four years until she could buy a Persian carpet for her dining room floor and raw silk turquoise living room drapes. For the most part, her demeanor towards her mother, husband, and Fay was upbeat, positive, warm, and relaxed. She appeared to most people to be blessed with a good nature and never compared herself to her more affluent friends, neighbors, sisters, or cousins. In an era when most people had brown wood kitchen cabinetry, Suzi Zweig had white cabinets. Her kitchen was her domain and she appeared quite content in her role as mother and wife, but not necessarily as a daughter.

Fay found her mother on the phone engrossed in a conversation. This was exactly where she had left her at 8:05 a.m., when her dad drove her to school. It sounded like her mom was talking to one of her sisters. She wasn't sure who was on the other end of the phone, because she didn't understand a word of Hungarian, which her mother spoke fluently. Suzi, her sisters Judy and Magda, and many others of her generation learned Hungarian from their immigrant mothers, most of whom took emotional solace in speaking their mother tongue as it served to remind them of where they came from, connecting them to their homeland, childhood, and family, including relatives who perished in the Holocaust. Their mother, Ava, was determined to remain loyal to her roots, often describing in vivid detail the life she led before she and her sisters were separated from their family and deported as teenagers to Auschwitz, the notorious concentration camp in Poland. She, never once described the 11 months she endured in Auschwitz. Her younger sister, Kati, shared more with her daughters, as did her older sister, Zita. Instead, Ava would opt to spend many hours on a Shabbos afternoon, painting images with words to describe her familial roots to her daughters. She would painstakingly describe how she grew up, how she helped her sisters-in-law with their babies and her mother with the endless housework. She talked so much about her own mother, DevoraLeba, that her three daughters truly felt like they knew their sainted grandmother who had perished at the age of 40. Though her modern, American-born daughters couldn't remotely relate, they listened dutifully as she described the tutor who came weekly to teach her and her sisters the German language. She explained how her father, Naftuli Baruch, was a Hasid who encouraged his children to study, both the girls and the boys. As a diamond merchant, he traveled frequently to Switzerland and Belgium and always brought back unique gifts for his ten children. Ava recounted how reading was her passion. Her crowning moment was when she was able to read Thomas Mann's *The Magic Mountain* in German. To hear Ava talk was to be imbued with the impression that she grew up in a villa in a cosmopolitan city. That was how she paid tribute to and honored her family—by glamorizing and embellishing every detail of her childhood. At the same time, she was ever so grateful to live in America. She loved democracy, revered nearly every American president except for Roosevelt—whom she felt, failed to act aggressively on any number of plausible rescue plans presented to him and tried hard to find balance between living in the present as an American citizen and in the past as a Holocaust survivor.

Ava, like most immigrants, never truly mastered the English language in all its nuances, but did a good job expressing herself nonetheless. That her daughters Suzi, Judy and Magda were trilingual, speaking English, Hebrew, and Hungarian fluently, was something she was pleased about. She never stopped admiring the way in which they diligently did their English and Hebrew homework. Often, she would feel sad that she couldn't help them and would simply sit alongside them for moral support as they struggled with difficult assignments.

Fay instinctively understood that her mother and her aunts, Judy and Magda, had a complicated relationship with their mother. It seemed like they were almost always worried about her. It wasn't anything specific, because Bobby Ava and her second husband, Imre, were both healthy and independent. Rather, their obsessive worry for their mother seemed to be a remnant from their childhood as children of Holocaust survivors. They worried that their mother was depressed, or had nightmares, flashbacks and survivor's guilt. This legacy, along with resiliency, courage, loyalty, commitment, and religious devotion was transmitted from Ava to Suzi, Judy and Magda, and to their daughters as well, including Fay. Only 25 years later did they come to know that scientific evidence existed to support the theory of the transmission of trauma from Holocaust survivors to their children. Epigenetics would further explain that this profound trauma was partly biological, and could genetically affect subsequent generations of Holocaust survivors. However, in the 1950s and 1960s, when Suzi, her sisters and their first cousins were growing up in Brooklyn, they never questioned their upbringing. They simply felt compelled to be the best daughters they could be to somehow make up to their mother for the horrific numbers tattooed on her forearm, for the unspeakable losses and nightmares, and for the disbelief that their mother was one of those who had lost everything, merely because she, like 450,000 other Hungarian Jews, was a prisoner of war until the Allies liberated the camps. Then the challenge and struggle to survive really started for their mother and aunts.

"Hi Mom," Fay said tentatively, not wanting to interrupt what might have been a genuine crisis.

"Oh, darling," cried her mother in earnest. "I can't believe you are home already! Wait, let me hang up."

"Magda," she said into the phone breathlessly in English, "Faygala is home from school. I must go now. I guess we will talk about it in the morning."

Suzi hung up the phone and turned to Fay, who from the age of three would not respond to any version of her name except "Fay." Her mother never got the memo. Though Suzi tried to please her daughter, she would lapse into calling her "Faygala" all the time, sounding more like her own mother rather than a first-generation American.

Suzi brought out a platter of sliced strawberries and honeydew and sat down to hear about Fay's day. She never offered her girls cookies or snacks, simply following the strict rules Ava set in motion decades earlier. Ava was like a drill sergeant when it came to watching the figures of the girls—and later women—in the family, especially Magda's girls Dani and Dini, who loved to eat. Though

Suzi was not overweight, she worried that her daughter Bethie had a tendency to become chubby—inheriting those genes from her father's family of course—and decided the best way to approach the situation would be to put everyone in the household on a diet rather than make Bethie self-conscious. It was something she discussed daily with Magda, especially around holiday time in the spring and fall when they would go shopping at Borland in Williamsburg for the little girls and at Mr. Martins for the preteens.

Suzi, Judy, and Magda, with Ava taking center stage, treated these shopping expeditions like a religious pilgrimage to Mecca. They would scour the racks for days on end and emerge triumphantly, assured that the eight granddaughters of Ava Kertesz would look like European princesses. Ava would then buy them the most elegant coordinated luxurious accessories at Bonwit Teller or B. Altman's, often depriving herself of new clothing, saving money for months on end. Her granddaughters, she insisted, would all wear the finest Italian kid-leather gloves and lace socks, satin headbands, or woolen berets, coordinated with their coats and shoes. When questioned by her sisters why she went to such extreme lengths to dress her granddaughters in such finery, her answer was always the same: "So I can erase the images of the children in Auschwitz." It was that important to her and she didn't care if anyone understood her reason.

In their small, crowded shul, reminiscent of a European *shtiebel* [little house]—as it was just a room in a *shtieb* [house]—nearly the entire congregation waited on Rosh Hashanah and Pesach to see the girls make their biannual debut. Ava, seated promptly for the start of prayers at 8:00 a.m., would look each daughter and granddaughter up and down as they entered the shul. She would carefully close her *Tzena-Rena* [the women's Bible] or Yiddish-translated *machzor* prayer book and look at her gems. Each of them would wait anxiously to see if Ava would smile or frown. Magda's girls, held in their stomachs for the duration of the inspection. If Ava smiled, they all breathed a sigh of relief, but if Ava merely pasted a superficial smile on her face, the girls would be miserable. Fay was glad she was slim. Bobby Ava always smiled at her.

Fay, like her sister Deenie, didn't particularly care about what she ate. She loved her mother's elaborate Shabbos, *yom tov* holiday meals, and her weeknight dinners. It was Bethie who minded—she wanted fried food and snacks, rich desserts, and delicacies that she was introduced to in her friends' homes and sleepaway camp. Bethie was happiest when she had access to bags of potato chips or Carvel soft serve ice cream, items that were strictly forbidden in their home, treated as if they were as unkosher as ham or bacon. Bethie absolutely detested her mother's healthy menu: the poached halibut without sauce, the grilled chicken without skin or ketchup, the fresh salad without oil, and fruit desserts without sorbet. She became adept at eating outside of the house to satisfy her cravings. Often, she would babysit long hours on Sundays or do homework for other kids to earn money to buy grilled cheese sandwiches and tomato soup at the little luncheonette near school that was owned by two Polish Holocaust survivors whose daughters also attended yeshiva. Their parents as a direct result of their wartime experiences wanted to shield their children from the world at large, among only Jewish children and not mixed in with the general population in the district public school.

3

"The woman who walks alone is likely to find herself in places no one
has ever been."
—Albert Einstein

May came home from school and put her book bag down. She took
off her Calvin Klein jacket, hung it up carefully on a hook in the foyer
and went straight into the kitchen. She poured herself a glass of
orange juice and opened a box of Entenmann's cookies. Before she
knew it, the chocolate chip cookies were finished. Feeling slightly
nauseous and guilty for devouring useless calories, she decided to go
for a run before tackling her homework and thinking about dinner.
As she turned on her Walkman and adjusted the volume, she
instantly felt better, listening and singing along with Rick Springfield,
Michael Jackson and Whitney Houston.

In between songs, she could not suppress her maudlin thoughts
about how much she hated her home life. Not once in 12 years of
school had she come home to find her mother waiting for her,
greeting her with enthusiasm. It was always the same routine. Her
mom worked part-time at a museum, volunteered at a nursing home,
and often met up in the evening with her friends for dinner and a
movie. On a rare occasion, she would notice May and offer to go to

the mall, but May knew from past experience that at the last minute, when they were already in the car on Flatbush Avenue, minutes away from Kings Plaza, the largest mall in Brooklyn, her mother would change her mind and the trip would be relegated to "another time."

Most nights, May ate tuna fish from the can or ordered pizza or Chinese food. She wondered, with a sinking feeling, what her best friends would think if they knew that she ate unkosher food. She knew her parents definitely did but only outside the house. In the house, they kept kosher, but not at all equivalent to what she observed at Fay's house, where there were two completely different sets of dishes, pots and pans, and even two sinks—one designated strictly for dairy food and one for meat.

There was never any food in May's house, mainly because both her parents ate out a lot and never considered where that left her. It was as if she had no needs simply because she was an only child; she was expected to figure it all out on her own. They weren't mean people, just ignorant of the needs of a child born to them 14 years after they married. By that point, their lives had become a comfortable routine, which they had no desire to change to accommodate a child. May did not have a clue how to cook and didn't have the time or desire to become Julia Childs. Maybe one day, as a wife and mother, but for now, she had no interest in cooking for herself. It was just too pathetic. Often, she would arrange to do homework with Ray or Fay and eat dinner at their houses a few times a week. Even Lucía's boring and predictable Mexican-flavored Sephardic food was better than what she could scrounge up by herself. Certainly, eating at Fay's house was a treat. Every dinner, even on an average Tuesday night, was prepared with so much care and love; whether it was broiled chicken and salad or hamburger with string beans and almonds, it was always delicious, hot, and freshly made. Suzi treated her like a daughter and when given notice that May was coming for dinner, would always make her favorite: Uncle Ben's rice with tiny French peas, and sautéed mushrooms and onions. She served only small quantities of the rice, since it was a starch. Fay openly laughed at her mother's dread of starch, as if it were the bogeyman, but May was touched that Suzi would go to such great lengths to please her by cooking food she didn't really want her family to eat, simply because it made May happy.

Tonight, however, she was on her own again, and it didn't feel good at all. Aborting the run when it got dark, May went back home. Again, she headed into the kitchen, this time to devour a container of Friendly's mint chocolate chip ice cream: the only one in the freezer and definitely not her favorite flavor.

From a young age, May decided that if she could, she would marry one of Ray's older brothers. She had no particular loyalty to her own American Jewish roots and found the Salem family lifestyle to be warm, spiritual, exotic and exciting. She knew she would have to dedicate at least three hours a day every single day of her life if she wanted to look like all the girls in the Syrian community, whose members referred to as SY. No Syrian guy, much less any of the Salem brothers, would ever look at her unless she was a perfect size four with a toned and tanned body, accompanied by flawless skin, courtesy of monthly facials, and the best blonde highlights that Ray swore only Mustafa could produce. That look would almost certainly give her instant acceptance into the large, insulated, tight-knit Sephardic community once she proved that she would follow the rules. May was ready for that and hoped that by the time she was 17 her life as a Salem bride would begin.

She would be a very different mother than her own—totally devoted, anticipating all of her children's needs and getting involved in school plays and functions. She would make her husband eager to come home from work, because she would be a great wife. She would make everyone proud by being a model daughter-in-law and the best sister-in-law ever, and she would wear the same designer clothes as Ray. She was even willing to give up her edgy, ripped jeans that she lived in day in, day out. Without a doubt, she knew she would adhere to the rituals of *mikveh*: the purity bath married women immersed in monthly, following the end of their menstrual cycle. These— alongside keeping kashrut [the Jewish dietary laws] and lighting the Shabbat candles—were the most important commandments directed at women in order to keep the family safe and well. She understood from Ray that the Sephardic community, especially the elders who illegally immigrated to the United States from Aleppo or Damascus in the 1950s, were very spiritual and believed fiercely in these traditions and she admired that spirit and loyalty. Fay on the other hand, came from an Ashkenaz family that appeared much less spiritual and more inclined to follow rules determined 5,000 years ago from the Torah that didn't factor in modern times that one day you would be able to generate light on the Shabbat by flicking a switch and not laboring for hours. That meant that in Fay's world, on Shabbos, time stood still—there was no usage of electricity of any kind, handling money or traveling anywhere.

May grew up celebrating only the High Holidays. The life she saw in Ray and Fay's communities would be a welcome change from the morass she grew up in, much more so Ray's, although she loved lots about Fay's family too. Often, May would daydream about being pregnant and pushing her perfect Perego baby carriage, all while talking to Ray about dinner and winter vacation plans in Cancun, Mexico, or Isla Verde in Puerto Rico. Those winter destinations were so popular that the SY community leaders arranged annually for a traveling Sefer Torah; the complete Torah scrolls would accompany them so that the men could attend services three times a day, exactly as they did at home in their Gravesend neighborhood, where a vast majority lived. Kosher catered meals were arranged too, so that the 50 to 60 families would not be inconvenienced whatsoever while on winter break.

Ray had invited May along numerous times and while she stuck out like a sore thumb due to her pale white skin, she was enthralled with all of it: the fabulous pool outfits, the designer sunglasses coordinating with expensive bikinis not meant to ever get wet, the daytime and nighttime resort wear, the food, the plans to raise money for the synagogue extension and the big families happily engaging with each other. It confirmed to her that she desperately wanted to become part of the Syrian community. She could put her entire childhood and miserable, dull life behind her, knowing she would have a happier, fuller life as an adult. She naively assumed that Ray would eventually embrace the community, family, and lifestyle she was born into, even if right now she openly despised her glamorous parents, whose definition of home was a place to sleep. That would be the icing on the cake—having Ray as her sister.

Sitting down to do homework, May's mind wandered. In her home, she was the de facto judge and intermediary between her two warring parents, who didn't see eye to eye on anything. Almost daily, they drew her into their arguments, forcing her to choose one over the other. She mostly pitied her father, a subdued man who worked extremely long hours as an accountant, not only during tax season but all year round, often drowning his melancholy in alcohol. He thought she was unaware of his habits: choosing to sleep in the spare bedroom and drinking as soon as he came home from work, even more so on the weekends. He was a quiet, sad drunk and didn't bother a soul.

For her mother, May had some empathy. She had endured six miscarriages before finally giving birth to her. Almost daily, she would remind May of this. Rather than spoil and adore that long-awaited baby, she blithely ignored her child—as well as her husband—spending her time on charity events and friends.

For the umpteenth time May wondered why she wasn't worthy of being loved by her parents. *Was she such a disappointment?* she wondered. *Was she not cute enough or smart enough? What would she need to be in order for them to notice her?* She didn't have the answer. Tears rolled down her face.

4

"Pessimism is a luxury a Jew can never allow himself."
—Golda Meier

Ray thought about her future. She had no great desire to go to college and definitely no desire to become a doctor like her parents. Looking around at her synagogue friends who were flirting outrageously with boys, she decided it was time for her to find a boyfriend. This would be her future: like most of the girls in her community, she would have a family and that would define who she would be. She was afraid to tell Fay and May, who talked incessantly about their SAT scores and jobs. She assumed they were on the college-and-career track and would attend Brooklyn College or maybe Hunter College in the city.

Feeling somewhat left out, Ray confided in her friend Mazal, who was also Sephardic. Mazal was honored to be invited to Ray's house. She was a beautiful girl who unfortunately could not attract any of the better boys in the community, simply because her parents were not wealthy. In the community, it was an unspoken rule that you needed to be wealthy to attract someone wealthy. All that the Shami's could fall back on was that their family were relatives of the well known Gindi's—that was their claim to fame. It gave her father a job, but not much more. Being Ray Salem's friend on the other hand, was something Mazal knew could work to her advantage. It could help her gain notice in her own community. Moreover, it was a chance for her to get to know Ray's older brothers—a bonus opportunity she would die for.

Together, the girls hatched a strategic plan; they would immediately go on the popular Atkins all-protein diet, attend the gym more often and start going to all the synagogue events to check out the boys. After Mazal left, Ray went into the kitchen to explain her dietary needs to Lucía who looked startled and upset at Ray's requests.

"What you mean, Ray?" she said tentatively. "Something is wrong with my food?" Ray felt sorry for Lucía, whom she loved merely because she was a constant in her life. Rather than hurt her feelings, she decided to include her in her plans.

"Lucía," she said warmly, "you know I am 16 years old, and I never had a boyfriend?"

"Si, that is true," responded Lucía. "So you get a boyfriend and bring him home and I cook for him too."

"Well," said Ray, "it's not that simple. I was talking to my friend Mazal and she said that there are a lot of girls and every one of them is looking for a boyfriend. So, I have to look better than them or I won't be able to get the right boy."

"Oh," said Lucía, who sounded like she understood but in fact was perplexed. *What in the world did Ray need to do?* she thought to herself. *Did she not know whose daughter she was or the house she lived in? Any boy would want her.* She kept these thoughts to herself because she wasn't paid to give her opinion. "So, how can I help?" she asked.

"Yes!" said Ray jubilantly. "That's what I was just about to tell you. I need to lose ten pounds very fast, before Purim—you know, the Jewish Halloween. I need to be sexy and show off my figure."

"Ray," admonished Lucía, "por favor, no use words like that please. And you don't need to lose ten pounds. You beautiful like this."

"Lucía, please listen to me," said Ray in a semi-hysterical voice. "The girls are all crazy skinny. Everyone wants to look like Cheryl

Tiegs or Claudia Schiffer. I am never going to be blonde or have blue eyes, but I am going to be stunning. So, here's the deal. I need to eat chicken, beef, or fish every night for dinner. No empanadas, no dumplings, egg rolls, potatoes, or rice. Just protein. And for breakfast, just eggs. And for lunch I need you to make me a huge salad with pieces of turkey, no dressing except oil and lemon. Okay? Can you do that for me?"

Lucía looked like she was about to keel over.

"I... I..." she sputtered. "Okay, but this sounds mucho loco to me, just crazy."

"Don't worry, Lucía," reassured Ray. "It's just until I get to 107 pounds. Then I will go right back to eating all your amazing food. I can't give up your tacos, tortillas and guacamole!"

Ray left the room, satisfied that Lucía would help her realize her goal. It never crossed her mind to reach out to her own mother for support or advice. It also never occurred to her that the feeling of being in control by restricting her calories might have a deleterious effect on her. Long after Purim and Passover, Ray was still limiting her caloric intake and doing away entirely with carbs. She never noticed when she got down to 100 pounds, neither did her parents. It was only when May and Fay insisted on a "chat", that Ray had an inkling that maybe she needed to stop the diet.

"But Fay," she protested weakly, "look at my cheekbones. Aren't they amazing?"

"Actually, no," said Fay with a sad look in her eyes. "You look weak and gaunt. My family is crazy skinny-conscious and even Bobby Ava said you are too skinny when she saw you last week."

"May," pleaded Ray, turning to her best friend, "is that really true? Do I look bad?"

May, ever the peacemaker, lied to Ray. "No," she said, "not that bad. More like you just got over a stomach flu and need to recover."

"Oh, okay," said Ray, not wanting her best friends to be angry at her. "Then I will. Hey, you guys, please don't worry about me. Honestly, I can stop this."

No sooner than ten minutes after the girls left, Ray went for a one hour run, followed by two hours in the gym on the elliptical. Then she got home and sat down to a small piece of chicken, carefully peeling off the skin. After finishing her chicken, she drank three glasses of water with lemon and turned on the TV to watch reruns of *The Facts of Life*. Like May, it was her favorite show. The girls on the show never had to deal with parents like hers. Instead, they all lived together with Mrs. Garrett while attending boarding school in a remote town in upstate New York. Similar to Tootie and Jo, she had her own crew, even if she didn't live with them.

While her stomach grumbled, she looked in the mirror and smiled with enormous approval.

"So what if I'm hungry," she challenged herself. "I look amazing. This is my body and I have every right to look this good."

She didn't see what others were seeing: that she was on her way to anorexia.

5

"I can be changed by what happened to me,
but I refuse to be reduced by it."
—Maya Angelou

Fay was in a terrible dilemma affecting her sleep and mood. The SAT test was coming soon and decisions had to be made about the year abroad in Israel, college, and her career. On the one hand, she desperately wanted to please her entire family and become a respectable teacher or speech therapist, but on the other, she adored fashion and wanted to design clothing. She knew it would not go well if she would try to get her parents' support. She could predict exactly how the conversation would go with her hysterical mother.

"But Faygala," her mother would say in a high-pitched voice, setting the stage for the pas de deux dance that was commencing, "do you know even one *frum* [religiously observant] girl in the fashion industry?" Suzi would continue, her voice building up to a mild crescendo. "Let's just say by a miracle, by an absolute miracle, you landed an internship while attending the prestigious Fashion Institute of Technology and now the clock has changed and sundown, when Shabbos starts at 4:08 p.m. How will you get permission from your boss to leave work at noon to get home before sundown? What happens if they want you to work on a Saturday? And where does that leave you on the holidays, the *yomim tovim,* when they fall on a weekday and are subject to the same rules as Shabbos? They will never hire you if they know in advance what your requirements are, and if they do, in two weeks time, when they see a pattern of you developing a headache or calling in sick nearly every single Friday, they will fire you before you can even pass 'go' and collect $200 in Monopoly money! And that, Faygala," Suzi would say hysterically, tears pouring out of her eyes, "doesn't even factor in your reputation. You would be working among *goyim,* Gentiles, and probably a few homosexual designers!"

With that, Suzi would beg her daughter to be smart and choose a safe career—one that would not interfere with her responsibilities as a wife and mother. Fay knew all this and more. The real world, outside their insulated community, was just not for her. Her parents made it patently clear to her, Bethie and Deenie that the world was not a safe place. One only had to reflect on Bobby Ava's experience. They would grimly remind their daughters that you could never trust anyone but family.

Growing up exposed to parents coping with PTSD, Suzi too was always fearful and vigilant. Without understanding why she felt so scared, Suzi took every precaution to guarantee that she and her family were safe, never once connecting her own childhood experiences with her adult behavior. Rather, every night, she routinely checked the elaborate alarm system in the house to assure that in the event of an emergency, the central station would send a silent signal and the 70th precinct policemen would dispatch to their home on East Eighth Street. For an added layer of divine protection, Suzi insisted the girls all say their night prayers, the *Kriat Shema Al Hamita,* with reverence. During the day, she exercised caution too, especially when she drove uptown to shop at Bloomingdale's with the girls. Like her mother did years before when she headed by bus to shop downtown at A&S and May's department stores, Suzi carefully hid her money in various pockets. And yet, Fay knew that given the opportunity, she could master the challenge of entering a world she was not part of. She wouldn't have to compromise her

26

religious standards; she would not run off with a goy or change in any way. She could still be Fay, because she had her grandmother's backbone. If Bobby Ava survived the war, then nothing would stop her either!

Fay thought about Ava and the myriad challenges she had faced post-Holocaust emigrating with Zaydy Lajos and baby Magda to America in 1949. From the stories that Ava herself told, Fay knew that it had to have been extremely stressful to leave behind everything that was familiar in Hungary in exchange for the vast unknown that was New York City, without any resources, language or parents to support and help her adjust. But Ava demonstrated an iron-clad resolve to face those challenges, and presumably she never once lost her way. Fay decided she had to present her case and get her grandmother's opinion. *If she got her grandmother on board, would that help?* she wondered idly. In many ways, Ava, with her European background, was far more sophisticated and open-minded than her three daughters. Despite having access to and the advantage of growing up in the most fascinating city in the world, Suzi and her sisters remained provincial. They adhered to a set of American rules imposed upon them in school that alternately mystified and amused Ava, whose family background was far more Hasidic and now, having been uprooted from her hometown, chose to live life by her own, inconsistent, modified rules. She routinely mocked the school's rigorous Hebrew curriculum, including requiring her daughters to study the five books of Prophets and the five books of the Torah in great detail, as if they were men studying to become rabbis. She was simply incapable of relating to an educational system so vastly different from what she observed in Bayamare. Instead, as a trauma survivor, whose personal boundaries were cruelly violated, she worked towards restoring her own sense of equilibrium in her own way, which was confusing and contradictory to her American-born daughters. In fact, much of what Ava did was often confusing to her daughters. At any given moment, Ava was strong but also weak, happy but also sad, mature and also childlike, scared but also fearless.

Fay decided she had to plead her case with Bobby. If Bobby was not on her side, she would become a teacher—a nice, safe career choice.

Fay sat in the den, dutifully took off her Dr. Martens before tucking her feet on to the brown velvet couch. She sighed, took out her SAT vocabulary list and randomly started studying the words beginning with the letter "U." She loved learning new words, but some of these were hard. She had no problem with words like "unyielding," "unabashed," or "unilateral"—all of which she could break down somewhat—but words like "ubiquitous" and "unctuous" were an enigma to her. Her nightly goal was to acquire ten new words a day until the test. As an avid reader—she read Tolstoy's *Anna Karenina* and Rand's *Atlas Shrugged* in the ninth grade, simply to please her grandmother, Ava—she typically borrowed an eclectic swath of books from the library, working her way through playwrights like Tennessee Williams and William Inge, novels by James Baldwin, Herman Wouk, John O'Hara, and Theodore Dreiser, to books on the Holocaust like *Night*, *In My Father's Court*, *The Diary of Anne Frank*, *BabiYar*, and *Treblinka*. Like her best friends, she also enjoyed the *Sweet Valley High* and *The Baby-Sitters Club* book series. Those were her guilty pleasures, imagining the life of these girls who never seemed to be plagued with acne, frizzy hair, or a yelling mother.

Every Friday, Suzi would allow her, Ray, and May to go by bus to the Kings Highway library after early dismissal at school. Fay would carefully select six to eight books to read over Shabbos. Reading was her salvation; it transported her to places and people that were totally alien and foreign to her own existence. Fay especially loved reading about complicated relationships, often crying bitter tears when young lovers were separated from each other by circumstances beyond their control. Fay was truly grateful to her mother for picking her up from the library, even though she had many errands and much cooking that needed to be done before Shabbos. For the most part, Suzi was gracious about picking up the girls by car and driving them home, but sometimes, she would get impatient and would start honking halfway down Ocean Avenue if she didn't spot the girls waiting outside. Sometimes Fay regretted the ride; her mother's outbursts were uncomfortable to say the least.

Fay had an excellent grasp of the English language, but she desperately wanted to excel. Similar to her mother and grandmother, she felt compelled to be productive at all times. It almost seemed as if this drive to be perfect was in her DNA. Fay knew intuitively—or maybe it was from all the books that she read—that her mother, who dropped out of college when she got engaged, was counting on her to do all the things she had been deprived of. Suzi rarely said anything negative to her daughters about Ava, but Fay was certain that her mother complained bitterly to her own sisters who understood exactly how she felt. Once, Suzi made a point of telling her that Ava as a grandmother was very different from Ava as a mother. Fay couldn't fathom what her mother meant. To her, Bobby Ava was the quintessential woman of all ages.

Fay had the impression that she was her mother's favorite daughter, or the one she could manipulate the best. Suzi never had to tell her anything twice, once was enough. Fay would do whatever her mother wanted her to do. In some ways, Suzi sometimes acted like she, too, was a survivor. That put Fay in the uncomfortable position of trying to please her mother in the same way that Suzi perfunctorily did with her own mother. As she got older, Fay knew that her mother's mood swings—characterized by outbursts, occasional rage, fears, anxiety, and temperament—were not healthy whatsoever and wished she could talk to someone about the family dynamics that sometimes suffocated her, but to even suggest that she wanted to see a therapist was something Fay knew would drive her mother insane. She could predict how that conversation would go.

"Are you kidding me, Faygala?" Suzi would ask. "Do you want to destroy any chance you have of making a good *shidduch* [Orthodox Jewish system of matchmaking]? Who will want to marry you if they find out you need to see a therapist? Your only problem is that you have it too good!" And with that, Suzi would launch into a monologue about how hard life was for her growing up with parents who were Holocaust survivors. After hearing one or two tales, Fay would swear that she would stop complaining. How could she compete with that?

The next day after school, Fay walked over to her grandmother's house. Bobby Ava lived on a beautiful tree-lined street within walking distance of her daughters. It seemed to Fay that living in close proximity to her family was what made Bobby happy, and nothing was more important than Bobby's happiness. When her beloved Lajos died suddenly, she sold their home, unable to stay there without him. Then, less than a year later, with three little girls to raise, when Imre begged her to marry him and allow him to take care of her, they bought a new home, to start a new life together. Imre had never married, claiming Ava was his one true love from BayaMare, and he fully embraced her and her family. The grandchildren adored him and his attention. He was a wonderful man and Ava had no complaints. The fact that she knew his family from "home" was a great source of comfort to her. They lived together in harmony and enjoyed each other's company, never talking about the past. Imre was a true Hungarian gentleman, not nearly as handsome as Lajos, but he was wealthy and generous. When he was not working, he was busy spoiling Ava—buying her outrageous gifts and looking for ways to make her love him.

Suzi arranged for Fay's after-school visit to Ava, not knowing her daughter's ulterior motive. It was not surprising that Fay would want to see her Bobby, who was getting ready to leave with Imre for Miami Beach for the duration of the winter. All the granddaughters were spending extra time with Ava, who adored the fanfare surrounding her relocation to a warmer climate to avoid the brutal cold. For Ava, the relocation was almost a necessity as the cold winter months in New York almost always invariably triggered horrific memories of the infamous Death March she and her surviving sisters had endured in January, 1945. Walking in minus 1 degree weather, through snow that nearly came up to her emaciated thighs, in a thin prison rag for days on end when she did not have the physical or emotional stamina to walk another step, was a memory she did not want to revisit. Thus, like many survivors of trauma, attempting to avoid reminders of that dreadful time was how Ava dealt with those harrowing memories and she was grateful to Imre that he could afford to whisk her away from New York, even pay for her sister's and daughter's airline tickets so that they could all visit frequently in the sunshine. Suzi was happy that she could give her mother such pleasure merely by sending over a beloved granddaughter, especially Fay, the oldest grandchild, who was tall and thin enough for Ava's Hungarian standards of beauty.

Fay got dressed very carefully in the morning. She was well aware of how her Bobby liked people and things to look perfect. She took her time, brushing her hair until it was shining and totally straight. Then she carefully put on the black velvet headband that Bobby bought her last year. She wore a pleated, woolen skirt with a leather belt that emphasized her tiny waist, a turtleneck sweater and knee-high boots. She knew Bobby would smile when she saw her. Bobby's beautiful brick house, the front of which was a showstopper that nearly everyone passing by looked at, was surrounded by a riot of pastel flowers, surrounded by a lily pond and a bridge crafted to resemble Monet's bridge at Giverny. Fay was glad to know that Ava's outrageous garden made her happy. As she stood at the door, she had a moment of regret and wondered if she was doing the right thing. *Was it fair to her own mother to ask her grandmother to decide her future?* She knew the answer, but decided to ignore her conscience, focusing instead on being enveloped by her grandmother's love.

"Bobby, I am so happy to see you," she said when Ava opened the door.

There stood Ava, at 4:40 p.m. on a Tuesday, wearing a camel-colored woolen A-line dress that accentuated her slim figure. She was five feet five inches tall, 116 pounds, and a very attractive woman with beautiful, expressive chocolate-brown eyes, a sensual mouth, and a patrician nose. On many occasions, people remarked that she resembled the very beautiful exotic Italian actress Sophia Loren and that pleased her. Ava had a flair for clothes. She could take any garment and make it look chic. She got dressed every single day, even if she wasn't going anywhere. She craved and lived by structure and routine. It made her feel normal. It was the antithesis to when she was held captive by the Nazis for nearly a year—subject to perverse, degrading, unspeakable rules, wild dogs, sights and smells she would never forget. Her life now served as a reminder that she was free and in control of her body and her choices. Today, she accessorized her outfit with a simple pair of coral-and-gold earrings, a necklace, and a print silk scarf tied around her neck. She wore sheer nude stockings and black leather pumps. She could have been off to the opera.

"*Hadd nézzek rád drágám*," she cried with pleasure. "*Gyere be drágaságomba. Szép vagy* [you are so pretty]." Lapsing momentarily into Hungarian, Ava forgot that her granddaughter did not understand one word of her mother tongue.

"Come, sit with me in the kitchen while I finish cooking," she said.

"Of course, Bobby," replied Fay animatedly.

She loved being in Bobby's kitchen. Every single thing that came out of the oven was a masterpiece. Ava was not only an amazing baker and cook, but also visually arranged the food artfully and elegantly. It didn't really matter what you ate at Bobby's house, because it always looked so nice. Of course, worrying about her girls' figures and Imre's sugar and cholesterol caused Ava to bake in limited quantities. She only made small batches of delectable pastries—the kipfels, *kokosh* cake and cheese *delkalach* that her own mother made —fearing they would add pounds onto her girls. Yet somehow, she always had something sweet on hand for whenever anyone dropped in.

"Ooh Bobby, what is that delicious smell?" asked Fay.

"Vell darling, I am preparing some food for Miami. You know how particular I am. I really don't like the kosher meat that is available there, so I always bring along my own *fasirt* [spiced ground meat] mix some veal schnitzel, and minute steaks. Later, when Mommy and your aunts come to visit us, they bring more. Vould you like a little taste?"

Fay was not really hungry, but mindful of pleasing Bobby, didn't want to disappoint Bobby, who loved feeding and, conversely, starving her family. "Sure," she said, mustering up enthusiasm. "How could I pass that up, with you going away for so many months? Just a little, please."

Ava took out a plate and served her. The table was already set for dinner with Limoges china. Fay knew that if she opened Bobby's huge Amana refrigerator, the Yarden wine imported from Israel would be chilling, the cucumber salad prepared and the chicken *paprikash* ready to go into the oven at precisely 6:15 p.m., to be served at 7:30 p.m., when Imre walked in the door. Fay reminded herself that one day she would absolutely have to find the time to compile a cookbook with all of Bobby's recipes. For now, she was content watching Ava finish what she was doing and then remove her apron and sit down next to her.

"So tell me darling, vat is going on in your life," Ava asked.

Fay inhaled deeply and decided to take the plunge. "Bobby," she said rather tentatively, "I am in a dilemma. I need to make a decision about my future."

"Vat decision, darling? You vant to be an astronaut or a brain surgeon? You vill get married and have a family, no?" Ava chuckled at her own wit.

"Well it's not exactly like that," said Fay. "Of course I want to get married and have a family! However, I want more than that. Mommy and Daddy also think I should have a career, but they will never agree to the one I want."

Now she had Ava's full attention.

"And vat kind of career do you vant, my darling?"

"Well," said Fay, gulping once, "I want to become a fashion designer."

"A fashion designer, vat a vonderful idea! I could help you," Ava said excitedly. "You know I learned how to sew at home and your great-aunts know how to make patterns and muslins. In our day, a proper young lady learnt at least one language, how to embroider, knit and walk like a lady... but that vas then and this is now... America," she muttered. "Oy vey."

Fay never heard the extraneous commentary. She was astounded. She had never taken the time to imagine what Bobby's reaction might be, but this unconditional support was overwhelming. "Oh my goodness! Really, Bobby? You can't imagine what this means to me! Mommy is worried about what the neighbors will think," she said tearfully. "I don't want her to be mad at me."

"Don't you vorry about Mommy. First show me vat you think you can do. Can you draw something for me, my darling? Or shall ve look in *Vogue* or *Bazaar* and you can show me vat you like in the magazines? After all, if I am going to help you, I vant to be sure I am backing a vinner!"

The next two hours flew by. Fay forgot the time, so engrossed was she in showing Ava her sketchpad that she always kept in her school bag, just in case inspiration came to her during the day. Ava, for her part, was the best cheering squad ever and Fay's face shone with happiness at Bobby's loud exclamations and praise. In the middle of their conversation, Ava abruptly got up to call both her sisters and excitedly shared her news that her darling Fay was surely going to become the next Donna Karan. Such was the relationship between Ava and her sisters; they who had survived together never made a move without each other. Meanwhile, Fay sat there, oblivious to anything but her grandmother's validation of her talent. She completely forgot that she had a test to study for until Ava's phone rang, shattering the festive atmosphere. Suzi asked to speak to her and Ava handed her the phone, whereupon Suzi grimly reminded her that it was a school night and time to come home. She listened without defending herself, reluctantly put her sketch pad away and jumped into Ava's arms.

"Bobby," she said, "a million thanks for being you. I am so happy I came over and I will miss you so much when you go to Florida."

"My darling, your happiness is my happiness. Don't vorry, we have a telephone in Miami too, you can call me anytime. I vill talk to Mommy before I leave. I promise."

At that moment, Fay knew the road ahead had just been paved for her. Nobody, least of all her mother, could stop Ava when she believed in something. That was just how things were in their family. No one ever challenged, argued or disagreed with Ava. Consciously or not, she always played the card of being a Holocaust survivor. In fact, her daughters went out of their way, at great cost to their own happiness, to assure that potential conflicts died before they ever had the chance to escalate into a fight. From considering out of state college on a full scholarship to attending coed parties or considering a musical career, Ava's daughters never once troubled their mother, knowing she would not be comfortable.

Fay fiercely hugged her beloved grandmother for what seemed like the tenth time and floated home. This was a day she would long remember; the day her grandmother encouraged her to pursue her dreams and study hard. One day, she would see her designs—her exquisite dresses and gowns—in the windows of the most exquisite stores in all of Manhattan, Bergdorf Goodman, Bonwit Teller and B. Altman's. *Yes*, thought Fay, *life was going to be good*.

6

"Choices are the hinges of destiny."
—Pythagoras

As usual, May was on the fence, this time about the future. On the one hand, she wanted to emulate Fay and pursue her passion, making that her immediate goal instead of marriage and a family. On the other hand, she wanted to imitate Ray, who was actively looking for a boyfriend with future potential. Being married would mean that she could stop worrying about the future and just enjoy her life. It would also mean having at least one other person in her life who would actually care about her. May longingly thought about how it would feel to love and be loved; she wasn't really sure that she knew what love was or whether she even loved her absentee parents and grandparents whom she hardly ever saw, as they pursued their own interests.

Both her maternal and paternal grandparents lived in Scranton, Pennsylvania. The women were best friends since grade school. They married two nice enough men, Mordy and Sal, and when they finished high school, opened a beauty salon together. They worked six days a week, only taking off Mondays, when most hair salons were closed. Saturday was their busiest day and while they did not observe the Sabbath, beyond lighting candles on Friday night, because they remembered their grandmothers Bubby Ida and Bubby Sadie doing so. May and her parents were usually invited to spend Thanksgiving, Rosh Hashanah, Yom Kippur and the first Passover Seder with them. Hanukkah was not considered important enough to make the trek to Scranton, so May and her parents celebrated at home by turning on the electric menorah that May's mom got from the nursing home.

The holidays that were deemed important enough, took place either in the Goldbergs' ranch house or in the Fineberg apartment, rotating every year. In May's opinion, both the Goldberg and Fineberg grandparents were nice enough people. They were traditional Jews who worked hard, but also enjoyed life. They saw their friends on a regular basis, played bingo one night, canasta the next, and they bowled in leagues every third night of the week. Fran Fineberg was a short, stocky, bleached blonde woman who was content with her life. Shirley Goldman was her exact opposite: a tall, thin brunette who, when not at the tanning salon, was always seen drinking coffee and smoking Camel cigarettes. Both of them were anticipating their imminent retirement and relocation to condos in Boca Raton, Florida. There, they would continue their activities without facing the harshness of winter. They seemed to have little or no interest in their only grandchild, certainly not beyond the holidays and even then, not so much either.

May knew she needed to make a decision as deadlines were fast approaching. She wasn't a great student, but she wasn't the worst either. With no one to turn to, she decided to make a list of pros and cons, leaving out emotions and using only logic to help determine her future.

One hour later, May had it all figured out. She decided that while a college degree was a lofty goal, it was not going to get her a husband, much less the kind of husband she wanted. She needed to finish high school and just get a high-paying job while she figured out how to meet the right type of men. For one brief moment, she entertained the thought that, like her grandmothers, she might like to open her own beauty salon one day. The idea of owning a shop was appealing and at the same time daunting. Where would she ever get the start-up funding to rent a space? How would she get clients? How would she know what to order? Who could she afford to pay to come work for her? It all seemed like a lot for a 16-year-old girl to contemplate and figure out. For now, she decided, the plan would be to graduate high school and try to land a job that would give her access to a broader world than the dreary one she lived in now.

She impulsively applied for and landed a yearlong internship at Jordache Jeans beginning in the fall. Looking back, May, who was not very religious, saw it as a sign from God that she deserved better. Until the internship officially started, she had to attend mandatory training sessions. Suddenly, she found herself caring about her appearance, anticipating that she would meet new people. During her internship, it didn't hurt as much to come home to an empty house, because she was exhausted. Her eight-hour training days and the commute with the subway to and from the city were grueling but do-able. When coming home, she actually appreciated the empty house. She needed the quiet to process her day.

When she was the only one of all the interns to be invited to the Sutton family's Hanukkah party, she thought she had died and gone to heaven. Even Ray, who typically shied away from Sephardic social events and thumbed her nose at them, was impressed. "May," she said, "this is your big chance. We have to start planning now. You have to dress sharp so you will be noticed." Ray ransacked her closet until she found the perfect dress that her dressmaker could alter to fit May's silhouette. Both girls cut school and Ray treated May to a makeover at Il Makiage, to a facial at Christian Valme and took her to her hairstylist Mustafa in Deal for a cut, highlights and a blowout. All told, what Ray spent on May's debut into the very same community Ray was trying to escape, cost more than what May's father earned in a week.

May's transformation was noticeable, especially because in the weeks leading up to the party, she cut back on junk food. Her skin was clear, her eyes were shining and she felt invincible. She was excited and came across as not only pretty and well-dressed, but also confident and poised.

May painstakingly took the time to memorize Fay's specific

instructions over and over: 1) don't be too friendly or they will think you are desperate; 2) show empathy and thoughtfulness; 3) bring your host a token gift; 4) mingle; and 5) smile. Fay said these rules came straight from the source: from the ubiquitously cultured Ava. Taking these rules to heart, May felt like she had nothing to lose and everything to gain. Ray also told her that her older brother Danny, who was casually dating Amanda Sassoon, would be there and would certainly be glad to help her if she needed anything. Though she never prayed—it was not mandatory in her very liberal-minded yeshiva—she did ask God to make the day a glorious sunny day, so her debut would go off without a hitch.

Later in life, when her entire facade fell apart, May would think of that day as the start of her destiny. It would take nearly 20 years for her to really find herself, on her own, unencumbered by Danny or the community, and truly find her way home to 770 Eastern Parkway: the world headquarters of the Lubavitcher Rebbe, whose philosophy and guiding principle was to welcome all Jews back into the fold, no matter how far astray they had gone. It was only then, that she was able to put those years as a pseudo-Sephardic wife aside and become the person she was destined to become.

7

"Success is not fatal, failure is not final: it is the courage to continue that matters."
—Winston Churchill

Ray felt a sense of relief. Having a plan was important and her plan to be the most looked-at girl at her synagogue's Purim festival was well on its way. She knew she needed a costume that would accentuate her unbelievable weight loss and decided her best bet would be to have it made by a tailor, because none of the ready-made Halloween costumes or masks at Party City appealed to her. Thinking for days on end, she finally decided to ask Fay for help. "I need you to design me a Cleopatra costume for Purim, so I can have Lilliana make it," she told Fay as they sipped freshly brewed coffee in the Salem kitchen,

Fay looked at her in surprise. "What's the deal, Ray-Ray?" she said affectionately. "Why so much effort when you loathe most of the boys in your community?"

"Because," said Ray slowly, as if talking to a young child, "that's my future and I might as well face it. I am not as talented as you or as smart as May. Getting married is the only answer. Looking fierce will get me what I want."

"I see. Of course I can get the fabric and sketch you a fab outfit, if that's what you want, but could we stop for a sec and discuss why you can't also go to college while you pursue these lofty goals?" Now it was Fay who sounded like she was talking to a child. "You don't even know what might strike your passion," she continued. "You shut yourself from anything that might remotely please your parents, but what about you? What would make you happy? I know you, Ray-Ray. Please, just give this some thought!"

Ray looked at Fay and her heart felt warm. Fay was such a loving, caring human being. She was like the sister she never had, more so than her future sisters-in-law would ever be and certainly more than her own mother ever was. Ray rose from her chair to get another cup of decaf coffee. "You know what, I really don't care about doing more with my life than crawling out of my parents' shadow, but I can see that it matters so much to you that I swear I feel like I have to think about this."

Fay burst into tears. "Oh, sorry if I came on too strong," she sniffed. "I am so hormonal today. But honestly, Ray-Ray, I can see the three of us now. I will be a fashion designer—you will hear about it tonight—May a business tycoon and I'm thinking, with your intuitiveness, you will be a killer attorney!"

"Me, a lawyer? Are you joking? How would I ever get into law school? How would I ever keep up with the classes? My dad has always said it's a good thing I'm pretty, because that's all there is to me."

"Well, you can start by 100 percent ignoring your father's ridiculous opinion and then you can start eating a little more. You can't focus on your studies if you are starving. It's that simple, Ray-Ray! And then, with your dad's dough, we get you the best tutors to coach you for the LSAT exam. You know it can happen," she thundered. "The question is whether you believe in yourself and really want to find your passion. I noticed that you have not rejected the idea."

"I can't believe I'm actually saying this, but oh my goodness, if I, by a miracle, became a lawyer I could be my own person and that really excites me, Fay-Fay."

"That's what I'm saying. We live in such unbelievable times. Who knows what technology will make possible in the next 20 years? Look at the World Wide Web and AOL. People say that it is going to change everything. Soon, we will use it for everything from research to shopping to sending documents and files of any size. We will be communicating by email instead of sending letters. Let's not limit ourselves. My God, just look at your own mother, what she made of herself, what a trailblazer she was back in the day! Should you do any less?" Fay paused, hoping her words would penetrate. "Find yourself, give it a shot. We are, after all, modern and emancipated women. Nothing should hold us back, certainly not our parents or grandparents and their archaic ideas. Let's just 'shout, shout, let it all out.'" Fay broke into song.

Both girls started laughing and dancing. They recalled the countless times they, along with May, with their arms wrapped around each other, sang the popular Tears for Fears song at the top of their lungs. It really felt good to just shout and let it all out, thought Ray. No more pretending that everything was okay. That would enable her father to maintain the fierce grip he had over her. Fay was so right. She was a perfect role model—relentless in her belief that she had the right to pursue her dreams.

"Okay, Ray-Ray. I'm leaving. See you guys for dinner and a sleepover tonight. We can definitely continue this conversation, but only after I give you my news," Fay said mysteriously.

"What news?" cried Ray. "Don't do this to me, Fay. I can't wait until tonight. I need to know now!"

"Nope," said Fay as she eased into her brown leather jacket. "Tonight is soon enough. What I want you to do now is think about your own future and please, no exercise today. You are too thin and if my outrageous creation doesn't look fabulous on you and your skinny bones on Purim, you will break my heart!"

Fay left and Ray started to reflect on what she said. In truth, she knew Mazal was not the best candidate to steer her future. She would go along with any plan just to be her friend, but it was Fay, her beloved book-smart Fay, with no ulterior motive other than genuine affection, who made her stop in her tracks and ask herself to consider what exactly she was doing. In doing so, she came to realize that things were not okay. Suddenly, feeling overwhelmed with emotion, Ray decided to skip her run and just relax. It felt good not to be so hard on herself. Tonight, she would connect with Fay and May. That would be wonderful. Tomorrow would be soon enough to think about her future. When her phone rang, she ignored it, sure it was Mazal calling.

8

"Now and then it's good to pause in our pursuit of happiness and just be happy."
—Guillaume Apollinaire

Fay was euphoric. She believed that this is how the recipient of the first New York State lottery drawn in January of a record $35,000,000 must have felt. First, she felt in every bone of her body that Ray had really heard her and that pleased her enormously, because she loved Ray and agonized over her alarming weight loss. Like her mother, she also had a strong compulsion to fix and heal her friends. Then, there was her own spectacular news. With Bobby Ava's endorsement, she felt confident that her mother would have no choice but to let her try to become a fashion designer. Now she could start to plan her career. Fay knew how persuasive Bobby Ava was and, more importantly, how powerless her own mother was in the face of her grandmothers determination. That part, while not a done deal yet, was not the insurmountable part. Fay was realistic: she knew that becoming a bona fide fashion designer was a long shot, but that was not going to stop her. She would methodically start the process, not procrastinating like so many of her friends. Instead, she made a note to herself to call FIT and Parsons to order their catalogs. She imagined herself poring over them and figuring out which school would offer her the best options.

Suddenly, not even her two sisters annoyed her. In fact, she noticed that lately she was actually nicer to both of them and tried to get closer to them. Her enthusiasm was short-lived in that both misunderstood her new-found interest and rejected her again, as they did in the past. Fay wondered why her two sisters were so difficult to get along with. Why was it that they were always so hostile towards her? As usual, she fell back on those who were actually interested in her. Bobby Ava never stopped stressing that family was everything based on her own life experience, but Fay saw that for her, true friends were everything she couldn't establish with her own flesh and blood. She would have her best friends ver tonight for a sleepover and share the good news with them.

After running downstairs, she found her mother in the kitchen.

"Mom," she said breathlessly, "is it okay if the girls come over for dinner?"

Suzi looked up from the pot of vegetable minestrone soup that she was preparing.

"Of course it's okay, Faygala," she said warmly. "You know how much I love the girls and how happy your relationship with them makes me. I will make something special for May. I know she always looks forward to my food."

"Thanks, Mom," said Fay. "I really, really appreciate it. And the girls are staying over tonight. I know it's a school night, but we have some major stuff we need to discuss that just can't wait. Okay?"

Suzi looked at her daughter quizzically, trying to figure out what the drama was about this time. She knew better than to ask and accepted how blessedly different her relationship with her daughters was than that with her own mother. Sometimes she was aware that she was imitating her mother when she didn't mean to. When she realized she was even remotely acting like her, she immediately censored herself. Over and over, she reminded herself that she was an American, not a Holocaust survivor like her mother. To expect her daughters to give her the level of deference she gave her own mother was foolish. Only her sisters, Judy and Magda, understood this unusual duality: loving, revering and resenting their mother at the same time. Some days, it seemed so hard to keep up the facade. While other days, the joy of her own family was a welcome reprieve from the burden imposed on her by being born to Holocaust survivors.

With a smile on her face, she continued to finely dice her mushrooms, onions, carrots and celery to add to her soup. This was one of Ava's best recipes and Suzi, a creative cook in her own right, did not tweak it whatsoever. It was a wonderful, hearty soup and her entire family loved it exactly the way Ava made it. That Ava didn't consider this soup a calorie trap was interesting, Suzi thought with some resentment, but that was her mother: hardly the poster girl for stability, especially when it came to food.

Suzi remembered vividly when, as a child, she accidentally stumbled upon Ava's secret goodie drawer. It was filled with little white paper bags of exquisite candies, nuts and chocolates from Schwartz *baci's* tiny candy store. The cocoa-dusted almonds, chocolate orange peels, sesame candies and cherry cordials looked beautiful. Suzi never told anyone what she found, but from that day on, she was conflicted when Ava would serve them fresh fruit for dessert night after night, knowing that at some point, her mother was having a very different dessert. Suzi remembered how uncomfortable it made her feel, wondering why Ava had the need to hide such delicacies from her children.

Suddenly, Suzi felt guilty for thinking such horrible thoughts about her mother. What was the matter with her? How could she be critical of her own mother who had suffered so much and had almost starved to death? Suzi was so lost in her thoughts that she forgot where she was for a moment. Realizing that Fay was still standing there, she shook herself out of her reverie. "Yes, sure, darling. I'll set up the guestroom shortly."

Fay smiled broadly. There were days like today, when she simply appreciated and adored her mother's positivity. Other days, when her mother's mood was foul, she wondered what set her off. All of a sudden, it dawned on her. Maybe her sisters didn't hate her. Maybe, just maybe, they couldn't cope with their mother's mood swings and were jealous of Fay's protected status. She knew she was lucky—her mother never got angry at her. Why she was so privileged she never understood or questioned, but the same didn't hold true for Bethie and Deenie. To them, their mother was someone they were scared of, not knowing when or why she might get angry at them. Their mother would sometimes yell ugly words at them.

As Fay left the kitchen, she felt a knot in her stomach. She had to reach out to her sisters and try to breach the gap between them. In the next few years, they would all be out of the house for good. She wanted to know that she at least tried to help them. She wondered why she had never thought about this before—probably self-preservation and fear. What was it about her mother that made her go off like a time bomb? Was it something about her childhood?

Fay knew better than to ask her mother. She would just deny it all. Aunt Judy or Magda would be more forthright and tell her the truth. She decided to follow-up with them instead. Did they know, she wondered, about her mother's yelling? Fay, practical like her dad, was anxious to find a solution to what she perceived was a communication problem in her family. In her naivety and desire for everyone she loved to be happy, the need to help people, something she repeatedly observed from her mother and grandmother and common in wounded people, truly believed that if they all expressed their feelings, they would feel much better. In part, Fay was right. There were untold horrors that Ava and every other survivor would never share and take to their graves. These tortuous secrets, while meant to protect their children, also kept them at a distance. At a minimum, children of Holocaust survivors were terrified of what they weren't told.

To Fay, the answer was therapy. An impartial professional could certainly sort this all out and help them all understand how their mothers childhood environment helped shape her personality. She worried that Deenie was too quiet and Bethie too rebellious. Maybe one day she could persuade her mother to see a therapist, she thought to herself. For now though, she needed to focus on her sleepover. Tomorrow she would make this a priority. Now that she gained some insight, she could no longer ignore the problem. That would make her complicit and if she learned anything at all from Bobby Ava it was how despicable it was, how utterly wrong it was, not to speak up when injustice was being perpetrated. She just had to make this right. No matter what it took or who got hurt, she knew she had no choice but to take a stand.

9

"The only way to have a friend is to be one."
—Ralph Waldo Emerson

Ray got in the car and sat back, inhaling the smell of fine leather in the Lincoln Town Car. In approximately five minutes, she and Earl, her designated driver for just about ten years, would arrive at May's row house in Bay Ridge and proceed to Fay's house in Midwood. She always picked up May, even though it was out of the way. Ray's parents had set up an account for her from the time she started first grade and Lucía had been dispatched to pick her up from a play group with a reputable car service.

There was no traffic and soon Ray and May were in front of the Zweig house. As they got out, Fay opened the front door, running out to greet them. The look of genuine happiness on her face was not lost on Ray. It confirmed to her what she deduced yesterday—it was Fay's advice she would take, not Mazal's.

The girls walked into the dining room where Bethie and Deenie were already seated, as was Fay's dad. To Ray and May, seeing a whole family assembled at the dinner table was an anomaly. It wasn't Shabbat or Thanksgiving. It was an ordinary Thursday night, but in the Zweig house they were having dinner together. Ray and May felt very comfortable in the Zweig house and the family members always welcomed them warmly.

Dinner was delicious. Suzi was delighted to feed them all and shooed the girls away when it was time to clear the table. The girls went upstairs. No sooner did they reach the guest room when Ray begged Fay to spill the beans. Fay was happy to indulge her.

"I visited Bobby Ava and she adored my idea of becoming a fashion designer!"

Ray and May were stunned. Not only did they have no clue that Fay had such grand aspirations, but knowing that her grandmother endorsed the idea made it that much more attainable. Fay was beaming and answered their many questions with a big smile on her face. Then, she pulled out her sketch pad and a board on which she clipped fabric swatches for Ray's Purim costume.

"So," she said breathlessly, "in the future you can tell your kids that you wore an original AvaFay gown! Do you like it?"

Ray studied the sketch. Fay had attached a magnificent train to the gown. It looked like it was made of luxurious velvet with satin and Swarovski crystals.

"It is the most beautiful sketch I have ever seen," she said in awe. "You really are a designer! I swear I would wear this to my own bridal shower."

May nodded. She was so overcome with emotion that she knew if she said one word she would burst into tears. The girls sat in silence for a moment. Then, May piped up. "Well, I'd like to report on my adventure at the party. It was amazing and everyone was so nice to me. I think I was possibly the only blonde, non-Sephardi there."

The girls laughed and May's eyes flooded with tears, first of laughter and then with emotion.

"And Ray," she faltered, now really sobbing in earnest, "I will never forget what you did for me. I would have been nothing without your help."

Ray tried to shush May, but Fay would not let her. "She's right, Ray-Ray. You have a heart of gold. I am so proud of you. You turned May-May into a babe!"

With that Ray took center stage. "Girls," she said seriously, "I need to tell you something. I know you've been worried about me lately and I was too stubborn to admit I had a problem, but yesterday Fay really made me see the truth. I want a lot more out of life than just snagging a guy. Don't get me wrong, I want that too, but I am going to do everything in my power to get into a decent college. Hopefully, if I can pull it off, I will go to law school or social work school. I really think that someone like me has to advocate for women across all our communities. I believe that our communities, in spite of the tremendous good that they do for the sick and the elderly, also hide a lot of things. Underneath the surface, there are women suffering, unhappy and intimidated by old-fashioned, arrogant fathers, brothers and husbands who act like we are their chattel."

The girls looked stunned. Like May's recent admission when they were at the library that things were less than perfect in her home, this came as a shock to them. Ray sounded like a feminist and Fay was bursting with pride. While she knew instinctively that something had to be very wrong if Ray was switching gears so radically, she also knew that if Ray believed enough in her own ability to have the life she truly wanted, that she would find happiness. One day, she knew Ray would tell them why she was so angry at her parents. When that day came, Fay would support her and help her through whatever hurt her so badly.

The girls crowded around Ray, all three crying. While May felt oddly left out for a second, she nonetheless was happy for both of her friends. She hoped that inspiration would come to her as quickly as it came to Ray.

The girls got into their matching pink baby-doll pajamas and put on a Kiehl's mask that the fashion editors at *Seventeen* and *Vogue* magazine swore would remove the impurities lurking on their young faces. Then, in bed, cozy and content, drinking Fresca and nibbling Bachman pretzel rods, they talked incessantly about their summer trip to Israel. Birthright Israel provided an opportunity for all Jewish teens to visit Israel. In addition, the newly formed International March of the Living arranged an extensive weeklong educational tour of Auschwitz and Dachau, the mass killing centers.

The idea of visiting these concentration camps in Poland and

Germany was daunting to Fay because of her grandmother Ava. However, discussing it with her friends helped her quell the slight buzz of anxiety she felt. She thought that traveling from Israel, the Jewish homeland where all jews belonged would somehow make a difference in how she would feel to literally walk on the ground where her great grandmother and relatives were murdered.

All three were thrilled at the prospect of going abroad. The programs guaranteed a free trip for any Jewish student to both Israel and Poland and May was relieved to know that she could apply for a scholarship for the extra costs not covered by them. That they would likely be attending different programs didn't bother them at all. It was no different in New York, where each attended a school that reflected their particular family backgrounds and ran the gamut from Fay's all-girls Orthodox school to May's Conservative one. What mattered to the girls was not whether they spent every waking moment together, but the bond they shared.

Yet, although they shared this special bond and fully trusted each other, there were things that they never talked about, topics that would have entailed facing truths that were simply too difficult to bear. The best part, Fay observed as she drifted off to sleep, was that Ray ate dinner with her usual appetite and practically polished off the bag of pretzels by herself. Fay smiled, hoping Ray was back to herself, stronger and more determined to live her life on her own terms.

10

"Don't walk in front of me, I may not follow. Don't walk behind me, I may not lead. Just walk beside me and be my friend."
—Albert Camus

The alarm clock went off at 7:10 a.m. The girls resented it mightily.

"Please shut that thing off," Ray groaned.

"Wait," cried Fay. "Isn't it Shabbos?"

"No, it isn't, you nutcase," laughed May, playfully throwing her pillow at Fay.

"Oh God," exclaimed Fay. "Then it's a regular school day! I wish you guys just lived here permanently. I would face the day so much better."

"You know what, me too," said May. "But such is life, sweetiekins! Maybe one day we will buy a ten-bedroom summer house in Belle Harbor, a block away from the beach, and live together under one roof for the entire summer."

"Actually," said Ray, "that would be amazing. Fabulous idea."

Fay turned the dial on her boombox to 95.5 FM. The girls slowly started getting ready for school. It was easier to "get into the groove" with Madonna; she definitely made them feel better.

Downstairs, Suzi was in the kitchen finishing her elaborate but healthy breakfast preparations. She was dressed in a simple black knit skirt, white cotton blouse and her new black suede platform Skechers. She worried that maybe the sneakers were too youthful for a mother, but so far none of her daughters had commented on them. On her head she wore a baseball cap, with all her hair tied back in a ponytail tucked into the cap. As an Orthodox married woman of Ashkenazic descent, she was required to cover her hair and she adhered to this custom fully. It was also what Zak expected from her. She was grateful to him for marrying her and letting her start a new life. Therefore, she was willing to do almost anything not to rock the boat. Why she never considered that Zak was also delighted to be married to her, grateful for the home she created and didn't require placating, was something she never thought about. Pleasing people, starting with her parents was a long-ingrained habit designed to eliminate conflicts and sadness. Perhaps it had to do with Ava's incessant litany of examples of women who didn't know how to keep their husbands happy. Ava was an expert of course. She was European and therefore much more cosmopolitan than her daughters. That, plus her keen observation of Hollywood and famous women gave her license to speculate. More than once, Ava informed her daughters that Jackie Kennedy was a naive woman to think she could keep the Hollywood actress Marilyn Monroe away from Jack. The way Ava said it made her daughters believe that Ava had some inside information, which they later realized came from the tabloid magazine *The Star*.

As Suzi waited for everyone to enter her kitchen, she looked at her breakfast table with fresh fruit cut up, boxes of Rice Krispies and cornflakes, ready to eat with skimmed milk and sliced bananas. She also made hot oatmeal with raisins and cinnamon and arranged a spot for the fresh rolls and mini danishes that Zak brought from the bakery, a daily routine he adhered too after he attended morning services at the shul. Though she had cream cheese and butter, because Zak insisted he had rights too, she was reluctant to put it out on the table and decided she would, but only on request. For a minute, Suzi questioned herself and wondered why she needed to be so vigilant, not only with herself and her daughters but even with

Fay's friends? To her knowledge, no one had health issues or was even mildly overweight, yet here she was imitating her mother and withholding cream cheese and butter as if they were the enemy. She felt uncomfortable and knew that her behavior was somehow related to Ava's attitude toward food. *Maybe*, she thought, it's time I actually address this insanity. *I should go to the Brooklyn College Library resource room and see if there is any research that links eating disorders to Holocaust survivors?* Of course, she didn't need to be a scholar to know that starving for 11 months had to influence a person's attitude toward food, but she wondered why her mother would not want to indulge others in an abundance of food, rather than restricting food? Was it possible, subconsciously Ava was reenacting an irrational fear that this might happen to them at some point in time and was preparing them to make do with less, like she had to? It was too much to think about. She decided she would for once do something without getting her sisters' or mother's approval. Maybe this time, she could do something independently without feeling like she broke some sacred cardinal sisterhood rule.

Fifteen minutes later, five girls surrounded her round kitchen table. They were all showered and dressed in their respective outfits and uniforms. Bethie and Deenie were used to having May and Ray in their house and barely acknowledged them. On some level, they attributed their mother's good mood to the fact that there were guests around. That Fay was allowed to have a sleepover on a school night, proved yet again that she was their mother's favorite.

For Suzi, rising at 5:45 a.m. was worth it. She loved looking at them all eating together and soaking up their voluminous praise for her thoughtfulness, delicious array of choices and the labeled lunch bags she prepared. After they hugged and said their goodbyes, Suzi ran after them to give Earl a bag too. If he was driving the girls, he needed energy, she thought. The gesture was not lost on Ray and May, each of whom felt lucky to have a second mom like Suzi in their lives. They were never witness to Suzi's volatile temper and thought she was hands down the best Mom ever, better even than Aunt Viv from *The Fresh Prince of Bel-Air*, the new Will Smith comedy show everyone was watching.

For Ray, seeing a mother figure in the kitchen in the morning was a rarity. In her entire life, she had never seen any woman besides Lucía in the kitchen. Even on holidays, her mother sat in the dining room, along with her own parents and relatives, as if she was a guest. It was abundantly clear to everyone that Dr. Victoria Salem had absolutely no interest whatsoever in being a cook, wife, or mother like her own mother Paulette or grandmother Marcella, both of whom had never really adapted to life in Brooklyn.

May was also not used to having a big home-cooked breakfast. Her mother was busy saving the world. Mundane things like breakfast were simply a nonissue. There was a cafeteria just about everywhere. There, you got what you needed. End of story. For Mrs. Goldman, food was something you needed to live, no different than filling the tank of a car with gas.

11

"One loyal friend is worth 10,000."
—Euripides

Just like that, the girls moved into a new phase. Each of them was calmer, anticipating the fulfillment of their goals while surviving the rigors of school and family pressure. Ray dreaded the upcoming charity dinner where her parents were the guests of honor. She wasn't proud of them or their contribution to the world of medicine. She looked at her brothers and felt sorry for her parents. Not one of their sons would continue their legacy and become a doctor; they would either marry wealthy girls or look for real estate properties and make deals. She knew her brothers were close with one another. She used to resent the fact that she was the outsider, the one whom they bullied when she was a child, but now she was at a place in her life where she was glad that they had each other. In some ways, the fact that her brother Danny was definitely after May was a plus. If they got married, May would be her sister and she would have a relationship with at least one of her brothers.

As Ray got dressed for the dinner, she looked at herself in the mirror. She saw for the first time that she was too thin and promised herself to see a nutritionist. Lucía certainly had no clue about nutrition, but was willing to do anything she asked her to do. Sadly, neither of her parents noticed that she had been skating close to the edge, rescued by her real family—Fay and May. Even Bobby Ava had called her once to ask if she was okay and wanted to come over to chat. Ray remembered that phone call with profound sadness and gratitude. Sadness, because none of her parents or brothers had noticed that she needed help, but so grateful for those that did.

She gently severed the relationship that Mazal had so carefully cultivated with her, recognizing that Mazal had little to offer her. She heard a year later that Mazal was engaged in senior year to an ultra-Orthodox Sephardic boy. Once married, she would wear a *mitpachat* on her head: an ornate scarf that resembled an African head wrap. It seemed extreme to Ray, but she was nevertheless happy for her friend for finding what appeared to be her authentic self. She recalled the teachings of the Rabbi who emphasized spirituality as the pathway to connecting with your soul. She envied anyone who found their spiritual self, knowing that she was devoid of that attachment to God. In fact, the only time she ever felt remotely affiliated to her religion was when she watched Suzi Zweig light her candles on Friday night. The depths of her silent prayer always moved Ray and she hoped that one day, she would find that level of blind faith to sustain her the way Suzi apparently did.

As she grabbed her fur bomber jacket, Ray smiled. There would no doubt be a lot of parents that would want to set her up with their sons or nephews. She decided that she would be open to meeting anyone, as long as they met her basic criteria.

In the town car, Ray thought about how much she relied on Earl. He wasn't simply a driver to her, but someone she could talk to. He was discreet and honest, qualities she admired. Often she wondered if he realized how dysfunctional her family was. Here they were all attending the same function and it never dawned on anyone to travel together to the Pierre Hotel. Instead, Danny, having dumped Amanda, was picking up May, and her other two brothers Ralph and Ikey were going straight from work. Her parents had slept over in the hotel the night before so that her mother's dresser from Bergdorf Goodman could get her ready for the event. All Ray had to do was show up for the pictures. At least she would have May with her. She hoped yet again that Danny was good enough for May, because she adored her with all her heart.

As Ray stepped into the lobby of the Pierre Hotel, she felt even more detached than usual. She accepted a glass of Perrier sparkling water from the waiter who approached her and anxiously scanned the room to see if there was anyone she might talk to. Thankfully, she spotted May and Danny and flew over to greet them.

"May," she said warmly, "you look drop dead gorgeous."

She felt as proud as a mother as she took in May's dress, shoes and bag. No doubt Danny had taken her shopping at Jimmy's or Charivari. She was glad to see that May's common sense had prevailed and she had not allowed herself to be tarted up for Danny's pleasure. May looked beautiful and happy. She tugged at Ray's sleeve and casually raised her hand so that Ray could see the delicate diamond bangle she now wore on her wrist. Ray examined the bangle with admiration and gasped.

"My brother bought you that bracelet?" She turned to Danny. "Wow, I am impressed."

Her six-feet-tall brother clad in an Armani suit and tie smiled. "Nothing's too good for my girl."

He possessively put his arm around May as if to demonstrate his ownership over her. Ray didn't like the gesture, but she could see that May didn't take offense at practically being mauled, but instead was pleased and happy. She couldn't believe how different May and she were. In her heart, Ray knew that May was desperate for attention and Danny Salem—even if he was her brother—was a catch. He was 22, handsome and charming. The dark side in him would hopefully never come out. Ray, on the other hand, was more clearly affected by her father's attitude to women and the verbal and psychological abuse he subjected her and her mother to. She was terrified of men and terrified that her brothers would turn into their father: drink too much and pinch, punch or slap their women behind closed doors. She would never, ever let that happen to her, she promised herself. How she would know that her husband-to-be could be trusted was a mystery to her, but she knew without a doubt that no man would ever be cruel to her. She would simply leave if that was the case. She would wait five years if necessary before starting a family to guarantee that she was bringing kids into a safe family.

She had this all figured out, thanks to Fay, who had helped her face her real demons without even knowing she had done so. In therapy, Ray continued, week after week, to painfully describe the horrible animal she considered her father to be. Coming tonight had been a choice. She knew she could have bailed, but decided to be there, not out of fear of her father's wrath after the party, but in spite of it. She was no longer afraid of him.

She was glad that May was also seated at the family table. If she had to make inane conversation with the girls her other brothers had brought to the dinner, she would have puked. They looked like twins in their mini sheath dresses, an abnormal amount of make-up and teased hair, talking loudly and stupidly.

Ray glanced at the center of the room, where her parents sat at a table for two by themselves. *How perfectly fitting*, she thought. *Exactly how they liked it: just the two of them, with no one bothering them.* She watched as people fawned over them, gushing with fake admiration and praise. No one she knew really admired the Salems. Most people came because it was important for their status. Taking out a journal ad for $750 allowed for two people to have dinner, be seen and mingle with those that could really afford to be part of this society. Ray swore to herself that she would have a meaningful life that absolutely did not pander to the artificial people she saw here tonight. The only positive thing was that the money raised this evening would help establish an orphanage for abandoned children in Israel. She knew her parents didn't care who the recipient of their largesse was, but to her it mattered. She planned on visiting the orphanage that summer and hoped she could convince May and Fay to join her. Randomly, she wondered how she would survive in Israel without Earl or Lucia who cared about her.

Ray laughed as she noticed her brothers' dates moving their salads around on their plates. No, she decided, I will savor my prime rib and scalloped potatoes. She enjoyed her food thoroughly and ignored the young man sitting on her right who desperately tried to engage her in conversation. The zucchini muffin on her plate had more appeal than this pompous 20-year-old son of a real estate tycoon who had no higher ambition in life than to drive a DeLorean and go into his daddy's business. She turned to May, who was glowing from Danny's attention and felt glad to see her so happy. She would call Fay the second she got home and tell her every last detail, including the dessert she ate. She glanced at the elaborate chandeliers overhead, looking to the heavens to thank God for feeling in control of herself. She finally had a clear-cut path to the future.

When Purim rolled around a week later, she attended all the parties in her community in her outrageous Cleopatra costume. She even gave her phone number to two guys, but was certainly not disappointed that this did not become the defining moment of her life. She knew that her time would come when it would come. For the first time in her life, she saw her on-going therapy sessions, not as a punishment meted out by her parents for her recalcitrance, but rather as an opportunity for growth. Therapy was no longer going to simply be a place where she could safely talk about how much she hated her parents, rather it would be a place where she could gain understanding and through that cognitive lens, choose behavior and feelings that made her happy.

12

"Let us be grateful to people who make us happy, they are the charming gardeners who make our souls blossom."
—Marcel Proust

May was ecstatic. Ever since the party and Ray's magical makeover, her life had transformed into one where she woke up every morning feeling happy to be alive. That Danny Salem really liked her was probably a modern day miracle. She was honored that he had chosen her out of likely 50 girls who would have done anything to snag him. She looked for the 100th time at the bracelet he gave her the night his parents received an award. She could not believe that he had spent so much money on her. That night, in the backseat of his car, May showed her appreciation. True, she wanted to, but he also clearly expected it and she was not about to mess up this rare opportunity to land a bona fide hunk like Danny. She knew Ray would never ask and Fay, being a naive religious girl, wasn't aware of the things a girl needed to do to keep a boyfriend interested.

The day before the party May used her babysitting money to go to the city. She went to Victoria's Secret, where she bought a silk teddy and the sexiest panties she could find. She was satisfied with her armor and left the store confident that this was what she was supposed to do. It never dawned on her to reach out to her mother for advice. She was on her own. She could definitely not share this with the girls, but accepted that without any remorse. Being with Danny would make Fay and Ray happy; what exactly she had to do to get there was strictly her business. Besides, she was hardly the first woman to use her feminine charms to get ahead. She comforted herself by thinking about the models, singers, gymnasts and actresses who—no doubt—did the same to advance their careers.

At 6:00 in the morning her phone rang, waking her from a deep sleep. She picked up, knowing it was Fay. "Hello," she groggily said. "I know you are going to kill me for not calling you last night, but I was with Danny until 4:00 a.m. Wait. Oh! Oh my God, what time is it, Fay-Fay?"

"No need to panic, May-May," replied Fay in a loving tone. "*Boker tov* and top of the morning to you, May Goldman. I am neither pissed nor hurt. Ray gave me all the details last night, so you are in the clear. And for your information, it's 6 a.m. Plenty of time to get ready for school, cookie. I'm just checking to see if you want to talk."

"Oh, thank you. I am so tired and my head is killing me; I guess I drank too much. I do want to tell you... No, I have to show you the bangle Danny bought me."

"I heard!" screamed Fay. "I am so pleased, May-May. You know what, I think we should all take the day off and celebrate. Ray of course doesn't need to clear it with anyone, neither do you, I imagine, but I will have to invent some illness for my mom. One that's serious enough to get the day off, but not so bad that she starts making phone calls to get specialist referrals from her circle of friends who volunteer at Columbia Presbyterian and Mount Sinai Hospital."

May didn't answer.

"So? May? Hellooo?" She stopped talking and heard the familiar sound of her beloved May breathing. "Oh, you are sleeping. Good. Don't say a word, I'll call you around 12, after I speak to Ray. Let's do Greener Pastures for lunch and Bloomies, then we can go over everything, including the bracelet!"

Fay softly hung up the phone, hoping the disconnect buzz would not wake May. She quickly dialed Ray who picked up on the first ring.

"We're skipping school today. Go do whatever it is you do in the morning and let's meet at 12, pick up May-May and head to the city."

"And good morning to you too, senorita," answered Ray, who was working on perfecting her Spanish. "Sounds like a plan!"

Ray was delighted to skip school and hang with the girls. They had a standing tradition every Sunday, but this day was special. She decided to skip her workout and rolled over, sinking deeper into her Pratesi sheets and down blanket.

"See you soon, Fay-Fay. *Laila tov*."

Fay smiled at Ray's use of Hebrew. Of the three of them, only she was decently fluent. Ray and May struggled to master the language. After Passover, she decided she would begin a tutorial program for the two of them so that they would be able to actually converse in Israel this summer, rather than just get by.

"See you soon, darling," she said, realizing she sounded exactly like Bobby Ava, without the accent. *Not the worst thing in the world*, she thought as she turned over and went back to sleep. I sound like Bobby, who is all light and love. How perfectly marvelous is that.

13

"There is nothing on this earth more to be prized than true friendship."
—Thomas Aquinas

Earl was used to picking up Ray's friends. Like Ray, he found them all to be mannered and polite girls. He enjoyed watching them as they settled back for the ride into Manhattan. He knew from past times that they would bring him lunch from whatever restaurant they would eat at before they began their own meal. He liked the Greener Pastures kosher vegetarian restaurant on East 61st Street, but he absolutely loved La Difference, which was good enough to compete with his own Mama's slow cooked braised short ribs. Who would believe, he wondered, that Earl Jones from Birmingham, Alabama, would eat kosher food and wear a jacket to work everyday, driving a Lincoln Town Car for the nicest Jewish family in New York.

He was so grateful to them; they had saved his baby sister's life when she had a mole that turned cancerous. He would never forget that, nor the surgical care they provided to his sister for free. These were special folks, he told Clara every single night. Thanks to the docs, his handsome salary would allow his kids to all get an education and earn decent wages. One day, when he would be too old to drive, he knew he would be okay, because Doc Salem took social security from his paycheck every week.

Earl laughed to himself when he thought about Ray's grandmas. Both of them were from the Old World. They didn't speak a word of English, only Arabic or something, and were kind of old-fashioned. He didn't blame the Salem kids for keeping their distance, but he was disappointed that the docs didn't do more for their parents. However, worrying about that was not part of his job.

As Earl expertly got off the 60th Street exit on the FDR drive, he found himself thinking about lunch again. He was more than ready for the vegetarian eggplant parmigiana, fresh salad with raisins and nuts, and delicious homemade rolls. Yes, he concluded, first lunch and then a nap while the girls ate.

Over lunch, May repeatedly showed off her bracelet. Both Fay and Ray were duly impressed and thrilled for May, who was under the impression that this was a major commitment from Danny.

"Do you girls think I should be buying him a gift?" she asked nervously. "I don't have that kind of money."

"Buy him a gift?" asked Fay, with Ray shaking her head in agreement. "Are you out of your mind? You are not engaged. There is no reciprocity here at all."

Ray started to laugh.

"I know exactly what you are thinking," Fay proceeded. "How does Fay know about any of this? And you might be right. I don't have first-hand knowledge of all the ins and outs of relationships, but I do read a lot and I have tons of experience just watching everyone in my family."

"Okay," said May, faltering. "It's just that I have no clue and I really want things to go the right way."

"Then just be yourself," said Ray. "He likes you because you are different from the girls he's used to. To be honest, I am *mucho* impressed with my brother. Picking you is the best thing he ever did. Now, we just need to move this along for a few months, until we get back from Israel, and you can be the first bride in your senior year!" Ray burst out crying. "Oh my God, can you guys believe what we are talking about? Our May-May a bride?"

Fay and May were tearing up as well. The three of them were lost in thought of the past and the future.

"May-May," said Fay, "this is really what you want, right? You haven't said a word about your parents and what they might say. I mean, this could never be my story, but what do you think your parents will say?"

"Sadly, I don't think it will make a difference to them one way or another. It's hard for me to say this, but I never felt like they or my grandparents ever needed me in their life. I don't know why they are that way, but my life is going to only be about family. Who knows? Maybe, once I'm out the door, they will miss me? Or maybe, they won't even notice that I'm gone and just continue killing each other, like they did before I was born."

This was the most revealing statement May had ever made about her parents. Both friends were stunned.

"I hope that you are exaggerating," said Ray sadly. "And that they will take the opportunity to give you away when you get married, like you deserve."

May nodded. "That would be nice, Ray."

Unfortunately, May was right. Thirteen months later, at the wedding and endless celebratory parties, the Salems treated the newlyweds like a king and queen, but May's parents attended like guests, with little emotion. Throughout the entire nuptial period, it was Suzi who went shopping with her, for everything from custom-made embroidered bed linens, to Hungarian down blankets purchased in the Hasidic neighborhood of Williamsburg where dozens of businesses sprang up, that catered exclusively to the needs of the community, honeymoon clothing and apartment necessities.

When Victoria rose to the occasion, Ray was thrilled that instead of thinking about her wedding, her mother was focused on Danny's bride. She was getting tired of the endless "soon by you" whispered into her ear. Ray saw a side of her mother that she didn't know existed. Victoria was happy, smiled a lot and actually made the time to fully welcome the new bride into their family. She registered May at Bloomingdale's and Tiffany's, and threw a magnificent engagement party at the newly renovated community party hall on Ocean

Parkway. No expense was spared; flowers and tablecloths were ordered to enhance the party room. She even bought May a beautiful Chanel evening bag to match her party dress.

In the days leading up to the wedding, Victoria arranged her future daughter-in-law's pre-wedding ritual immersion ceremony. She sent out exquisite pale peach Crane invitations to all the bride's relatives, her mother, grandmothers and closest friends, as well as her own friends and family. Everyone accompanied May to the ritual bath *mikveh* and stood outside the room while she immersed in the pure waters with the help of her attendants. After the immersion, a lavish party followed, accompanied by traditional candy and other sweets to symbolize a sweet future. May loved every moment of these strange customs. Fay, however, looked faint from the lack of privacy May had. Suzi whispered to her during the ceremony that this was totally the opposite of their Ashkenazic traditions that included a very private mikveh immersion. Mikveh, a time-honored tradition, was meant to sanctify marital relations by requiring women to immerse in pure rain water, after their periods ended every single month and prior to their wedding.

A day later, Victoria presented May with a gorgeous black velvet dress, heavily adorned with pearls, jewels and metal threads to wear to the pre-wedding party where all the guests enjoyed a beautifully catered meal. Afterwards, Victoria arranged for an artist to come and paint designs and symbols on the palms and hands of the bride, using henna dye: a brown liquid used for centuries for decorating the skin of Middle Eastern brides. Victoria was satisfied with the way her lovely Ashkenazic bride was surrounded by sufficient symbols of fertility and protection from evil. After so many rituals, parties and lavish Sephardic celebrations, the wedding was almost anticlimactic. And, while May was exhausted, she was exhilarated and felt very special, reveling in her moment as a bride. It made up for all the loneliness of her childhood. Danny was almost incidental.

The girls quite literally hopped back into the car after they invaded Bloomingdale's, the giant department store on East 59th Street that sold everything a trendy teenager could possibly want or need. They also went to the famous Forty Carats restaurant located on the lower level where they always stopped for the soft frozen vanilla yogurt with melba sauce that they all devoured in seconds. It was a wonderful afternoon and everyone was satisfied. Ray was relieved that no one mentioned calories or sugar. It was only later that day that May realized Danny hadn't called her yet and she felt uneasy, terrified that maybe the bracelet meant nothing more than a token gift and not a commitment at all. When May hadn't heard from Danny the next day, she called Ray in tears.

"Should I be nervous, Ray-Ray?"

"Absolutely not. He is just a *schmuck*, typical jerk. It's possible he is busy with a new deal. Let me find out, but swear to me that you will not call him again and stop panicking!"

May hung up the phone feeling better, but still nervous. If he really liked her, wouldn't he want to hear her voice? Maybe, she wondered, he didn't respect her for her behavior in the backseat of his car, when she allowed him to touch her all over. While she knew she could never share that with anyone, much less her best friends who would kill her, she resolved to act like a lady from now on. In 15 minutes, Ray called her back sounding happy.

"May-May, it's all good! I spoke to Ralphie and he knew all about you, even about the bracelet. He says Danny's smitten!"

"No! Are you serious?"

"I would never joke about this. He likes you. Now, when he does call, just be cool and don't say a word about what I told you. Also don't question him or ask him why he didn't call until now. If you are going to be part of the clan, you might as well get to know right now that many, not all mind you, but a lot of Sephardic men believe they are superior to women. They have an attitude, May-May, but most of the girls ignore that because they give them a good life."

"Seriously, Ray-Ray," said May, practically stuttering. "I am a little terrified about my dream coming true. It all happened too easily. I hear you, it might not be easy, but I'm definitely up for the challenge."

She thought to herself that she needed a total do-over with Danny. He had to know she was a good girl, one worthy of being his wife and the mother of his children, not a cheap slut.

14

"Thinking is difficult, that's why most people judge."
—Carl Jung

Fay knew as soon as she walked in the door that Bobby Ava had spoken to her mother and it was going to be a battle. There was an electrical charge in the atmosphere. Belatedly, she realized that her aunts' cars were triple parked in their driveway. That was the giveaway. If the three of them were together, it could only be a sign of impending doom. Fay recalled many instances growing up when her mother, no doubt imitating her own mother, sought out her sisters when she needed help with the kids or her husband. It usually worked, because the three of them together were formidable, like their own mother and her sisters.

"Hi Mom!" she called cheerily. "I'm home!"

"Yes, I can tell," called Suzi dryly from the den. "Why don't you wash up and come join me in the dining room."

"In the dining room?" squeaked Fay, thinking to herself that this was going to be a bigger battle than she had anticipated. No one ever sat in the dining room unless they gathered for Shabbos or holidays. It implied the matter to be discussed was very serious.

"Sure will, Mom," she replied, trying hard not to sound nervous or anxious or even that she knew her aunts were in the house waiting for her to enter the room.

In less than five minutes, Fay found herself in front of the firing squad, shocked that her father was there too. Fay began to sweat profusely and her stomach clenched in earnest. "Hi Dad. Hi Judy. Hi Magda." Fay dutifully hugged and kissed each adult. "What a lovely surprise to see all of you."

"Well," said Suzi, clearing her throat, "let's get right to it. You made a terrible mistake, Faygala. By going to Bobby you thought you wouldn't need our approval?"

"No, please, Mom," cried Fay earnestly. "It's not like that at all. Bobby asked me why I was upset and I told her the truth. In a million years I didn't expect her support. She offered to talk to you. I never asked her to get involved!" Pleading, she turned to her father and aunts who all sat stiffly. "Dad, don't you trust me? I know who I am and where I come from. I would never embarrass you, ever," she said emphatically.

"Well Faygala," her father replied, "if it's not you we are worried about, it's the people you will come in contact with. They don't have our history or background of having to run on a moment's notice when persecution, round-ups or pogroms start."

"But Dad," sobbed Fay, "I can't live like that. This isn't Czarist Russia or Nazi Germany! I am a New Yorker and we are less than ten years away from the new millennium. We live in a fantastic world. Please, I beg of you, let me live my life."

No one at the table seemed to hear her. Her aunts and her mother openly laughed in her face, speaking in Hungarian, using the words "*kitchi bolond*," which she knew meant "a little crazy." They dismissed her as if she was a moronic child who had no clue about the dangers lurking in every corner. Fay inhaled and made her final pitch.

"Mommy, Daddy and dearest aunts, I know that growing up you had a different life. Maybe you never got the chance to find your way in the world because Bobby hovered over you, but I am asking you to think about this. I can handle myself and no one, and I mean no one, will influence me. I just want a chance to go to fashion school and see if I can make it. I promise I will still get married and do everything right. Nothing will change."

She was in tears, but to her utter dismay, it appeared as if she had not said a word. No one responded or moved from their seat. Fay looked at her father, hoping he would rise to the occasion, but he did not. She looked to her mother who refused to even make eye contact with her. Suddenly, it dawned on Fay what the real issue was.

"Wait a second, this is not about me at all," she cried. "You are furious with Bobby for overstepping, for acting like she's the mommy, completely overriding your right to decide my future."

Fay saw that she was right, because now her mother's face was bright pink and both her aunts looked extremely uncomfortable.

"You know what, Suzi," said Magda as she rose, "Faygala has a point. I don't want to be here. This is really unfair to her. I will leave, and Judy, I suggest you do the same." She walked over to Fay and pulled her so close that Fay could smell her Giorgio perfume. "I am sorry, Mamala," she crooned. "You are right. I would feel sick if my daughters were in this position. It's bad enough how Bobby feels about their weight and drives us all insane. This is too much."

Fay felt her heart melt at her aunt's words. Finally, someone honest who was willing to admit to their insane family dynamic. Not that anyone meant harm, but her mother and her aunts were literally mimicking the behavior they observed growing up from their European, immigrant, Holocaust survivor mother and aunts. The problem was that not all of Bobby's actions were grounded in rational thinking and who could blame her? For being overly protective, for distrusting goyim, for being slightly paranoid? Even for being so Hungarian and look-conscious.? That's who she was, but it shouldn't mean her granddaughters had to be like that as well. Fay watched her aunt Judy rise. She did not say a word, just blinked rapidly and nodded. It was too much to expect from both of her aunts to acknowledge what she said, but Magda's words were enough for her.

As soon as her aunts left, Fay turned to face her parents. "Are we done here or may I be excused?"

Suzi looked at her daughter as if it was the first time she saw her. "Faygala," she said heavily, "I am stunned. I never, in my whole life, until today, made any connection between how I was raised and Bobby's suffering, and how I raised you and your sisters. I was on autopilot. Somehow, because I had two sisters just like Bobby, I think, it made it seem so natural to do the exact same thing as my mother. I never had a grandmother, so I had no blueprint of how things were supposed to be. The way Bobby did things was the way I assumed everyone did things. I love my mother, but maybe I need to reevaluate some things." She faltered, took a deep breath and continued. "I really need some time to think this over. Just recently I promised myself that I was going to find some research and now I am convinced that it is really crucial. I don't want to burden you like that." She looked sad. Then, she turned to her husband. "But you, Zak, where is your good *sechel* and common sense?" Lapsing into the Yiddish words that peppered her mother's English and Hungarian, she looked at her husband and berated him for not using his sound logic. "Why didn't you tell me this was wrong? Why did you automatically take my side against our child?"

Zak looked grimly at his wife. "Why, you ask? So that I could keep you from exploding. You aren't the easiest person to live with when you are challenged."

"Oh my God," gasped Suzi. "My father! I never ever realized. I am just like him. Bullying everyone." Suzi was practically in a daze, remembering things she had long since buried, like her hopes to become a world-famous singer. Her father had quashed those dreams forever, to the degree that she never sang again. Now, to think that she was even remotely like her father left her feeling extremely uncomfortable. Suzi turned to her daughter who sat quietly. Fay watched recognition unfold and truly admired her mother for her honesty.

"Fay," she said, finally using the diminutive form of her daughter's name, "I don't know where to start, except to say that I am sorry. I know you have talent and I hate myself for holding you back. Yes, you have my full support. I trust you and I will be the proudest mother ever when you become famous. I will even volunteer to be your secretary or your manager or your buyer. I will do anything to help you succeed."

Fay looked at her father who merely nodded his head in agreement.

"Okay ladies, let's not get carried away completely. We are still observant and Shomer Shabbos and many Fridays will pose a problem when the sun sets at 5:00 pm." When he saw their stricken faces he hastily added, "But do not worry. My friend Avrom is a constitutional lawyer, he will tell us what to do. After all, we are Americans and we have the right to practice our religion without discrimination."

He excused himself and left the room. Fay looked at her mother and burst into another round of tears. "Mommy, Mommy, Mommy," she kept saying over and over. "I will never forget today. What you said took so much courage. In my eyes, you are a real *Aishes Chayil*, a woman of valor, exactly what the sages meant."

In that instant Fay forgave her mother for all the inconsistencies of her childhood. The two hugged and stayed welded to each other for many minutes, neither wanting the moment to end.

"Okay," said Suzi, wiping her tears. "Let's go tell your sisters the big news, and then, we must eat supper before it..." As she said the words, she changed her mind. "No," she said emphatically, at which Fay looked at her puzzled. "Tonight we are going to Schmulka Bernstein's on the Lower East Side. I am having a fully loaded hot dog, French fries and a pastrami sandwich on club bread, calories be damned! Go tell your sisters and your father, Fayg... I mean Fay, while I turn off the oven."

Fay ran out of the dining room feeling like a great weight had been removed from her chest. This was the absolute best possible outcome that she could ever have dreamed of. Not only was she allowed to pursue her dream with the full support of her parents, but at the same time, she had opened the door to changes in her mother's understanding of herself. This would likely have major implications for all of them, but mostly for her mother.

She arrived at the foot of the stairs and called her sisters. Going to Schmulka Bernstein's was a rare treat; it meant that her mother was consciously breaking with some aspects of her own upbringing that had no place in their life.

15

"In dwelling, live close to the ground. In thinking, keep to the simple. In conflict, be fair and generous. In governing, don't try to control. At work, do what you enjoy. In family life, be completely present."
—Lao Tzu

The days before Passover, Fay, Suzi, Ava, Deenie and Bethie, as well as Magda and Judy and their daughters, were all busy. They were cooking, cleaning and dieting. Everyone was excited and anticipated spring shopping. It was the holiday that men and children loved the most and women dreaded the most. The work was back-breaking. As a cooperative, the three sisters divided much of the cooking between them. Ava made her famous Pesach chicken soup, noodles and gefilte fish, Judy did the baking, Suzi did the roasts and Magda, by default, was left to come up with amazing sauces, dressings and salads.

Suzi attempted to explain to her two sisters how she felt about the critical moment she shared with Fay and Zak. She talked to them about the aftermath of her revelations and her determination to live her life differently. She invited them to come along on the journey, which she was positive would help her with her mood swings and feelings of helplessness in the face of her mother's alternating displays of symptoms of PTSD, suffering and vulnerability, as well as resilience and lust for life. However, neither of her sisters was ready to embrace change and she accepted that. She knew that she needed to do what she needed to do, without fanfare or her sisters. She began to read a lot. When she could not find all the answers she sought, she found herself a therapist who had experience with secondary trauma.

Suzi began to implement new ideas this Pesach. Like other first-generation Americans, she was invested in bringing a modern twist to all aspects of her life, including how she celebrated the holidays. While Ava recreated the Passover holiday of her Baimare childhood in Hungary, Suzi enjoyed experimenting with many of the traditional foods and presented them to her family as her own version of how the meal should be. The first time Ava saw Suzi mix mayonnaise into the freshly grated horseradish, a condiment served with the gefilte fish, she nearly choked on the water she was drinking, but Suzi was as adamant as her mother in her desire to take it up a notch and Ava conceded.

Ray liked Passover, it was a time when her family got together with as much fanfare as in Fay's house. May was invited to spend the holidays with the Salems. She knew that this invitation was an important statement and that she had to do everything right. In her conversations with Ray and Fay, she found out what she had to bring, what she had to wear and how she had to act. They told her to offer to help at every meal even though Mrs. Salem already had much help, waiters and extra staff to accommodate the entire family. When May told her parents she would not be going with them to her grandparents, they looked at her with mild surprise.

"Oh," said her mother, "where in the world will you be?"

"With my boyfriend's family," she said icily. "Apparently it's a thing in their family that everyone celebrates the full seven days of the holiday together and as Danny's girlfriend that means me too."

"Okay dear," said her father, and to her surprise he added, "Maybe you want to bring this fella around so we can meet him sometime? Sounds like you are sweet on him."

"Sure Dad," said May, dismissing the idea before the words came out of her mouth. She did not need her parents' approval or want

Danny to meet them before he popped the big question. Not that he would care, but she didn't want to take a chance. Things were going very well with Danny and he behaved like a perfect gentleman every time they were together. Neither mentioned the episode in the car and he continued to buy her exquisite gifts from The Green Door, an exquisite jewelry store owned by a lovely family from her community. May was excited about Passover. She took copious notes on everything she observed, so that next year, as Danny's bride, she would be familiar with the routine. She loved learning and doing it right mattered to May. This was her big chance to have the life she dreamt of, no sacrifice of her own wants and needs was too big.

16

"What you think you become. What you feel you attract. What you imagine, you create."
—Buddha

Ray finished her mounds of homework, showered and got ready for bed. She had a migraine headache and wanted to sleep. She had been suffering from migraines for as long as she could remember. One of her mother's colleagues told her to avoid all dairy products, another told her that they would disappear during menopause, while her therapist said they were a function of stress. Before going to bed, she was rifling through a bunch of catalogs that she ordered. Among them was one about degree requirements for undergrad programs leading to a master's degree in social work as well as JD programs for a degree in law. She also leafed through *The Jewish Week*, a weekly publication that her father brought home from his Manhattan office, and noticed an ad for SAR-EL. Not knowing anything about it, she read on and was intrigued. SAR-EL, she found out, was a fairly new program whose mission was to bring volunteers of all ages and from around the world to Israel. The volunteers would become support staff on various military bases in Israel, preparing medical kits, repairing mechanical equipment, as well as packing and inspecting a variety of field equipment. It sounded unlike anything Ray had ever contemplated and she decided impulsively to fill out an application for September 1991. Maybe after graduation, while Fay was in a religious seminary, she would take a gap year at SAR-EL. She decided to share her thoughts with the girls, knowing full well that yet again their plans diverged.

As she closed her overhead lamp, her Hello Kitty telephone rang, startling her. She knew it wasn't Fay or May, or even Mazal, because they all had a personal ring code. Picking up the phone, she heard a guy ask for her hesitantly.

"Ray," he said. "This is Sammy BenAdin. You gave me your number a few weeks ago. Is this a good time to talk?"

She was shocked, having practically given up on the idea of anyone ever calling her spontaneously. "Well hello, Sammy BenAdin," she said, pronouncing his last name correctly. "How very nice of you to remember me."

"Well," he said, "if you promise not to hold it against me, I'll tell you a little story about how I got your number again."

She listened with half an ear, expecting some lame excuse. What she heard instead was more interesting than she could have imagined. It turned out that Sammy's grandparents were close friends of her Salem grandparents and his mother had been pestering him to call her. He had no idea that the number in his tux from the night he met her at the dinner honoring her parents was the same girl. Dreading the familial pressure, he decided to get over the obligatory date until he realized that the two girls were one and the same.

Ray felt her heart beat rapidly. This was no ordinary boy at all, and if memory served her correctly, he was very good looking and more importantly not part of any of her brothers' circles. He just graduated from college in Israel and was going to start a master's degree in political science at Harvard University in September.

Impulsively, she told him about SAR-EL and miraculously discovered that he not only knew about the program, but had attended it when he studied at Bar Ilan University. Ray nearly gasped. Could the universe actually be sending her the perfect guy? One who seemed to have character, a brain and was from the right background too? When Sammy asked her out for Saturday night, she said yes immediately, knowing she was dead wrong for letting him know she was so available. She knew the girls would interrogate her and kill her for being so easy, but Ray didn't care. She was happy. There was something about Sammy that she instantly liked and the fact that he was 24 years old and attending Harvard in the fall thrilled her.

Sammy called her in the morning to wish her a pleasant day. He was thoughtful and down to earth. When they discovered that they both loved the zany humor of a new comedy show called *Seinfeld* about a group of friends living in the city, it started to feel increasingly nice together. As expected, the girls bombarded her with questions, most of which she had no answer to. Nonetheless, she loved their advice, concern, enthusiasm and most of all, their happiness for her. She even for one mad moment considered telling her mother, but instead, chose to confide in Suzi. It was a good decision. She found herself enveloped in Suzi's arms.

"This is wonderful news, darling Ray," cried Suzi. "When will you bring him over so I can meet him?"

Ray could not get over how her life had changed from the moment she truly heard what Fay had said to her about how skinny she looked and took it to heart. She was now back to a healthy weight, looking forward to a fulfilling career and a relationship that made her happy. The only thing that concerned her was her father. All her life he was there, menacing and threatening, never hearing her or interested in what she wanted out of life. While she never shared her thoughts with him, she knew he had to be aware that she was dating someone. Sammy was at the house almost every night. Ray waited, dreading the moment when her father would fabricate a reason to end the relationship. He would probably say that Sammy wasn't good enough for her. Sammy was the complete opposite of her father. However, she knew that the real reason her father would object to Sammy was to demonstrate his control over her.

When the two men met, Sammy was respectful and calm. He refused to engage in any combative conversation. She knew this annoyed her father. He was used to his patients fawning all over him and expected Sammy to need his approval and prove his worth. He questioned Sammy repeatedly about his plans in the political arena, failing to hide his disdain. He even had the audacity to suggest that he was concerned that Sammy would not be able to support a wife as a political strategist.

When after three months it was evident that Ray and Sammy were truly serious about each other, Dr. Salem made his move. Without consulting his wife or daughter, he invited the BenAdins over to the house for drinks to meet and talk about the children. In reality, it was to intimidate them and show them what a successful doctor he was. He had never heard of the BenAdins and assumed erroneously that they were beneath him socially. When they arrived, he was wearing a navy cashmere blazer, gray Armani woolen slacks, a Charvet white shirt, Brioni tie and handmade leather loafers. He was a successful doctor and he looked the part. He had instructed Victoria to buy herself an expensive Valentino caftan, so the stark difference in their respective status would be obvious.

The BenAdins were low-key people. They were not ostentatious and sought only to meet Ray's parents, not impress them. When Dr. Salem looked at them, he smiled, thinking he had the upper hand. He let Ray know that afternoon that she and Sammy could join them and they arrived moments later. The six of them sat in the living room, where Dr. Salem held everyone hostage while bragging about his accolades, his speaking engagements, his first-class trips and his collection of paintings, antiques, fancy watches and cars. The BenAdins looked uncomfortable and said very little. Then, Dr. Salem went for the kill.

"I am sure you are eager to get to know more about my daughter, so let me tell you about her. She's a beautiful girl, as you can see. With my reputation and success, she can have any boy in the community, and I don't mean the nobodies. I'm talking about the top people."

In his excitement, he lost any semblance to the carefully cultivated image he had forged for himself since becoming a doctor. While Ray looked like she wanted to float away in embarrassment, it got worse. He proceeded to regale them with stories of Ray's awkwardness as a child and need for various therapies.

"You should have seen her back then, or maybe, better you didn't." He chuckled. "We tried everything except shock therapy. In fact, when Ray was 12, I told my wife that we may actually have to pay someone to take her off our hands."

Ray wanted to die. How cruel could her father be? What was the purpose of bringing all of this up now, if not to humiliate her to the core? The room turned quiet until finally Mrs. BenAdin spoke.

"Ray, sweetheart, you and I have so much in common. When I was growing up in South Africa on our estate, I was such an awkward girl. I couldn't stand all the servants hovering around and my poor parents, besides themselves with worry, also took me from therapist to therapist! They even bought me a pony, hoping that riding would calm my nerves. Just like you, I turned out alright."

Ray just gawked at her future mother-in-law. At that moment of sheer gratitude, the beginning of her spiritual connection to God was developed. Surely, this was a modern-day miracle. Not only did Mrs. BenAdin save the day and rescue her from the embarrassment her father had subjected her to, but she also subtly was letting her father know that she was not impressed with him, his status or his wealth. Suddenly, everything was back to normal and Sammy stood up to make a toast.

"To our families getting together on many happy occasions. To life, *Lehayim*!"

As the group drank, Sammy looked straight at Dr. Salem and in a quiet but dignified tone he said, "I don't know where you grew up, sir, but where I come from, we don't speak about our beloved women like that at all. I would ask you in the future to consider your words when talking about Ray."

Dr. Salem looked mummified; his face frozen in fear, admiration and shock.

Sammy took Ray's hand and asked her if she wanted to go for a walk. His parents stood up and politely said their goodbyes. Ray was trembling as she left the house with him. The worst had happened and not only had she survived, but she was supported and not left to flounder on her own in the face of her father's verbal abuse. She looked at Sammy and couldn't talk. Tears slowly fell down her beautiful face. His heart broke.

"Ray," he said slowly, "I am thinking that tonight's performance was not the first of its kind. I hope I am wrong and your father was just nervous and it all came out so poorly."

"No, that's exactly how he is. I knew he would try to ruin my happiness just to remind me that he makes the decisions for me. What I didn't know was what kind of mother you have and what kind of person you are, Sammy."

"To be honest, Ray-Ray," he said warmly, imitating her best friends' childhood habit of doubling their names, "if I could, I would have you move into our home until you leave for Israel. I always suspected that you were afraid of your father, but I never wanted to pry or make you feel uncomfortable. All I can say is that I feel sorry for a man who has such a wonderful life and needs to degrade and humiliate his daughter to feel powerful. He won't ever do that again. I won't let him."

"Sammy, thank you for shielding me. I don't know what I ever did to deserve you and your mom. I can't believe what your mom said" she sputtered. "She is simply an angel. To share such personal things about herself in order to make me feel less self-conscious! Oh my God, you must be appalled at what kind of family I come from."

"No no no, please Ray, do not concern yourself for one minute about that. My parents adore you! You are not responsible for your father. Obviously, he had a very troubled childhood of his own and in spite of his success, fortune and *mazal* in life, he is still an unhappy, insecure person," he concluded. He would never tell her that his mother had crafted that entire scenario merely to defend Ray.

"Oh Sammy, no wonder I love you," said Ray and then gasped as she realized what she had just said.

"Well well well," said Sammy, broadly grinning. "So this night is going to have a very different ending. I am in love with you, Ray Salem, and have been since our first phone call. I want you to have everything your heart desires—your trip to Israel, your senior year and whatever career you want. Just know this, I will be in Boston for two years. I will wait for you and when you are ready, we will get married." He reached into his pocket and took out a tiny silver box. "My grandmother, my mother's mother, wore this ring all her life and my mother wanted you to have it," he said as he gave the box.

"Oh my God, I don't know what to say," Ray replied. She opened the box and saw the most exquisite sapphire ring.

As Sammy put it on her ring finger he said, "This is my pledge to you. I love you. I will care for you and protect you as long as I live. You would make me the happiest man alive if you agreed to marry me someday."

Ray was in such shock that she could not breathe and felt as if her heart was bursting out of her chest. "I will, Sammy. I will."

He took her into his arms and held her for a long time.

When Ray stepped back into the house she wasn't sure what to expect. Both her parents were waiting for her, her mother looking sad and rubbing her upper arm. Dr. Salem looked at his daughter and in an instant spied the ring on her finger.

"What is that?" he shouted angrily. "He gave my daughter a trinket!" He moved closer and pulled roughly at Ray's hand so that he could properly look at the ring. He stood in shock. "This ring! This is a very valuable ring. In my estimation, this might be a 20-carat sapphire ring. Where would Sammy or his parents get that kind of ring and have the audacity to give it to a 17-year-old girl without her father's permission?"

Ray took a deep breath. "This ring is a pledge. Sammy's mother wanted me to have it even if I don't wear it until I am older. It belonged to her mother: Mrs. Rothschild from London."

Ray knew that the Rothschild name would get her father's attention.

"Well, I for one don't like them at all. I have no intention of socializing with them. Even if they have one big ring to try and show off with," he postured.

Ray saw that in her father's bravado, Sammy was absolutely right about her father. He was still an insecure person. Because the name BenAdin was unfamiliar to him, it never dawned on him that they could possibly be exactly the kind of people he enjoyed mingling with. It was the first time in her life that Ray saw her father look uncomfortable. She glanced at her mother and made eye contact with her.

At that moment, she realized that her mother, for all her accomplishments as a respected plastic surgeon in her own right, was trapped by a patriarchal cultural mindset that forced her to be subservient to her husband. But Ray knew that she was never going to be a submissive little girl, not to her father or her husband. She was going to leave this house and have a wonderful life in a marriage where her opinions mattered, where she was respected and valued. She felt sorry for her mother and vowed to help her find the strength and courage to leave her father, if that's what she wanted. Ray was doubtful that her mother would have the wherewithal or courage to confront him. She turned to her father and savored the words she was about to impart as if they were droplets of the finest, most exquisite aged wine on her tongue.

"Well Dad, I don't think you will have that many opportunities. They flew in today on their private jet just to meet you and Mom. They have four homes around the world and when they are in New York, they stay in their Upper East Side pied-à-terre, next door to the Safras, not here in Brooklyn."

Ray exhaled and grinned. She knew she had just delivered the knock-out punch. Had her father known in advance who these people were, he would have played this all differently. He was smart enough to know there was no do-over, not with the BenAdins, not with Sammy and certainly not with her. Dr. Salem looked miserable, like a bully who met his match and knew he lost.

"Well, next time they can stay here," he blustered. "In fact, I will invite them for dinner when you come back from your trip and we can start over."

He knew, however, that the BenAdins would never step foot in his home again after the way he treated his daughter in front of them. He looked defeated and Ray felt vindicated for the first time in her life.

As she made her way to her bedroom, she hummed "Roll With It Baby." She had rolled with it her whole life and now, by the grace of God, things were finally changing.

After taking off her beautiful Carolina Herrera floral dress and her brand-new Charles Jourdan pale pink leather pumps from Ira's shoestore on Bay Parkway, she took off her make-up and replayed the events of the evening in her mind. For one brief moment, she almost felt sorry for her father, but then she reminded herself of her mother rubbing her upper arm and shook the pity away. She would save it for someone who truly deserved it. Finally, at 1:00 a.m. Ray decided to have a three-way conference call with May and Fay. She would tell them about the drama that unfolded with her father on the flight to Israel. For now, she had plenty of other things to tell them. As expected, the girls were enthralled with Ray's ring. More than that they were shocked to hear what kind of family Sammy came from. This made them admire his humility all the more.

17

"In Israel, in order to be a realist you must believe in miracles."
—David Ben Gurion

The girls shopped for Israel in earnest, going to Lester's at least five times to find the perfect accessories. In just two weeks they would board their flight. School, final exams and the New York State Regents exams were over and summer was officially in full swing. The daily phone calls were fast and furious. The lists of toiletries and odds and ends were growing by the minute.

Then it was June 24th and time to head to the airport. The girls would meet up with their individual groups in Israel, but they were flying together. It was a night flight, leaving at 11:55 p.m. They were flying directly to Tel-Aviv from John F. Kennedy Airport and needed to be there three hours in advance for El-Als security boarding.

Ray and May were anxious to get the goodbye time with their parents over with, while Fay dawdled when saying goodbye to Bobby Ava, her aunts, cousins, parents and sisters. Ava, for the first time in her life, looked old to her and slightly vulnerable. Fay felt guilty that her going away for four weeks was so frightening to her grandmother. It made her feel all the more compassionate toward her own mother, growing up with parents who were always scared, always anxious about something. Ava was always expecting a disaster, catastrophe or calamity. She was practically waiting for the other shoe to drop. However, her mom was great. Fay was enormously proud of her mother, who had made such obvious progress in taking stock of herself.

"Now, Anyu," she said in English to her mother, as if she was a nurse and her mother a patient. "Fay is going to be just fine on her trip. She will write and she will call when she can."

Suzi was exceedingly cautious not to make promises of daily or weekly phone calls, so as not to commit Fay to that pressure. Shockingly, Ava allowed herself to be outwardly mollified by Suzi's assurances, but in her heart of hearts she was truly scared, even more so because of the recent 1987 intifada in Jerusalem. Not wanting to upset Suzi, who had become much nicer to her of late, she held herself back from expressing her fears. However, looking at her beautiful Fay, she started to panic and her thoughts escalated to a degree where she started to imagine that every Arab in Israel was readying to kidnap Fay. Looking at her granddaughter, an American girl born to luxury and privilege, she was terrified that in the event of an emergency, her Fay would not know how to protect herself. She wondered why the girls needed to go on this trip ; causing her this unnecessary stress. But then she looked at Suzi and tried hard to control her racing thoughts.

"So, my darling Fay," she said, biting her trembling lower lip. "Go and have fun and take pictures everywhere."

Fay hugged her grandmother. Crying openly now, she whispered, "I love you so much Bobby, please don't worry about me or I will feel terrible for going."

It seemed as if those words penetrated into Ava's terror-stricken heart because she dried her tears and said, "Okay, everyone line up for a picture."

Dutifully, everyone did and the moment was memorialized. When Fay looked around, she saw May buying magazines and Sammy hugging Ray. It was time for the three of them to leave.

The girls did not sleep the entire flight. Fay insisted they talk only in Hebrew and that in itself caused them to burst out laughing every few minutes. It was hopeless, thought May. She just couldn't grasp the grammar or remember the words. Ray was hardly any better. They were glad that on their free weekends and midweek breaks Fay, the apparent linguist, would be their spokesperson.

As they got ready for landing they put away their snacks and put their shoes back on. They were taken aback by the emotionality of the moment when the entire flight crew started singing, dancing and welcoming them home—to Eretz Yisrael, the land of Israel. All three girls, as well as most of the passengers who had never been to Israel before, were openly cheering, some crying. The girls took their backpacks and left the plane. As their groups were not meeting for two days, they were proceeding to the King David Hotel in Jerusalem where Sammy's father kept a permanent suite for when he traveled to Israel for business. Mr. BenAdin had personally called Ray and told her that his suite and driver would be available to her for the duration of her stay. The generosity, but mostly the warm, calm and loving way in which he spoke to her was not lost on Ray. Could it be possible that there were actually fathers who just loved their daughters and accepted them, without trying to control them every waking minute of the day? As she brushed those thoughts aside, she smiled, excited to finally be in Israel. The girls got through customs quickly and stepped into the limousine waiting for them.

"I miss Earl," said Ray, laughing.

"Me too," said May. "But to be honest, these guys are hot! Don't tell Danny, please."

In 45 minutes, the girls were in the center of Jerusalem, overwhelmed with the myriad of sounds and sights of the Holy Land. In their suite, which had three bedrooms, a parlor, a kitchen and an incredible view of the Old City, there was also a magnificent oversized bouquet of exotic flowers with a card attached to it.

"Shalom and welcome, my precious Ray, to our homeland. I hope you and the girls enjoy every moment. Love, Sammy."

Ray was touched. She felt so loved and cherished. The girls opened the door for the bellhop and as soon as he deposited the assorted pieces of luggage, they opted to go have breakfast and see Jerusalem. It was going to be the most spectacular day ever.

"Oh my God," said Fay an hour later. "If Bobby was here, she would *plotz*, literally faint from this breakfast. It was so delicious. I can't believe how much I ate."

"Me too," said Ray laughing. "That coffee-flavored Leben was so delicious, and the hummus and tahini with the *lafa* and pita so fresh!"

"Okay," said Ray, ever practical. "Here's an idea. Let's skip the Monit taxi—ha ha Fay, see, I'm actually using Hebrew words—and at least walk off breakfast before we stop for falafel and pizza. Okay?"

"What a great idea!" cried May. "I will take my brand-new Canon camera and we can start taking pictures right now."

The girls left the hotel and started walking. They posed on Rechov Hamelech George Street, at Jaffa Gate and at Machane Yehuda, the amazing market—commonly referred to as the *shuk*—where over 250 vendors sold the freshest vegetables, delectable exotic fruits, baked goods like baklava and halvah, cheeses, nuts, seeds and spices. It was a cornucopia of delights, designed to tantalize the hundreds of tourists and locals who shopped there. Eventually, they found themselves at the Kotel—the Wailing Wall. It was beyond any description they had read. The *mechitza* partition separated the men from the women. They watched men of every age and background fervently praying in unity on one side and observed the dozens of praying women on the other side. As they approached the wall itself, which was an outer wall and the last remaining connection to the Beit Hamikdash, they saw the crevices filled with thousands of tiny pieces of paper—prayers that people from all over the world left in the wall.

Fay took dozens of pictures that day. By the time they got back to the hotel, they were achingly tired but also exuberant. In addition to lunch and praying at the Western Wall and leaving their own heartfelt notes, they toured the Old City, the Tower of David, the Dome of the Rock and the Armenian, Christian and Muslim Quarters. They also passed through the ultra-Hasidic quarters of Mea Shearim and marveled at how ancient it all looked. They ordered a light mixed grill dinner from room service and fell asleep the minute they got into their beds. Fay remembered to call her mother, who promised to call Mrs. BenAdin, Mrs. Salem and Mrs. Goldman and, of course, Bobby Ava, who had already called the hotel five times, anxious to hear Fay's voice.

The girls rose early the next morning, excited to see more of the city of Jerusalem. Once again, they thoroughly enjoyed a lavish Israeli breakfast, this time of *shakshuka*, smoked fish, assorted cheeses, delicious finely chopped *salatim*, asparagus, artichokes and unbelievable desserts and coffee.

"Oh my God, we must all get pregnant at the same time so that our kids can do this together too," said Ray.

Fay burst out laughing. "That would take some planning, Ray-Ray."

Fay was touched that Ray wanted their children to be as close as they were and experience Israel in the same way as them. The few days together were over all too soon and the girls tearfully said their goodbyes. They planned to meet every Monday for dinner on their designated night off and every weekend. In fact, Mr. BenAdin had graciously given them carte blanche to use the suite for their weekends in Jerusalem, while Ray's parents arranged for them to stay at the Hilton Hotel in TelAviv when they found themselves in that vicinity. Ray knew her father's largesse was only about competing with Mr. BenAdin and had a hard time thanking him for his generosity. The girls each assimilated into their programs, but were happiest when they were together.

18

"There are no beautiful surfaces without a terrible depth."
—Friedrich Nietzsche

All the schools hosting American and European teens would be going to Poland together in two weeks' time, after touring extensively up north. May was happy she and Ray would be there in case Fay had a hard time facing the past realities of the Holocaust. Her intuition was spot-on. Fay was a wreck from the moment they arrived.

At check-in at the hotel in Warsaw, she turned pale when she heard the staff speaking Polish. Then, when they arrived at Auschwitz, the largest concentration camp built by the Germans, she could not bear to look at the infamous overhead iron sign that boldly stated "Arbeit Macht Frei"—the blatant lie perpetrated to make people think it was a work camp instead of a death camp. She could not handle the actual March of the Living, when all of them walked from one end of the camp to the other: from Auschwitz to Birkenau, nearly two miles in total.

Then, it was time for the agonizing visit to the on-site Auschwitz museum; to the display of piles of leather suitcases and shoes, the artifacts and memorabilia housed in glass to preserve them forever; the artwork, often crude drawings done by children and adult prisoners depicting their thoughts, hopes and fears; pictures of the sun shining and the outdoors, of mass graves, of rabid dogs set on children and of menorahs and wine goblets, of what once was a life of innocent, good Jewish people. She could not bear to look at the striped prison uniforms and pictures of the Nazi officers in their uniforms, smiling, confident and exuding power and a maniacal discipline to fulfill their führer's explicit mandate to rid the world of Jews, but not necessarily of their property or wealth. Nor could she handle the tour guide showing them the crematoria, bunkers and barbed wire.

The fact that she was surrounded by Jewish teens from Israel, Canada, Australia, Argentina, Brazil, Panama, South Africa, France, Belgium, the United Kingdom, Hungary, Austria, and Poland made no difference to her. At the same time, it was not lost on her that this was an incredible opportunity to meet and share moments of both sadness and joy with others. She was made aware that there were third-generation German teenagers there, one of whom told them all that her mission in life was to atone for the sins of her grandparents and to make sure the world knew what unchecked racism could do.

Fay did not eat or sleep much the entire time they were in Poland and only perked up as they left Auschwitz, wrapped in Israeli flags, arm in arm, singing the venerable age-old song, *Am Yisrael Chai*,our Jewish people live. To think that her great-grandmothers had both perished right here was unfathomable to her. To know that her grandmother and great-aunts had been subjected to the will of the most evil men and women was equally unbearable. How, she kept wondering could the entire world have stood by while millions of innocent men, women and children were systematically being murdered. Fay was bereft of all emotion; incapable of talking, sleeping or eating. Ray and May held her close and were extraordinarily protective of her. They were glad the trip was coming to an end and they would fly to Paris together before heading back to the States.

Fay kept a diary and drew sketches of everything she had seen at Auschwitz. She attempted to call Suzi every single day, but was unsuccessful in getting through. When she finally did, she could not stop crying the entire time.

"It is so bad here, I can't bear to think that Bobby Ava was really here. Oh my God, Mommy, I can't take it."

Suzi was alarmed at Fay's reaction. She immediately contacted the program director, who assured her that there were counselors available to talk to the teens. For Fay, nothing helped. She was stunned beyond comprehension at man's capacity for evil. She made vows about what she would try to do in her life to somehow right this wrong, to make sure the world never forgot what happened. At the same time, she knew there was nothing she could ever say that world-famous humanitarian and Holocaust survivor Elie Wiesel hadn't already said in his autobiographical account of all that he had endured as a teenage boy. He was an eyewitness to the atrocities of the Holocaust and a noted author and Nobel Prize winner. Fay learned about him in school and Ava talked about him ever since she could remember. Almost immediately after the war, he became the face of Holocaust survivors. He lectured around the world, met presidents and monarchs and pressed for reform in places like Rwanda and Darfur, where genocide still existed. He talked in his lectures about his own survivor's guilt for having survived while millions died, and the doubts he had about a God who would allow such atrocities to happen.

Fay, like her mother, was socialized to put the needs of others before her own, and made every effort not to spoil this unbelievable aspect of their trip. She forced herself to enjoy the three glorious days their parents had agreed to let them have in Paris. As planned, they checked into the more modest and budget-friendly, but still very French, Westin hotel, toured the Palace of Versailles, the Louvre Museum and the riot of spectacular flowers in the Tuileries Garden. They took countless pictures at the fabulous haute couture Chanel, Ungaro, Dior and Yves St. Laurent windows on Rue Saint-Honoré and bought adorable gifts, souvenirs and knick-knacks at Galeries Lafayette. They heartily enjoyed the divine hot cocoa at Angelina's Salon de Thé and kosher food courts in the Marais district on Rue des Rosiers. They ended their spectacular day by visiting the Eiffel Tower.

At night, the nightmares of Poland terrorized Fay. On top of that, the graphic images she had seen at Yad Vashem, the remembrance museum in Jerusalem on Mt. Herzl dedicated to the Holocaust, haunted her. The museum was a monumental testament to the six million Jews who had perished. It also paid tribute to the thousands of righteous gentiles who had risked their lives to help save Jewish neighbors or friends. It was also a resource center for Holocaust education. In its explicit mission statement, the museum elaborated on the need to provide a historical perspective and an in-depth analysis of the events that led to the implementation of Hitler's Final Solution. But it was the three-year-old newly constructed pavilion dedicated to the one-and-a-half million children who perished during the Holocaust that completely overwhelmed Fay; it was more than she could handle. The hall was designed in such a way as to provide a reflection of lights. As guests moved through the room in the sparse light of candles, they could hear the names of the deceased children and adolescents, with their age and place of death, recited over and over by an on-going looped tape recording.

On the plane ride home to America, while the girls napped, Fay pondered again and again, how her grandmother remained sane and how she had the stamina, fortitude and ability to emigrate to a new country at the age of 22 and start over, raise a family and remain a devout Jew. Was it the desire to live for those who were murdered? Was it her youth? Was it her upbringing which gave her such a strong foundation of faith that not even the Holocaust could destroy that? Fay knew that there was no one answer to her questions. She developed a newfound respect for her grandmother, whom she thought she couldn't love more than she already did. She also felt a fierce kinship with her own mother for everything she did to make Bobby Ava's life pleasant, even if that meant not eating starchy foods.

When she arrived back in New York, after greeting her relatives who were all at the airport with signs welcoming her back, Fay went straight to Bobby's house and fell into her arms, sobbing in such wild abandon that Ava was taken aback.

"Please, please, my darling girl. I am okay. You see me here. I am okay. Please don't cry. It hurts me to see you so sad."

"Oh, Bobby," sobbed Fay. "Why? Tell me why. How could those monsters do this? Where was the world to stop them? No one cared. No one."

"I know, my dearest darling girl. I asked myself the same questions, for many many years. I used to wake up from my sleep crying to your grandfather asking him to explain to me how it could be possible that the people who gave the world the most exquisite classical music and the most profound philosophers and talented artists could be the very same nation who could also torture, starve, beat and murder six million Jews and at least that many millions of Roma gypsies, homosexuals, persons with disabilities and political dissidents. The mind can not grasp this, my precious one. It is beyond understanding. But please, my angel...Just know that our people have survived and we will prevail, because we have our own homeland and that's all that really matters."

"Yes, I agree with you Bobby. We deserve our own homeland, where we are safe and where our citizenship can not be revoked. I love Israel and I feel very connected to our people when I'm there. But still, I personally have to do something. Please Bobby, tell me what can I do?" asked Fay desperately. "There must be something I can do!"

Fay, in her desire to try and process her tumultuous feelings, was determined to find a way in which she could express her sorrow and at the same time help the world remember what happened when good people stood idly by.

Out of nowhere, it occurred to her that she could use her talent for painting. Her art would itself be a memorialization of the Holocaust. As much as she adored fashion and designing clothes, she loved painting too. From that day forward, Fay used oil and chalk for her paintings. She created scenes of ordinary Jewish people: husbands and wives, children and young lovers, synagogues and rabbis. She also painted villages and towns she had never seen first-hand, but imagined them from talking to Ava and reading books about life in Hungary, Poland, Romania and Germany before the war.

She studied the photos of the life and culture in the shtetl [Jewish villages] of Eastern Europe between 1935 and 1939 extensively. Many of them were captured by a Russian-Jewish street photographer named Roman Vishniac, who had emigrated to Berlin with his family before the Holocaust. Vishniac had amassed a collection of thousands of images of Jewish people. After witnessing the devastation of *Kristallnacht* and the way in which German Jewish citizens lost their status merely because they were Jewish, Vishniac devoted himself to using his camera as a means by which to document the Nazi parties rise to power. He took pictures of the swastikas rapidly rising everywhere and the cities and people they were rapidly destroying. Fay learned that Vishniac, under the auspices of the Joint Distribution Committee, traveled extensively throughout Eastern Europe to photograph Jewish communities. The commission took him to cities and shtetls in Lithuania, Belarus, Poland, Czechoslovakia and Hungary, and to Jewish farming communities in the Carpathian Mountains. He traveled an astounding 5,000 miles in total. His most famous book, a pictorial documentation published in 1983 called *A Vanished World*, captured the faces of innocent men, women and children with much respect and dignity. Fay was fascinated with Vishniac's determination to use his talent to create a legacy of a world that no longer existed. She found his ambition to return to Europe in 1947 to document the Jewish displaced persons camps astounding. These places were crudely set up to house survivors in former concentration camps like Bergen-Belsen until they had the wherewithal to emigrate and continue their lives. She learned that during this time, he also recorded the efforts of Holocaust survivors to rebuild their lives. Here was someone who understood the gravity of being a survivor, someone who needed to rebuild a broken psyche in a world that had no idea how to help. Fay was disheartened to learn that Vishniac had recently died at the age of 92. She imagined wistfully what an opportunity it might have been to speak to him face to face.

Fay started to have serious doubts about whether she could continue what she now referred to as her frivolous quest to become a fashion designer and focused instead on producing art as a political statement. However, Ava asked her to reconsider and go forward to the life she wanted and not what she felt compelled to do. In the end, after discussing it with her father, she decided she would not make a decision just yet. In time, she would know how to proceed or if she could do both.

By 1994, when director Steven Spielberg created The Shoah Foundation to record the oral testimony of all the remaining survivors, Fay was one of the first volunteers. The need to be involved had not abated one bit.

19

"I have learned that to be with those I like is enough."
—Walt Whitman

The summer was an experience that the girls knew they would never forget. It left an indelible impression on all three of them, even though May and Ray did not express their emotions anywhere near to the degree that Fay did. For Ray and May it was Israel that captivated them and they knew they would return often. They loved the people, their fierceness, their passion and their loyalty to their convictions and right to live as Jews in their country, promised to them by God. Not once did the girls feel afraid while visiting Haifa, the Negev, the Dead Sea, the Galilee and various kibbutzim, or while walking the ancient streets of Tzfat, the Golan Heights, Meron and Rosh Hanikra, or when climbing the stronghold at Masada, or even when their bus tours were close to the borders of Lebanon, Syria or Egypt.

When they got back to New York, they made multiple copies of their hundreds of pictures and looked at them daily, then weekly and finally, occasionally. Soon though, it was Labor Day and senior year. Ray and Fay were taking Advanced Placement courses while May was busy at Jordache and reading bridal magazines.

Things were going very well with Danny. Although he occasionally drank a little too much and was a tad too possessive, she loved him and looked forward to marrying him and taking her place among the Salems. She was horrified when Ray shared the incident that had occurred the night the BenAdins had met and consequently kept her distance from her future father-in-law. Her only concern was Danny, keeping him happy and having a fulfilling life. Nothing else mattered, not the permanent marketing job she was offered or even her desire to become more observant and to visit Israel often.

The girls each breezed through 12th grade. On the weekends, they went out as a group: Danny and May, Ray and Sammy, and Fay. At first Ray and May were concerned that Fay would feel awkward, but she wasn't. She was not ready for a relationship yet. When the time was right, she would be set up on a *shidduch* date with any of her mother's friends' sons. For now, she was more than happy to hang out with her friends and their boyfriends, who liked her as much as she liked them.

She was also hyper focused on her artwork, dabbling in various shading techniques to give her work more depth. She knew she needed guidance and had already decided that she would take art classes, regardless of what her ultimate career track was going to be. Often, she would paint in Ava's house while wearing the Israeli flag that she had worn on the trip to Auschwitz , wrapped around her thin shoulders. She increasingly felt the need to be in Ava's presence.

Before Chanukah, she finished the first in a series of portraits of Ava and her great-aunts. She had worked painstakingly, capturing the hollowness in their eyes, the faint smile on their lips, the shattered hearts they possessed and the tattoos on their arm: A20014, A20015 and A20016. The tattoos were a permanent reminder of that moment in time when madness took over their world and they were stripped of their clothing, possessions, names and identity, relegated to being branded and treated like slaves.

As the days grew colder and the first snow fell, Fay dreaded the impending separation that was rapidly approaching. Ava and Imre would relocate for the winter to Miami. Fay resolved to spend her winter vacation with her grandmother in Florida instead of joining her family or the Salems in Cancun, or going skiing with May and Danny in Vermont. Being with Ava was extremely important to her. Not even skating at Rockefeller Center, the Rockettes at Radio City Music Hall or the annual trek to see the spectacular revolving Christmas window displays at Saks Fifth Avenue and Macy's cheered her up. To Fay, these were distractions. Only Ava and her art mattered right now.

20

"A true friend is the greatest of all blessings,
and that which we take the least care of all to acquire."
—Françoise de la Rochefoucauld

Rosh Hashanah, Yom Kippur and Sukkot were a time of celebration. Danny was getting ready to propose to May, so it also became a time when their families finally met. May dreaded the moment. Knowing how Dr. Salem had treated the BenAdins, she could not imagine what kind of performance he would put on for her parents. One thing she was sure of, if Dr. Salem embarrassed her, Danny would not rise to the occasion like Sammy.

The day after the holidays ended, with the Sukkot decorations packed away, Dr. Salem invited the Goldmans over for a drink. Victoria braced herself, but shockingly, Dr. Salem behaved. Not only did he greet the Goldmans as if they were his equal, he actually went out of his way to make them feel comfortable. By the time May and Danny arrived, the parents were relaxed and laughing. May looked at her parents as if she was seeing them for the first time. What, she wondered, had actually transpired here? She turned to look at Danny, to see what his reaction was to the sight of their parents getting along so well, but he was oblivious. He approached Mr. Goldman and deferentially asked his permission to propose to May. She watched in amazement as her father gallantly gave his permission and her future father-in-law raised his glass. It was all surreal.

Ray and Sammy came over with Fay and then the party officially began. Danny got down on his knee and presented a magnificent diamond ring to May. As the girls cried "mazal tov" and "*mabrouk,*" May glanced at her happy parents. Was it possible that she didn't really know them? Why were they suddenly so invested in her happiness? Coming to no conclusion, she took a sip of champagne and ate a chocolate-covered strawberry.

Ah, the good life, she thought as she accepted a square toast point with black caviar covered with a sliver of black olive from the waiter who was passing hors d'oeuvre to the many guests from the community who descended on the Salem house to congratulate them. If anyone wondered why the bride's parents weren't hosting the event, they kept it to themselves. May was happy, happier than she thought possible and it was all thanks to Danny. He was the vehicle by which she acquired a true sister like Ray, brothers-in-law, prestigious parents and status in the community. She vowed to herself that she would devote every day of her life to making him happy. When the rabbi made a speech, she listened to every word of advice that he offered to her and Danny. Nothing, absolutely nothing, would stand in the way of her happiness.

From this day forward, May became a permanent fixture in the Salem home. A month after their engagement, her in-laws presented her with a red Volvo, a key to the house and an American Express card for her personal use. May was flabbergasted. This was beyond her wildest dreams. The Salems treated her like she was a princess and in return she treated them like royalty. So far, she had yet to see the nasty side of Dr. Salem. From her vantage point, he was charming, generous and good-natured. However, like her own parents, it appeared as if there was another side to him that he chose not to reveal.

In truth, Dr. Salem was playing a game. He was well aware of who the Goldmans were. In being the gentleman by offering to pay for the wedding, he made himself feel better after the debacle with the

BenAdins. In fact, he personally invited the BenAdins to the nuptials and wedding, but they did not respond. Instead, they sent an antique Menorah from Christie's auction house for the young couple and expressed their regrets directly to May for being unable to share in her happiness.

The snub was not lost on Dr. Salem, but he pretended it didn't matter. It was only in the privacy of his bedroom that he expressed his true feelings to his wife. At first, he ranted and raved about the BenAdins and how much he loathed people like them. Then, he attacked the Goldmans, including May. And finally, he blamed Victoria for everything, saying he was sorry he married her, saving her from obscurity, because she failed to impress the BenAdins. She just looked at her bedspread while her husband spewed his venom. She hoped he would tire himself out and leave her alone. That was all she ever wanted—to be left alone.

Tonight though, that was not on the agenda and Victoria submitted to her husband. That was what her mother and her own Sitti taught her before her marriage. Glancing at her husband of 25 years, Victoria wondered where the boy she thought she married had disappeared to. Certainly, the man lying here in her bed was not the handsome, charming boy she thought he was, or wanted to believe he was. How did her own parents not know what they had done to her by arranging this match without her consent? She, being a dutiful daughter, never once complained or told them. Instead, she let them and the world believe that being a doctor was her number one priority. Sadly, she had done such a good job trying to keep her husband happy that even her own children believed that she had no interest in them or in being a mother.

However, that wasn't true. It was all a facade to impress her husband who decided that if they both became doctors that would really insure their status in the community. No one would ever recall the poor homes they came from once they became successful doctors. Victoria gave in to her husband to keep the peace. Her professors were amazed at her ability to do rounds and rotations while being pregnant and right after giving birth.

Satisfied that her husband was finished with her and asleep, she quietly left their bed and went to the kitchen where she made herself a cup of tea. Tomorrow, she would be at work again. That, and the thought of the birth of her first grandchild, made her happy to be alive. All that she had endured, never able to defend her precious daughter or herself from the abuse heaped on them by her husband, would pale by comparison when she would become a *naaneh*. She hoped her first grandchild would be a girl. She would spoil baby Victoria May and give her the world. No one, not even her bully of a husband would get in the way of her last chance at happiness. It was bad enough that she had betrayed Ray all these years by acting oblivious to her husband's behavior. She would fix all of that if she could; one day, when she was able to do so. For now, she hated the submissive coward that she was and cried bitter tears.

That's how Ray found her when she and Sammy came into the kitchen. Alarmed at seeing her ever-composed mother so vulnerable, Ray immediately held on to Sammy for support.

"What is it, Mama?" she cried. "Why are you crying?"

"I'm crying from happiness," her mother replied, trying to reassure her. "I am so thrilled that Danny is marrying May. She is so lovely."

She knew the words were empty and Ray was not fooled, but this was not the time. Both of them knew that.

Sammy looked concerned and said, "Victoria, is there anything I can do?"

"Yes, just continue being yourself. Seeing you with Ray means everything to me."

With that, Ray looked shocked. *Who is this? And where is my real mother?* Then, Ray figured it out—menopause. Yes, her mother's waning estrogen was changing her in some weird way. Ray hoped this was a one-time occurrence. She wasn't sure she could deal with a softer version of her mother, not after a lifetime of wishing her mother would be more present. At least, she consoled herself, she might be an amazing *nanne*.

Ray and Sammy took some bottled water from the refrigerator and said good night to Victoria. This was their nightly routine, after dinner and drinking they had a mutual understanding that water would wash away anything unhealthy. As they sat in the den, Ray curled up to Sammy and leaned her head on his shoulder.

"Do you want to talk about it, Ray?" Sammy asked gently.

"I don't get it. If my mom has a vulnerable side—and clearly she was having a moment—why has she hidden it from me all these years?"

"I can't answer that, sweetheart, but I think that someday you, at the right time and in the right place, you should ask her. My hunch is that she has a lot to say that might surprise you."

or who to impress. The unexpected bonus was his family. She adored her younger sisters-in-law and Sammy's parents were the kindest, most loving people. On her first trip to London to their palatial home, replete with tennis court and stables for their horses, she found herself in a newly decorated bedroom stocked with an array of amenities found in world class hotels, simply to make her feel comfortable. She found American branded toothpaste and mouthwash, her favorite brand of Opium perfume, a typed list of phone numbers to various shops, lovely soaps and a hair dryer. There were no adequate words to express how valued and cherished she felt. Her future mother-in-law, who managed a household staff of ten and was the chair of three international charities, took the time to personally take her on a shopping spree to Piccadilly Circus, Bond Street and Carnaby Street, and to lunch in the Jewish quarter in Golders Green. They ate the best fish and chips Ray had ever tasted and had a delightful day. In the afternoon, at a very formal high tea at which the invited guests were dressed in suits and hats, they enjoyed an array of finger foods and cucumber rounds served with tea and crumpets. These were her mother-in-law's closest friends, and they were gathered to make her acquaintance.

Ray panicked at the thought that she might come across as American, low class or spoiled. After calling Sammy, who was doing some work for his dad and laughed off her concerns, she called the arbiter of all things European: Ava. Ava set her straight within minutes, reminding her to speak slowly and reflect on her words rather than speak hastily.

"And darling, remember your posture and cross your legs at the ankles, not at the knees, much more refined," said Ava firmly and lovingly.

"Now tell me, Ray," she asked conspiratorially. "Is it true they live in a palace or was Fay exaggerating?"

"Bobby, Fay was not exaggerating. It is a palace! I lost count after 16 bedrooms. And one of my future mother-in-law's best friends with whom they summer together in their Herzlia 'cottages'—as they call them—is Lady Jacobsen."

Ava smiled at Ray's calling her "Bobby." All of her

granddaughters' friends did and she loved it. Now, though, she was suitably impressed. After all, she grew up in a country that had a monarchy and all the pageantry associated with royalty. Hearing these details from Ray gave her deep pleasure and Ray could hear it in her youthful breathlessness. It lit a fire under Ava and in the next sentence she let Ray know exactly what was on her mind.

"Listen to me, Ray," she said urgently. "We need to find a good boy for Fay. I would have no objection vatsoever to an international *shidduch*. Keep your eyes and ears open please."

"Bobby," said Ray emotionally, "you know how much I love Fay. If I am lucky enough to find a boy that deserves her, I promise you will know before Suzi."

"I imagine in that case you vill need my telephone number in Miami?" asked Ava, assuming Ray would drum up a candidate within weeks and would want to keep her apprised.

"Yes, of course," said Ray enthusiastically. "That would be helpful. Also, I might need one more etiquette lesson. I am lost at the table with all the miniature forks!"

"Not to vorry," reassured Ava. "Call me anytime you need me. *Servus*, darling." She lapsed into Hungarian, something that only happened when she was very excited.

Ray knew Ava would immediately call her own two sisters and tell them the news. She was thrilled that in some small way her good *mazal* and fortune somehow extended itself to making Ava and her sisters happy. Ray already knew Fay's Bobby was extraordinary, but as she got older, she appreciated her even more. That generosity of heart, that boundless enthusiasm for life, was inspiring. Ray truly felt honored to know Bobby Ava and her sisters.

As the days of her first trip to London during winter break came to an end, Ray looked back on everything she had experienced in the span of ten incredible days. She simply adored "the tube"—as the British referred to the subway—and all the tourist traps. She was so overcome with joy that in addition to buying Fay, May, Bethie and Deenie wonderful gifts, she also bought carefully selected token gifts for each of her brothers and their girlfriends at Harrods, which was the British equivalent of Bloomingdale's. The one extravagant gift she bought was an oversized beige, red and black Burberry shawl for Bobby Ava. It was made from the finest, softest cashmere and wool. She knew Ava would love it. To Ray, happiness was something she wanted to share with others and Ava had been and continued to be a guiding, comforting presence in her life, much more so than her own grandmothers. Further, it was her way of paying tribute to Fay—whom she thanked every single time she spoke to her—for never backing down on her unwavering belief in her right to a more meaningful life. Fay's determination was what saved her from a vacuous, empty life. Perseverance was recognised as post-traumatic growth in some survivors—a legacy of the Holocaust that was generationally transmitted alongside trauma symptoms. It was that strength of character that would one day also save Fay's own life when in one drunken moment, which Danny Salem would regret for the rest of his life, he threatened to shatter her already fragile psyche. She refused to psychologically wither away.

Perhaps the nicest evening Ray ever spent with her new family was when the entire family dressed formally and went to West End Avenue to see *Cats* on Broadway. There was no bickering or quarreling, everyone simply enjoyed the night out together and the elegant dinner afterwards. Similarly, on Shabbat, the whole family attended service at Bevis Marks: the oldest Sephardic synagogue in London. It was the first time in Ray's entire life that she was spellbound by the environment of a synagogue. It was opulent, majestic and elegant and she felt privileged to sit with the BenAdins as their future daughter-in-law.

She was dazzled and distracted by the ornate carvings, the oversized menorahs and ceiling moldings that reminded her of the Sistine Chapel in Rome. She only had devastating memories of that trip: her father yelling at her and her mother in the museum for not knowing proper attire and wearing shorts even though other tourists were equally ignorant of the dress code expected of female tourists regardless of the fact that it was 101 degrees. Erased from her memory within seconds was the stay at the villa-like Art Deco style Hotel Lord Byron near the Piazza del Popolo with its view of the entire city from the balcony, the gelato they indulged in, the leather gloves and pocketbooks they bought while shopping on Via dei Condotti, the Coliseum and the fountains at Trevi, the camaraderie of seeing hundreds of tourists like themselves enjoying strolling for hours on end on the cobblestone streets and shopping in the open markets. Ray recalled fleetingly how happy she had been with the delicate filigree sterling silver ring she had bought that day, agonizing over her choice and finally loving it to death. All that vanished and in its place the only memory to surface was the sinking feeling that yet again somehow she and her mother had, according to her livid father, once again ruined their special trip, which had cost him thousands of dollars of his money.

By contrast, the most inspiring moment she observed on that first trip to London was the succession, day and night, of throngs of people—mostly men—of all ages and backgrounds. Sephardic, Ashkenazic, Hasidic and Modern Orthodox Jews who came to the house to see her father-in-law. In her naivete, Ray initially thought, based on his warm greetings of his guests, offering food and beverages at all hours, that these were all highly esteemed business colleagues or partners. It was only years later when Ray found out inadvertently that all of these individuals were people who came for *sedaka*—collecting money for themselves or for the needy.

The humility, the kindness, the devotion to family, all that she observed in her father-in-law was nearly overwhelming. She was sure that one day the queen would knight him for his services to the Crown, because in his banks in England, Ireland, Scotland and Wales, he treated every single customer, big or small, with the exact same grace and dignity and often went out of his way to help failing businesses succeed. To Ray, he was the epitome of a man and she was ecstatic that he was Sammy's father.

This is what gave her the confidence to let go of the past. Had Sammy asked her then and there to move to London after they were married, she knew she would have agreed. Barring Fay and May, there was really nothing in New York that kept her tied to the city. She adored the British accent of the locals and all the gossip swirling around the formidable queen and "the people's princess" Lady Di, who did things her own way and tirelessly worked to help AIDS patients get treatment. The thought of being married no longer terrified her, but she was relieved that Sammy wanted to finish grad school first. By the time he returned from Harvard, he would know whether Washington DC or London would strategically be best for his career and Ray could finish undergrad at Oxford or George Washington University. The idea that she would have a career was intoxicating to Ray. Her father's derogatory remarks from childhood and on led her to believe that all she was suited for was marriage and babies. Sammy, however, believed in her and wanted her to reach her fullest potential, including being his wife and the mother of his children.

It never ceased to amaze Ray how her life had changed so radically and she never forgot who it was that made it possible: her soul sister Fay who never gave up on her. In therapy too, she worked hard on repairing her bruised self-esteem and slowly came to the realization that her mother had sacrificed a lot for her and her brothers, doing the best she could under difficult circumstances.

Ray asked herself often what she might have done if she had been married, had four children and no emotional support whatsoever. Assuming her mother was even brave enough to contemplate divorce, back then when her mom was a bride, it was virtually unheard of for a woman to be granted one. To begin with, by Jewish law, only the husband could release the wife from marriage and Ray was sure that for her heavy-handed father, that was never an option. The impression she got was that her grandparents, on both sides, were also intimidated by her father's grandiosity and rather than rock the boat, they all—especially her mother's parents—pretended not to see their daughter's unhappiness. Instead, they acted the part of proud grandparents and marveled at their daughter's good fortune and wealthy lifestyle. That was probably why they stayed away, except for the holidays— to avoid seeing what they were powerless to change. One day, she would have a conversation with her mother. In her heart, she wished but knew it was likely never going to happen that her mother would simply pick up and move to London. She was positive that the BenAdins would help her start a new life and if

Ray's destiny was to live with Sammy in London, she would be there for her mother.

Letting go of the past made Ray feel invincible. Every day, she felt motivated to do her best and it showed. She looked radiant and confident and people commented on it all the time. The comments made her cringe and laugh in alternating measures. Some people said she landed a great guy and that was why she was so happy while others, perhaps a bit more astute, attributed the change in her to maturity and self-awareness. Only Sammy, May and Fay knew the truth: she was simply relieved that life had finally dealt her a decent hand.

23

"Gam zu l'tova. This too is for the good."
—Nachum Ish Gamzu, Talmud, Taanit, 21a

The dreaded day came upon Fay, as she knew it would. Chanukah was over and Ava was packing for Florida. Fay started packing too. Ava and Imre were booked on Pan American Airways on Christmas Day, a week after Chanukah ended, which would give them enough time to settle in before Fay's arrival for winter break.

While doing some research, Fay found that exactly one year ago an incredible memorial to the Holocaust had opened in Miami Beach. She learned that not everyone, even some survivors living in Miami, wanted this memorial in sunny Miami and she resolved to see it with her own eyes. She called the museum and was able to have a brochure sent to her that provided details on the architecture and what would soon become the world-famous four-feet-high sculpture of an outstretched hand. Fay regretted that once again fate had intervened and she had missed the opportunity to be there last year for the opening ceremony at which Elie Wiesel was the keynote speaker. She read his powerful words combined with the images in the brochures of emaciated grandparents lying in the street, of naked mothers shielding their children and groups of SS men enjoying themselves while tormenting helpless, innocent Jews. This served as inspiration for future graphic works of her own. She was especially moved by Wiesel's keen observation about the future: "One day, a man or a woman will enter this sanctuary of remembrance and wonder 'Was it all true? Were the killers really that cruel? And the victims helpless? That lonely? That abandoned?' Will this museum, or any other, bigger or smaller, make a difference? I hope that visitors will bring their children. I hope they will look at the pictures."

Fay understood exactly what Elie Wiesel was trying to convey to the world. It was urgent and up to her and every successive generation to swear to the veracity of these pictures, so that in time people would not view the Holocaust as just another tragic period in Jewish history.

Oddly, the thought of visiting the newly opened museum on Meridian Avenue was comforting to her. She desperately wanted to ask Bobby Ava to accompany her and decided to ask her Aunt Magda's opinion, even before asking her own mother. She had wanted for some time now to have the opportunity to talk to Magda alone, privately and confidentially, about her mother's childhood. This might just prove to be the opportune moment.

Fay dialed Magda's phone number. She loved her aunts fiercely. Even when they sided with her mother, she found them to be loving, supportive, caring and thoughtful. She would never forget how Magda had stood up for her that fateful day when her career was on the line. Ironically, as it turned out, her new career path was one that was far less complicated. True, her art classes were subject to the same issues regarding Jewish holidays and observance of Shabbos, but there was far less mingling with students than the path to becoming a fashion designer. While she still had not determined exactly what she wanted to do, in planning her fall 1991 schedule, she was looking for an undergraduate degree that would ultimately lead toward a Master of Fine Arts. She might someday design clothes for friends and family, but for now, she wanted to paint.

"Hi Magda, *haj vaj*," she said, exploding in laughter while mangling the Hungarian she didn't speak but picked up from her mother's morning conversations. The words, trying to convey "how are you," served as an icebreaker.

Magda started laughing. "Hi Fay, darling. I love your Hungarian! Almost as good as my Spanish. How are you?"

"I am great, Magda Nene," she replied. "I am sure Mommy mentioned to you that I am planning to go to Miami for winter break and I wanted your opinion on something. Can I come over today?"

"Sure," agreed Magda, intrigued.

Later that day when her niece joined her in her kitchen for coffee she asked her, "Any reason you didn't go to Mommy first, which I imagine would be the right thing to do?"

"Well, that's the thing, Magda Nene. Mommy has been amazing lately, but growing up she wasn't always like that. If you don't mind and if it's too painful or sad, I totally get it, but I was wondering what it was really like growing up with survivor parents."

"Well," said Magda slowly, "I didn't see that coming whatsoever. It wasn't easy, not for Anyu and not for us. We, we..." She cleared her throat and started again. "What did we know, we lived in Crown Park, almost like a ghetto. Nearly everyone we went to school with had mothers with accents and numbers on their arms and no one had grandparents. We never talked about those things, ever. It was like a public secret, like what you would call the pink elephant in the room. We spoke English in school. We recited the Pledge of Allegiance. We learned geography and American history. Then we came home and answered our parents in Hungarian and watched Bobby Ava or Zita Nene make strudel or Dobos torte, never apple pie. We helped our parents fill out English medical records forms, drivers license applications and even their citizenship papers. We saw them cry when they lit those strange candles every year to commemorate their parents who perished and sometimes we heard them scream in their sleep when they had nightmares. At home, we were often reminded that we belonged to two separate worlds that had nothing to do with each other. Do you understand what I'm saying, Fay?"

"Oh my goodness," answered Fay, astounded by Magda's candor. "In five minutes you have told me more than my own mother was able to in 17 years. Not that I blame her, but I always wondered about certain things, which brings me to this: I understand that on top of everything else, you were also first-generation Americans. The difference, I guess, is that your immigrant parents didn't just decide one day to leave their home for a better life. They left because their way of life was gone, along with their families. That must have been insanely hard to put together and deal with."

"Yes," said Magda, nodding her head in agreement. "We all suffered on some level. Look at Judy, she went through hell. Even after years of therapy, she is still a timid rabbit; she lets everyone walk all over her. Me, I'm obese, and your mother is a hothead and aggressive."

"So you know about my mother's moods and temper?" gasped Fay.

"Sweetheart," said her aunt softly, "it's not as obvious as my weight, but yes, I've seen it many times and your father and Bobby have both complained to me many times over the years."

What she didn't divulge to her niece, knowing she had no right to cross that boundary, was that Zak had threatened to leave Suzi many times and stayed only because of the girls.

"According to your mother, Bobby tells her daily that my weight problem is killing her and that she can't take how Judy acts like a *lemala* [a scared timid rabbit]."

"Wait," said Fay, confused. "Why does Bobby tell you what she doesn't like about Mommy and Judy Nene? Why doesn't she just tell you she's worried about your weight and tell Mommy she's too aggressive? Wouldn't that make much more sense?"

"Yes," sighed Magda. "Of course it would. I can't tell you how Bobby was before the war, I can only tell you how she was after, while we were growing up. She tried her best, that's for sure, but in truth, she never got help because no one wanted to talk about the war. Now, today, the vets in our country are getting some help adjusting to life post-combat, because some psychiatrist finally realized that when people are a witness to near-death experiences or catastrophes and survive, that they can develop reactions to that trauma anytime in their life, not just when it happened. However, in 1945, no one was thinking about what the survivors needed. The only thing that mattered was that they survived."

"So, you're telling me that in 45 years, no one, not one Jewish agency, thought the survivors needed help in dealing with the memories of their experiences ?" asked Fay incredulously.

"Yes, Fay," replied Magda. "That's what I'm saying. It's a little more complicated though. There was nothing remotely like this in the history of mankind. The doctors themselves didn't know how to go about treating survivors. I read once that in Germany, after the war, psychiatrists were hired to assess the survivors for damages the Germans knew they would have to pay as war reparations. They referred to the symptoms they observed as 'concentration camp syndrome.' The only people who probably got help were those that completely broke down and were institutionalized. The rest, like Bobby, Kati Nene and Zita Nene, were trying to put it all behind them. So they did what normal people their age did: they got married and had babies. They needed husbands and the men wanted wives and most wanted to leave Hungary for good. So they applied for visas to Israel and America. The first group of children were born in displaced persons camps Bergen-Belsen, including me. And over time, we children, being the only ones who lived with them from birth, absorbed their panic, their fear, their depression, anxiety, mistrust of strangers or officials in uniforms, their endless headaches and stomach aches, food issues, nightmares and physical pain. What they didn't tell us, we read in books. It didn't matter how old or young we were, or whether the stories we heard scared or repulsed us. We listened, because we were a captive audience. All we ever wanted was to go to school and be normal. Believe me, darling, Bobby tried very hard. She always put us first, but when she inevitably had a flashback or dream or nightmare, she simply shut down. We were lucky that she shielded us from her sorrow, but at the same time, in trying to protect us and never telling us the truth—that she was sad or missed her mother—she often looked so stern and unapproachable. That, I can tell you, was scary! She wasn't really stern, though. She was as loving as you know her today, but she could only truly let her guard down and laugh when she was with her sisters, because that's probably when she felt most alive—with those with whom she almost died. Oh, I can tell you stories, but what's the use? Your Aunt Judy, did everything she could to make Bobby laugh. She didn't know why as a child it was so important to her, but now as an adult, we all understand that she must have felt that if Bobby would laugh, then we would all be okay. We could not be happy as long as our mother was sad."

Fay felt like she was about to faint. She was breathing hard. Her face was red and she felt like a rocket was going off in her head. Magda was like a gushing fountain of information that she needed to turn off for a while. It was a lot to absorb and Fay wondered if Magda talked this much with her own daughters.

"Magda Nene," said Fay, the physical trembling of her anxious body reaching her throat, "I am in shock. First of all, I honestly feel like I just went to college! I feel like you explained so much to me that I never knew and it helps me understand my own mother so much more, let alone Bobby! Oh my goodness, I am so sorry for your pain."

She burst into tears. Her aunt was silent and then the two of them cried together for a long time. When they both calmed down, Magda made coffee. As they drank it, Fay continued hesitantly.

"As you know, I am going to Florida for winter break and I am planning to visit the new Holocaust Museum there. I am sure Mommy told you that this has become my focus ever since my trip last summer? So, I wanted to hear your opinion. Do you think it would be okay for me to invite Bobby to come with me or would it be too much for her? I feel like if I can see her, in that context, being free, alive and well, then I can separate her from what I saw in Auschwitz, which was more terrifying than I can even say. I've thought about this for months. It's like I need to liberate Bobby in my mind, because I feel like she never left Auschwitz. Does that make any sense?"

"I honestly don't know, darling. Again, I don't want to cross a line and decide anything for my mother who, *baruch Hashem* [praise God], can still make decisions for herself. My advice is to ask her, but I think what would be very hard for her is seeing your reaction. Your emotions might be taken for pity and that Bobby certainly doesn't want from anyone, least of all her grandchildren. Now," she brightened as a thought occurred to her, "if you invited all of her granddaughters, that would be a different story. The focus would be on her explaining, teaching and showing, and not on her reaction."

"Oh Magda Nene, I love you! You are a genius! What an amazing idea," said Fay excitedly. "Do you think we can pull it off? As the oldest girl, you know you can count on me. I would gladly coordinate the details and I think it would be such a fantastic experience for us third-generationers."

Fay hugged her aunt. She was so happy to have an aunt as wise as Magda, grateful for all she shared and for the idea that would grow, flourish and garner so much attention that it would grow into a small story in the *Miami Herald* and *Miami Jewish Times,* and create a platform for Ava, who would be invited to speak repeatedly.

When Fay got home from Magda's house, her mother already heard about the plan and was talking to Judy. The moms, after some logistical and financial discussions, were all on board and the girls very excited. No one mentioned being nervous or afraid and Fay kept those emotions to herself. Her cousins, except for Dani, were all a little bit younger than her and none had yet been on "the March," as she referred to it. Maybe this excursion with Bobby on American soil would prepare them for when and if they would do the March of the Living. In fact, the more Fay thought about it, the more she liked this plan!

That night, she talked about her trip to Israel and Poland for the first time at the dinner table. Shockingly, both of her younger sisters actually cried and felt bad for her. Fay was taken aback by their reaction, and felt really glad that she had shared what was painful and difficult for her, when she was hesitant to do so. Maybe there was still time to have a better relationship with her sisters. Certainly, the more her mother learned about her own behavior and treated them all equally, the better they would all get along. Fay wondered yet again why her mother had always singled her out and treated her differently? One day, she would hopefully find out. For now, that her mother was trying to be calmer, and more even-keeled was apparent. Both Deenie and Bethie looked noticeably less guarded to her and definitely excited about the upcoming cousins trip. That night, for the first time since Fay got back from the trip last summer, she went to bed without painting or thinking about the Holocaust. She had a strong feeling that this trip might help her put things into context, one in which she could function without falling apart or obsessing over Bobby's suffering.

24

"Never marry at all. Men marry because they are tired, women,
because they are curious: both are disappointed."
—Oscar Wilde

May went for her first fitting at Vera Wang in April, shortly before
Passover. Her mother, mother-in-law, Fay and Ray accompanied her.
She felt a pang akin to regret when her dresser, judging simply by
Victoria's enthusiasm and open checkbook, assumed Victoria was her
mother. Soon, that would be the case, she thought. Observing her
mother sitting so comfortably among the women who mattered most
to her, annoyed her. Now she wants to be more involved, she thought?
She tuned her out completely when she oohed and aahed over the
sight of her in her majestic bridal gown, veil and headpiece.

How ironic, thought May, Victoria, whom she was told by Ray often
enough was a cold fish, was the one who cried and hugged her and
repeatedly called her "daughter" and lovely words she would have given
anything to have heard from her own mother. In fact, watching Victoria
gushing with pride at how magnificent she looked in her custom Vera
Wang ornate silk organza gown, with a full layered tulle skirt and train
with lace and crystal embellished details, she could not fathom what
had brought on this sudden change in her future mother-in-law. She

knew it couldn't just be the menopause that Ray had alluded to recently; there was something about Danny getting married to her that made her future mother-in-law happier than she had ever seen her.

That night, still thinking about Victoria, when she, Fay, Ray, Danny and Sammy met up for dinner at Lou G. Siegels in the Garment District of Manhattan, May innocently brought up the topic. She quickly realized it was a terrible mistake when Danny's handsome face darkened.

"Why," he said through gritted teeth, "are you dissecting my mother like a lab experiment? Isn't she good to you?" When May nodded her head in agreement, he looked to the others at the table and implored someone to back him up, but in his desire to defend his mother, he went too far. "I mean, let's face it, guys," he said sarcastically. "My mom is pulling out all the stops here while yours gets a free ride and you think it's okay for you to criticize or speculate why my mom is happy or sad or anything at all? I'd say that's pretty damn nervy and plain crazy, May."

Everyone at the table was uncomfortable, especially Ray and Sammy, who knew that Danny had just morphed into Dr. Salem in front of their eyes. Fay looked appalled and May just sat there mute. Ray instinctively knew that this time, she needed to step up like Sammy had done when his parents came to meet her parents. In a calm but assertive manner, calling into mind her mother-in-law, who was her hero, she turned to May.

"Darling, I think that you did not make yourself clear and Danny misunderstood you, because just today, you told me how much you appreciate my mom and yesterday, I was there when she received the most gorgeous pale pink tulips, Japanese mums and king protea floral arrangement that you sent her to thank her for all her help and involvement."

May looked at Ray and understood the brilliant lifeline she was offering her. She was afraid to look at Fay, knowing that this act of contrition would not sit well with her. Fay, while never combative, was fiercely assertive, a trait she claimed was inherited and passed down to her by Bobby Ava. May, knowing she had no choice, mentally apologized to Fay for being a coward and grabbed the olive branch Ray offered her.

"You know what, Ray? You are absolutely right," she said, smiling brightly. "I adore Victoria and I absolutely did not mean to imply in any way, shape or form that she is less than perfect."

She smiled at Danny who was valiantly trying to control himself and succeeded just barely.

"Well, you know," he muttered. "We all make mistakes."

Not exactly what Ray was hoping for, but good enough. They ordered appetizers for the table. The worst was behind them, but Ray was worried. Fay was mortified and May acted as if nothing had happened. Sammy, too, was concerned. He adored Ray's best friends and saw too many similarities between the Salem father and son. He wondered why a smart, talented, pretty girl like May didn't see her own worth and tolerated Danny's behavior. Then again, so did his future mother-in-law and he knew better than to think that he was privy to all the facts or that the respect and mutual admiration he saw between his parents was commonplace.

He surmised that the bond his parents had was indeed rare, but something he was determined to bring to his own marriage with Ray —the light of his life and the most sophisticated girl he had ever known. He knew how passionate Ray was about the things she believed in, because he validated her right to think and choose for herself. He could see her fighting social injustices, helping to create legal remedies for battered women. In his mind, she was everything he could ever have dreamed of and while their nuptials were a way off, he knew it would all turn out well for them. He didn't know then that it would take five long years, including two years of premarital counseling, before his beloved Ray would finally be ready to fully commit to marriage.

When May got into the car, she continued the pretense that everything was fine, but she could not shake the feeling that tonight was a cosmic warning and she felt scared. She knew this was absolutely not the right thing to bring up with Rabbi Dweck, nor could she afford to say one word to Ray or Fay. Ray would tell her in no uncertain terms to postpone the wedding and Fay would urge her to totally reconsider the marriage.

May stole a look at Danny as he expertly drove his newest toy: the Mercedes S600. She knew nothing about cars and that had annoyed him when he asked her how special she felt sitting in his new Mercedes. Sometimes, she wanted to tell him to just give her a list of responses and she would say them to avoid another incident. Of course, that was insane and she knew that even thinking that was not a healthy thing whatsoever, but what else could she do to make him happy? Not talk? That for sure wouldn't work, she argued with herself.

From the way his jaw was set, she could see that he was still angry and decided to wait for him to speak. He did and what he said shocked her. He parked the car in front of her house and looked her straight in the eye. Bracing herself for what she knew was going to be nasty, May waited for him to insult her. He took her hand, which surprised her. "May, that was uncalled for. Totally inexcusable," he began.

May, terrified now that Danny might call off the engagement, began to cry in earnest and trembled. "Danny, I am so sorry. I love your mother. She has been beyond wonderful to me. The dresser thought she was my mother. I—"

Danny interrupted her by putting his fingers on her mouth. "Shh, listen to me, sweetheart. You misunderstand me. I'm talking about my behavior, not yours. I do not ever want to turn into my old man and tonight I could see that if I don't do something drastic, then I will wake up in a few years and be him. I'm not doing that, because it would kill my mother for sure."

May, being young and inexperienced, didn't question why Danny wouldn't consider her as his primary reason for change, but Fay did when she recounted the entire conversation. By then, May was so grateful at this turn of events that she laughed off Fay's concerns and almost regretted bringing up the whole topic, knowing she did so only to allay Fay's concerns.

"Fay-Fay," she said endearingly, "all the doom and gloom, please lose it. Danny would never hurt me. He told me he will handle it."

"Well," said Fay slowly, "before I even try to accept what he says, what exactly is his plan? Did he say he will see a therapist for anger management, because May-May, he is not going to be able to change his behavior if he doesn't get professional help."

"Oh my God," groaned Ray, who was so quiet that the other two assumed she had fallen asleep, which she was known to do from time to time. "Did I not warn you, May-May, about SY boys? This is how they are! I have to say, I am really impressed with my brother's insight. If he was really sincere, then he is A-OK. If he said it just because he knew he was wrong, then he's a jerk."

"Girls," cried May, "please, I can't take anymore of this. Has it ever occurred to either one of you that maybe, just maybe, I was the jerk for talking about his mother in public? I mean, to him it might have just made no sense. I can see that, honestly."

"And he wouldn't have had time to tell you that after dinner when it was just the two of you?" Fay said, furious with May's defense of Danny. "Please, May. I am begging you, just don't defend him. That scares me more than anything. Even if you were wrong. Okay, I will go so far as to say that my mother and my aunts all said that it was a tiny mistake on your part. You never talk about a guy's mother in front of him, much less others, ever, but that still doesn't give him the right to take such a swing at you in public."

"Well," said May laughing, "now we can officially put this to rest. The jury of Suzi, Magda and Judy has voted. I am guilty."

She laughed again so that the girls would know she wasn't upset and calmly ended the call. She mulled it over one more time and decided to simply let it go. She was getting married in 16 weeks, there were many more important things to think about. Men, she knew from her own father and grandfathers, are very different from women. While it made her laugh that Suzi Zweig had actually taken the time to consult with her own sisters about her, she knew it was a tactical error she would never make again. If Danny was sincere in his desire not to turn into his father, there was nothing to worry about at all.

25

"A man cannot be comfortable without his own approval."
—Mark Twain

Fay looked around at her gaggle of first cousins. All solemnly lined up for the group photo that Judy was about to take. She was thrilled and secretly loved being in charge of her cousins. She loved the girls and hoped the trip would create an indelible bond between them. They were all checked in and sitting at the gate, ready to board their flight to Miami. Ava, in Miami Beach, was anxiously checking her watch to see if, somehow, it was already time for her and Imre to go to the airport to pick up the girls. She was alternately excited and apprehensive about having all her granddaughters en masse at the same time, concerned that their high pitched voices, peals of laughter, natural exuberance and sisterly fights might be a little too much for Imre.

She had noticed lately that he wasn't himself; little things that by themselves weren't cause for concern but altogether seemed a little troublesome. She resolved to make an appointment with their internist, Dr. Schwartzman: a Hungarian physician who had emigrated to America before the war. Ava had a close, personal relationship with her. Dr. Schwartzman would most certainly run some blood tests, just like she always did when Ava went into panic mode and needed reassurance that Imre was fine. That was all she wanted, to live out her golden years with this good man. Anything else was unthinkable.

The girls made their final goodbyes, most of them unable to hide their desire to be rid of their overprotective mothers and start their adventure. As they boarded their flight, they all instinctively looked to Fay for direction, as the de facto adult in the group. In fact, Fay was turning 18 while they were in Florida and though initially Suzi was terribly disappointed, she took hold of her unbridled emotions and calmly told Fay they would have a marvelous celebration on her return. It was far more about her than Fay.

Fay found this new and improved version of her mother to be refreshing. Suzi had revealed to her that in therapy, she had already uncovered many things that never made sense to her. That in itself was a relief, but she still had a long way to go to come to terms with many conflicting behaviors she assumed were average, like Ava's coping mechanisms. These were designed to help Ava deal with her painful memories, none of which were Suzi's experiences and therefore they were not applicable to her challenges.

Suzi had become more honest with herself and her daughters. She even shared that she was seeing Magda's therapist. She only told Fay this, because she had yet to rid herself of the habit of treating her like a privileged confidante who was routinely rewarded by being privy to information she didn't want or need. Her mother confided in her that Magda said she was ready to get help in understanding her obesity and Suzi was hopeful that Magda would find her authentic self. While Fay felt this was privileged information and that Suzi might have betrayed her sister's confidence, she nonetheless felt a pang of joy for her favorite aunt.

Of Ava's three daughters, Magda, in spite of her weight, which limited her in so many ways, appeared to be the best adjusted. Her two daughters, until now, had never found fault with her, as she devoted her life to making theirs easier. Her marriage was not a good one, having married Hershel Baum right after graduating high school, like most of her peers. Hershel, she would often tell her sisters, was in far worse shape than she was. After meeting his parents for the first time, she understood why he was the way he was. He shrank in the face of his mother's authority and pitied his passive father. When Magda met him, she saw none of his moodiness or negativity. All she saw was an appropriate boy she could bring home to her parents and start her own life. Like his brother-in-law Zak, Hershel too, often threatened to divorce Magda. That he cheated on Magda before their first anniversary never seemed to matter to him or Ava, who firmly let Magda know that there would be no divorce.

The only sister of the three who even had the semblance of a good marriage was Judy. She, after a difficult childhood, married the son of two Polish survivors. Judy was madly in love with her husband and he adored her. Their girls appeared to be well-adjusted young ladies, all of whom were on an academic track. They were the only ones who did not live in walking distance to Ava. Instead, Judy dutifully called her mother in the mornings, six days a week. Judy had close friends besides her two sisters. She also belonged to the PTA and was on at least two committees in her neighborhood that attracted modern Orthodox Jews from various backgrounds. In fact, one Shabbos, when she invited Ava and Imre to sleep over at her newly decorated home, Ava nearly fainted when she walked to the table and saw a motley crew of six strangers whom Judy invited without mentioning it to her beforehand. To Ava, this symbolized Judy's complete switchover to becoming American.

"Next," she darkly said to her daughter, "you'll tell me you aren't making the roux for the vegetable soup or that you are following the instructions on the Manischewitz box for ferfel instead of first toasting it in oil."

Judy smiled at her mother. "Okay Mamuka, let me get the smelling salts. I have an announcement to make. Are you ready? I do make the ferfel your way because my family loves it like that, but here's the newsflash, I am American and so are my children. We aren't being disloyal to Hungary because that is your homeland, not ours."

All of a sudden, shy little Judy, the proverbial "lemala," as Lajos used to call her, had developed a backbone. Ava wasn't sure if she liked it, but she was wise enough not to confront her daughter. Instead, in Hungarian, at a feverish pitch she shared her true feelings and thoughts with both her two sisters Kati and Zita and then with her two daughters, Suzi and Magda.

"You just won't believe what Judy said to me," she said as if she was revealing classified information.

Each of the recipients, feeling privileged to be in Ava's orbit, waited to hear what Judy said. No one ever asked Judy about her side of the story. They knew from experience with their own daughters that sometimes it was hell raising them, especially these spoiled American girls who got to sleep on beautiful sheets every single night, take a shower or bath as often as they liked and have unlimited access to books, music, friends, movies, skating, parties and trips. They had every luxury at their fingertips without a war or a madman interrupting and changing their existence forever. For Magda and Suzi, whatever Ava said was the gospel and they never questioned her. She was, after all, their mother and her role as leader, captain and wise one was never challenged. On some level, the power she had over her daughters' lives was cathartic.

Ava and Imre walked into the terminal at Miami International Airport and waited for the girls to arrive. Ava kept sneaking glances at Imre to make sure he wasn't sweating or breathing heavily. He looked nice in his beige linen pants and navy polo shirt. Yet, she had an uneasy feeling about his health and made a mental note again to call Edith first thing in the morning and make an appointment. She had neglected to do so since hearing that her princesses were all coming to visit her.

Then, they were in front of her eyes as they exited the plane. Ava started crying on cue as they all laughed and shouted, enveloping her with kisses and hugs. Imre was beaming like a proud grandfather and told the Pan Am airline personnel, the staff at the baggage claim and at the restaurant they went to that all these beauties were his. While Ava thought her heart could only belong to Lajos, it was moments like this that endeared Imre to her. These were his grandchildren and he loved being their *zaydy* [grandfather].

The girls laughed when they saw the minivan Imre had rented at

Hertz. Ava was pleased that there would at least be no fighting or shouting over space. When she turned to look at the girls, the symmetrical rows in the vehicle instantly caused a flashback. Each of her granddaughters strapped in with their seatbelt on, vividly reminded her of that fateful day in May when she and her family also sat in a row when they were forcibly deported from the ghetto into cattle cars ill equipped to carry the hundreds and thousands of Hungarian Jews from every city and town except Budapest, into cattle cars. Would she ever forget the stench? Not only of human waste and dead bodies, but of fear and terror? She and her family were packed into those cattle cars with less dignity than the animals normally transported in them. She wondered again if these flashbacks, which came at the most inopportune times, would ever go away for good. She quickly shook her head, as if to dispel the thoughts ruminating in her mind, and was once again in the moment. When she had a flashback. she was gone, transported back to hell.

"Shall we go straight to the apartment?" she gayly asked the girls. "Or maybe first for ice cream?"

She craned her neck so she could see her precious girls. The "apartment," as Ava called it, was actually a beachfront condominium on Collins Avenue close to the Fontainebleau Hotel. It was an entire floor of three penthouse apartments that Imre had converted into one huge apartment so that all of the family could feel comfortable and never crowded. There were numerous bedroom suites, pull-out couches in the den, a library, living room, bunk beds in two more bedrooms and a total of 12 bathrooms. Ava and Imre's wing was on the opposite side of the 6,000-square-feet apartment, with a small living room and kitchen so that Ilonka, their live-in housekeeper, could prepare their breakfast and espresso coffee in their Illy coffee maker in private.

Throughout the winter months and in years to come, everyone came down to Florida, a never-ending parade of visitors paying homage to their matriarch who now held court in Miami Beach. The apartment accommodated everyone, including the infant great-grandchildren who spent weeks away from the brutal cold of the winter. To Ava, ten years of time had indeed caused her to slow down a bit, but more than her health, she was troubled by the fact that Fay, her eldest granddaughter, at that time 28, was still unmarried and eclipsed by her younger sisters and cousins. For now, however, this was heaven on earth and she never stopped thanking God for granting her enough years to enjoy life and a wealthy man like Imre by her side to make all of this possible. So what if he wasn't her first choice?

Dini, Magda's youngest, who was nine years old, started chanting, "Wolfies, Wolfies!" The rest of the girls soon joined in.

Ava laughingly said to Imre, "Driver, you heard my princesses."

He proceeded to drive downtown. While Wolfies was not a kosher restaurant, its owners were Jews. Ava decided a long time ago that having ice cream there was perfectly acceptable. She didn't overly concern herself about complicated kashrut dietary rules. She, of course, was fastidious in the stores she shopped in for meat and groceries, only patronizing stores where the owners were strictly religious Jews. Although over time, she had become far more lenient than all of her daughters when it came to treats. Zita claimed it was her best friend Rose who influenced Ava into exploring the world beyond the narrow confines they were used to. Imre would happily indulge her and bring her cherry cheese cake, Black Forest cake and Nesselrode pie from the finest Italian, French and Hungarian bakeries in Manhattan on Second and York Avenue just to make her smile, but her daughters never saw those cakes, ever.

As Ava watched the girls enjoy their ice cream sundaes and banana splits, smothered with hot fudge, caramel, whipped cream, maraschino cherries and bananas, she said to her husband in Hungarian, "*Nu* Imre, who would have ever believed that one day we would be sitting here like this?"

Imre, who had been in slave labor for four long years in the Hungarian army, just shook his head. He was similarly enthralled watching the girls, never once in his entire life burdening anyone by divulging a word about his own torturous experiences and losses. He felt sad thinking of his dear friend Lajos, the biological grandfather of these beauties, and wished he was alive. It was, remarkably, the first time Ava did not notice or care who ate what. She was mesmerized by their excitement and simply euphoric that they arrived safe and sound. She sipped her coffee and nibbled on a delicious biscuit.

The next few days flew by. Ava was in her element, instructing Ilonka on what to cook and bake for her guests. They started the day with her idea of a nutritious breakfast, followed by pizza at the pool for lunch, snacks all day long and dinner either at a local kosher restaurant or in the apartment. Imre rented a yacht and one day they had a picnic lunch on the boat. The girls tanned for hours, while Imre fished and Ava took pictures and painstakingly applied and reapplied suntan lotion every two hours on every one of the girls. It was only when she approached Imre, that she noticed for the first time a raised bump on his left earlobe. It was pearly white and she could see blood vessels inside it. It alarmed her because it was a new growth and not small at all. She again made a mental note, but now it was to call Mt. Sinai Hospital's referral hotline. She needed the name of the top dermatologist in town, and hopefully, not a cancer surgeon.

After two days of frolicking at the pool, walking on Lincoln Road, going to the movies and shopping at Jordan Marsh, the girls voted to get the museum over with. No one came close to expressing the level of trepidation Fay had, but clearly they were all aware of her trip to Poland and how it had affected her. Even Dini was concerned about seeing Bobby Ava sad.

After breakfast, which hardly anyone touched, the girls got dressed. They all dressed conservatively, out of respect for the museum. There were no shorts, tank tops or jeans, which Judy's girls, Lisa, Malka and Daniella, routinely wore in the summer and on non-school days. Instead, they were all dressed in a going-to-the-city-to-a-Broadway-show-or-museum garb. Not quite Shabbos, but better than their everyday garb. Fay wore her first official suit: a Bill Blass pink cropped jacket and straight skirt that Ava had found in a basement store whose owner she knew from "home".

Rifchu Pearlman was a brilliant businesswoman. She would finagle her way into the showrooms in the garment center on Seventh Avenue in Manhattan and refuse to leave until she spoke to a manager. Then, in her broken English, she explained who she represented; hundreds of affluent, sophisticated shoppers whose only requirement was modesty. In fact, she convinced Harry Benard, Alvin Nipon and Bill Blass to modify their lines with appropriate necklines, sleeves and skirts. For over 30 years, generations of shoppers scoured her basement when they needed better clothes. Rifchu, with her keen eye, could immediately size up the best outfit for every single one of her customers. She offered tailoring advice and dieting tips before a date, but also tactfully dressed the chubbier girls.

When the girls reappeared, dressed and ready to go, Ava nearly fainted at the sight of them. At that moment, she felt overwhelmed with love.

"Imre, *shnell*!" she shouted in Yiddish. "Hurry! We must take pictures before we go."

From the urgency in her voice, one might have assumed they had an appointment or specific time to enter the museum, but they did not. The urgency all emanated from Ava; an internal reaction that caused her to get flustered and panicked. Imre brought the camera, took dozens of pictures, and then asked Ilonka to take one so that he too would be in it. It was a picture like no other.

As they approached the museum, Fay prepared her grandmother and cousins. In a quiet, but authoritative voice she told them, "I don't know what you are expecting, but today you are going to see pictures, documents, artifacts and artwork that will shock you. It is really important that our generation sees this for ourselves. One day, we will tell our children and grandchildren what Bobby, Zaydy and our whole family witnessed and suffered." She took Breindy's hand. "I think you are a little too young for all this but we didn't want to leave you out! I remember when we went to Disneyland and you and Lisa didn't meet the height requirements on some of the rides and were so sad. Well, this is a little like that. You will definitely get old enough soon to see this, but for today, Bobby and I felt it would be best if you wait in the reception area with Ilonka."

Breindy, who adored her big cousin, gulped. She didn't want to cry in front of everyone to confirm that she was a baby, but secretly, she was relieved. Last night, Hedy scared her.

Imre bought the tickets, maps and guidebooks and they made

their way outside to the first sculpture to that of a mother and her two nestling children. From there they made their way to the memorial wall engraved with the names of thousands of souls annihilated in Europe. They stopped at each sculpture: one of three very young children crying from pain, hunger or fear; one of emaciated naked men; one of dead skeletal bodies shot down.

Ava looked stunned, pale as a ghost and incapable of talking. She held onto Imre as if she couldn't walk without assistance. In a millisecond, she was transported back to her arrival at Auschwitz. She saw the harsh lights overhead from the watchtower, scanning the entire perimeter. She saw the barbed wire. She heard the crying and guttural screaming. She smelled the acrid air and she remembered the encounter with the nefarious malevolent Dr. Mengele who shoved her to the left when she attempted to join her mother and baby nieces and nephews on the right. There, Kati and Zita waited for her.

Ava forced herself to breathe. It helped. She looked at her granddaughters and saw the agony on their faces, the horror and fear, the pain and confusion in their beautiful eyes. Her heart broke and tears rolled down her eyes. Fay noticed and felt sick to her stomach. *What was I thinking, what have I done?* she asked herself.

She turned to Ava and instead of crying and needing Ava to comfort her, she calmly said, "Bobby, please don't be a martyr. Let's go to the Botanical Gardens next door, get some air and decide exactly how long it makes sense for us to stay. The fact that we got here, that we are witnesses that this memorial exists in the world is enough. Nothing is more important than you."

All the girls looked more relaxed when Ava agreed to leave. In five minutes flat, she revived. "Now listen here, all of you. This is not a picnic, not for me, not for you, but we owe it to the six million who were murdered. We will go through the entire museum and tonight we will light candles just as I do every year to commemorate the death of my loved ones. Tomorrow, the sun will shine and we will spend the day at the EdenRoc Hotel. We will get manicures and facials and we will go out to The Crown Hotel for a beautiful steak dinner."

Fay could not believe what Ava said and started to smile broadly. She was so incredibly proud of her grandmother. Seeing Fay, their role model smile, all the cousins did too, until Leah started to cry. At 16, she was a very serious teenager, slightly introverted and a voracious reader. She apologized for crying and Ava took offense. "Nonsense, my darling. That's how you feel. Please don't ever deny your feelings. We will be fine, all of us. We will live to see another day."

At that moment, Fay knew that was the truth. They would all be fine, because they, too, were survivors, having inherited that resiliency, and were obligated to live their best lives while never forgetting what happened.

After that, they were able to complete the tour of the museum, pairing off and walking around. True to her word, Ava stayed in the moment the entire time, listening as the girls whispered questions to her. She was quite thankful when the tour was completed.

At dinner that evening, everyone was quiet. As they headed back to the apartment, Ava felt a sense of peace envelop her. This was exactly what she needed: to confront the past in a benign setting surrounded by the future generations of her family, not by stepping on the hallowed ground at Auschwitz-Birkenau or Dachau, where precious blood was spilled relentlessly. While some of her friends and acquaintances had made the decision in the past five years to actually go back to Auschwitz with their children and grandchildren, she and her sisters were adamant that they would not. Instead, they took a trip to Hungary and Romania with their spouses and went to the cemeteries to pay respect to their ancestors, who had died before the war, some living until age 100 in 1912.

Ava remembered vividly how she felt in Budapest with her sisters. Strolling on the Vaci Utica, they looked like typical American tourists. They stayed in the newly built Forum Hotel and drank espresso while listening to the exquisite sound of the strolling violins. By day, they traveled with Istavan, who was delighted to hear them all speak fluent Hungarian. At night, they fell into A Konyha, literally "the kitchen," which was the only kosher restaurant in town. The food was plain but delicious and eating there brought back memories of their own tiny kitchen in Bayamara, when their mother DevorahLeba cooked many of the same dishes. Kati was quite subdued while Zita, eating the delicious potato *krumpli*, was excited and talked a lot. The husbands largely kept quiet, used to being in the shadows when the three sisters were together. They stayed for four days and even visited their childhood home, but only from the outside. No one had the courage to knock on the door and talk to the current owners. When they left Budapest, all three were relieved that they would be going directly to Israel for two weeks. That trip to Israel was extraordinarily meaningful to Ava. As she stood at the Wailing Wall, the Kotel, and put her hand on the wall, she felt a sense of peace and closure. The movies, the literature, the books and even the survivors themselves could never adequately describe what had happened in those tumultuous years. While nothing would ever compensate for their suffering and losses, Israel was and always would be soothing to Ava.

She knew that someday she would live in Israel, not just visit. And in fact, many years later, as an aged woman living in Jerusalem, Ava discovered AMCHA, a social services agency dedicated to providing social services and psychotherapy to survivors and their children. She was fascinated by the fact that every single therapist, social worker and psychologist was a child of a Holocaust survivor. There, she addressed for the first time in her life the post-traumatic stress symptoms she lived with since 1945. She adored Dr. Tauber. She read her book *In the Other Chair* four times and sent copies of it to her sisters, daughters and granddaughters. Then, after years of individual therapy, she invited her three daughters to join her in session, in Israel, to address how they grew up. She had come a long way and continued to surprise everyone she encountered with her resilience.

Ava described her trip to her daughters in great detail, almost glossing over the excursion to Hungary. Now, judging by Fay's experience, Ava knew that she and her daughters could never be part of that contingency of people who felt they needed to honor their loved ones who were murdered at Auschwitz by going there. Looking at her oldest granddaughter, Ava smiled. Fay smiled back. This trip was one neither of them would ever regret or forget. It contextualized what Fay needed in order to make sense of the Holocaust without destroying herself. For Ava, it was the perfect compromise between showing her granddaughters what she endured without actually being back at Auschwitz.

As promised, Ava took the girls to the Eden Roc Hotel. She preferred the Eden Roc over the Fontainebleau. She set Imre up on a lounge chair with his newspapers, suntan lotion, radio and Breindy to keep him company while she and the rest of her granddaughters went to the salon. It was an absolute pleasure watching the happy girls pick their nail polish colors. This is what she lived for, the sound of their laughter, not the intrusive memories of Auschwitz.

When it was time for the girls to leave Miami Beach, Ava was reluctant to let them go, but realistic enough to know that they needed a day or two before the spring semester commenced to go shopping for Pesach. The girls were already anticipating the excitement of the plane ride home, seeing their friends, and the upcoming holidays, but Lisa was reluctant to go until Ava reassured her that she and Imre would return to New York shortly before Pesach and they would all be together once again. Now, as she and Imre were getting older, Ava agreed to move into one of her daughters' houses for those days. Kati did the same, so that they would all be together for the duration of Pesach.

For a few days, before the holiday, Ava cooked food she would bring to her daughters home.Even though they would not be home for Pesach, she prepared her own kitchen by putting down silver foil over every square inch on her countertops, took out her Pesach pots and pans and cooked the Hungarian delicacies that her own beloved mother used to prepare, each day waiting patiently until 4:20 p.m. for any of granddaughters to be dismissed from school so that they could help her, merely by being there and watching her. Ava loved when they came over. Leah would fastidiously write down everything she said, because she wanted to replicate every single one of Bobby's recipes in the future. For Ava, that was life-affirming, that her granddaughters would carry on her traditions.

26

"When all the dust is settled and all the crowds are gone, the things
that matter are faith, family, and friends."
—Barbara Bush

On the day before Passover, May moved into her in-laws' house. Her
parents had left for Scranton that morning and she was eager to be in
the kitchen with Lucía to help and learn all the dishes that her new
family would prepare for the holidays. She knew from spending so
much time in the Zweig house that the Ashkenazim had very
different customs than the Sephardim, especially about *kitniyot*, the
dishes made of legumes and rice, corn, millet and chickpeas. Lucía
was happy to have company in the newly scoured kitchen. She
showed May the menu cards that Dr. Salem had given her many
years ago. It shocked May to know that Victoria had taken the time to
write out exact details and precise instructions on how to prepare the
Seder plate, the lamb stew, the amazing white rice with apricots,
prunes and almonds, among many other holiday foods.

That night at the Seder, May felt like she was in an alternate
universe. Never in her life had she ever been exposed to customs and
rituals like those she was now committing to be a part of. Sephardic
Jews, it seemed to May, fiercely believed in ancient Biblical folklore

and customs that seemed quite out of place in the modern world they lived in, but that didn't stop them. When the Seder plate was brought in and placed on the head of Danny's youngest cousin, Moses, she nearly gasped. *What were they doing?* Danny just looked at her. While he wasn't upset with her, he did little to make her feel included. When the ceremony began with the matzah passed around in a sack, May was enthralled. She decided she would get a book and read up on all the customs and traditions, or ask Victoria. She wanted to belong, not be an outsider. That night in bed, slightly drunk, she turned to Ray.

"Why didn't you prepare me, Ray-Ray?" she asked playfully. "I had no idea that your traditions were so old-fashioned. Oh my God, I was sure that sheep and goats with a shepherd were going to make an appearance too."

May exploded in laughter and Ray joined her. "Welcome to my world," she said gleefully. There was no undertone of sarcasm or hostility in Ray's words and May knew it was because of Sammy. He made her so happy and May loved her brilliant future brother-in-law. She admired him a great deal.

Although May had been given her own bedroom in the Salem house, she chose to sleep in Ray's newly decorated pale gray and silver bedroom, as she had done all of her life on sleepovers. The girls would not see Fay until the first part of the holiday was over and they tearfully said goodbye over the phone. All three of them had officially gotten their driver's license in the past month, but none were ready to actually get behind the wheel and drive.

"Fay," said Ray as they attempted for the fifth time to end the call. "Please come after the *chag* is over and we'll have an old-fashioned sleepover. We have to do one soon, because May-May is going to be a married lady and I doubt Danny would allow her to have a sleepover with us."

"I would love that," Fay replied. "But I'm not sure my cousins would appreciate me leaving. Let's play it by ear. Who knows, by then I might be dying to get out of my house!"

The girls said their last round of goodbyes. Fay was especially thrilled that this year Bobby Ava was moving into her house. Ever since she got back from Florida, she yearned to see her grandmother and hoped that at the Seder, Bobby Ava and Imre would tell them about their own personal liberation and redemption. Fay knew this didn't come easy to either of them, but it was a tradition in the family and now more than ever, she wanted to learn more about her great-grandparents. On some level, she felt it was her responsibility to carry on the legacy. The more she heard first-hand, the better she would be able to tell her own children and grandchildren.

For Ray, having May move into the house for the duration of the holiday was a joy. She never realized to what degree she had missed out on not having a sister. For the 100th time, she wondered why Fay was so dismissive of her two sisters and was determined to talk to her. Without being able to fully express why this mattered so much to her, other than it fundamentally felt right that sisters stuck together. Bobby Ava and her sisters, mother and aunts were very close. Why wouldn't Fay want that with her sisters? It never dawned on Ray that maybe it wasn't Fay who was responsible for her relationship with her sisters, but Suzi. Fay explained it to her.

"It's not me, Ray-Ray. I've tried so many times. I think my mother's favoritism is what did it. I am trying hard to understand why my mother not only favored me, but also made a point of showing my sisters that they could never live up to the standards she forced upon me."

Ray wasn't satisfied with Fay's response. "In that case, if there is no major issue between you guys and it's only your mother's stupidity, then you need to talk to Bethie and Deenie and end it now," she argued.

"You know what, you have a point," said Fay with a huge smile on her face. I can't thank you enough, especially now with the wedding around the corner, for caring enough to bring this up. I give you my word, I will borrow my mom's car and I will drive the girls to Kings Highway to look at shoes at ShoeBox and then take them out for pizza at J-2. I will put all my cards on the table and hopefully it will make a difference."

Fay hugged Ray. "Thanks again, *amiga*," she said, grinning, knowing Ray loved her occasional use of Spanish.

Victoria sat at the resplendent Seder table looking every bit the matriarch. She was wearing a brand-new navy blue silk caftan and a pair of sapphire and diamond earrings that twinkled in her ears. She looked happy and content, knowing there was a wedding in the near future and hopefully a baby nine months later. It was all she thought about. She gazed around her glass dining room table at the three generations assembled and showed no emotion whatsoever, knowing that was going to change in the near future. May was her savior.

May was delighted to meet both sets of Danny's grandparents. While she dutifully answered all the questions they asked her, she could tell they didn't know what to make of her. She knew she would likely not have much to do with them, but for her husband's sake she would try hard to get to know them. Thereafter, every single Friday until the day she was divorced, she visited them before Shabbat, always bringing a book, flowers, cookies, challah bread or fresh fruit. Danny told her that they decided that for an Ashkenazic girl, she was okay.

From the time Passover concluded, May was counting down the days to her wedding. She was on a juice fast two days a week, working out daily, still doing the internship at Jordache and had officially earned the right to a spot in the highly coveted managers training program. She never discussed it with Danny, choosing to push off the conversation as long as possible. Graduation came at the beginning of June and the girls all attended each other's ceremonies. It was a very happy time. In years to come, all three would look back at those pictures and marvel at how great the future seemed back then. People were routinely using the World Wide Web and it seemed as if everyone was getting a mobile phone, not just doctors.

Then, it was the day of the wedding. All of the grand festivities of the past few days that led up to this moment went off without a hitch. May looked stunning in her gown. Her hairstylist convinced her to go for a soft flip and when Victoria looked at her, she knew they made the right decision.

"May, my dearest daughter." Victoria choked, unable to hide her tears. "You look magnificent."

May adored her mother-in-law and wondered how Ray could

have painted such a horrible portrait of Victoria. Not once in all these months had she ever seen an aloof, cold, disinterested woman. Victoria was the mother of her dreams; she could tolerate any situation as long as Victoria would be there. Many years later, when Victoria left her husband and moved in with her, she would remember this moment. Victoria was the epitome of love, praise, advice and assurances when May was overwhelmed. It hurt her to know that Victoria could have been a far better mother, but chose a career over her children. She knew right then and there that she would not make the same mistake.

The wedding was at 5:00 p.m. that Sunday evening in July. It was a beautiful day at the Lido Beach Hotel, a Moorish-style building with 300 rooms, designed to look like the Riviera. It was an exclusive seaside country club in Long Island, grand in its own right before Victoria's crew descended and added massive amounts of flowers and couches to enhance the setting, ready to host the event of the decade.

Victoria had truly outdone herself, especially in dealing with the cantankerous owner, Mrs. Harriet Bloom, as she was known to the housewives in Connecticut and New Jersey who considered her their exclusive European party planner, who had an opinion on everything.In the many meetings held before the wedding , Mrs. Bloom rejected every idea Victoria presented to her, practically laughing in her face. With her thick Hungarian accent, the four-foot ten stocky redhead was a formidable opponent who brooked no interference with her operation. Each event she executed was a personal win for the Holocaust survivor originally from Hungary known then as Hinda-Baila.

Most people understood that Mrs. Bloom was eccentric but incredibly talented and that she and she alone called all the shots, regardless of what the contract stipulated or how much money exchanged hands. "Harry, this lovely doctor is going to tell me how she wants the *chuppah* canopy to look, where the musicians will set up and what kind of food she wants at the reception," she yelled to her partner, who was also the head chef, in English, so that Victoria would hear her.

Harry just nodded, having learned 25 years ago never to argue with Hinda-Baila who had Americanized her name to Harriet Bloom. At one point, Victoria was so desperate to get through to Mrs. Bloom that she considered calling Fay's grandmother for help, assuming naively she would know Mrs. Bloom from Hungary. However, it was the bride herself who won over the hotel owner.

"This little girl, your bride," she said to Victoria, "I like her and I vill make for her the most magnificent wedding." She turned to the terrified May. "So tell me, sweetheart, what do you vont your vedding to look like?"

She proceeded, in her tiny chaotic office loaded to the gills with books, samples, pictures and oversized poster boards, to pull out pictures of ice sculptures, white doves, a canopy crafted entirely out of plexiglass, of the most exquisite satin, velvet, embroidered tablecloths and candelabras. May was sold.

"I love everything, Mrs. Bloom. I think you have the most exquisite taste I have ever seen. You remind me of my best friend's grandmother, Ava. She is also Hungarian and has amazing taste. She told us many stories about where she grew up, in a village called Bayamare."

Mrs. Bloom looked stunned. "Do you by any chance mean Ava Reiss?" she asked.

"I'm not sure, but it's possible that was her name before she remarried."

"Of course it is!" shouted Mrs. Bloom, positive that it was her Ava. "If it is who I think it is, I know her very vell. Oh, you should never know from vere I know here. Vonce upon a time, ve vere *lager* camp sisters. Her sister Zita took care of me like I vas her child, because I vas alone and so so scared."

"I know Zita Nene!" cried May. "I love her almost as much as Bobby Ava."

"Vell then," decided Mrs. Bloom. "It's settled. You must invite them to the chuppah ceremony and you vill see vat I vill do for you."

May shook her head in agreement.

"It is our pleasure," Victoria said. "I understand from May that Fay's grandmother is an extraordinary woman. It would be an honor to have them."

147

Harriet did not disappoint. She outdid herself primarily to show her adopted sisters just how far she had come in life thanks to them. They were duly impressed with her. The unusual coincidence that brought them together made Hinda-Baila very happy. It was the first time in her life that she looked forward to an event without thinking once about the many tragedies of her own life, including the murder of her own angelic baby who was brutally snatched from her arms. As she sat in her office, chain-smoking, Hinda-Baila was pleased. This wedding would put her on the map.

How this prestigious Sephardic family came to her door was an absolute mystery to her, but she was no stranger to mysteries or miracles, having been the sole survivor of a plane crash on the first transatlantic flight from Germany to France after the war. She would call a few caterers who specialized in exotic food and outsource the reception. This crew would be responsible for creating an unprecedented international food bazaar at the smorgasbord that would have people talking for months.

As she lit yet another cigarette, Hinda-Baila felt an emotion akin to satisfaction. The bride was a sweet girl; she was as blond as her own baby Ruchala and that was reason enough to go all out for her. Had she survived the Holocaust, Ruchala would have surely been a mother by now, which meant that Hinda-Baila would have been a grandmother.

Better not to think of the past, she admonished herself, knowing that in a minute she would start thinking about her husband, her real husband, the love of her life, Shay-Duvid, whom she had married before the war. He was gone and so was her baby girl. Instead, life had given her Mr. Bloom, a man 20 years her senior who sat on the boardwalk most days. She also had Harry, her business partner with whom she had a relationship that met most of her needs. Each wedding and each bar mitzvah was to her and Harry like the birth of a child; it was all consuming and never boring.

Before each event, Hinda-Baila bought herself a new piece of jewelry and an exquisite brand-new designer cocktail dress in Boro Park, where other religious women who could not go to work were now starting to sell clothing from their basements. When Ava, Zita and Kati Reiss would see their little camp sister, they would be speechless. Impulsively, she picked up the phone to call her cousin Yenta in Brazil and in rapid Hungarian ordered three diamond bracelets to present to the Reiss girls. They saved her life in Auschwitz, feeding her, and caring for her when she could not do anything for herself. They never saw each other after the war, when Hinda-Baila was taken on a children's transport to Sweden and the sisters were waiting for visas to America or Palestine. Time had flown by and they had all moved on. This occasion would prove to be very interesting.

The wedding started late, which caused Mrs. Bloom to start yelling at her staff in a pitch that caused many to start trembling. She irrationally held them responsible for the Syrian custom for guests to arrive late. Hinda-Baila could not control her temper when things were out of her control. She took a glass of schnapps and tried to regroup. The main course would have to be revamped and the desserts put back in the refrigerator. Instead of the 5:00 p.m. start time, it was close to 7:45 p.m. The singing and dancing went on until 4:00 a.m., when most affairs usually ended at 1:00 a.m.

While the customs were very different from the typical Ashkenazic or *New York Times* society weddings that Hinda-Baila was accustomed to executing,this one stood on its own merit. The international food court was an overwhelming success and the guests raved about every single dish. For Hinda-Baila, seeing Ava, Zita and Kati was the moment she had been waiting for. They had assumed Fay had imposed on May to invite them to the ceremony so that they could see Fay in her role as bridesmaid in her pale pink chiffon gown.

When they came into the Lido, oohing and aahing at the pink bricks, sure that this castle-like edifice must have had a Hungarian architect, they decided the trek was well worth their while. None of their husbands had opted to attend and the three sisters unanimously decided to enjoy this night out together. They dressed for the occasion in black beaded and lace cocktail dresses and looked beautiful. Ava looked at her two sisters. They were older and a little rounder. She wondered if Mamuka, their beloved mother, would even recognize them. Ava forced herself to stop this dangerous trajectory. She accepted a glass of sparkling champagne from the waiter while her sisters sampled the food. As they sat down on one of the plush luxurious leather couches set up for the guests, a woman approached them. She was very well-groomed. Instinctively, all three of them checked her out from head to toe. The woman looked nervous. She started speaking in Hungarian.

"My sisters," she cried, "it's me, Hinda-Baila."

Kati and Zita stopped eating and Ava's fluted glass slipped out of her fingers.

"Hinda-Baila!" Ava screamed. "Am I seeing things? We looked for you for years! We searched every Red Cross list. We wrote letters..."

Ava could not keep herself together. Looking at Hinda-Baila brought everything back to her. Zita, too, was openly crying. Kati sat in silence. As if on cue, they rose and smothered Hinda-Baila with hugs and kisses. When they found out that Hinda-Baila was the legendary Harriet Bloom, they were astounded. They had heard about this incredibly formidable Jewish business woman named Harriet Bloom who was a creative caterer and brilliant party planner long before any woman entered the male-dominated industry.

Hinda-Baila proceeded to tell them about her life, including her inability to ever have children again, her permanent limp, her life with Mr. Bloom and her career. There were simply no words to describe how the four of them felt at this reunion. When Hinda-Baila presented them with the matching bracelets, they were overcome with emotion and joy. For each of them, the moment was surreal. For the next 25 years of their lives, they would spend Passover and Sukkot at the hotel with Hinda-Baila and she would become an honorary Bobby to all of their grandchildren. On those happy occasions, Hinda-Baila would be calm and not smoke or drink as much as she was inclined to. Instead, she would be busy buying linens for her sisters' suites, ordering flowers for their rooms and creating a menu that they would enjoy in her dining room.

Later, on the ride home, Zita softly said what they were all wistfully thinking. "I know that for many years, I would pray to Hashem, to God, for a miracle and we would find out that Mamuka's sisters were alive. In discovering Hinda-Baila, even though she's not our blood sister, to me it feels like we almost found Chancsy, Chayala, Leahla, Zissy and Sheindy again," she said, remembering their sisters and baby nieces who were murdered at Auschwitz.

"Yes, I agree completely with you. Who would have ever thought that May's wedding would bring Hinda-Baila back into our lives," said Kati nearly astounded.

The three sisters unanimously vowed right then and there to include Hinda-Baila in the family, sharing their children with her and welcoming her into the fold. They had done so in Auschwitz when she was a starving nine-year-old who miraculously had been allowed to live through the notorious first selection of Dr. Mengele and they would do it again.

27

"Love does not dominate; it cultivates."
—Goethe

The seven days following their spectacular wedding, Danny and May received guests in their new apartment on Avenue S. Immediately thereafter, they left on their four-week-long honeymoon to Greece, Italy and Spain. For May, who had only flown once in her life when she joined the girls on their trip to Israel, this was a view of the world that astounded her. That Danny planned the whole trip without consulting her was immaterial, since she certainly had nothing to offer. Then too, she knew that Danny asked Ray to help him plan an itinerary that she would love.

Ray and May were aware that, like his father, there were two sides to Danny. On their honeymoon, though, he was romantic, sexy and attentive. He also liked showing off May and taking pictures of her. He bought her six new bathing suits to wear on Santorini, in Greece. One was more revealing than the next and May felt quite self-conscious as she modeled them.

"I don't know about this one," she said to her husband as she looked in the mirror. She was wearing a red one-piece halter bathing suit that was extremely low cut.

"Babe," said Danny with a beer in his hand. "You look great. Flaunt it!" He grabbed her and twirled her around. "Oh, yes," he said playfully, licking his lips. "This is all mine."

They left their opulent honeymoon suite and headed to the beach for a day in the sun. May was happier than she had ever dreamed she could be. Her only concern was that on three occasions, once in Marbella and twice in Portofino, Danny had suggested she eat less at breakfast. Knowing she had never been slimmer or more toned, May was confused. Why would he say that? Granted, she was short, but she did not have a weight issue, especially nowadays.

She had given up a lot for Danny, quietly quitting Jordache the day before her wedding and her Entenmann's cake and rocky road ice cream from the time they got engaged. She hoped she would be enough for him. It was a worry she expressed to the girls, especially when she gained weight in her pregnancy and Danny's comments became quite pointed and obvious. She was uncomfortable and felt torn between nourishing her unborn baby and scared to gain weight, fearing her husband would find fault with her, have an affair or worse of all scenarios, simply lose interest and ignore her like her parents did.

28

"A wise man makes his own decisions.
An ignorant man follows public opinion."
—Chinese Proverb

Ray woke up the morning after the wedding with a huge smile on her face. Last night was one of the best nights of her life. It started with Sammy. The more she got to know him, the more she liked him. He was smart, handsome, compassionate and, most of all, confident in his own abilities. Being at the wedding merely heightened her sense of how right this all felt. May and Fay adored him. And of course, there was the bride herself, so achingly beautiful. Ray hoped for the 100th time that Danny was good enough for May. And finally, beyond the wedding itself, was her mother.

There was no doubt in Ray's mind that her mother was undergoing some kind of transformation. It was subtle, but it was there. While at home she maintained her usual aloof facade with her husband, with her daughter and sons she appeared friendlier and more approachable. Ray found that her mother's new schedule at the office gave them time to have coffee in the morning. The quality and depth of those morning conversations were almost astounding. She caught a glimpse of her mother as a person with thoughts, hopes and dreams beyond her scope as a doctor. She was helpful and encouraging when Ray shared her concerns about her future career. They never discussed Ray's dad; he was a topic neither was ready to confront. Ray was confident that day would arise and relished her mornings with her mother. When May returned from her honeymoon, it was the first thing Ray told her.

"I told you, Ray-Ray," exclaimed May. "I adore Victoria. She makes my heart sing."

"Well, May Salem, it's you," said Ray happily. "It all started when you and Danny got engaged. It's as if that released something my mom was holding inside! To be honest, I am just so happy for her. She seems more hopeful and a lot happier. That's all I care about."

"I can't imagine what my getting engaged did," said May. "But I'll take it! She deserves to be happy; she is the greatest mother-in-law ever."

For Ray, who had decided to start at Baruch College in the fall rather than do the Sar-El program in Israel, these were glorious summer days. For as long as she could remember, the family summer home in New Jersey was her haven. It was a beautiful spacious house. Her best memories were created there. May and Fay would spend weeks on end with her and her family, especially when Fay gave up sleepaway camp altogether.

Ray fondly recalled the summer jobs they got at Sephardic Temple as junior counselors when they were 15. Fay, whom she worried would be out of her element among the SY crowd, surprised her. In her knee-length summer skirts and elbow-length cotton t-shirts, she flirted with the boys, laughed with the girls and the campers adored her. Now, here they all were, just a few years later, spending endless days at the beach in Long Branch.

Sammy joined them as often as he could, while Fay, May, Danny and her brothers Ralph and Ikey and their girlfriends swam and tanned. They barbecued at night and thoroughly enjoyed each other's company. She felt nervous that Fay and Sammy were soon leaving, though both reassured her numerous times of their proximity by phone, by the ever evolving email correspondence and by plane. Ray impulsively decided she would surprise Fay and spend

Thanksgiving with her in Jerusalem and winter break with Sammy in Boston or Cancun.

Looking at May, Ray felt a slight sense of anxiety. It was nothing she could pinpoint, but a vague sense of something being off-kilter. That night before dinner, she approached her sister-in-law.

"May-May," she called from her bedroom, "can we talk for a sec?"

"Sure," said May, sauntering into Ray's bedroom while wearing one of her honeymoon string bikinis. "What's on your mind? Need advice from your big sis?"

May was clearly loving her new role as sister-in-law. Though she and Ray were only three months apart, her new marital status automatically gave her a leg up, which she reminded her friends about daily. Neither Fay nor Ray had ever asked her about her sex life with Danny, respecting that boundary, but May herself could barely contain herself from telling them how happy she was. She told Ray and Fay once that married life was better than *Ghost*, *Sixteen Candles*, *Dirty Dancing*, *Moonstruck* and *Splash* combined. As the girls reminisced about Patrick Swayze and Patrick Dempsey, they understood clearly that May was delighted to be married.

When May stood in front of her, Ray cleared her throat. "May-May," she began, "probably Fay should be the one having this conversation with you, because she is so much more observant than both of us, but as your sister, I have to know if my brother is forcing you in any way, I want to know."

"Whatever are you saying Ray?" asked May, genuinely puzzled. "Just spit it out."

"Okay, May-May," said Ray. "That bikini you are wearing. Sure, on your honeymoon, in St. Tropez or Ibiza, but here in Long Branch, isn't it a bit much?"

May took a deep breath and hesitated. In that second, Ray knew she was right, regardless of what May might choose to say. It was that schmuck Danny who engineered this!

May turned to Ray and with a huge grin on her face she said, "Well look who turned into a prude. I know with all my heart it's not jealousy about my hot body, because you just have to look in the mirror. So what's the deal, Ray? Why so uptight about my knock-out bikini?"

Ray curtsied to May and said, "Well done, Mrs. Salem, you are so clever. You turned this whole thing on me! I'm not a prude. Hardly! I just know this isn't you at all."

"Well, maybe you don't know me as well as you think you do," said May seriously. "Am I not entitled to please my husband even if he happens to be your brother?"

Ray knew then that May was not going to expose Danny, that she was intimidated and would cover for him.

"Okay," she replied. "Let's say I don't know you as well as I think I do. Just look me in the eye and tell me that if Fay was here instead of shopping again for another 100 shapeless skirts for seminary, what would she say to the bits of fabric barely covering your privates?"

"Why do you pick Fay?" asked May, laughing. "You and I know she is *frum* and would never go for this, even in private. Let's ask someone who brings no bias, like Victoria."

As soon as May said the words, she knew she had made a fatal mistake. Ray would love to ask her mother, because Victoria, being refined, classy and honest, would tell her the truth: that this bikini was trashy.

May knew she lost this round and rather than drag Victoria into this mess, she decided to tell the truth to Ray because she owed her that much. "Okay Ray, busted," she said, grinning. "In truth, this is 100 percent not my look."

"I knew it!" screamed Ray. "He's a copy of my father!"

"No, no, no," interjected May quickly. "It's true, this was Danny's doing and I hated it at first, but now I love it. I look hot and I like the attention."

"Do you really mean that?" asked Ray skeptically. "Because I will bust his chops if he is making you do things you don't want to."

"I swear, Ray-Ray."

While Ray chose to believe May, she wasn't entirely sure if May wasn't covering for Danny. That night, she told Sammy about the conversation.

"Well, I'd at least need to see the heinous bikini in question," he teased.

"No jokes," pleaded Ray. "I am worried about May. If she gives in to Danny on this, then who knows what other demands he will make?"

"I hear you, darling," replied Sammy, taking her into his arms. "I think you need to believe May and trust her, but at the same time, keep an eye on her. If you notice anything else, then confront her again. For now, respect her right as a newlywed not to be scrutinized. Remember, one day you will be in the same position. You won't want everyone speculating and drawing conclusions about your behavior or clothing or attitude."

"You know what?" said Ray, feeling totally better. "That is so true. Thank you for being the sole voice of reason in my life."

Sunday night at the movies Fay was miserable. Behind her mother's back, she had agreed to be set up with Sammy's roommate at Harvard just so she could feel normal when the couples decided to go into the city from New Jersey for a movie and dinner. In theory, hanging around Ray and May had broadened her perspective and she was open-minded. In practice, she loved her Orthodox lifestyle and didn't feel like she was missing anything. What she didn't like was the compromise she made, lying to her mother in order to better enjoy the evening out.

Jared Natan was a really nice guy. He was decent looking and dressed like a preppy, which Fay noted that she liked. She enjoyed talking to him, realizing then that except for Sammy and Ray's brothers, she rarely, if ever, talked to boys. She didn't think Jared was interested in her, assuming she was too religious, but he was polite enough not to show it. In fact, the entire evening he was extremely solicitous of her feelings and made sure she was comfortable. He did not attempt to put his arm around her in the movie theater and Fay realized for half a second while glancing at Ray and May that she actually wished he had. It dawned on her that she wanted a boyfriend, exactly what Ray had: a commitment for the future, but someone she could have a relationship with here and now. Knowing that was not possible, and there was no way Jared was interested in her, she decided to enjoy the date for what it was: a one-time deal.

That night, when the couples returned to New Jersey, Ray invited Jared to join them for a drink. Fay was surprised but pleased. She didn't want the night to end just yet. The girls kicked off their heels and all of them trooped into Victoria's summer kitchen, which had a massive floor to ceiling wall of windows overlooking the garden. The lights revealed Ralph and Ikey at the pool with their girlfriends and a few of their friends. They were having a pool party. In minutes, they joined the crowd.

Jared found a secluded spot and waved Fay over. She was taken by surprise. Surely the date was over and he was under no obligation whatsoever to still be so polite. Fay was intrigued by his good manners.

"So tell me," Jared began as he cracked open a beer and took a sip. "What exactly are you going to do with the rest of your life?"

Fay was pleasantly surprised. If she didn't know better, she might have thought this guy was actually interested in her. She shrugged that off and assumed that he was either just out of a relationship or bored.

"Well," she said, "I always wanted to be a fashion designer, but that changed in the past year."

"Oh, and why is that?" asked Jared amiably. He sat back in his chair and stretched his long legs in front of him, his body language indicating that he wasn't going anywhere and wanted to hear what she had to say.

"Well, it's complicated," said Fay. "Last year, when my friends and I went on the March of the Living, it had a really big impact on me. I am the granddaughter of a Holocaust survivor."

"That's fascinating," said Jared, leaning forward to be closer to Fay, who was curled up in a giant wicker chair. "But how did that experience change your career track?"

"Well," said Fay, "in addition to sketching clothes, I've always dabbled in painting. When I got back, I found myself painting a lot and after a time, it occurred to me that I wanted to somehow use my talent as a vehicle by which I could share my feelings and at the same time honor my grandmother. Have you ever met any Holocaust survivors, because if you did, I think what I'm saying might make a little more sense."

"In fact, I have," said Jared.

"Now that's interesting," said Fay. "Where?"

"Where?" said Jared, laughing. "At my bar mitzvah, at every family occasion and every time we go to Israel to visit my grandparents."

"Wait a second," exclaimed Fay. "You are not SY?"

"No," answered Jared, smiling at her. "What gave you the idea that I'm Syrian?"

"Oh my God, you are going to think I am a real Valley girl," said Fay miserably. "I assumed since you were Sammy's friend that you were Sephardic like him."

"Well," said Jared, "you know what they say about assuming. Hey, don't feel bad. What's the difference?"

"Wow," marveled Fay. "We actually have a lot in common except that I'm probably a lot more religious than you are."

"That you are," conceded Jared. "My grandparents on both sides are Polish survivors. My dad's parents emigrated to Israel after the war and settled in Haifa, the only non-religious community in all of Israel," he joked. "They are happy and so am I when I see them. My mom's parents live here in Jersey and they are what you might call conservative. They attend services at their synagogue and are very involved in raising money for Israel, but after six years in the ghetto and fighting as partisans, they just didn't connect to formal religion or God anymore. In my family, we don't judge them, or anyone for that matter."

Fay looked at him aghast, desperately hoping he couldn't read her mind, because at that exact moment she could hear Ava, Judy, Zita, their newly acquired sister Hinda-Baila, her mother and her aunts dismissing Polish survivors as if they were beneath them. She could also hear them attacking her just for mentioning it to her mother, who would be sure to tell Kati, who would tell Magda, and from there on it would be downhill. Of course, that was if she was insane enough to even tell them about Jared's family. They were extremely judgmental. Fay was determined not to be like that.

Turning to Jared, she said reluctantly, "My apologies for even slightly implying that being more religious means anything. I think every person has to make a choice. Our grandparents did, our parents did and we get to also. It was nice to meet you, Jared. Good luck at Harvard." She stood up and walked away.

Jared looked stunned, but kept his composure. He quickly got up, not sure what to do. Should he hug this intriguing, gorgeous girl, shake her hand or kiss her? Knowing none of those were appropriate he instead said, "I enjoyed meeting you too, Fay. I look forward to seeing your future exhibitions at every important gallery in every city in the world. Have a good evening."

As Fay waved to the others, she was crestfallen, but glad she had ended the night. Here was a really great guy, but to her family he might as well have been a Reform Jew or Roman Catholic. If he wasn't exactly like them, he would never be accepted. For the first time in her life, Fay felt mildly annoyed at the imposition her family put on her. Was it some sort of pact that Hungarian survivors made with themselves? Did they feel responsible to populate the planet only with Orthodox Jews and did she need to go along with the program because of something that happened 46 years ago?

Fay scrubbed her face with Pond's cold cream and got ready for bed. She knew there would be no hashing over these new details. Ray would be with Sammy until 6:00 a.m. and then sleep away half the day. And May would be going to bed with Danny. Reluctantly, she got under the covers, closed the light and recited Krias Shema, the night prayers that Ava taught her when she was three years old. Oddly, tonight it gave her little comfort and she merely said the words by rote.

Fay was wrong. Just as she fell asleep, she heard voices. Ray and Sammy were in her bedroom.

"What's going on?" she said, struggling to open her eyes.

"You tell us," said Sammy, glaring at her as if she was his incorrigible bratty little sister. "Would you care to explain to us why you blew off just about the nicest guy in the world who, I might add, is mad about you."

"What?" screamed Fay, trying to make sense of what Sammy had just said, forgiving him instantly for practically wagging his finger in her face disapprovingly. "Jared liked me? He didn't think I was a religious freak?"

"No," said Ray as if she was talking to a dumb girl, which is exactly how Fay felt. "He thought you were great until you dumped him. He was shocked!"

"Well, first of all," said Fay, pulling the blanket up to her chin, conscious of the fact that she was in her pajamas in front of Sammy, "I thought he was SY like you guys and was being proper all night. Then, when he sprung the news on me that he wasn't but also isn't Shomer Shabbos, I figured there's no way he could be interested in me."

"Well, you figured wrong, you stupid idiot," said Ray, who sounded exactly like when she was eight years old and mad at Fay. "And now you have to fix it!"

"But Ray, honestly," said Fay. "What's the point? Do you even know what a commotion this would cause in my family? Forget about me lying about the whole date! The idea that I might marry out? My mother would literally rip off her jacket and sit shiva for me, mourning me as if I had died."

"Okay," retorted Ray, annoyed. "Stop this nonsense right now. You aren't getting married. You are just going to get to know this guy and enjoy his company, because he's a great guy and I know you like him."

"And how do you know that?" asked Fay belligerently because Ray was, of course, right.

"Because I saw the look on your face when he offered you a piece of cake from his plate at dinner," said Ray triumphantly, daring Fay to deny it.

"Yes, Ray, it was nice to have a date. Tagging along with you guys has been okay until now, but tonight I realized I want more and I'm sick of my family's rules," she muttered, stunning herself with this admission.

"All change is possible if you want it enough, Fay," said Sammy quietly. "You have every right to find your happiness, just like your mother and grandmother did. You honor your grandmother in the most profound way I could ever imagine. If you date a guy like Jared, do you think that's what will do her in? I think not."

Fay sat back rocking her body lost in thought. Sammy was the most logical person she ever met, after her own father. She recognized what he said as the voice of truth and she was hit hard with the realization that once again she needed to evaluate her life. Here she was weeks away from going to Israel for a year and now this.

"You guys, I love you. Let's go to sleep and continue tomorrow. I really appreciate you waking me up because now I will dream about Jared!" she crowed.

She waited for Ray to bend over and kiss her cheek and fell back asleep with a smile on her face. Ray and Sammy shut the light and tiptoed out of the bedroom. Ray looked at Sammy with so much respect, love and admiration.

"How about getting married next weekend and coming to Boston with me?"

Ray laughed and Sammy let it go, pretending it was a joke. What he wouldn't give for her to be ready to marry him right now.

29

"All happiness or unhappiness solely depends upon the quality of the object to which we are attached by love."
—Baruch Spinoza

The summer flew by and suddenly it was Labor Day. Sammy left for Boston the last week of August for orientation but came back for the final barbecue of the season. Fay left for seminary, feeling quite emotional at leaving behind those she loved, including Jared. From the night they met until the day she left, they were either together or on the phone. Though Fay adored everything about Jared, she was noncommittal. There was no way she would ever disappoint Bobby Ava, even if it meant giving up Jared. She also knew she was nowhere ready to make a commitment of any kind.

She told Ray and May that her going away for nine months was a blessing in disguise.

"He will be in Harvard, he will move on and I won't have to be the mean one by dumping him."

Ray nor May argued with Fay, as neither were sure of her true feelings. Though Ray knew for sure from Sammy that Jared was crazy about Fay.

Saying goodbye to Fay at the airport brought tears to their eyes, especially when May revealed that she was pregnant.

"Oh my God," screamed Fay. "That's my niece or nephew in there!" She gently tapped on May's tummy. "Hello little one, please wait for me to come home for Pesach."

The girls burst out laughing, all three happy and excited and at the same time aware that life was moving at warp speed. Ray was excited to start college and with Sammy at Harvard, she spent all her spare time at the college library studying. She found that, contrary to what her father had always told her and exactly what Sammy believed, she was a great student and a quick learner. She loved her schedule. She loved her professors. She loved college and going into the city. Earl drove her and picked her up. At least twice a week she met Victoria for lunch. Those were precious days. Occasionally, May joined them, often saying she was too tired or that Danny liked her to be home when he came back from work.

May was busy playing housewife and following through on the rabbi's suggestions. She was taking classes, getting to know other women in the community and volunteered at the center. She got herself a few tried-and-true cookbooks. Nearly every night, she treated Danny to a wonderful dinner. Most nights he was effusive in his compliments. Some nights he said nothing, almost daring her to ask. For May, cooking anything was a big deal and she wanted to be sure he liked her food. When he told her to stop nagging him, she realized it was a mistake and simply pretended he had never shouted at her. Instead, she concentrated on making even more elaborate meals, just to get his approval.

Considering her own background, she was ecstatic to learn just how simple it was to prepare a nice meal. She also found Victoria's guidance to be a blessing. Every week, like clockwork, she got a delivery from Sutton's Meat Market. Her mother-in-law made life so much easier for her and she never stopped thanking her. In late October, May got a phone call from her mother who had yet to see May and Danny's apartment. Her mother informed her that her father had decided to take early retirement and they were moving to Boynton

Beach, Florida. May was flabbergasted. The purpose of the call was to allow her the opportunity to visit the house and see if there was anything she wanted to keep. She was numb. As much as her parents weren't a part of her life, they were still her parents and the idea that they were moving to Florida pained her. That night over dinner, she tearfully told Danny. As soon as she saw his reaction, she knew she made a terrible mistake. She was furious with herself. By now she should have known what might set him off. Yet, she wondered, was it so awful that she just wanted a little sympathy from her husband? Instead, he treated her to a 20-minute diatribe about her parents.

"Why," he asked exasperated, "do you even give a damn if they are here or there? Look around, Dum-Dum." This was his new nickname for her. "Do you see anything in this apartment that they bought or offered to pay? Even an ashtray or roll of toilet paper?"

May couldn't help herself, she was extremely hormonal in these early days of her pregnancy. She burst into tears and got up to leave the table.

"Hey, wait," called Danny.

May thought he was sorry for his mean comments until she felt his grip on her arm.

"Where do you think you are going, Dum-Dum? Did I say you could leave the table in the middle of dinner?" he asked in absolute rage. "I mean, is it not enough that your useless parents don't do a thing for us? Now you also allow their departure to ruin our dinner?"

"Danny," pleaded May, "please let go of my arm. You are hurting me, for real."

"Am I?" he asked incredulously. "Then it's really very simple. Even you can understand that you just have to sit down and apologize to me."

May started to cry again, caught in an awkward position, half standing in an effort to get away and trapped by Danny's grip on her upper arm. She knew what she had to do.

"I'm sorry, Danny," she said in a meek tone. "I don't know what I was thinking."

Danny released her and she slid into her seat. She began rubbing her arm.

Later, at bedtime, when she put on her nightgown, she noticed a blue mark. It made her sick. She felt scared and alone, knowing there was no one that she could tell. All that she could do, she decided, was use her head and try not to irritate him. He was her husband. He was the one who gave her this incredible life. *Maybe he was right*, she thought, *maybe I am a dum-dum. Who else would be stupid enough to make waves?* She vowed to be a smarter wife.

The next morning, May impulsively called Victoria and asked her if she wanted to join her at her third month ob-gyn appointment later that week. Victoria, who was scheduled to present at a medical conference, immediately canceled her engagement and told May that she would be honored to go with her. From that point on, she accompanied her every month. May felt happy and comforted. Being Victoria's daughter-in-law made up for having Danny as a husband.

As she entered her fourth month, May started to feel self-conscious. When she heard the news that Ray was leaving for Israel before Thanksgiving, she became emotional.

"Please, Ray-Ray," she begged her sister-in-law. "Don't go. I need you here. Fay will understand."

Ray looked at her beloved sister-in-law. "May-May, you are hormonal. You knew I was going. I promised Fay and also, I want to look into that Sar-El program again. You'll be fine," she said encouragingly. "After all, you have a husband now."

Glancing at May, hoping she would get a hold of herself, Ray caught an expression on her face that she could not identify. It occurred to her that in addition to the pregnancy, May was perhaps subdued about the fact that her parents had moved, quite literally, out of her life. *Yes*, she thought to herself, *that's it*. She hugged May and promised to bring back from the shuk the rugelach pastry that May adored and all the freshly blended spices for her Moroccan stew and kibbeh. May looked at Ray and smiled, deciding at that moment to hide her anxiety. She would be okay, because this was her life; a life she had prayed for. If all she had to do was be good to her husband, then that's what she would do.

30

"I shall argue that strong men, conversely, know when to compromise and that all principles can be compromised to serve a greater principle."
—Andrew Carnegie

Fay was not happy in seminary. She knew it had to do with the glorious summer she had spent in Long Branch and, of course, meeting Jared. Spending a gap year in Israel before *shidduch* dating and college, immersed in her Hebrew studies, away from home, was something she had been looking forward to for the past six years and now it was simply anticlimactic. The girls she was acquainted with from home and those she met from France, England, Canada and Israel, all seemed so rigid to her, so unworldly and uninterested in anything except taking notes in class and scoring points with their guidance counselors.

On top of that, she was worried about Ava and May. Neither of them were comfortable with her being so far away, even though she called weekly. For Ava, as she got older, the need to be surrounded by her children and grandchildren was paramount and Fay understood that. Yet, she knew that in this rare moment she had no recourse but to put her own needs first and leave home to create distance between herself and Jared and to allow herself time to truly reflect on what she wanted out of life.

It was easy to love Jared and dream about a future with him. He reminded her of her father, whom she adored. They were both understated, principled, devoted and kind. Jared, however, was also sophisticated. He didn't need a makeover, as Suzi often noted about her husband when looking at his wardrobe, which she had revamped from the day they met. Jared wore his clothes well. He was tall, lean, muscular and had wavy jet-black hair. He was comfortable in his own skin and that was extremely attractive to Fay. The fact that he was not Shomer Shabbos though, was hard for her to accept. Keeping Shabbos was a fundamental principle of Orthodox Judaism. It meant no driving from sundown on Friday to sundown on Saturday night, no cooking, no turning on lights, no handling money or business of any kind. On some level, she felt utterly disloyal to Bobby Ava. She knew that after all Bobby Ava had endured that she could not subject her to that kind of betrayal.

"Vat do you mean he isn't religious?" Ava would say. "Vere is he from. Who are his parents and grandparents?"

The moment Ava would hear that Jared's grandparents were from Łódź and Białystok, it would be over. Growing up, Fay had heard enough to know that Hungarians cornered the market on suffering and she was not going to be the one to heap one more portion onto Ava's brimming plate. Even if Jared agreed to a religious makeover, Ava would never consent.

Daily, Fay went through the motions. She got up at 6:30 a.m., made her bed, *davened*, prayed with her classmates, had a light breakfast and settled in for a long day of classes and lectures that ended at 10:00 p.m. During the midday break from 1:00 p.m. to 3:00 p.m., she often wrote letters and made lists of the things she needed to focus on.

Going off campus was something she looked forward to every week. She enjoyed doing the required *chesed* charity hours, which she primarily spent babysitting for a young pregnant woman in Mea Shearim who already had 13 children. She noticed that they were all helpful kids. They were curious about her and that gave her a new perspective. Chava-Sara was a third-generation Sabra. She was born in Israel, was 35 years old and had never seen the world outside of Mea Shearim. She did not complain or appeared bothered by the circumstances of her life. On the contrary, she often tried to persuade Fay to look at the richness of her life, ignoring the blatant poverty she lived in.

Fay rounded out her hours by volunteering on a kibbutz cooperative farm every other week, which was exhausting but also exhilarating. It exposed her to a broad range of hardworking, technologically savvy Israelis, many of whom were originally from Russia and Ethiopia. Finally, every Friday morning she helped prepare the Shabbos meals for elderly Holocaust survivors who had no relatives and depended on the community to help them.

When Fay first met Mimi and her sister Ibu, she was taken aback. Both of them were Romanian survivors, practically old enough to be Ava's mother, but the polar opposite of her wonderful Bobby. Where Ava was optimistic, Mimi and Ibu were pessimistic. Where Ava was the height of fashion, Mimi and Ibu never wore anything but housecoats: a simple floral cotton robe that snapped on. Fay gave thanks to God for Ava's disposition. She wondered if Mimi or Ibu had been different when they were younger, before war had turned their life upside down. Were they ever young and carefree and now bitter and miserable because they were old, lonely and in pain? For Fay, these interactions made the week that much more tolerable and interesting and helped her in her determination not to contact Jared. It also showed her that there was so much she did not understand about how Holocaust survivors repaired their broken psyches. One would imagine that living in Israel would have reignited a spark. And yet, for Mimi and Ibu that was surely not the case.

Fay was happy that her Hebrew was good enough for her to communicate and understand everyone she came in contact with. Some of her roommates had a hard time with the language and Fay laughed when she reminded herself of Ray and May's desperate attempts to master the nuances, diction and grammar of Hebrew. She missed her girls! She missed hanging out with them and thought of how May's pregnant body was changing. Her heart swelled when she thought of May, knowing this was the life she wanted. Ray, too, was in a very happy place, confident and secure in her relationship with Sammy and excelling at her studies at Hunter College, determined on becoming an advocate of change for women by acquiring a dual degree in law and social work.

Fay noted the time and took out her siddur: her prayer book for afternoon services. Her father laughed when he heard that she prayed twice a day, saying it was hardly necessary for a girl to do so. However, Fay liked her prayer time; it reminded her of her relationship with God. She looked at the peach leather exterior of her siddur and was thrilled that she had also ordered them for her sisters, her cousins and, of course, for Ray and May. They would be ready before Ray's arrival. She was excited for Ray to be in Israel over Thanksgiving and had gotten special permission to leave the dorm to spend every minute she could with her. She knew that the winter in the little town of Beit Shemesh would be long and tedious without the distraction of television or movies, but later she would be going home for three and a half exciting weeks by which time, hopefully, May would have her baby! Overall, Fay recognized that, like her grandmother and mother, she would always find that smidgen of optimism and resilience to weather any storm. She did not yet know how much of it she would soon need.

31

"Be happy for this moment. This moment is your life."
—Omar Khayyam

Thanksgiving, 1991

As Ray stepped off the plane and headed into the bustling airport, she felt excited and happy to be back in Israel. She couldn't wait to see Fay and catch up with her! As she headed out, she thought she heard someone call her name and smiled. The plan was for her to meet Fay at the King David Hotel in Jerusalem and yet, someone was calling her. Ray took off her sunglasses, perched them on her head and looked around. There stood Fay, in a navy pea jacket and checked skirt, navy suede loafers, holding a huge hand-lettered sign that read "SHALOM RAY SALEM AND WELCOME HOME."

Ray ran to Fay and the girls hugged and openly cried. It was the longest stretch of time that they had ever gone without seeing each other: nearly three months. Seeing Ray made Fay realize just how much she missed her and everyone else that she held dear. Then it occurred to her, if she felt this way, how in the world could Bobby deal with the pain of always missing someone you love? It was something she would have to think about.

In the taxi, the girls excitedly talked over each other.

"Fay," she said conspiratorially, "I brought you some contraband to help the time pass."

"What are you talking about?"

"You'll see when we get to the hotel. The good news is that as soon as I give you my presents and everything your dear mother and grandmother sent, I will have an empty suitcase, so I will have plenty of room to shop at Heathrow Airport in London on my way back."

When they arrived at the hotel, the girls went straight to the BenAdin suite. Sammy's father had insisted they use it. Once again, the suite was filled with fragrant, fresh flowers that Sammy had arranged for Ray. Fay could barely control her excitement when Ray opened her brand-new black and white Halston tweed luggage (a gift from Victoria) and pulled out a stack of books.

"Oh my goodness, are you kidding me Ray," whooped Fay. "This is amazing!"

As an avid reader, Fay was thrilled to get her hands on the bestseller books Ray had so thoughtfully and lovingly shlepped for her.

"You can thank Sammy," said Ray happily. "He is a huge reader and said that since he has no time to read, he'll be happy knowing you are reading them."

Fay opened the box and looked at the selection of books as if she was meeting long lost friends. "Oh, Ray-Ray," she chortled in delight. "I can't wait to read these." She recited the titles aloud as if to confirm their deliciousness. "I can't believe you got me *The Firm* by John Grisham, *Loves Music, Loves to Dance* by Mary Higgins Clark, *As the Crow Flies* by Jeffery Archer, *The Kitchen God's Wife* by Amy Tan, *The Sum of All Fears* by Tom Clancey and *Heartbeat* by Danielle Steel! Oh Ray, thank you so much! These must have cost you a fortune. I appreciate it so much. Every night I'm tired enough to go to bed, but on Shabbos the day is so long. I will have to hide my contraband very well. If Mrs. Kramer or Mrs. Levy find them, they will kick me out for sure!"

"Well," drawled Ray, genuinely puzzled, "in my community the girls don't do this sort of excursion away from home. They do what

May did: they get married and have babies. To deny you books, what's the point? I mean, it's not like you are becoming a nun?"

"I know," said Fay. "Maybe I should have gone to a more liberal school, but this one was highly recommended. One thing is for sure, I will see to it that Bethie and Deenie look into other options."

"Oh, Fay," said Ray. "You are an amazing sister. Speaking of which, did I tell you about our sister May-May?" She excitedly dug into her suitcase to take out a beautifully wrapped box and a small photo album which she presented to Fay. "These are from May."

Fay was taken aback. The box was from The Green Door, her favorite jewelry store. Inside, nestled in the signature green box, was an exquisite white gold infinity necklace with a card that read, "Our bond, like this necklace, knows no limits. Missing you and waiting for you to come home to my heart. Kisses and hugs, May." Fay stood there in silence, touched by May's words. Then, she opened the photo album and gasped. "Oh my goodness, she is really pregnant!"

She loved the candid shots May had sent, some of them by herself, in her kitchen, cooking, in her living room with her feet propped up on her gray velvet kidney bean shaped couch, and some with Danny as they were heading out to a movie or to dinner. To the naked eye, May looked very happy.

Yet, Ray, while looking at the pictures over Fay's shoulder, innocently asked, "Do you think May is happy?"

"Duh, yes. I mean, look at that rock on her finger, that belly in front of her, her Gucci moccasins and her fabulous balayage highlights! I'd say our girl has done pretty well."

"Okay, I hope you are right," said Ray slowly. "I am not all that sure, but maybe it's because Danny is my brother and he reminds me of my father."

"Don't do that," said Fay sternly and emphatically. "He is not your father. He's May's husband and over the summer, with rare exception, he was unbelievable. Even Jared remarked that he thought they were a great couple and, I quote, 'with great potential in spite of the fact that young couples statistically don't make it.'" "Speaking of whom, I am so torn, Ray. Some part of me knows that what I love about Jared is how different he is from my family and that's not a reason to rock the boat and fight to marry him."

"Marry him," said Ray incredulously. "Have I taught you nothing? What marriage? Can't you finish out your jail sentence here in Israel, come home and start your life without planning the chuppah?"

"It's funny you say that, because with the exception of your parents, everyone in your community does exactly the same as in mine! The girls can dabble in a career, but marriage is the real goal. I have been doing nothing but thinking the past 12 weeks and I am still not sure. For my family this would be too much to comprehend and I just can't do this to Bobby, who sacrificed and suffered so much."

"But Fay, why is there no compromise? Remember how supportive Bobby was when you told her you wanted to be a fashion designer? Maybe you don't give her enough credit? She loves you so much. If she meets Jared, I am positive she will change her mind. Anyway, who says Jared isn't willing to meet you halfway?"

Fay carefully considered Ray's logical argument and saw the validity in her words. "I suppose you are right. Why am I assuming and deciding for two people who I know and admire?"

32

"There is only one way to happiness and that is to cease worrying
about things which are beyond the power of our will."
—Epictetus

Ray enjoyed every moment in Israel. In particular, she loved Eilat, the
beach town that Fay insisted they visit even if only for one night.
Although it was a plane ride away, the girls were thrilled that they
had made the effort to take a 6:00 a.m. flight and enjoy a full 24 hours
in the sun. The rest of the days flew by and saying goodbye to Fay was
especially hard on Ray, knowing that she was in a turmoil about Jared
and her future. Fay being Fay, reassured Ray repeatedly that there
were many aspects to her life, even at seminary, that pleased her. She
was positive, even though Ray was not sure if everything would work
out. Days after Ray left, Fay started to seriously reconsider whether
Jared and Ava could each be persuaded to bend a little. She knew her
parents would need some time to adjust to Jared, but she was far less
concerned about them than she was about Ava. Once again, Fay
turned to one of her aunts for advice. This time she called Judy and
was quite shocked by her comments.

"Faygala, darling," she screamed with delight, so much so that Fay didn't even bother correcting the use of her old nickname. "How wonderful to hear from you! Wait, are you okay?"

"Yes, Judy Nene," replied Fay. "I am totally fine. My friend Ray was just here and it was so wonderful to spend time with her. She brought me a ton of books and gifts. I'm really good except for one teeny tiny little thing."

"Oh," said Judy relieved, swelling her voice, "so what's the teeny tiny thing? You don't know what to buy your mother or Bobby?"

"No, Judy Nene, not at all. I might as well just tell you. I hope you won't be disappointed in me. No one knows about this."

"Oy vey," said Judy breathlessly, "now you are really starting to scare me."

"Well," said Fay, dreading what she was about to say, "last summer I met a guy and I really like him, but he is super modern and his grandparents are Polish."

"I see," said Judy slowly. "Anything else you'd like to add? Like, are you in love?"

"I don't know for sure, but I do really really like him. He reminds me of my father."

"Well," said Judy, "let me get right to it. Bobby is going to freak out. It's no secret that she favors your mother and you are your mother's favorite, but she will draw the line very severely in this case. If you don't marry the type of boy she expects, she will never stop hounding you and making you feel guilty." Judy paused and sighed. "Fay, there are a lot of things about Bobby Ava that I, your mother and Magda Nene never talk about. Nothing crazy, but for example her inability to change except when she feels it's right, like marrying Imre Baci. She won't budge! And my own *nenes*, Zita and Kati, know it very well, but they will never go against her. Even if we asked them or Imre for help, it's no use, darling."

"But," cried Fay, "I'm not even sure I want to marry Jared, I just don't want to hide him like he is some sort of wrong person, because he's not. He is so kind and fair. He is a product of his own environment, just like I am a product of mine."

Judy could tell Fay was upset and tried hard to make her

understand that her way of dealing with Ava's hysterics and drama was simply to go about her own life without defending it.

"Easy for you to say, Judy Nene," retorted Fay. "You have a husband to back you up and you're not my age. Plus, it's not like my own parents will endorse this relationship either."

"All too true," said Judy. "I believe that being in Israel will give you time to figure out what to do. My advice is to do nothing right now, especially because you are so far away. When you come home for Pesach, I think that should be the time to make some decisions."

"Thank you, Judy Nene. I really appreciate this conversation and I can't wait to see you and the girls and tell you all about sem."

"That would be wonderful, Fay," said Judy. "But don't be surprised if your cousins opt out of 'sem,' as you call it. I have decided to let my girls have their own opinion and make choices for themselves. Seminary is a long way off. I'm sure they will be enthralled by your stories. If they want to go, that's fine and if not, that's fine too. At some point, we all need to take responsibility for our own lives and recognize that Bobby's perspective is not necessarily ideal for all of us."

"Wow," gasped Fay. "Judy Nene, I am so impressed with what you just said. I have nothing but time on my hands and I started to think about my choices. I am going to see a therapist in town, because I can't possibly tell my guidance counselor about any of this. I am sure any therapist would agree with you."

"Fay darling, you are right," said Judy. "I have been seeing a therapist for years and Magda has finally seen the light. You won't recognize her when you see her! She has lost a ton of weight, but more than the weight loss, she seems so much more confident and assertive. I am so happy for her."

"Maybe you guys could convince my mother," asked Fay plaintively. "Honestly, Judy Nene, the way my mother spoils me and favors me has definitely affected my relationship with Deenie and Bethie. Right before I left for Israel, after they came home from Camp Rina, I took them out for lunch and they outright said they are jealous of me, that I can do no wrong in Mommy's eyes."

"This," said Judy slowly, "I wasn't aware of. Yes, your mother sings your praises all the time, but I had no idea how bothered your sisters were. Does your mother even know?"

"Not yet," said Fay grimly. "There was no time before I left and with Imre needing surgery and Bobby so nervous, I didn't think Mommy needed this on her head."

"You are truly a wonderful daughter," said Judy. "So mature. I hope my girls continue to look up to their cousin, because you really are extraordinary."

"I don't think I'm extraordinary," laughed Fay. "But thank you for the compliment. Stay well, Judy Nene. Kisses to everyone and shalom from Israel."

Fay hung up the phone, feeling determined to find a therapist to talk to. She needed an unbiased opinion and wanted to understand more of how it was that as a Holocaust survivor, her grandmother had certain needs that she imposed on her daughters and even granddaughters. She thought it would be good if everyone in the family would learn more so that the negative aspects of being descendants of a Holocaust survivor didn't outweigh the benefits.

33

"Happiness depends upon ourselves."
—Aristotle

January, 1992

Ray was excited to see Sammy in Cambridge, in his academic environment. On some level, she was glad to know that Jared had gone skiing with friends. Not only would it give her and Sammy total privacy, but it would spare them all the awkwardness of Fay's choice to put the relationship on hold. Ray was beside herself, believing Fay was making a huge mistake, but also supporting her in her desire to come to terms with her choices. Nevertheless, she and Sammy adored Jared and were uncomfortable in their inability to offer any insight into Fay's decision-making.

Ray arrived at Boston's Logan Airport in a heavy snowstorm and loved how picturesque the town looked. As she saw Sammy in the baggage claim area, her heart felt like it would burst with love. In spite of the heavy security at the airports and so many restrictions—it was post-9/11—she was glad she made it easier on Sammy by joining him instead of him coming to NY. She knew, although Sammy never said a word, that he was a brilliant student and devoted much time to his studies. She would be that kind of wife, she decided, who understood her husband and considered his needs first. She knew that her own parents had never had that kind of bond and felt sorry for her mother, who—she was learning more and more—was someone she admired. Sammy and Jared's apartment on Fifth Street was everything a bachelor could ever want. It had a large living room that overlooked the square, three large bedrooms, a study and an open, airy kitchen stocked with microwave-ready meals. It was centrally located and in walking distance to the Harvard campus. Sammy had thoughtfully booked Ray a room at the Hilton Copley, but Ray had already decided she would stay with him. With Jared out of town, she felt there was no reason for them to be apart anymore. Being intimate with Sammy seemed like the most natural thing in the world and when she asked Victoria for her opinion, she was stunned at her mother's candor.

"I am so honored that you trust me and want my opinion. Naturally, compared to you, I am old-fashioned. I was, of course, a virgin at my wedding, your father and grandmother would have stoned me otherwise," Victoria said jokingly, but with a tremor in her voice. "I think that what is much more important is who you are marrying. If you are going to sleep with him ahead of your wedding, make sure to use birth control."

Now, having packed her birth control pills, and looking at Sammy as he expertly navigated through the traffic and the snow, Ray was sure. Sammy had never once pressured her, often saying he would wait for her forever.

"Do you want to check into the hotel now or later?" he asked.

"Definitely later," said Ray with a smile on her face. "I can't wait to see your digs!"

Sammy gave Ray a full tour of the apartment. When they got to his charcoal-gray and burgundy bedroom, Ray pretended she dropped something. When Sammy bent to retrieve the blister pack, he looked puzzled. "Do you always carry your vitamins with you?"

"Actually, no, I don't carry my vitamins on me," said Ray. "But I do carry essentials with me."

She removed her tote bag from her shoulder and proceeded to unpack her toiletry bag, cosmetics, slippers and a robe. While

Sammy watched her open the closet and deposit her things, he looked again at the packet in his hands and recognition hit him.

"Happy holidays, Sammy," said Ray softly. "I do prefer the right side of the bed if that's okay with you."

"Oh Ray, this is more than I could have dreamed of." He took her in his arms. "These pills... How brave of you to do this all by yourself."

"A girl's gotta do what a girl's gotta do," said Ray. "I might add that not only are May and Fay on board, but even my mother approves."

"I see," said Sammy dryly. "Anyone else? Like my mother, your neighbors, Earl, Lucía?"

"Sammy, don't be silly. This is private, just between us," said Ray, not considering sharing her decision with May and Fay or her mother a breach of that privacy.

"Well future Mrs. BenAdin, I have a suggestion that I want you to think about. My marriage to you means the world to me and you being ready to give yourself to me without that legality is incredible. How about though, if we get married tomorrow in the rabbi's office? Then you can be a kosher bride and when the time is right, we will get married civilly with all the pomp you want."

Ray was shocked beyond belief and knew that what Sammy had suggested was the best of all possible worlds. Although she was not particularly observant, in her heart she wanted to do mikveh and lighting the Sabbath candles and start off her life with Sammy properly.

"Is this a proposal, kind sir?"

"Indeed it is, mademoiselle. We can go to Tiffany's right now and pick out wedding bands."

"Yes," cried Ray. "A thousand times yes. I will be your Jewish bride tomorrow! And sorry, but I will sleep in the hotel until the wedding, because I have a lot to do before you will become my husband!"

Sammy called his rabbi and made the arrangements. The two of them put their coats and boots back on and made their way outside.

"I honestly don't know if life could be better," said Ray as she began to cry. "There must be a God, one who really loves me."

Within 72 hours, Sammy and Ray stood before Rabbi Benzion, a distinguished man who coincidentally was well acquainted with the BenAdin family. As he wrapped the tallit on both the bride and groom to bind them as one, he asked them again why they were choosing to be married so impulsively and without family by their side.

"Rabbi," said Sammy, speaking for himself and his pale bride who was wearing a brand-new, beautiful, white woolen suit trimmed in satin, "this is what is right for us. Those who love us will understand and I am confident that the ones we care about the most will rejoice in our *simhah* [joy.]"

The rabbi looked at the beautiful bride standing in front of him. He was perplexed, no doubt, but trusted that this indeed was the right thing for this couple. That they had made all the arrangements in three days was a sign of their deep commitment to each other and their religious foundation. Ray Salem was a pure kosher bride and he would give her the ketubah she now owned as a married woman.

In lieu of family, the young BenAdins hosted a lavish dinner that night for the members of Temple Beth Shalom. It was surreal to both of them, but totally perfect. In years to come, they would look back on this moment and appreciate their choice even more. Ray knew that not having her father attend her wedding was exactly right for her, even if it also meant excluding her mother and her in-laws. When Sammy called his parents, the BenAdins were ecstatic and never once questioned his choice. They did say they would give a kiddush celebration in London in their honor and hoped they would be together over Pesach to celebrate. When Sammy called Victoria, she cried with joy.

"Sammy, *mabruk!* I am so happy!"

Victoria instantly understood why they had chosen to get married and she was grateful to know that they would start their intimate life according to *halacha* [Jewish law].

Ray loved being married to Sammy. It was blissful to fall asleep in his arms and wake up next to him. Inevitably, when it was time for her to leave, she became sad.

"I can't leave you," she moaned late into the night.

"Then don't," he said. "We can try to get you into Boston U. for the spring semester. It might take some doing, but I am fairly confident it can be done. Then, over the summer, you can decide which uni offers you what you want. If Boston U. doesn't work out, you can still do volunteer work at a domestic violence center or apply for an internship and cook dinner for your husband."

Ray started to laugh.

"Is this a dream? Because if so, I don't want to ever wake up. Naturally, I will have to go back to New York and pack up my whole closet," she said seriously. "And of course, I will have to be at May-May's shower, but oh my God, Sammy, that sounds amazing."

"Well then, Mrs. BenAdin, as it appears, you are pleased with my performance as your husband, perhaps we can mutually please each other."

Ray groaned with pleasure as she turned to face her husband. "Mmm," was all she said.

By the time Jared returned to Boston, he was amazed to find out he now had their apartment to himself. Sammy had already rented an exquisite, furnished townhouse for him and his bride for the next two years.

34

"Happiness is not something ready-made.
It comes from your own actions."
—Dalai Lama

March, 1992

May lay in her bed at 10:30 a.m. and sighed deeply, feeling quite content. She was nearly eight months pregnant, her baby was kicking all the time and Danny was on his best behavior. For her, life couldn't get better. Today was her baby shower and though she felt sick that Fay wouldn't be there, she felt certain that she would understand. That was the nature of their relationship. It even seemed to be getting better with time, as they all moved in different directions, because in its foundation, the girls loved each other and were fiercely loyal to each other.

May smiled as she thought of Ray's visit when she returned from Israel. Hearing Fay's reaction to the necklace thrilled her! As she reluctantly got up to pee yet again, she decided to have a light breakfast before showering and getting ready. That Ray was now also married was more excitement than she could bear. Ray was scheduled to arrive at Penn Station on Amtrak within the hour and had offered to pick May up. She was touched by the gesture. Earl could have easily driven her to Victoria's house and Ray could have met her there. Yet, like a true sister, Ray wanted to be by her side. It was not lost on anyone that May was like an orphan, with no relatives of her own ever participating in any event.

Ever since her parents had moved, May had chosen to keep her distance from them. The stress of their abrupt departure, coupled with Danny's outbursts, had caused her severe stress and uncontrollable vomiting that her ob-gyn doctor was quite concerned about. When May found out that the stress could affect her baby, she made up her mind to immediately take hold of her emotions and simply pretend that her parents were in Africa on a peace corps mission. In her fantasy, they were at least caring about someone.

Ninety minutes later, May was ready. She struggled into her maternity pantyhose, white leather knee-high boots, put on a black Wolford bodysuit that, miraculously, stretched over her tummy, and slipped into the oversized Courreges white woolen A-line jumper with huge pockets. She was glad Danny wasn't home this Sunday. She hated him watching her get dressed now that she was this big. True, he had been on his best behavior and was affectionate to a degree, even if he didn't attempt to have any kind of intimacy with her. May looked in the mirror, barely recognizing her full face, but grateful to her hair stylist Mustafa for creating height on top, which definitely elongated her face. Satisfied that she looked her best, she reached for her shearling mink jacket that Victoria bought her for Hanukkah and waited for Ray to arrive. Within minutes, Earl was at the door, insisting that he walk her to the car in her condition. As soon as May saw Ray, she gave out a shout.

"Ray-Ray, my sweetest sister, I am so happy to see you! I can not believe that you are married. Let me look at you, married lady."

"Well," laughed Ray, "I hardly think I'm the one to look at."

"Oh Ray, it's so good to see you," said May, nearly crying. "I am so lucky Victoria is so good to me, but a girl needs her sisters and Fay is so far away and you are in Boston, living the good life with that hunk of a husband of yours. I'm here all by my lonesome."

"Shhh," soothed Ray. "We are almost at the house. Calm yourself,

Angel Face. We will talk after the shower. Okay? For now, let's just have a blast."

The two young married ladies walked into the Salem house, which was temporarily transformed into a baby shower winter wonderland that took May's breath away. A professional photographer was taking pictures of everything. May was delighted that she would have pictures to send to Fay. She didn't know where to look first. There were white and silver balloons cascading from the ceiling. It had an ethereal winter wonderland feel, with sugar icicles on the huge dessert table. There was a magnificent fondant cake made to look like a Silver Cross baby carriage, the body of it navy blue with huge silver wheels and a white blanket. In fact, all of the miniature cakes, cookies, candies, and flowers were evenly divided between shades of blue from navy to sky blue and pink from fuchsia to pale pink. It was gorgeous and May could not even begin to thank Victoria and Harriet Bloom for the planning and execution of the event. Mrs. BenAdin was also there, deciding to spontaneously join them and spend a little time with Ray. May was delighted to make her acquaintance. She seemed to be a very nice woman and she clearly adored Ray. Victoria had invited a number of her own friends in addition to May's and she proudly showed May off to all of them. This meant the world to May: a mother who was proud of her and genuinely interested in being in her life.

May sat down and ate heartily. She loved the mini quiches, the salads, pastas and of course the desserts. It was a beautiful brunch and it was one of May's happiest moments. Karina, Ralph's girlfriend, made herself very useful, as did Nicky, Ikey's girlfriend. In the past few months, May had invited both couples over for dinner, wanting to get to know them better. Today she felt glad that she had made the effort. Both of her future sisters-in-law were helpful. They organized all the gifts right beside her, so that she could open them without exerting much effort. Nicky dutifully recorded the gifts, so that May could send thank you cards after the event. Mrs. BenAdin had sent a five-feet-tall Paddington Bear and it was a huge hit. Other gifts ranged from rockers or a mobile for the crib, to exclusive custom-made embroidered burping cloths with a capital "S" for Salem. No one bought clothing, as this was considered a bad omen before the actual birth.

"You don't need a bunch of things you may not like," assured Ray. "You really want my mother to choose your layette at Lester's! Trust me, knowing my mother, when the time comes she will call and everything the baby could possibly need will be delivered within hours of you giving birth."

"Yes, Ray," said a tired but very happy May. "That's exactly what I want."

After all the women left, Danny came to pick up May. His younger brothers were also with him. They packed up all the gifts so that Danny could focus on taking May home. Once again, May found herself in the uncomfortable position of having to say goodbye to Ray.

"May-May, don't be sad, please," pleaded Ray. "We speak daily and Sammy and I are coming to New York for Shabbat in two weeks and then we will be here for the whole Passover, when you are due."

Ray was profoundly grateful to her in-laws, who agreed to come to New York for the holidays so that Ray could be with her sister-in-law the entire time, rather than in London. Those were some of the things her father-in-law did that Ray never failed to be grateful for. He anticipated her needs and without any fanfare, simply did what needed to be done. He was the exact opposite of her own father.

35

"Between stimulus and response there is a space. In that space is our power to choose our response. In our response lies our growth and our freedom."
—Viktor E. Frankl

It was *bein hazmanim*, literally translated from Hebrew as "between the times," the term all schools in Israel used to refer to the period from right after Purim until a week after Pesach. Fay was anxious to leave, to have nearly five weeks of free time to paint, having neglected her art while in seminary. She also wanted to see her sisters, with whom she established a great pen pal relationship that she hoped would translate well in person, and see her extended family of aunts, uncles, cousins and, most importantly, Bobby Ava.

While she had been hopeful to find guidance with a therapist, she had not yet been successful in finding one who met her needs, namely one who spoke fluent English, accepted her health insurance as payment and seemed open-minded enough to understand her. If she returned after spring break, Fay was determined to find that person.

She headed to the airport by herself. Her roommates were all flying out the following week, most not eager to go home and help their mothers. Fay realized how fortunate she was to have a mother who was not overwhelmed with life. Over the course of seven months, in addition to perfecting her proficiency in Hebrew, Fay learned a lot about her roommates, which enlightened her significantly. One, who lived in Los Angeles, was also a granddaughter of Holocaust survivors. The other two were from *frum* families whose grandparents escaped Europe before the war, and one of them had grandparents who were themselves first-generation Americans. It was like being with May and Ray, finding that what they had in common was much more important than their differences.

Pessi, for example, hated being the youngest in her family of eight. Everyone treated her like a child. Ruchy, on the other hand, hated being the oldest in her family of seven and expected to come home and literally roll up her sleeves and start cooking or baking. When Fay innocently said that all that baking sounded like fun, Ruchy glared at her and retorted, "So come to my house *erev* Pesach, the night before, and join me in the kitchen that is not heated, because it is really a garage, and start sifting through ten dozen eggs at 4:00 a.m. for all those delicious cakes and kugels. And don't get me started on peeling 100 potatoes."

Fay recognized frustration when she heard it and could only mumble an apology. She, her sisters and her cousins were never expected to do anything except set the table for the Seder and help bring the dishes to and from the table during the meal. But similar to her seminary friends, she was also slated to finish seminary and dabble in an approved career until she got married. Debbie, whose close-knit family of four lived on the Upper West Side of Manhattan, was not even expected to attend college, just simply appear at weddings , do good deeds and a good *shidduch* would be sought for her. Fay sometimes felt like an impostor when the girls talked about marriage. She was not dreading the dating process, like Pessi, or overly excited, like Ruchy, to get out of the house. Like Debbie, she enjoyed her home life and if not for Jared, she would be excited about dating and finding her *bashert*, the one who was destined to become her husband and the father of her children.

The whole journey home, Fay was lost in thought. The plump middle-aged woman who sat next to her gave up trying to make conversation when she finally got the message from Fay's closed eyes and siddur on her lap, that she was otherwise engaged.

At JFK International Airport, Fay passed through customs easily and came out of the terminal. She was flabbergasted to see Bobby Ava standing next to Deenie and Bethie. She ran into Bobby's arms, overjoyed to see her. Bobby's genuine smile made her incredibly happy and she was sorry that she hadn't dressed for the occasion, never once thinking that Bobby would leave Imre's side as he was recovering from a quintuple coronary bypass operation. Yet here she was, looking as beautiful as always. Fay, subconsciously imitating her mother's near obsessive worry about her grandmother, scrutinized Bobby's beautiful face, looking for signs of age, but all she saw was a glow that permeated straight to her own heart.

"Bobby, Bobby," she cried, all while holding on to her sisters. "I can't believe you came to the airport before Pesach, with all that you have to do!"

"My oldest grandchild comes home from *Eretz Yisrael,* the land of Israel ,and you think I vouldn't be here to see that with my own eyes?"

"I am so grateful," said Fay, sobbing as she walked with Bobby and her sisters to the parking spot where her father was waiting for them.

When Zak saw his oldest daughter, he felt an enormous sense of pride and relief. In a household of women, he had come to accept that he was outnumbered in terms of the surging female hormones in his midst. In truth, he was emotional too, but kept it carefully hidden. He knew plenty about emotions, but chose to keep them inside. Yet now, in this moment, he allowed himself, his mother-in-law and daughters to see his true feelings. He sprinted over to help his daughter with her bags and hugged her tightly, tears pouring from his shiny eyes.

"Oh, am I happy to see you, Fay Zweig," he said. He stared at his daughter, seeing a new maturity in her that he admired. While he loved his wife and her sisters, he felt that none of them had ever risen to their full potential, living in the shadow of Ava who commanded centerstage. He hoped Fay and his younger daughters would have a better chance at self-fulfillment.

When Fay looked at her dad, she instantly thought of Jared. There was actually a slight physical resemblance that she had never before picked up on. Now, after not seeing her father in such a long time, she saw other similarities; it was a gesture, a smile, a look that instantly made you feel accepted, loved, admired and heard. She pushed Jared out of her mind, there would be plenty of time for that.

When they got onto the Belt Parkway heading west, Fay became animated and giddy. She realized that between worrying, packing and insomnia, she hadn't slept in 36 hours. She held Ava's hand the whole way home, while laughing with her sisters. She found both of them to be very receptive to her and she was hopeful that she could continue to get closer to them.

When they finally arrived, Suzi came running out onto the street to see her daughter. Once again, a cascade of tears came gushing down everyone's faces as mother and daughter embraced. Fay felt a profound gladness that this was her family. They supported her and she hoped that when she shared her news, they would have the ability to put prejudice and bias aside and continue to support her. It was not, after all, like she was suggesting marrying Jared or even becoming less religious. All she wanted was the freedom and opportunity to get to know him better without sneaking around.

36

"Out of difficulties grow miracles."
—Jean De LA Bruyere

Fay thoroughly enjoyed her homecoming dinner and all the questions thrown at her. Her mother prepared all her favorite foods, even though it was three weeks before Pesach which meant she typically was scaling back on cooking and instead focusing on a rigorous cooking, cleaning and baking schedule, 12 hours a day. When Fay took out her gifts, every single person was thrilled. The girls loved the *siddurim* prayer books and her father the hand-painted *tallit* bag that housed his prayer shawl. Her mother adored the turquoise earrings and Ava was touched by the beautiful *mezuzah* that Fay bought for Imre. The parchment inscribed with specific verses from the Torah was contained in an ornate, hand-carved sterling silver case. Ava assured her that she would have it hung by the door of their home that night to guard her and Imre. Zak was quite impressed with his daughter that she had gotten the parchment scrolls that fit inside the mezuzah case in Mea Shearim [the ultra-Hasidic quarters in Jerusalem] to ensure its authenticity. For Ava, Fay bought an exquisite oil painting of the city of Jerusalem signed by the renowned artist Huvie who, rumor had it, started dabbling in oil ever since she was a toddler. It was shipped to her parents' house and when Fay gave it to Ava, she began to cry.

"Vat did I ever do to deserve such a vonderful family and a granddaughter like you?"

"Oh Bobby," said Fay, as emotional as her beloved grandmother. "You have it backwards. It's we who are the lucky ones for being your children and grandchildren."

After dinner, Bethie and Deenie joined Fay in her bedroom as she unpacked and they spontaneously decided to have a sleepover. Fay, although quite tired from her travels, was absolutely delighted to stay up for hours more as they laughed and enjoyed each other's company while noshing on cookies and fruit. When her sisters fell asleep, Fay set her alarm clock for 7:00 a.m. She wanted to be at May's door by 8:00 with croissants and cappuccino.

And precisely 8:00 a.m., she rang the doorbell of May and Danny's apartment. Fay was surprised to find Danny at the door, assuming he would be at prayers or on his way to work in Jersey. He told her that as May was in her ninth month, he wasn't comfortable being so far from her for so many hours and had arranged with his partners to work from 10:00 a.m. to 2:00 p.m. until May had the baby. Fay was shocked, never once thinking Danny possessed such sensitivity. She broke out into a huge smile and impulsively hugged him. "Danny," she said. "I am so impressed with you! That is absolutely the right thing to do."

Fay wondered why Ray nor May had bothered to tell her, knowing how happy this would make her. Then May rolled into the kitchen. She looked at Fay and rammed her soft rotund body right into her arms.

"Okay, *bebe*," she said in a fake French accent to her protruding belly. "You may now officially arrive any day now because Auntie Fay is here."

The girls had a marvelous reunion, gossiping, laughing and eating. Fay could not believe how much May could eat in one sitting and then also have a snack an hour later. She was thrilled to find May relaxed and looking forward to the baby's arrival. Although it was hard to say goodbye to May, who seemed so vulnerable, Fay eventually left as she had an early morning train to Boston to visit Ray and Sammy. She was going to spend three days in Boston and Ray was excited to show her around each afternoon after she finished at the clinic.

When Fay arrived at the stunning townhouse Sammy had rented, Ray was overjoyed to see her. Fay was overwhelmed by Ray's happiness. She was a changed person. Ray insisted they go out to celebrate Fay's arrival and the three of them had a lovely evening. Like May, Ray adored her personalized siddur and Sammy was touched that Fay had gotten him a hand-painted pale gray silk challah cover with the words "*Lchvod* Shabbat *Kodesh*" embroidered in silver silken threads to honor the holy Shabbat. He assured her that he and Ray would use it every single Shabbat. Fay was enormously satisfied with how everyone loved the gifts. It had been a labor of love going all over Jerusalem to find the perfect gifts, but in retrospect, Fay felt it was well worth her time. The only gift she still had in her possession was Jared's.

At dinner, Sammy broached the topic they had been avoiding ever since Fay had arrived.

"So Fay-Fay," he said with great affection and a twinkle in his eyes, "you've had quite a few months in which time I might add Jared has never once complained or tried to contact you, right?"

"Right," said Fay nervously as her mouth went dry. "That in itself illustrates exactly what I like about him."

Fay couldn't bear to say Jared's name for fear she would fall apart right there in the restaurant. "I made up my mind," she continued. "I am going to speak to my parents first, then to Bobby Ava and then to Jared."

"Would you like to reverse that order?" asked Ray. "Maybe see Jared first and confirm your feelings for each other?"

"You mean like while I'm here?" asked Fay despondently.

"Yes," said Ray sympathetically. "Like right now, as in tonight, this minute."

"I don't know," said Fay in anguish. "I just don't know!"

"Then maybe let those who know and whom you trust help you come to know," suggested Sammy.

"Sammy, you are the brother I surely would have wished for," said Fay seriously. "Do you think you understand my situation fully?"

"Actually, I do," responded Sammy. "Coincidentally, one of my professors is the chair of Holocaust studies and a close friend of Elie Wiesel. He talks about him in class all the time. In fact, Jared and I actually met with him and told him about Ava."

"Are you kidding me, Sammy BenAdin? Your professor had nothing better to do than discuss the antics of one Hungarian grandame?" asked Fay in sheer disbelief.

"Yes. Not only was he available to talk to us, but he invited us to his office at BU, where we had a pretty fascinating discussion. He was very interested in this apparent transmission of trauma from one generation to the next, saying that he believed that in addition to educating the world about genocide that still exists globally, that we must also inform the world of the potential impact of living with survivors and inheriting not only their DNA and eye color, but also their anxiety, stress, feelings of terror and need for control."

"Oh my God," said Fay. "I am in shock! There are educators who are actually commenting on the impact of the Holocaust on future generations? This is truly mind-boggling."

"My professor thanked us for the illuminating chat and made us promise that we would keep him informed of any future research that we found, as he was most interested. But most importantly, Fay, he had a piece of advice for you."

"Really?" cried Fay. "I can't wait to hear it."

"I think," said Ray slowly with an odd look on her face, "that we should order dessert and some more wine while you digest this news and then we can relay his exact message to you."

"That's fine by me," said Fay reluctantly. "Although I am not sure I can eat or drink until I hear what he said. I think that since he has a close relationship with Elie Wiesel, who as a survivor himself must have doubted his relationship with God and Judaism, his insight would be very meaningful to me."

"In that case," said Sammy, "let me ask Jared to tell you what he heard."

"What?" said Fay, confused. "Did Jared record the conversation?"

"Actually, great idea, but regretfully, no," said Jared, who came over to their table from the far corner of the room where he had been patiently waiting for a signal from Ray or Sammy for the better part of an hour.

"Fay," he said softly, "let me look at you."

Fay jumped out of her chair and ran into Jared's arms, not caring that she had just violated *negiah,* being touched by a man before marriage. It felt no less right and equally as important as the hugs she gave any member of her family. She was so shocked that for almost five minutes she could not speak.

"I think this has to be the all-time biggest shock of my life," she eventually said hoarsely. "Next to the possibility that some more of my grandmother's family survived the Holocaust. Bobby used to tell my mother that she was secretly hoping that her own mother had mysteriously survived Auschwitz and that they would meet by chance in Israel or America."

Fay knew she was rambling, but she couldn't help it. She was trying to convey to those present that seeing Jared and him loving her and not being hurt by her need to stay away was tantamount to a miracle.

"Fay," said Jared as he gently moved to sit down, "how are you, my sweetheart?"

"I am... I am... I don't know, Jared. I really don't know how I am," stuttered Fay.

"Can we order dessert now?" said Ray in a jocular tone in an effort to lighten the atmosphere. "And drink some vino?"

"Yes, yes, of course," said Fay magnanimously, aware suddenly of the three pairs of eyes trained on her. "Eat cake and get drunk, while I try to come to terms with what just happened here. And please tell me you didn't make that whole thing up about your professor."

"Almost guilty as charged," said Jared. "We wanted to get your undivided attention and now that we have it, I will tell you that I did meet with a neuroscientist in New York City who is doing brilliant work on post-traumatic stress disorder of Holocaust survivors. It is fascinating, to say the least, and very real."

"You spoke to someone," said Fay, shaking her head. "Not because you have questions about your family, but because you have questions about mine?"

"Correct," said Jared. "My family, while not impervious to nightmares and occasional bouts of anxiety and depression, especially my grandparents, *savta* and *saba* in Israel, related to war and such, are for the most part fairly well adapted. Hey, if you ask me —and I'm no expert, but I am pretty logical—after six long years in multiple camps, preceded by internment in the ghetto, I think the Polish survivors were generally stronger and heartier, having sustained themselves far longer. I think but I can't say for sure that after so many years of suffering, it created an unshakeable desire to live and gave them more of an incentive to move on than the Hungarians, who were remanded to the concentration camps in late 1944. My grandparents on both sides anglicized their names, left their *tefillin* phylacteries on the ship that brought them to America and rarely, if ever, looked back. Now, admittedly, I don't know how they might feel when they are older, but for these many years, they seem to manage and adapt and certainly have never in any way imposed conditions on me, my siblings, or my parents."

Fay was astounded on many levels. "This is the most surreal experience I've ever had and I'm trying very hard not to feel crazy or say something inappropriate. I am overwhelmed. This is too much to process," she concluded.

"I have an idea," said Sammy. "Why don't we all go for a nice drive and show you our town? Enough heavy stuff for one night."

Everyone agreed and the couples got up to leave the restaurant with Fay quickly saying the Birkat Hamazon [the prayer for after meals]. It was a beautiful evening. They strolled through the length and breadth of Faneuil Hall and the conversation was light. As they walked back to the parked cars, Jared asked Fay to join him for a drink and she quickly agreed.

"Don't wait up for me, Mrs. BenAdin," she called out merrily to Ray, absolutely surprising herself as well as Ray and Sammy, who were horrified that they might have overstepped their bounds.

Over coffee the next morning, before Ray and Sammy left, Fay admitted to making a serious effort to compartmentalize all that she had taken in and mull it over later. She enjoyed being with Jared and simply wanted to be in his presence without the shadow of the Holocaust dominating and ruining their unexpected reunion. It was then and there that she knew she had the ability to control her thoughts and decided that she would. *One day*, she ruefully thought, *Bobby won't be here and it will be up to me to keep her experience and her memory alive, but not at the cost of my own life.* As much as Fay was excited to see Jared again, she couldn't wait to get home and paint. She wanted to express in a riot of colors, in a cacophony of hues, all that she felt, all that she understood now. Painting was then and would always be the vehicle by which she kept her sanity.

Jared and Fay agreed to shelve any serious talk until Fay impulsively invited him for Pesach.

"You could stay with the Salems and as their guest you could come over with Ray and Sammy to meet the clan and sample their fabulous Pesach creations," she exclaimed.

"Ah, the old Trojan horse thing," said Jared, half joking, half serious. "You know what? I believe this plan has merit on the face of it. Possibly, conceding, more so than what we cooked up in the restaurant, with all due respect to Elie Wiesel."

Fay was thrilled. Everyone she loved would be together, if not under one roof then at least a short distance away.

"Uhm, Jared," she said nervously. "I need to ask a favor."

"Have no fear, he glibly replied, knowing what Fay was about to ask. I have my *kipa sruga*, my knitted yarmulke from Israel. I will certainly wear it at your house and for your information, I kind of think it's really cool to show respect to God by covering your head and blessing your food before and after eating."

Fay looked at him in wonder. "So stop me please if you think that I have no right to critique your grandparents , but is it possible that in an attempt to start a new life, without reminders of the past, your grandparents withheld their own heritage from their children? A generation later, you actually crave what is in your DNA?"

"Whoa, Nelly," said Jared playfully. "Hold your horses! That was quite astute, but please have no fear, I don't feel like my grandparents deprived me of anything and while I don't know what the future will bring, I do know that I am not yet ready for any change."

All Fay heard was the word "yet,". She could wait. When Jared would see how seamlessly her father integrated his religious standards into his secular life, she felt strongly that Jared would recognize it was not old-fashioned or cumbersome to be Orthodox.

Jared proposed that Fay fly home instead of going back on the train, so that they could spend another evening together. Fay was happy to agree and Jared made the arrangements.

As she said goodbye to Ray and Sammy, Ray asked her anxiously, "Tell me, Fay-Fay, are you upset with us or are you okay with where things are now?"

"Actually," said Fay, carefully considering her words, "I am grateful for how much you care and thrilled that you, Sammy and Jared will spend at least some part of Pesach with me. If your mom is okay with it, it would be sensational if you guys could come for one Seder or lunch."

"I think if Jared gave up going to Israel, then the least we can do is spend a good part of the holiday with you. I believe everyone is going to fall in love with him."

"Me too, Ray-Ray," said Fay as she zipped her small suitcase shut. "I can't wait to see you in 16 days and who knows, by then we might be aunts!"

"Yes," said Ray. "Fabulous things are coming our way! I love my life here with Sammy, away from New York, without prying eyes watching every move I make. I'm starting school this summer and this volunteer work has really helped clarify what I want to do with my life."

"I think that all sounds wonderful, Ray-Ray," Fay said seriously and solemnly. "You will be the best advocate for our women, Ashkenazic and Sephardic, who need a voice. No one, and I mean no one, should ever have to go through being abused alone."

As ironic as a Shakespeare tragedy, that was exactly the fate Fay consigned herself to for the next 14 years of her life.

37

"Fortunately, analysis is not the only way to resolve inner conflicts.
Life itself still remains a very effective therapist."
—Karen Horney

The holiday was in the air and so was spring. Mothers were shopping and preparing for their guests and Suzi Zweig was in the throes of it. When Fay asked if she could have her three friends for lunch and one Seder, Suzi was as expansive as always.

"Sure, Fay. I would be delighted to meet Ray's husband and his best friend."

Fay was thrilled and decided to give Bobby Ava a heads up, so that she would be comfortable and relaxed by knowing in advance who would be joining them. She knew Ray of course, but not Sammy or Jared. When they came over for Seder, Ava began her seemingly innocent interrogation by asking Ray why she and Sammy had elected to be married by a rabbi and forego a lavish wedding with friends and family in attendance. Shockingly, before Ray could reply or Sammy intervene, it was Jared who chimed in.

"With all due respect, Mrs. Kertesz, I think that Ray and Sammy don't owe any of us an explanation. Don't you agree?"

Ava, while surprised and taken aback, looked more carefully at this exceptionally well-bred young man and recognized that he could be a potential foe if ever they had cause to disagree. While she had no reason to speculate, she had a tiny suspicion that Fay had a crush on this boy. *Well*, she rationalized to herself, *my Fay could do worse*. He was after all a boy studying at Harvard with a successful family business to fall into. The fact that he was of Polish descent didn't concern Ava whatsoever, because he was charming, sophisticated and clever. She was not aware of his religious standards but simply assumed he was Modern Orthodox.

Even Hinda-Baila liked him. She had moved in with Ava for the duration of Pesach, having recently parked her husband whom she oddly referred to as Mr. Bloom instead of by his first name, Mechel, in a long-term care facility in Williamsburg, in Brooklyn, in the heart of the Hasidic community. Hinda-Baila was a realist. Mr. Bloom, at 82 years of age, needed a lot more care than she was willing to provide and as a thank you for all the money he had invested in many of her failed business ventures over the years, she saw to it that his every need was met by generously tipping the orderlies and bringing the nurses expensive colognes, chocolates and gifts every time she visited. In truth, Mr. Bloom looked happier and healthier and Hinda-Baila felt liberated yet again in her life, having only married him by default when no other suitable candidates appeared.

It was Hinda-Baila who first recognized that Fay and Jared had a connection, one that she once had with her first husband. While Ava was innocently questioning Ray, merely by looking at Fay's lovely face that was glowing every time Jared glanced at her, she knew they were in love. She remarked on it in Hungarian when the women all left the Seder table en masse, midway through the reciting of the Haggadah at 11:00 p.m. to assemble the lavish feast that the family would proceed to eat.

According to the chart that Bethie had constructed weeks before the holiday, everyone had a responsibility for the meal and Hinda-Baila was touched to be included. She and Ava were making chicken *paprikash* with authentic smoked paprika from Sighet, which Hinda-

Baila personally purchased twice a year when she went to Budapest for the mineral baths. They also made a huge potato kugel and tongue polonaise. Judy was meticulously combining and whisking the dill, garlic and lemon dressings for the avocado, spinach, artichoke and Caesar salads. And Magda was stirring the bottom of the crock pot in which a lamb stew with chunks of potato and carrots was simmering, while also occasionally basting the apricot-glazed ducks and garlic-infused minute steak roasts that had been seared and braised rather than roasted, to avoid the prohibition of eating roasted meats resembling the Passover sacrificial lamb. Meanwhile Suzi steamed the asparagus, sautéed the mushrooms, and checked on the zucchini marinating in tomato sauce.

"Hát drágáim, tudjátok, hogy a mi kis Faygalánk szerelmes a vendégünkbe?" Well my beloveds, said Hinda-Baila, are any of you aware that our little Faygala is in love with our charming guest?

"Nem yo, Hinda-Baila," said Suzi in Hungarian. "Not good what you are saying. Why do you say that, because he's a boy and she's a girl?"

"I think Hinda-Baila is absolutely right, declared Ava. I was too busy with Ray and her adorable husband Sammy but now that I think about it every time he talks, Faygala looks away, as if she's afraid she will give away how she feels" Ava said. With that pronouncement, the topic was closed for discussion, regardless of whether Suzi, Fay's mother, agreed or disagreed. What Ava said took precedence every single time and no one knew that better that Suzi.

They all fell silent and focused on the most immediate task ahead of them, bringing the oversized platters of gefilte fish, carp and white fish to the table and preparing Ava's green and white oversized Herend soup tureen with a piping hot potato onion leek soup that was Ava's annual specialty and Imre's favorite. Hinda-Baila was no less a contributor, bringing a veritable smorgasbord of cakes and tarts, pies and cookies, all made from potato and tapioca starch, rather than flour, which was forbidden for the duration of the holiday. It was the first Pesach she was not with her business partner Harry who was more like a husband to her in that he soothed her when she could not control her mood swings, far more so than her legally wedded husband who chose to drink rather than deal with her volatile temper. She seemed genuinely happy to be with the Reiss sisters and secretly considered herself one of them.

38

"All happy families are alike, each unhappy family is unhappy in its own way."
—Leo Tolstoy

Jared effortlessly charmed everyone at the Seder table. He insisted on taking on the role of pouring the wine for the traditional four cups to be drunk at different intervals throughout the Seder. He listened attentively when Zak spoke, when Fay's uncles gave a *dvar* Torah and when Imre spoke briefly about the gratitude he felt toward America for the freedoms he enjoyed with Ava. He was also effusive in his compliments regarding the meal, declaring it fit for kings and better than anything he had ever eaten in all of Europe, China, Japan and Australia.

Ava took that information in, wondering idly if perhaps Jared did not keep kosher, because where would he find kosher food in Japan or China? She would have to have a little chat with Fay, she decided. For now, she would let it go, because Fay was going back to Israel and Jared to Boston. In case it fizzled out on its own, why bother anyone? In spite of concern that perhaps Jared was not appropriate for Fay, Ava and Imre both liked this young man with the deep voice, inquisitive eyes and lovely manners.

That night at 2:00a.m., when the Seder was over, Ava turned to Imre and said, "Probably he has some Hungarian ancestors that he doesn't know about. This boy is definitely not Polish," she said, laughing.

"And if he is darling *Dragam*, Ava," asked Imre. "What's the difference darling? We are Americans now. We don't live in Hungary anymore, not in Dej, Bayamare, Sighet, Cluj, Djalu or Marmarosh. If Fay loves him, that's all that matters."

Ava looked at her husband and felt very close to him. It was true. He was not her first love, but certainly he would be her last love.

"*Igen* Imre," she murmured softly. "Yes, you are right. Now tell me, did you see how vonderful Magdala looked tonight? So slim and thin! I am so happy."

"Ava," said Imre wearily, "don't start at 2:00 in the morning."

"Start vat," said Ava genuinely puzzled. "I am just saying how happy I am that she finally came to her senses and now she can vork on her daughters who are very chubby."

"I rest my case," said Imre, throwing up his hands. "I knew this is where that was going. Can't you just be happy that Magdala feels good and not worry about the girls?"

"Okay, Imre," said Ava, patronizing him. "I can see you are tired. I will stop talking for now, because you know I always have something to say."

"Yes, I know. Sleep well, my darling."

As Ava drifted off to sleep with a smile on her face, her mind wandered. Tonight's Seder was a dream come true, it almost made up for the first Seder after the war when she and Lajos had been married for six months. It was just them, Kati and Zita and Lajos's best friend Ziggy. Ava remembered how she and her sisters sat at the tiny table without a flower or even a tablecloth and cried through the entire Seder, missing their parents and siblings. Nothing Lajos said made it any better. That was 48 years ago, thought Ava as she fell asleep. It still hurt her heart.

Next door, in her navy blue and white polka dotted bedroom, Fay was still awake, also thinking about the Seder. It was perfect. From the exquisite floral arrangements that Hinda-Baila sent, to the pristine white tablecloth and silver brocade cloth napkins and the sparkling stemware. In the center of the table closest to Imres seat was the oversized ornate Seder plate that had slots for the symbolic food eaten on Pesach from a shank bone, to a sprig of lettuce, a hard boiled egg and bitter herbs; respectively representing the Pesach sacrificial lamb, the lettuce symbolizing how initially life was soft in Egypt and then turned hard and bitter as the Jewish became slaves, and finally the egg as a symbol of the circle of life. It was warm and inviting and Fay was thrilled that Jared, Ray and Sammy had been there. She was sure that her family liked Jared. In fact, from the way Bobby was watching her all night, she had a hunch that Bobby knew Jared was there for her. Bobby was like that, thought Fay. She knew things ahead of everyone around her. She had the uncanny ability to ferret out information and make sense of it. Fay often wondered if this trait was one she adopted in Auschwitz in order to survive. Either way, thought Fay, as she sunk into her pillow, if Bobby had an inkling that she liked Jared, she would surely broach the topic and ask her directly.

Across the hall, Suzi finally reached her bedroom. It was 4:00 a.m. All the Grande Baroque sterling silver flatware was accounted for, the table newly set for lunch tomorrow, the meat she would need for tomorrow night defrosting in the refrigerator and everyone in the house sound asleep. Suzi got into bed quietly and Zak opened his eyes.

"Beautiful Seder, Suzi. Everyone enjoyed it," he said.

"Yes," said Suzi reluctantly. "But I can't figure out why Sammy's friend chose to be with us instead of his own family."

"Well," said Zak, ruminating, "maybe there isn't any deep-rooted, mysterious reason for it, maybe he doesn't have the same relationship with his family as we have with ours."

"Actually, that makes perfect sense," said Suzi, "When I was growing up, the emphasis on family was so strong that I was afraid to tell my mother I needed friends beside my sisters. Her sisters were her best friends. I assumed that was the norm."

"Okay, now that we have that squared away, shall we go to sleep?" asked Zak.

"Am I stopping you, Zak?" said Suzi, slightly annoyed and overtired. She went into the bathroom. When she came out, Zak was sound asleep. This time, she didn't wake him up.

In the Salem house, Ray, Sammy and Jared sat in the den and agreed that the Zweig Seder was a fantastic experience.

"I have to admit," said Jared, "I was raised without all that hoopla because my grandparents didn't want any reminder of their previous life. Those memories of a Seder and family were erased when they changed their names. In all honesty, I thoroughly enjoyed tonight and while I can't say right now what I would want for my own family, I can safely say that watching the Zweigs, I feel cheated, like I missed out."

"That's quite interesting," said Ray. "Didn't Fay suggest something like that when she visited us? Is my girl a genius or what?"

"Yes," replied Jared. "She did and she was right. I will tell her so tomorrow. My grandparents eliminated the source of what they viewed caused their horrific suffering, but in doing so, I think they shortchanged my parents, me and my siblings."

"The good news," said Sammy, practical as ever. "Is that it's never too late to change. Certainly, marrying a girl, someday, who comes from a religious background would make it that much easier."

"I am totally with you, brother," replied Jared. "On that happy note, I bid you all a good evening. I ate so much tonight, I can barely move."

"You and I both," said Ray. "I have been in Fay's house many times, but tonight was incredible."

39

"In spite of everything, I still believe that at heart, people are good."
—Anne Frank

May sat at the Salem Seder and never got up once to help. No one expected her to do anything. In fact, she was glad she made it to the table, feeling uncomfortable and ready to have her baby. She was sorry to see Ray and Sammy leave, especially because they would be with Fay, but in the end, the Salem home was warm and noisy and she thoroughly enjoyed the lavish meal and all the components of the Seder that was designed to include the children. In bed, May told Danny that she was nervous, as her due date had already passed and Dr. Pearl had told her last week that if she didn't go into labor within three days, he would induce her.

He looked at her and sarcastically said, "And now at 11:30 p.m. you tell me this, why exactly?"

"Because," said May stammering, "you are my husband and I'm scared and I don't even have Ray to talk to."

"Well, fatso, pick a better time. I'm about to go to bed and I hope that the second you have the baby, you start a starvation diet. Have you looked in the mirror lately?"

May thought she was hearing things. Could Danny really be so thoughtless and mean to insult her at the end of her ninth month? She had watched her calories all pregnancy long. She gained 21 pounds, which by anyone's standard was not a lot, and yet Danny looked at her as if she had gained 60 pounds! She started to cry and felt sorry for herself. She closed her eyes and said nothing.

Three hours later, May woke up, feeling very strange. She tapped Danny on the shoulder and before she could utter a word, he slapped away her hand.

"Are you effing kidding me? Now what? More pity?"

"I think," gasped May, "that I am in labor. I need to go to the hospital."

"I doubt it," said Danny. "I think you didn't like what I said before or maybe you ate way too much at the Seder and you have heartburn." He turned over and went right back to sleep.

May looked at him in shock. He was her husband; he was supposed to be so much better than this. She wanted to cry, but knew she didn't have that luxury now. *How*, she thought, *can I wake up my in-laws and tell them I need their help without raising their suspicions? What would they possibly think about why Danny wasn't taking her?* Nor did she want to involve Ray and Sammy. She decided right then and there to take matters into her own hands. Ray and Fay had been warning her for months now that being so submissive to Danny was not going to accomplish anything. This time, looking at him sleeping peacefully, she realized they were right. She had a child to think of and she wasn't going to tolerate Danny's foolishness anymore. With a sense of purpose, thinking only about her child, she walked over to Danny's side of the bed and yanked the covers off him.

"Get up and take me to the hospital. Right now!" she said in a stern, authoritative voice. "And don't even think about raising your hand to me ever again or you will regret it. That is a promise."

Danny glared at her. "Don't threaten me, bitch. I'll excuse you because you are in labor, but don't think I will forget." He quickly put on clothes and helped May, who was in pain now, down the stairs.

· · ·

She gripped the door handle of the car and kept hold of it the entire way into the city. Her ob-gyn was at Lenox Hill Hospital. Thankfully, there was no traffic from Brooklyn into Manhattan. She was silent the whole ride, thinking how Sammy or Jared or even Danny's own brothers might behave in this situation. She knew there was no way any of them would have acted the way Danny had. Then it occurred to her, the one person who under similar circumstances might lash out at his pregnant wife was Danny's father. He was distant with May and never once said anything offensive. It was as if they had a pact to simply avoid each other and any potential conflict.

When Danny reached Park Avenue, May was relieved. As hospital staff approached their car, she thought she would vomit when Danny called out, "Please help us! My beautiful wife is in labor. Please help her. I can't bear to see her in pain."

Was this the same man who wanted to hit her when she woke him up an hour ago? Was he crazy or was she? He was so charming that the nurses ran to get a wheelchair and speed up the admissions process, especially when Danny casually said, "Oh, my parents, doctors Isaac and Victoria Salem, will be so pleased when they get here."

In seconds, May was escorted to a private suite on a private floor of the hospital where she would deliver her baby. Every comfort imaginable was present, as were all the monitors to assess hers and the baby's condition. Upon examining her, the resident on duty announced that May was not in active labor and could technically go home, but when he looked at May's distraught face, he amended his statement, especially after the head nurse reminded him whose grandchild this was, waiting to be born.

"On second thought, I think it would be best for you to stay put, Mrs. Salem. Your doctor sent an email saying that he is about two hours away, but he will be here and decide what the next course of action will be. For now, just relax and we will keep monitoring your baby's heart and give you some meds to help you relax."

If you could evict my husband, thought May, *I wouldn't need medication.* Instead, she softly said, "Thank you, Doctor Freed. I appreciate everything."

The doctor adjusted her IV lines and May received a dose of Valium, an anxiolytic sedative given to treat anxiety, which almost immediately calmed her. She closed her eyes, mainly to avoid Danny. At this moment she didn't care what he was thinking or feeling. Now it was about the baby. Eventually, May fell asleep and so did Danny, sitting in a chair across from her.

"What a husband," remarked one nurse to everyone congregating at the nurses' station.

"He is so handsome and devoted to her," another said. "What a lucky girl!"

At 5:00 a.m., Dr. Pearl arrived. He frowned as he disposed of his latex gloves. "We will give you Pitocin to help induce your labor, but at this point it looks like we have at least 30 hours to go. In the next eight hours, we will decide if we should do a C-section or wait. Now, you go back to sleep and I will see you later."

"Thank you so much," May whispered so that Danny wouldn't wake up. She did not want to deal with him just yet.

The next eight hours flew by, with various doctors coming into the suite to determine if mother and child were progressing well. Dr. Pearl felt they should wait, as May had dilated just one more centimeter.

Victoria arrived. She'd heard Danny's car and figured they had left for the hospital. May was happy to see her and held on to her hand. Victoria found her very agitated and was concerned. "Rest, sweetheart," she said soothingly. "I am here and I am not leaving your side."

When Danny opened his eyes, she looked at him and suggested he go home to get some rest. She would keep him appraised of any changes.

"Do you mean it, Mom?" he asked incredulously.

"Yes," said Victoria, "I don't think there is anything you can do for May right now."

Danny looked at his sleeping wife, who looked exhausted. "Okay Mom, I'm out. Call me when I should come back."

He left, kissing the top of May's head for his mother's approval. "Take care of her, Mom. She is my life," he said seriously.

But he didn't fool his mother. She knew he was a lot less than the ideal husband. However, he was still her son. When Dr. Pearl arrived, she spoke to him after he examined May.

"Please doctor, do not hesitate to take my daughter for a C-section. On top of fetal distress, I am monitoring my daughter's emotional status and I'm not sure she can hold on much longer."

"Yes, Dr. Salem," said her much younger colleague. "We are devoting all of our resources to ensure a smooth delivery."

Thirty hours later, when the doctor determined they could no longer wait, the operating room was booked for a C-section.

May was sedated. Danny, as well as Ray and Fay, who had joined Danny on his return to the hospital, were all asked to leave the room. Only Victoria remained. When her granddaughter was surgically removed from May's body, she received her and thanked God.

"May," she sobbed. "Our little girl is here and she is perfect."

May, who was still sedated, smiled at her mother-in-law. "Please call my parents," she said.

Victoria's heart broke when she heard May's request. Regardless of their total indifference, May still wanted to share this moment with her selfish parents. Victoria couldn't figure them out; a girl like May was a gift that they simply didn't appreciate. She also noted that Danny was acting weird. When he and the girls returned, she was astounded at his disappointment upon hearing that he now had a daughter and not a son.

"Surely you aren't upset, Daniel," she said sternly.

"No Mom, I'm not. I'm just tired."

"You are tired," Victoria said in disbelief. "What should May say?"

Victoria lambasted her pathetic son who had still not acknowledged or held his daughter, but May was in Nirvana, holding her precious daughter with Fay and Ray by her side. As she gazed at her baby, May smiled. It had all been worth it. She turned to Ray and May.

"Girls, one of you should go home now, get some rest and come back. I know you both too well. You are going to stay with me until I'm discharged."

"You bet, your bippy," said Ray. "I'll stay and Fay can come back later."

"Are you sure, Ray-Ray?" said Fay. "I'll call my dad to come pick me up."

"No need," said Danny gallantly. "I need a shower and a change of clothes. If you want, I'll drop you off."

"Oh, okay," said Fay. "That would be great." Fay leaned over the bed and gently hugged May. "You are a superstar! This is the most exciting day of my life. I will never forget it!"

That was truer than Fay knew at that moment.

41

"Rules for happiness: something to do, someone to love,
something to hope for."
—Immanuel Kant

Five years later, 1997

Ray was ecstatic to finally be marrying Sammy. Her heart overflowed with joy at the thought of being legally married to him. Her career was firmly established, as was Sammy's. They lived in Manhattan and loved what the larger community had to offer them. They went to the theater when they were in the mood, to Lincoln Center and to the Met. Life was exciting and she was madly in love with her husband, who was the darling of the district attorney's office and being touted for a rising political career. It was all quite fabulous and amazing except for Fay's shocking decision to stay in Israel permanently, studying art at the prestigious Shenkar College of Engineering, Design and Art. Further, Fay also decided to move to Mea Shearim, to be closer to Chava-Sara and chose to practically become Hasidic to fit into the community. Ray and May, along with Suzi, Ava, Jared, Sammy and Victoria, all pondered this mystery and worried about Fay endlessly.

At the time when it became clear that Fay did not intend to return to New York, Ava insisted that they go to Israel and drag her home, take her to a neurologist for a full scan, convinced that only a brain tumor could have caused such a radical change in her beloved granddaughter's behavior. What could have made Fay abandon her loved ones like this and barely stay in contact with any of them? May in particular was devastated by Fay's utter metamorphosis. She complained often to Ray that talking to Fay was like talking to a robotic version of their former best friend.

Now, with the wedding invitations ready to go out, Ray wondered if Fay would come back for her lavish civil ceremony. Would she abandon Ray after all that they had been through together? When Ray received Fay's email later that day, she cried so hard that she couldn't breathe. When she forwarded the email to Sammy, he promptly called her from work.

"Ray, I know you are devastated, so am I, but please calm down. Fay isn't doing this to hurt you. I am sure that it is just impossible for her to get away right now. She says that she is preparing for her first exhibit in London next week. You have to believe her and let it go."

"I don't know, Sammy. Something is really wrong with her. It just doesn't make sense. I keep going over everything, the events before she left. The Seder was wonderful, Jared made a commitment to meet Fay more than halfway on their differences and the family adored him. What could have happened to make Fay run back to Israel and transform herself?"

"My feeling is that when she is ready, if ever, she will let us all know. We have to accept it. You have your work and our life. Can you imagine how Ava and Suzi are handling this?"

"Actually, I can't. I think I want to go to see May. Hugging those adorable little girls will help, even though I dread the thought of seeing my brother. I don't know what's gotten into him. In fact, I am worried about May."

"Why?" asked Sammy. "She is busy with the children. She looks great. She's involved in the community. What doesn't seem right to you?"

"Well, to begin with, she's too thin. I know she thinks that's how she needs to be to keep up with Nicky and Charlotte, but she seems edgy to me. And a lot of times, she sounds robotic, exactly what she accuses Fay of!"

"Let me ask you something, Ray. Is it possible both of them are simply getting older and coming to terms with how they view themselves?"

"I suppose so," she said reluctantly. "I mean, look at me. Once upon a time all I ever wanted was a husband and my own home, just to get away from my father. Now, I'm a lawyer and a social worker. I work for a not-for-profit that deals with Jewish women with domestic violence issues. I suppose if I've changed, so can they."

"Well then," said Sammy, "there you have it. Give it time. What you three have is truly extraordinary. Go visit May after work. In fact, have Earl take you and I'll meet you in Brooklyn. We can go out to dinner, maybe stop in to visit Suzi and Zak and tell them about Fay's decision in person?"

"You know something, Sammy BenAdin," she said. "I must be insane that I postponed marrying you for so many years. You are the best husband I could ever have hoped for. Ray, also a victim of trauma, never lost the need to idealize anyone who loved her. You are absolutely right, I will reply to Fay tomorrow and I will find the right words. See you in a few hours."

Ray hung up the phone and directed her attention to a new case at work. It was the plight of a young 24-year-old Ashkenazic woman with two small children whose husband refused to give her a *get* [a Jewish divorce]. Without the legal undoing of the Jewish marriage, her client would be prevented from ever remarrying another man. Ray did her research and found that nearly a decade before, a bill had been passed in Congress that clearly prohibited the withholding of a get. The sponsors of the bill, Sheldon Silver, Marty Connor, Harvard professor Alan Dershowitz and members of Agudath Israel, all fought for the estimated 150,000 women in New York State who were civilly divorced but waiting in limbo, often for years, for their husbands to give them a get. The men had the upper hand, because Jewish law stipulated that only the husband could end the marriage, allowing many to demand exorbitant sums of money or complete custody of their children in order to grant their wives the get. If their extortion demands were not met, many of these husbands left their *agunah* wives chained and tied to the shell of a marriage.

Ray was astounded when she met her client. Aviva was a soft-spoken, yet articulate Orthodox woman who tried hard to control her emotions, but was clearly stressed out. She explained that she could not afford to hire an attorney to represent her and was worried about her children. She had to take a job to support herself and her children. She also couldn't cope with being the center of attention in her community. Ray was determined to try and find a compromise that would appeal to Aviva's recalcitrant husband, Shlomo. There had to be a way.

May was happy that Ray was popping in for a visit. Now that Ray lived in the city and worked full-time, she didn't see her as much and she missed her. Compounded with Fay being 10,000 miles away, totally immersed in art and religion, May felt deserted once more. Other than her two vapid sisters-in-law and superficial friends from her classes, she really had no one to connect with. She was closer than ever to Victoria and loved her to pieces, but there were many things she couldn't share with her. She yearned for the intimate bond she once had with her childhood friends, a bond that made all the loneliness bearable. Sadly, her marriage didn't afford her one either. She knew Ray had it with Sammy. Even Mazal, stuck in a religious life, seemed enamored with her husband.

Danny was a changed person ever since Victoria May was born. She didn't recognize him anymore whatsoever. He came home late most nights, was always on edge, smoked and drank a lot and started taking pills to help him relax. May tried her best to be supportive, because that's what good wives did, but she had no clue what was bothering him and found that she didn't care.

A shocking turn of events in their household was that May no longer cowered in fear when he walked in the door. Being the protector of her three precious angels made her fierce. Once, in the park, an older child began to taunt Vicky. Immediately, May was all over this bully and only later realized that she had been a second away from slapping the child. In order to protect her children, she stood up to Danny. Nothing he said, nothing he did, scared her anymore. On top of that, she was thinner and fitter than when she got married and feeling confident. Danny almost didn't know how to deal with this new, aggressive May. So, like his father, he called a truce. They seldom talked, but there was no violence. For May that was enough, because her children were everything to her.

42

"Aki a kicsit nem becsüli a nagyot nem érdemli."
[Who doesn't appreciate the little does not deserve the big.]
—Hungarian folk quote

Fay's routine was always the same. Today, it was Thursday. After painting in the early morning, she would find her way to the busy streets of Geula. There, she would go shopping for Shabbos like many other women her age, except that she wasn't married and was shopping for Chava-Sara. She waved to a few of the women she recognized. They grudgingly accepted her in their midst, but were uncomfortable, because she barely spoke Yiddish and was not married with children.

Later in the day, she would go to the *shuk* and shop for Ibu and Mimi, who were largely bedridden at this point. She visited them every other day to minimize the overwhelming ache in her heart when she thought about her own beloved Bobby. Fay tried hard not to dwell on the past. She put in 15-hour days so that she would be exhausted and immediately fall asleep with no time to think. Yet, random thoughts would come to her at the oddest moments. Often, she cried for herself and for everyone she loved, whom she knew she had inadvertently hurt by trying to protect them.

When she flew back to Israel five years ago during Chol Hamoed of Pesach, making an excuse that one of her roommates was going through a crisis, her family was disappointed, especially Bethie and Deenie, but trusted that if Fay said she needed to go back, she did. They assumed that they would have contact with her and that she would be back at the end of June. The hardest person to say goodbye to was, of course, Bobby Ava. Fay was nervous that she would not be able to maintain the carefully curated image that everything was fine. It was a close call, but Imre was very helpful. At least two times, Fay considered confiding in him, trusting him implicitly, but then she decided it was too much of a burden to put on a man with congestive heart failure and who never kept any secrets from his wife.

When Fay told Jared that she was returning to Israel, he immediately assumed that she was leaving him and the potential for them to have a serious relationship. Like his best friend Sammy, he felt that no good would come from pressuring Fay. He offered to drive her to the airport, but she declined. In parting, she said something that puzzled him.

"Jared," she said in a sad voice. "I admire you more than words can say. I will never regret meeting you and caring about you, but the timing isn't right. I hope you will move on with your life, as I plan to do." When he looked puzzled, she shook her head. "That's just how it is." Barely audible, she then said, "Please don't forget me."

Jared was besides himself, playing her words over in his mind repeatedly. He knew he had passed the test with the family. He could not figure out what motivated Fay, a fearless girl who had so much character and integrity, to give up on them. However, he did heed her words. Not right away, but three years later, he accepted a job in London and made a life for himself. He found another expat from New York and they moved in together. He was somewhat satisfied, content with his career and having a partner he liked being with, even though she didn't come close to being Fay. When he finally came to terms with the fact that he was not really satisfied with his life, he decided, a few years later, that he wanted to try and keep kosher and Shabbat and see if that added a layer of depth and meaning to his life. It was ironically Fays mother Suzi Zweig that he called for guidance, advice and tips before he totally immersed himself in converting to Orthodoxy and making Aliyah to Israel permanently. Knowing Fay was in Israel comforted him, but he knew he would never reach out to her; she had made it patently clear that she had no desire to be with him.

When Fay got back to Israel, she went straight to Mea Shearim. She knew Chava-Sara would not question her and would help her in whatever way she needed help.

When Chava-Sara heard Fay's voice on the phone, saying she was back in Israel, she was surprised. In Hebrew she asked Fay, "Why did you leave so soon? You were so excited to go home! Was it that boy you told me about?"

"Something terrible happened to me," Fay said. "I can't talk about it yet, but I need your help."

"Then come right now."

When Fay got out of the taxi, Chava-Sara was waiting outside for her. She took Fay into her arms.

"Whatever it is, it will pass. God will help and you will recover. I know that for sure."

Fay just stood there, incapable of speaking. When they walked inside, she knew what she needed.

"I am not going back to seminary. Do you think I can stay with you for a while until I figure out what I want to do with my life? I can sleep with the girls on a cot or a mattress."

Chava-Sara was quite worried about her American friend. Fay was running away from herself, that much was clear.

"Motek [sweet one], for my part, of course, you can stay with us, but I need to ask my husband. He will no doubt ask his Rav if this is appropriate. One thing I can promise you is that I am here for you."

Fay felt relieved after verbalizing her jumbled, scattered thoughts. At the same time, it dawned on her that she could not move into Chava-Sara's apartment, because she was not a family member and Chava-Sara's husband could never be alone with her at any time. She was glad she had saved up all her bat mitzvah and babysitting money and had the foresight to withdraw half of it from the bank before she left. She would find an apartment and survive. She was, after all, Ava's granddaughter.

Later that day, Fay made her way back to seminary thinking how much she had changed in a few short weeks. She had left Jerusalem so excited for May to give birth, to see Ray and Sammy, to tell everyone about her adventures in Israel, so full of hope for a reunion with Jared, surrounded by her family and enjoying every aspect of Pesach from the food to the traditions of the afikomen and the *Ma Nishtana*, the four questions the youngest child asked during the Seder, to the beautiful songs of Hallel. In just one cruel moment, Danny had erased all of that and robbed her of all joy. She could not imagine how he could live with himself and she hoped he suffered.

As the taxi pulled up to the dorm, Fay felt numb. She didn't care that she was back, she just wanted to disappear. She was relieved that all of her roommates were still away and that she didn't have to talk to anyone or be anywhere because, technically, the seminary was closed until a week after Pesach. That night, for the first time since Danny raped her, she went over the details, trying hard to understand why it happened. She knew that she did not, in any way, cause this to happen. That Danny was lucid and insane enough to suggest that she had hugged him in order to seduce him was preposterous. His saying that was merely a pathetic excuse to shift the blame and make her culpable when, in fact, it was all about his lack of decency and impulse control.

As she relived the horror, she began to sweat profusely, felt her heart racing and couldn't breathe. The room seemed to close in on her and she felt a sense of dread like she was about to die. Though she didn't realize it that night, she had experienced the first of many panic attacks that would eventually lead her to seek out a psychiatrist. Art became her salvation, even more so than when she had returned from Poland. She painted pictures of the devil with Danny's face and of broken hearts, shattered and bleeding. She also painted a lifeless girl, whose body was broken, a girl who could not fight off her attacker.

Within 24 hours, right before the second part of the *chag* began, Chava-Sara found her an apartment. It was not ideal, but it was reasonably priced and a block away from Chava-Sara's apartment , which offered Fay some emotional relief. She couldn't explain why, but Chava-Sara was her lifeline and she clung to her. Talking to her, being in her presence, ultimately would prove to have helped Fay more than much of the therapy she received for three years, more than the anti-depressant medication she required for six months when she could not eat, sleep or stop crying. At the end of four months of therapy, when her therapist asked her to consider sharing what happened to her with someone she trusted, she did.

When Fay told Chava-Sara what had happened, Chava-Sara sat there in disbelief.

"This is the same man you've known your whole life, who is married to your best friend and is the brother of your other best friend" she asked incredulously? And you never told your parents or reported him to the police?"

"He was drunk. I'm not excusing him, not now, not ever, but he was frustrated and humiliated that his first-born child, his *bechor,* wasn't in fact a son. In some Sephardic families, that is a really big deal. Of course, how raping me helped that, I don't know," said Fay, relieved that she could say the word "rape" without the familar heart racing, or literally fainting or vomiting.

"Now I see why you came back to Israel," said Chava-Sara, desperately attempting to hold back her tears and not succeeding. "I am so sorry for you."

"I know you care," said Fay, also crying. "I also know with all my heart that being near you will give me the strength I need to move on."

"Oh, Fay," said Chava-Sara. "I am honored that you feel this way. Come, let's go to my father right now, *chick-chock* [Israeli slang for quickly], for a *bracha*. He is quite famous here in Mea Shearim and a blessing from him will do you wonders."

"But," said Fay nervously, "will I be allowed to be alone with him?" She had learned about the laws and customs of *yichud* for any female over age 12 when Chava-Sara had to turn down her plea to allow her to move in with her and her family.

"You will not be alone," said Chava-Sara gently. "My mother will be there with you. In fact, you will speak to my mother and she will speak to my father on your behalf. My father will not look you in the face but he will hear every word you say. Tell him whatever you want to share with him, he has heard many things in his years."

Chava-Sara was right. Because of her father, Rabbi Shanzer, Fay was able to gather the courage to return to America for Rosh Hashanah, Yom Kippur and the whole Succos. After hearing her story, and in particular her desire not to ruin many lives, he told her that her decision to have distance initially was a wise one. He advised her to do *chesed* [good deeds], to continue painting and calling her loved ones as often as she could manage, to say Tehillim Psalms every single day, and to pray at the Kotel as often as she could. For Fay, these concrete suggestions were life changing in that they were simple constructive ways in which she could channel her pain and sorrow. Rabbi Shanzer for his part, was drawn to his daughter's protégé, sensing her vulnerability and admiring her determination to survive a most horrific chapter in her young life. He was determined to help her succeed and find meaning and joy in her life. Within a brief amount of time, when Fay shared some of her artwork with the Rabbi and Rebetzen, it was he who found a wealthy financial backer in Golders Green in London, a *chosid* who was his follower, to invest in her talent. This chosid was honored to do his *Rebbe"s* bidding at whatever cost it would take to mount an exhibit of Fay's work.

It was after a long hot summer in Jerusalem that Fay started to consider and visualize how she would feel being at home for three weeks and how she would avoid Danny while still seeing May and the baby. As a way of postponing the inevitable, she asked her mother in desperation if there was any way that instead of her coming home, her immediate family could come to Israel for the holidays, but her mother gently reminded her that the girls could not miss school and her father could not take off that much time from work. Suzi was also shocked that Fay could be so thoughtless about Bobby Ava, who missed her fiercely and was counting down the days until she came home. In those first few weeks, when Fay was just glad she was able to care for herself, she almost conceded to Suzi's offer to visit. Her mother offered at least weekly to come for a four-day visit to see her, but Fay turned her down each time. She had told her mother that that was exactly why she had chosen to live on her own: to grow up and fend for herself. Unlike seminary, where meals were arranged and she was not faced with responsibilities, this new lifestyle afforded her the opportunity to grow up. To Ava, Magda, Judy and Suzi, this sounded plausible and they convinced the rest of the family that Fay wanted to be independent before she got married. *Of course,* thought Suzi resentfully, *Ava would never directly criticize Fay's decision, even pretending it was a good idea; but daily she would nag Suzi to bring her granddaughter home.*

For months, until Fay came home for the *yomim tovim* [the high holidays], Ava incessantly badgered Suzi and Zak, worried that Fay was missing out on her first dating season. She even forced Imre to call Suzi and Zak and threatened to get on a plane herself to find out the real story. That was when Fay knew she had to go home. Ava would not let up. If Ava did not see her, she would continue questioning Fay's motives in remaining in Israel and eventually she would find out that Fay was not doing Shana Bet [a second year in seminary], training to be a Hebrew teacher, but was instead holed up in a one-bedroom unit in a brand-new apartment complex in Mea Shearim, trying to hold on to her sanity day by day.

A week before Rosh Hashanah, Fay tearfully said goodbye to Chava-Sara. All the children lined up to say goodbye, even the older boys, who never talked to her directly but knew she was a coveted and respected *bat-bayis* [a daughter of the house]. As Fay hugged the girls and waved to the boys, she felt anxious about leaving them; they with whom she had bonded and felt safe among, they who served as her 'family'. Armed with the *Tehillim* that Rebbetzin Shanzer had given her on that first fateful day when she arrived, which now never left her side, she left for Ben-Gurion Airport.

She was glad that she was flying through Paris and could follow Ray's explicit 'rules' about airport shopping for gifts at Charles de Gaulle Airport. Her heart was not into the shopping, but when she found the most beautiful French lotions, perfumes, soaps, creams, berets and silk scarves, she began imagining the joy it would bring her family to receive these gifts. Suddenly, Fay felt like she could manage this trip. If Bobby Ava could survive Auschwitz and the loss of her beloved husband, then she too could survive her trauma.

Looking in the shop window, she was confronted with her own reflection and for one minute didn't recognize herself. She didn't look like Fay Zweig. She looked like an ultra-Orthodox girl in her long, gray, shapeless skirt and navy-blue argyle sweater. She was not wearing a stitch of make-up or nail polish on her short-clipped nails and her long, beautiful, chocolate brown, straight hair, that she used to blow out three times a week to achieve a curtain-like effect, was tied back in a ponytail. She repeatedly told her therapist Dr. Steiner that she was not punishing herself or trying to look unattractive. Her motive was to dig deeper into herself in an effort to achieve the blind faith that Chava-Sara seemed to possess. She argued with her therapist that when secular people went to an ashram or began to meditate and follow the teachings of Buddha, people applauded them for their discovery of their essence and purpose. That was what living in Mea Shearim would, hopefully, do for her too.

43

"Courage is knowing what not to fear."
—Plato

At the airport, Suzi seemed to have morphed into Ava, unable to stop herself from criticizing Fay's appearance. As soon as she saw Fay, she laced into her. "What is it?" she shrieked. "Purim? Halloween? Why are you dressed like that?"

Fay's hand tightened around her Tehillim. She was upset with herself for not anticipating this moment. She had used all her emotional resources just to get herself to this point. She should have, she realized in hindsight, warned or prepared her mother or herself by discussing this in detail with Dr. Steiner. She felt uncomfortable being scrutinized and stood there awkwardly, not wanting to defend herself, preferring to become invisible and not having to deal with questions. Her mother's shrieking was a throwback to her mother of old, except then, it was typically directed at everyone but Fay. She laughed to herself, her mother yelling at her and embarrassing her in public was some sort of progress. She had finally taken Fay off the pedestal she had erected. Fay looked at her sisters. They were fascinated with their mother yelling at her and didn't say a word. It was only when they reached the car and her father had a look of utter shock and a hint of revulsion on his face that Fay knew she needed to come up with some explanation so that her parents could warn Bobby and her aunts of her drastic change in appearance.

"I know I look different, so let me explain what happens when girls like me go to Israel for a gap year. There are those who hang out on Ben Yehuda Street in Jerusalem and party. Many are in schools that turn a blind eye to their behavior and those schools that don't condone such behavior, ask them to leave. Then there are the girls like me, who want to fit in and really pay close attention to everything our guidance counselors are trying to teach us."

"But you don't come from a home like those teachers," argued her mother in a high-pitched voice.

"Is it possible for you to accept me like this?" asked Fay in a deferential voice. "It may be permanent, it may be temporary. I can't say for sure, because I am learning about myself every single day." She took a deep breath. "And, there is no doubt in my mind that I'm going back next year for Shana Bet, for the whole year."

"What?" screamed Suzi. "I thought it was only going to be until December! What are you thinking? What is wrong with you? Don't you want to start college and dating? Even your modern friends are married!"

"Mom," said Fay wearily, "I just got off a plane, I haven't slept in days and I have a lot on my mind. Can we discuss this calmly tomorrow?"

"There is nothing to discuss, Fay," said Suzi. "Tomorrow we are going shopping and to the beauty salon. You can not, let me repeat that, can not see your grandmother the way you look, unless you want to give her a heart attack. You can call her when we get home and tell her your stomach hurts from the plane food and that you will come over tomorrow afternoon instead of tonight."

"You want me to lie to Bobby because I became more religious?" asked Fay in wonderment. "Does that make any sense to anyone in this car? So, if I came home wearing a tank top, ripped jeans, smoking and drinking that would be okay?"

"Stop talking!" screamed Suzi. "You are being ridiculous! If this is what that seminary taught you, you can be sure your sisters are staying far away from there."

Fay closed her eyes, drained from her mother's vitriol. Her heart ached. She wanted to be accepted as she was. It seemed so unfair that she was being attacked and ridiculed when all she was doing was trying to find her way back to herself. She did not open her eyes until they reached Brooklyn and then she avoided making eye contact with her parents and sisters. *Someone*, she thought sadly, *should have attempted to stop my mother's rant.* How many times had she defended her sisters when her mother would get on their case? That neither even bothered trying was upsetting to her. And her father, she understood, was caught between a rock and a hard place.

When she walked in the door, she saw the homemade signs, but could not muster up the energy to pretend it thrilled her. "I'm really tired," she said. "I'll go upstairs and rest, if that's okay.

"Go rest," said Suzi. "Let's hope you come to your senses when you wake up."

Fay drew a long, deep breath, thinking of Dr. Steiner. That calmed her. She visualized the spectacular beach at Eilat and performed her imagery exercises to help her stay focused on happy memories, rather than allow her mother's disappointment and her father's disapproval to put her in a dark corner where the memories of Danny's mouth and hands still existed.

This time, her sisters did not come upstairs to help her unpack and Fay was in no mood to give any of them her gifts. For now, she needed to be alone, in her own space. She called her grandmother, who totally commiserated with her gastric event. Ava suffered from irritable bowel syndrome.

"Sure, my darling. Go rest and have some tea. Tomorrow I vill see you. I can't vait to go shopping with you next week. Flamm Baci called me yesterday from his store. He put aside the nicest dresses for us!"

Ava didn't know it, but her words served to soothe the torment in Fay's heart. She decided in that moment to give in to her mother's demands that she change her appearance simply for Bobby's sake. When she got back to Israel, she could be her own person again.

As she undressed to take a luxurious shower in her own bathroom, she tried to figure out how Dr. Steiner would interpret her mother's behavior. She felt that maybe her appearance was scary to her mother on a level she couldn't understand. All she knew was that if she ever had children of her own someday, she would never be so judgmental, harsh and disapproving. She felt a pain in her gut thinking that this was how her two younger sisters grew up. No wonder they had such pinched faces. It made her sad. By the time she came out of the shower, she felt much stronger and quickly called May and Ray via conference call. It almost felt like old times and Fay felt her mood lift. For the first time since baby Vicky was born, she felt the tiniest glimmer of hope that maybe one day, she could leave the past in the past.

44

"It does not matter how slowly you go as long as you do not stop."
—Confucius

Although Ray and May were hurt by Fay's past decision to distance herself from them, neither could stay angry at her. Ray informed them that she and Sammy would be staying in Brooklyn for Rosh Hashanah and the girls tried to make a plan that worked for all of them. Fay felt a knot in her stomach. How would she see May and Vicky without also seeing Danny? Was this the challenge God meant for her to face? She tried to imagine how Bobby Ava might have reacted in this situation. Then, she had an epiphany. She realized that hiding and hurting those she loved, only continued to fan the flames of her own pain. She needed to face her fear, quash her panic and live her best life in spite of what had happened. That, she knew, was what Bobby Ava did. It didn't mean for one second that she forgot or forgave Danny, it just meant that she chose life.

The girls decided to meet for brunch the next day, after Fay visited Bobby Ava. Hanging up the phone, Fay breathed. She could do this, even if it sapped all of her energy, she could do this. Two hours later, she woke up from her nap, disoriented for a minute, not sure where she was. Then, she remembered that she was home. She opened her drawer and, without thinking, pulled out a pair of sweatpants and an old Camp Beverly Hills sweatshirt. She looked at herself in the mirror and said one word to herself: "Rome." That served to remind her that it was totally justified to dress differently while among people who dressed this way.

Putting on her old favorite Lancôme, pink lipstick and blush, she was ready to face her mother. She knew that once her mother saw her, she would be relieved and consider her attack at the airport as her way of getting Fay back from the clutches of the cult-like environment she had been in. Fay felt sad that her mother did not have the capacity to understand that the surface changes she observed in her daughter were all self-imposed. Not once did anyone in Israel ever insist she dress differently; not once did anyone ever suggest that she wasn't good enough the way she was.

When Fay walked into the dining room, there was a collective sigh and everyone welcomed her to the table as if she had woken from a coma, not a two-hour recharge.

"Oh, Fay," squealed her mother. "You look adorable. Have you been to the gym in Israel?" This was her way of saying, "now you are my daughter and you look good and worthy of my love and consideration."

"No," said Fay in a light tone. "Just walking all over town and eating my main meal at lunchtime. Israelis eat well, but very healthy. The different *salatim* they eat are delicious!" Feeling confident, Fay began to describe in detail the salads she ate daily.

"Yes, dear," said her mother slightly sarcastically. "We've all been to Israel and eaten out numerous times."

"Oh, right," replied Fay amiably. "I guess the fact that I shop at the local grocery store and prepare it myself is why I mentioned it."

She began to eat dinner with her family, making sure to wash her hands before eating bread and saying Birkat Hamazon, the blessing after the meal. If her father thought these were unnecessary for a girl, he didn't show it. He didn't say a word and she felt accepted. Internally, though, she felt extremely conflicted and wished she could call Dr. Steiner. They had discussed her trip home and he had generously said that he was available if necessary, but Fay wanted to work through this herself. She knew who she was meant to be and her family, on some level, was not entirely wrong. They were annoying sometimes, and judgemental, yes, but that's who they were, and they hadn't changed. It was she who had drastically transformed.

She decided then and there to think about her strategy, not brood or feel sorry for herself, just think. By the time she returned to Israel, she decided she would enroll at Shenkar, the well regarded college of engineering, art and design, to learn as much as she could. She also brought back beautiful good quality wools, cottons and knit fabric to make fashionable modest skirts for Chava-Sara's daughters, thinking that maybe she could parlay this into a small business to derive an income. This would also provide an opportunity for some of the women in Mea Shearim who, for religious reasons, would not work outside of their home in a secular environment that they or their culture deemed inappropriate for them. The creative side of Fay was slowly awakening. She was glad.

The next morning, true to her word, Suzi got Fay a 9:00 o'clock appointment at Studio 19. Two and a half hours later, Fay emerged from the posh beauty salon looking almost like her old self. She wasn't entirely comfortable, but also not unhappy. Her mother had given her permission to drive her car and she drove straight to Bobby's house. To say that Bobby's embrace revitalized her broken heart was to underestimate the power of love. She stayed in her arms, never wanting to let go.

45

"With every true friendship, we build more firmly the foundations on which the peace of the whole world rests."
—Mahatma Gandhi

"Let me look at you, my beautiful girl," said Ava. "I am so happy to see you! You look different somehow. Are you really okay?"

"I am fine, Bobby. I've been through a lot," she truthfully replied. "Life in Israel teaches you a lot; not everyone lives the way we do in America."

"Yes, I know that darling, but my family shouldn't have to verk so hard, because I paid in for ten generations."

Fay knew that expression; she had heard Bobby say it often when she was growing up. It was as if Bobby needed to believe that her past suffering would somehow protect her family against any future pain of their own. She wondered how Bobby would react if she found out what had happened to her. Would she be angry at God? More so than when her own beloved 40-year-old mother and two infant grandchildren were sent to the left by the malevolent camp doctor who decided who would live and who would die, while she and her two sisters were sent to the right, to live another day?

"Come," said Bobby happily. "Sit down and talk to me. You left so

239

suddenly, I didn't even get to tell you how much I liked Sammy's friend, Jared. Such a nice boy."

"Yes," agreed Fay, determined to stick to the truth as much as possible so that her authentic voice could be heard. "He is a really nice guy. We actually spent a lot of time together in the summer while you were in Budapest at the spa."

"So, vots the problem here?"

"There is no problem, Bobby. I told him the timing wasn't right."

Fay adroitly moved the conversation to inquire about Imre's health. If Ava noticed how skilfully Fay moved the conversation, she said nothing. Later, when talking to Hinda-Baila and Zita, Ava noted that something was different about Fay that she couldn't quite put her finger on. She told Fay that Imre was watching his diet and going to the cardiac outpatient clinic at Columbia-Presbyterian Hospital. His doctors were satisfied with his progress. For the first time in her life, Fay noticed a slight crack in Bobby's steel veneer.

"Don't tell your mother, my darling," said Bobby tearfully. "Because she vorries about me too much, but I am very nervous about Imre. I don't know vat I vould do if something happened to him."

"Please Bobby, don't worry in advance and have faith," said Fay urgently. "You always taught us to never let fear hold you back. Just take one day at a time."

"My granddaughter is not only beautiful, but brilliant too," said Ava gleefully.

For Fay, the message was clear: Bobby was very vulnerable and she certainly would not add more to Ava's worries by revealing what had happened to her.

As she kissed her grandmother goodbye, she told her how much she was looking forward to the holidays, that sitting in the shul and praying with her was going to be the highlight of her trip. "Not even the Kotel compares to being with you, Bobby," she said while smiling.

In that brief moment, Fay felt happy that she was home.

As soon as she left Bobby, Fay drove to Avenue J., where she was meeting the girls for a casual brunch at the newly opened Kosher Cafe. Thankfully, Bobby had only served coffee and freshly made cheese *blintzes* [a light crepe filled with ricotta cheese and vanilla sugar]. It was Fay's absolute favorite dish. She was ecstatic that the girls were meeting in a public place and that Danny would be nowhere in sight. When Fay saw Ray, May and baby Vicky, she gasped with pleasure. *Oh my goodness*, she thought, *these girls are my life!* She resolved yet again to protect them and spare them from the agony she had been through.

As soon as Ray and May spied her at the table, they ran towards her, all while navigating Vicky's orange compact stroller. The girls hugged and it was as if life had never changed. Yet, Fay was quick to note that May indeed had changed. She was far more assertive, not the shy May-May she once was. And baby Vicky was the most adorable infant you could ever dream of.

"Let me hold that baby!" shouted Fay, instantly infatuated with the blonde, blue-eyed, chubby-cheeked little girl dressed in an adorable pale pink velour Petit Bateau onesie. She smelled like heaven; Fay was intoxicated.

"May-May," she said, "how do you ever get anything done? Do you play with her all day?"

"No, Fay. I have things to do," May replied while laughing. "There's plenty of housework and cooking and Danny has deteriorated into a slob of the greatest magnitude. Honestly, it's like having two children."

She said all this jokingly, but truly meant it. As she spoke, Ray and Fay saw something in May's expression and worried about her.

"Okay," said May. "I know that silence. Please forgive me if I am not on cloud nine like Ray with the perfect man and the perfect career."

"May, please," said Ray. "Don't be like that. I know that Danny and his behavior ever since baby Vicky's birth is despicable. I can't tell you how many times Sammy and I have told him to get over the fact that he didn't have a *bechor,* a first born male child to continue the family name! What an ass."

"Is that what it is?" asked Fay in a strangled voice.

"One would think so," said Ray. "I mean, look at May-May: an absolute knock-out, fabulous mother, daughter-in-law of the century, community darling and a wife that other men would kill for! What else could it be besides his hubris, that insane arrogance and pride, that his firstborn child is not a male to carry on his name."

"Please, girls," begged May. "Let's not waste our time talking about Danny. Fay, you have no idea how happy I am to see you. Is there any chance that you might give up *Shana Bet,* since so few girls go back for a second year?"

Fay looked at May and was in turmoil. To return to New York now was unthinkable. It would be like opening a veritable Pandora's box. To stay in Israel for the time being, was definitely the safest route.

"A second year immersed in my studies is definitely warranted. I love where I am right now," she said sincerely. "I didn't know that I would feel so complete living in Jerusalem. Of course, missing you guys and Bobby is hard, but I will do better with my phone calls. That's a promise!"

Ray nodded in agreement. Fay knew what she needed. She then proceeded to tell the girls about her work, describing her newest client, A., without of course, mentioning her name. She was curious if the girls knew about the plight of *agunahs*. Both were fascinated and saddened to learn about these Jewish women, held captive by recalcitrant husbands who refused to grant them a Jewish divorce. They were stunned by the small but still significant number of battered women, women without options or recourse, women terrified to rock the boat.

Upon hearing about how these community women were struggling, May decided right then and there to hold a fundraiser tea in her home. This would provide financial assistance to women who needed it until a court ordered child support. Ray was utterly delighted and proud of May.

"You know, by bringing awareness to the community, you might save someone's life," she said. "So many of our women just think this is how it has to be. I could kill myself that I told you the same exact thing, May-May!" she said shuddering.

"Don't be silly, Ray-Ray, not the same at all. Of course, I remember that conversation," said May in an affectionate tone. "Please don't beat yourself up. I knew who I was marrying, but I am thrilled to share with both of you that while Danny is not the same anymore, neither am I. I am fine. In fact, I would marry him all over again just for the bonus of having Victoria as my mother."

Fay and Ray smiled, happy for May to have acquired a true mother figure. They knew Victoria unabashedly loved May and baby Vicky. In fact, May told them that Victoria had officially amended her surgery schedule and took a day off midweek every single week, so that she could spend the afternoon with Vicky. She often picked up her granddaughter and walked with her, the entire length of Ocean Parkway from Avenue Z. to Church Avenue. According to May, it was the happiest part of her week.

46

"It is not the strongest of the species that survives, nor the most
intelligent. It is the ones who are most adaptable to change."
—Charles Darwin

As luck, fate and karma would have it, Danny was out of town on
business between Rosh Hashanah and Yom Kippur. During Sukkot,
on Chol Hamoed, Fay met up with May and Vicky at the park daily.
Baby Vicky was now five months old and adored going out. It had
been a long and cold winter. May wanted to take advantage of being
outdoors as much as possible and Fay was thrilled not to have to even
see Danny's car in their driveway, much less him.

Ray and Sammy met Fay in the city and took her out to dinner.
Fay loved seeing the life they had made for themselves. When she
saw the wedding album of their Jewish marriage in Boston, she cried
and hoped that when Ray had her civil wedding one day, she would
be there. As Fay sifted through the few pictures in the rabbi's study,
she felt a pang of regret when she spotted Jared, who was one of the
edim [witnesses] at the wedding ceremony. He looked so handsome
and dignified in his navy blue suit and silver-gray tie.

During dinner, Sammy tried a number of times to talk about

Jared, but Fay was not receptive to him. "Fay, can I just ask why," he asked gently but persistently for the fifth time.

"Because," explained Fay, "the timing isn't right."

In truth, that was what it came down to—timing. Like if she hadn't gone home with Danny the night Vicky was born, or the fact that her grandmother's family was unable to flee from Europe while there was still a small chance. But who could control timing? Only God.

As Fay once again said her goodbyes, she felt she had accomplished a lot on this trip. She had not fallen apart and that buoyed her strength to keep afloat. She was reminded that like her grandmother, she was alive and she had choices. Rabbi Shanzer and Dr. Steiner had pointed that out to her often. All she needed to do was find balance between healing and moving forward, and to stay connected to those she loved, because she needed them in her life as much as they needed her.

She was now also looking forward to winter break, because Bobby Ava had promised her an extravagant birthday present: a trip to Europe. The plan was that they would meet in Switzerland for Chanukah if Imre got medical clearance to travel. They would tour Zurich and explore Lake Lucerne, as well as Geneva and Bern. The thought of climbing the Jungfrau mountain was exciting, as was staying for Shabbos in picturesque Grindelwald at the famous kosher Silberhorn Hotel whose owners were relatives of Imre. Imre would then stay on in Grindelwald, while Ava and Fay flew to Barcelona and Rome for four nights. Whether Ava knew it or not, the trip was a fantastic incentive for Fay to look forward in life instead of backward. It reminded her too that there was a whole world outside of Brooklyn.

Her father Zak was the family trip planner. He kept Fay updated about the itinerary every few weeks and took the opportunity during each of these calls to casually check in on his eldest daughter. Suzi was a little more blunt and reminded Fay that when she traveled with Bobby, she had to dress well, the way Bobby expected her to look, like a proper young lady. Fay understood that Ava was a European woman and that those standards were extremely important to her.

Somehow though, these standards had also become Suzi's even though she was not of European birth. Fay understood that her appearance at the airport, dressed so radically different, was almost heresy to her mother, who was simply mimicking her own mother's attitude. Fay wondered if Bobby Ava was aware of just how limiting this was. Could she accept any change at all?

47

"Do not dwell on the past, do not focus on the future, focus on the moment."
—Buddha

When May found out she was pregnant again, she was delighted, regardless of how she felt about Danny, she was going to have a family of her own. The need to fill the emptiness of her own childhood was still of paramount importance to her. The first person she called was Victoria.

"Good morning, Mom," she said cheerily. "How are you on this beautiful pre-winter day?"

"I am fine, May," answered Victoria warmly. "How are you and Vicky doing?"

"Oh," said May nonchalantly, "we are great. Earl is driving us to Fifth Avenue in Manhattan. We plan to first go to the incredible FAO Schwarz toy store and then we will head over to see the giant Hanukkah menorah and, admittedly, we are also going to view the gorgeous Christmas tree at Rockefeller Center! We were wondering if you could meet us for lunch at Greener Pastures or anywhere closer to your office if time is an issue?"

"Let me call Donna and check my schedule," said Victoria excitedly. "That would be lovely!"

"Wonderful," replied May. "We'd love to see you, if it works out. If not, how about dinner in Brooklyn this evening, just us girls? Anytime that works for you. I can thankfully get out because Dahlia is the best, most flexible babysitter ever. I can't thank you enough for finding her."

"That sounds like two great options. I will confirm in the next 20 minutes," said Victoria happily. "Enjoy your day with my angel and please take pictures, even in front of the Christmas tree ! My piano ledge needs more pictures."

"Well," said May while suppressing a giggle, "I am certain I can help you fill up your piano ledge. Bye Mom, love you."

After May hung up the phone, she called Dahlia, a lovely 18-year-old girl in the community who was, shockingly, not contemplating marriage yet. She was graduating high school and in no hurry whatsoever to be saddled with a husband and children. She was thrilled to be Vicky's steady babysitter, as she came from a very poor home and was in desperate need of money. She came every day straight from school and adored May and the baby. Mr. Salem, not so much; he looked at her in a way that made her uncomfortable, but Daahlia simply shrugged that feeling away, because everything else about this job was perfect. Often, May didn't even leave the house when Dahlia came, but simply attended to her own agenda while Dahlia played with Vicky. She was determined to become a vital part of the community by volunteering in some capacity or another in helping others.

Ever since Ray had told her and Fay about the plight of *agunahs*, May felt compelled to do more. She felt that raising money to help these women was the right thing for her to do. She vividly recalled how she often felt lonely and scared in her childhood, with no one to rely on.

She invited six community women to her house for brunch, which Lucía helped her arrange and Earl delivered hot and fresh straight from Victoria's kitchen. In no uncertain terms, she asked these influential women to help her start a not-for-profit organization that would provide money, toys, clothing and food for *agunahs* or women who were otherwise in dire straits. To her immense surprise, all six women were ready to commit and each wrote out a check for $18,000. The amount represented the two primary Hebrew letters "*chet*" and "*yud*," which together formed the Hebrew word "*chai*," meaning "life." May also approached Victoria who immediately wrote out a check for thirty times chai or $5,400 and referred her to a dozen other women whom she knew would respond equally as generously. When May walked into Citibank a few weeks later to open a business account, she already had over $100,000 in deposits. May was astounded at how the community rallied so generously and with so much passion to do good deeds, helping the needy, the sick and the frail. Ray, on hearing what May was doing was speechless, when May shared the goals of her initiative.

"I have no words to express my gratitude," she said. "I can not tell you what this support will mean to my clients. For them to know that there are people who are there to help them in such difficult times is enormous."

Ray offered to pick up the expenses for forming the legal entity known as a 501(c) not-for-profit which May named "*Nashim Ozrim Noshim*", literally "women helping women." May never imagined that NON, as the organization was referred to, would eventually become a major social services agency dedicated to helping women on multiple levels. For now, the meetings were in her home and she felt purposeful that she had found a way to give back for the life she was so fortunate to have. When she sent Fay an email describing NON, Fay burst into tears. Not only was she proud of May, but she was relieved that desperate women, across all communities, would have access to the services they desperately needed. Occasionally, Fay worried if Danny had ever raped anyone else, before or after her. She knew that by never reporting him, she was guilty on some level of aiding and abetting a criminal. However, when sharing her feelings, Rabbi Shanzer, who functioned as her spiritual counselor informed her that Jewish law decrees that one's own life comes first.

. . .

"You will one day face your accuser. That I know," he reassured her in their weekly calls.

Fay was glad that one day meant someday when she would be ready, not today.

That night May met Victoria at an amazing Israeli restaurant on Avenue U. She was starving and ordered the *kufta* kabobs, the Yemenite soup, salad, hummus, tahini and falafel balls. Just when Victoria thought May hadn't eaten in days, she also ordered the *senya* steak.

"May," she said playfully, "if I didn't know better, I would think you were pr..." She gasped. "Are you pregnant?"

"Yes, Mom," said May joyfully. "I am so happy to tell you that you will be a *sebbah* again in seven months with God's help."

"This is fantastic news," said Victoria. "I hope you will have another little girl, so Vicky has a sister."

"I had the exact same thought," cried May. "I want my girls to be there for each other like Fay and Ray are for me."

"Are you feeling well?"

"I am really fine," replied May, understanding in that moment that this was how real mothers acted; it didn't matter how old their children were. She recalled the many times in Fay's house when she observed Bobby Ava and how concerned she was for everyone in her family, young or old. May felt satisfied, both with the huge meal she had just consumed and with her life.

When she got home, Danny was pacing in the foyer.

"Where have you been, May?" he asked in an accusatory voice.

"Calm down, Danny, and breathe," replied May as she unhurriedly unzipped her hunter green woolen jacket. "I will not talk to you while you are acting out. I've said that before."

To see the effect of her words on Danny was mind-boggling, even to May. It never ceased to amaze her what becoming a mother had done for her. It had given her the confidence and determination to be her own person in spite of the fact that neither of her parents had ever taught her self-worth. Sadly though, becoming a parent had the opposite effect on Danny. He never came home straight after work, choosing instead to go into the city with friends for drinks. May pitied him for missing out on a home life she was so desperate to have, with or without him.

"Danny," she said in a straightforward manner. "I am pregnant and I was at dinner with Mom telling her the news."

"Pregnant?" said Danny. He was about to make a snide comment about her figure, but he abruptly changed his mind. "Well, it looks like you have another chance to make up to me for not giving me a *bechor*." A while back, when Danny realized that this was what May assumed was the cause for his depression, he decided to go with it. After all, it was true, he was humiliated in the community for not having a son. "*Mabruk*," he said kindly. "I am glad to know that our lovemaking has brought us to this point."

May looked at him as if he were insane. *Our lovemaking*, she thought, *is that what he called 15 minutes of fumbling?* She decided to control her impulse to respond sarcastically and simply said, "*Mabruk* to us."

Danny awkwardly kissed the top of her head and went to email family and friends. He was happy that he was home tonight. When May offered him dinner after he drove Dahlia home, he gratefully accepted. It was seldom that he ate at home and tonight he wanted to show his wife that in spite of everything, he was happy to be married to her. He rarely allowed himself to think about Fay, preferring to put the incident in the car behind him, but last year, as Yom Kippur approached, he remembered vividly the words she had uttered to him that fateful night. He was utterly terrified that they would remain with him forever, haunt him and cause terrible things to happen to him. He hoped that Fay would never come back from Israel.

48

"Music is very spiritual, it has the power to bring people together."
—Edgar Winter

Ray was thrilled when May shared with her and Sammy that she was pregnant again. Although it slightly concerned her that Danny seemed disconnected in some odd way, as if this was just May's child. Ray wondered if this had anything to do with their father and their childhood. She also thought about why she wasn't yet ready for a child herself. She loved Sammy and was truly looking forward to their big civil wedding sometime in the future, but a baby didn't seem to fit into her schemata just yet.

That night, over dinner at an Indian, vegetarian restaurant on Lexington Avenue that they both adored, she broached the topic with her husband.

"Would I like kids?" he asked her, munching on roti bread. "Most definitely! I had a marvelous childhood and each addition to our family made my parents very happy. That's precisely what I want for us. I can wait until you are ready."

"Thank you," said Ray. "If only my mother had been half the mother she is today when I was growing up, I might feel differently," she said with sorrow in her voice. "I love her and I am grateful that

Vicky's birth heralded a new day for her, but, selfishly, I wish my birth had been the catalyst for her."

"I understand, Ray, but I think dwelling on the past is not productive. The future is ours," he said jubilantly.

"Yes, agreed," said Ray. "But remember what Santayana said: 'Those who forget history are doomed to repeat it.' I just don't want our children to ever feel unwanted or unloved because I didn't prepare myself for motherhood."

"And how do you accomplish that?" asked Sammy. "Is there something I can do to help?"

"You, Mr. BenAdin, are just perfect the way you are. I am so grateful for you being in my life. This is all on me and I am cautiously optimistic that it's simply a matter of time."

"In that case you do your thing and I am here for you anytime you want to share your thoughts."

Ray felt better than she had in a long time and the following day at work, she made a mental note to try to limit her emotional involvement with her cases. She worried that the stress and anxiety many of her clients were going through potentially might trigger memories of her father's physical and verbal abuse. When a colleague at work suggested therapy, she laughed. I've had enough therapy to last me for a while. It was common practice in the office for all staff to learn detached concern in order to maintain professional boundaries with clients. Ray wondered what else she could do to help herself.

One night, while walking past the Carlebach Shul on West 79th Street, she impulsively decided to step inside. She vaguely remembered Suzi Zweig humming a few Carlebach tunes on Shabbat, but what she found there in the shul was far more than music. The unbridled passion and spirituality of Rabbi Carlebach was the balm she had been seeking all her life. It was the people, all of whom welcomed any fellow Jew with open arms, and then it was the rabbi himself. He was larger than life, a dynamic, inspiring human being whose love of his fellow Jews and his belief in the power of love was everything she could have asked for.

Ray dragged Sammy there for Friday night services and in time they became devoted members of the congregation. She felt like she was finally home, her precious *neshama* [soul], was finally on its way to being at peace. The words of every song the rabbi sang pierced her wounded self and she began to flourish. By the time May gave birth to her second little girl, Ray was practically reborn, ready to get married and start a family. Later in life, when Sammy and Fay asked what the catalyst was, she had an answer. She swore it was the rabbi's *nigunim*: his soulful, haunting, Hasidic, melodious music that was reminiscent of the folk music of legends like Bob Dylan and Pete Seeger, mixed with the holy words of the psalms that she listened to daily. She felt stronger and more able to help her clients and she was gaining a reputation in all the boroughs and beyond for the work she did with battered women.

49

"Don't wait around for other people to be happy for you. Any
happiness you get you've got to make yourself."
—Alice Walker

When Fay got back to Israel, Chava-Sara noticed the change in her.
She was delighted. She loved Fay with all her heart and was excited at
the idea of her starting a business and employing neighborhood
women. She promised to round up a few candidates for Fay to
interview. Although Chava-Sara begged her to stay for dinner, Fay
was anxious to go to her tiny apartment, unpack and start sketching
her first line of AvaFay skirts. First though, Fay wanted to confirm her
classes schedule at Shenkar. She was excited to be starting her degree
and grateful that they had allowed her to start the semester late. She
hugged Chava-Sara tightly and promised to be back in the late
morning, after she visited Ibu and Mimi to give them gifts from
America. She had promised to bring them new model coats from
Williamsburg and head scarves from Boro Park, the two heavily
populated neighborhoods that catered to the needs of religious
women. She had begged Ava to help her select them. When Fay left,
Chava-Sara was so happy at seeing the enthusiasm and radiance on

Fay's face, that she immediately called her parents to share the good news with them. They knew that Chava-Sara had taken a special interest in Fay. Rabbi Shanzer requested that she send Fay over to his house. Chava-Sara promised to give Fay the message. When Fay arrived at the Shanzer home the next day, she was taken aback and uncomfortable to hear that Rabbi Shanzer wanted to bring her a potential *shidduch*.

"The Rebbe feels this is a good opportunity for you," said Rebbetzin Shanzer, speaking deferentially on behalf of her husband. "He would like for you to meet the young man here in our house."

Fay was stunned and felt quite honored. "I don't think I am ready to meet anyone," she stammered. "Although I will never forget this incredible kindness, treating me like a daughter."

"The Rebbe and Chava-Sara both see something great in you," the Rebbetzin said sincerely. "It's the way you care for others tirelessly and selflessly, never failing your responsibilities and your studies, and how your eyes light up when you talk about your grandmother. These, my child, are the indicators of character and a special *neshama*. We are honored to have you in our midst. All that we ask is that you think it over. How could one meeting hurt? He is a tall, nice-looking young man, a good learner and he comes from a wonderful family."

Fay left the Shanzers in turmoil. She could not tell them that she still dreamed about Jared or that she had occasional nightmares about Danny. She knew it wouldn't be fair to any young man to present herself as available and ready to get married when in fact she was neither. Besides, how would her parents react? Wouldn't they be hurt that she would take such a monumental leap without them? *No, she decided, better to tackle school and start a business before dealing with the formidable task of finding a husband.*

The next three months flew by and it was time to pack again. Fay was overcome with joy that Imre's doctors had okayed the trip. Ava insisted they would travel in business class, using all their mileage on Pan Am, so that Imre would be comfortable. When Fay arrived at the Zurich airport, she nearly fainted at the size of it. It was huge and it held so many exquisite shops that she didn't know where to look first. She decided to wait for Ava before purchasing anything so that they could enjoy it together.

When Fay saw Ava and Imre, her heart leaped with joy. How lucky was she to be the oldest grandchild, to have the privilege of such a special trip. She knew she had a unique bond with her grandmother. As she ran into her outstretched arms, she prayed to God that Ava would live for many years to come.

Imre loved how excited Ava had been for the trip. She was like a young girl gushing while packing, discussing every outfit on the phone with her sisters. When Ava kissed her daughters and granddaughters goodbye at the airport, promising each one a trip of their own someday, she had felt relaxed and happier than she had ever been. Life, in spite of so much loss, had its moments of indescribable joy.

Zak had outdone himself on the itinerary. Imre had given him the green light to book the world-famous five-star Dolder Grand Hotel in Zurich and it was beyond Fay's wildest imagination. Ava delighted in her excitement, the spectacular suite, the views of the lake and the Alps, and the exquisite Parisian shops lining the corridor of the main lobby.

They bought the best Swiss chocolate at Sprungli and Lindt. Imre took pictures of them in Interlaken and Bern. And in Jelmoli, Zurich's finest department store, they shopped to their heart's desire while studiously noting fabrics and colors for Fay's future designs. Imre was laughing and having fun the whole time, but he wasn't laughing when the platform of the train that took them to the top of the Jungfrau mountain let them out to see the breathtaking views of the Eiger Mountain was full of snow. The ladies were totally inappropriately dressed, wearing their chic, silk dresses and open-toed sandals.

"Ava, I begged you," he said exasperated. "You need to be wearing boots and jackets."

"I am sorry," said Ava, stifling a laugh. She was shivering even with Imre's woolen coat draped around her shoulders. "I hate snow boots, they vould just ruin my outfit and Fay's also. It's fine, darling. Please don't vorry, ve are strong."

Fay was thrilled that her carefully curated wardrobe met Ava's approval. She realized lately that she not only wanted to please her grandmother, but she liked dressing a certain way for herself too. When she told Ava about her new business venture, Ava was beyond excited.

"This is marvelous, my darling! Ven we go to Rome, we can look for fabrics. Maybe you can eventually design a line of children's skirts too! The fashion in Israel is not that spectacular. Anything you create for the vomen in Bnei Brak and Mea Shearim vould be a huge mitzvah."

Fay looked at Bobby and right there, on top of the Jungfrau mountain, started to cry. "I don't ever remember a time in my life when you didn't encourage me to follow my dreams. Sometimes it wasn't easy, because life got in the way, but Bobby, thanks to you, I am going to live my dream."

"Fay, my darling girl," said Ava passionately. "I love you more than you can imagine. I vould give you my life. Whatever you vant, I support you".

As the three of them approached the finest kosher restaurant in Zurich, Fay realized she was starving. Imre insisted they try the exotic, mouthwatering cuisine of the region. Over the course of the next two nights, they indulged in kosher adapted meals of veal sausage with hash browns, Wiener schnitzel and beef bourguignon with a traditional Swiss *spätzli*, a delicious homemade pasta. Ava ate heartily without once mentioning calories or salt.

When they neared the town of Grindelwald, Fay was enthralled with the main street. It was a quintessential Swiss Alpine village. It had wooden chalets with sharply pitched roofs and windowsills adorned with colorful pots. Imre noticeably perked up. Being a gentleman, he never complained when the ladies were shopping, but now, as they rapidly approached the Silberhorn Hotel, he was reminded of his own youth and the wonderful times he had spent with his cousins at the family château. He would definitely enjoy himself while Ava and Fay wandered around Europe. And certainly, he would enjoy eating for an entire week without Ava monitoring his every bite.

50

"If nothing is going well, call your grandmother."
—Italian Proverb

When Fay and Ava arrived at the Rome Cavalieri Hilton, they both gasped at the grandeur of the hotel. Ava was mesmerized by the extensive priceless artwork hung on the walls. Zak had outdone himself by placing them in the heart of the city. From their palatial room, decorated in various shades of peach and green, they had views of the Eternal City and St. Peter's Basilica. They enjoyed every minute of their time together and Fay knew she would cherish this trip for as long as she lived. Not once did Bobby pressure her or ask intrusive questions she couldn't answer. It was the most memorable experience of her life and she would rave about it for months on end. It was also the moment when she saw Ava as more than just her grandmother. She was a very sophisticated woman whom others recognized as a refined lady. She noticed how people automatically treated her with respect, simply because she was gracious.

Fay adored seeing all the famous sites, but was especially fascinated with the Jewish Quarter, where the Jews of Rome lived in the ghetto. She visited the Great Synagogue and its museum, which displayed silverware and textiles, parchments and marble carvings from the private collections of the Jewish community of Rome. It inspired the artist in her and she sketched in her notepad daily. There was something about the spirit of the Italian Jews that resonated with her own desire to not let anything stop her from succeeding.

By March, Fay had all the components for her business set up. Rabbi Shanzer gave her some space in a warehouse. She set up production with the help of Bathsheva Katzenstein, the former manager of Gottex bathing suits, a very successful company founded in Israel by Hungarian Holocaust survivor Miriam Gottlieb that sold swimsuits and cover-ups worldwide. Fay had full confidence in Bathsheva. She was astute and knew exactly how to organize the production of Fay's first line of skirts.

Six Hasidic women showed up for orientation. Not one complained about the hours, grateful for the job and the opportunity to be part of an exciting new venture. The atmosphere in the shop was optimistic and friendly. Fay loved working among the women, their enthusiasm inspired her and she wanted this to succeed for them as much as for herself.

She was especially grateful for Imre's financial backing. On the trip, she had carefully outlined her plan and he immediately set up a $250,000 line of credit at Bank Leumi. Fay knew she was exceedingly lucky to have a benefactor like Imre, who wanted nothing in return but her happiness. She was, though, determined to pay him back.

Within half a year, she was able to hire six more women and started going on trips with Bathsheva to buy beautiful fabrics in Italy and France. In between buying trips, Fay made time to go home to see her parents, Ray and May, her sisters and Ava. Not once did she bump into Danny and that suited her perfectly. In therapy, she found that she was no longer afraid to face him, but she still was not ready see him. It meant making a choice, missing Ray's gorgeous wedding, but that was a sacrifice she knew she had to make. In truth, she was more afraid of seeing Jared than Danny.

51

"From beginning to end God's law teaches kindness."
—The Talmud

12 years later, 2009

Fay booked an emergency ticket to New York. She was heartbroken to be returning to America for Imre's funeral. He had lived a long happy life with Ava. She knew he had no regrets. He had told her so when she last saw him. As she settled back for the duration of the nonstop flight, Fay reflected on her successes in the past decade. She had graduated from Shenkar with honors and her first art show was a major success. Her agent had booked her next two exhibitions in Sydney and Melbourne. She was wildly excited.

She recalled vividly that first show in London. Her entire family, Ray, Sammy, May, even the Shanzers and Chava-Sara had all flown to London to celebrate her success. This touched her beyond mere words. Once again, as she reflected on that day, she thanked the heavens above that Danny had the sense not to accompany May. How she would have handled seeing him then was something she simply would not dwell on.

Fay remembered the day her business was in the black and her accountant had told her she was financially stable. True to her word,

Fay had repaid the entire loan to Imre. AvaFay was a phenomenal success, written up in *Forbes* and *The New York Times* as a millennial company run by a woman that solely employed minority Hasidic women, from the bookkeeper to the fabricators to the in-house designers. It made Fay very happy. Though she no longer had the time to be at the factory every day, she was confident that it was being run properly. One day soon, she would have to find a new general manager. Bathsheva had recently announced her retirement. For now though, she intended to stay in New York with Ava.

Fay's homecoming was different from the previous ones. She got into a taxi and went straight to Ava's house, where the family was gathered. One look at Ava's crumpled face and she was completely undone. She tried hard to compose herself so that Ava would not have to console her, but it was impossible. Seeing her beloved Bobby, still elegant and chic at 88 years old, but so distraught, tore her apart. She cried bitter tears for Imre and for Ava and wondered why God in his infinite wisdom didn't have a better plan to spare couples the pain of loss; especially for this generation who had survived Auschwitz. How much more suffering could they bear?

After two hours, it was time for them all to go to Kennedy Airport. Imre was going to be buried in Israel on the Mount of Olives and they would be escorting the coffin to the airport. Zak and Heshy would travel to Israel for the burial, while Ava would observe the mourning period, the seven days of shiva in New York. It was during the shiva, when Ava said she was inconsolable that Imre would be so far away from her, that Fay had the germ of an idea of asking Ava to move to Israel and get involved in managing the business of AvaFay. She knew it was too soon to bring it up, but in a few weeks, after the *shloshim* [the 30-day mourning period for a spouse], she would present it to her parents, aunts and Ava herself.

When Ava finally heard what Fay had in mind, she nearly jumped for joy. "Yes, a thousand times yes," she cried. "It was always my dream for Imre and I to live in Israel in our old age, but that time never came."

"But Anyu, Imre was 96, when were you thinking of making the move?" said Magda to her mother, trying to hold back a laugh.

"Never mind, Magda," replied Ava, glaring at her.

The topic was shut down temporarily.

Ava was anxious to move to Israel and begin to manage the business that Fay had built. Of course, she would have at least two capable girls to assist her, a driver and a live-in companion. All of her daily living needs would be met. She was confident that it would be the right move for her. The family would visit often. She was, however, a little disconcerted to know that—as luck would have it—Fay was planning to stay in New York for an extended period of time, but she accepted that. Fay needed her help with the business and that was enough for her. Furthermore, for Ava, the plan had great merit. It distracted her from thinking about Imre. The thought of influencing dozens of young religious women and helping them grow into competent professionals was also appealing to her. She decided she would enroll in Ulpan, so that she would become proficient in the Hebrew language. She was realistic about her own limitations, aware that she was 88 years old, but confident that her will to live would see her through every new challenge.

Suzi and both of her sisters, on the other hand, were beside themselves with worry. It was only when Zak pointed out how happy and excited Ava looked that the three sisters calmed down a bit. The plan was outrageous, but who were they to decide what would make their mother happy? Sitting alone in her gorgeous condo in Miami Beach or thriving in Israel? It was another opportunity for Ava to leave her mark on the world. All three made plans to help their mother settle in and Judy, who was newly divorced, mentioned numerous times that she was considering moving to Israel too, since her girls were out of the house and busy with their own lives. It was when Suzi and Zak were in Israel with Ava for an indefinite period of time, that Fay knew the time had come for her to confront Danny. It was something she had mulled over and knew she needed to do in order to achieve true closure. It was not about financial compensation. In fact, if she was to be awarded any money, she planned to give it away. She wanted nothing from Danny, only the chance to face him in front of witnesses.

52

"There may be times when we are powerless to prevent injustice, but there must never be a time when we fail to protest."
—Elie Wiesel

Fay texted May and Ray and asked them to meet her. She asked Ray if they could meet in her firm's conference room. Though Ray could not figure out why Fay was looking for such a formal setting, she acquiesced. When May walked in, Fay nearly lost her resolve. May was now a certified public accountant, the mother of three beautiful girls and the chief executive officer of NON, which had grown from a fledgling business in her dining room to a thriving social service agency that received government funds. NON was endorsed by Ashkenazic and Sephardic rabbis and community leaders, local politicians and social workers. The organization provided therapy and housing assistance, essential aid, babysitters and home-cooked meals to battered, abused women. Fay worried about how her bombshell would impact May and her marriage and family. And there was also Ray, a successful attorney, mother of adorable twin boys and wife of the first Sephardic Congressman. How would the news about her brother affect Sammy's career? Was she wrong now after all this time to bring shame on those she loved?

"My dearest sisters," she began in a low trembling voice. "I asked you here today because I have something to tell you. Something that I hid from you these past 17 years, ever since Vicky was born."

"Fay," cried May, "what is it?"

She almost couldn't speak, fearing that something was going to be said that could never be taken back. "I want you both to know that everything I did these past many years—at great cost to my own happiness and at times sanity—was designed to spare both of you from pain. Now, I have reached a point in my life where I need to find total peace and that can only happen if I take the necessary steps to bring a lawsuit and seek justice. I have allowed a criminal to walk free for too long."

Ray was alarmed and intrigued at the same time. "What crime, Fay-Fay?" she asked, reverting back to their childhood days.

"The night Vicky was born, I was raped," said Fay stoically.

"Oh my God," cried May. "Why didn't you tell us?"

"I couldn't," said Fay woodenly. "You just had a baby."

"Why didn't you tell me?" cried Ray. "I would have done anything to help apprehend the guy."

"I couldn't tell you either, because I didn't want to hurt you."

"But Fay, how would you telling me hurt me, other than my sorrow for you?"

Fay took three deep breaths and asked her best friends to hold her hands. "I don't know what the next few minutes will do to our sisterhood. All that I know is that I love you both and always will." She told them then about the devastation that had befallen her in Danny's car that night.

There was utter silence in the room.

May's face was drained of blood and she ran to the bathroom to vomit.

Ray started shaking. "My brother... my brother Danny raped you? Oh my God, Fay." She was sobbing. "I want to die, right here, right now. Tell me this is a nightmare and I need to wake up! My brother raped you? she repeated. And here I have helped so many women and there you were, in front of my eyes, alone in so much pain and I didn't know."

When May came back into the room, she looked as if she had aged 20 years. She walked straight into Fay's arms. "There are no words, Fay, no words. But it all makes sense now. How he changed, how you changed. I could never understand the drastic change in him. He was never what I fantasized he was, but after Vickie's birth, he went downhill. Oh my dearest Fay; I am sick thinking of what happened to you. May then turned to face both Fay and her sister-in-law Ray and said in a clear and level-headed manner, "Fay, forgive me for making this about me at this moment. I want you to know that what I am going to say and do is primarily in solidarity with you." With that she continued. "Ray, will you represent me or recommend the best matrimonial attorney you know? I am filing for divorce today. Not tomorrow. Not after I speak to our rabbi. Today."

Fay was astounded. She turned to May and said wistfully, "I wish it had never come to this. I just know that if I am to ever find happiness, I need justice. I am so sorry that this will change your life, May-May."

"Let's be honest," answered May. "Both of you know that I never had a real marriage. Would I like to say this is a blessing in disguise? Yes, sure, maybe someday I will be able to look back and see that perspective. Today though, that's hard. The reality is that for the girls it will be very hard. Any father is better than no father and knowing Danny, he may just love the single life and forget about them altogether."

"You can always move to the city," said Ray. "We can find you a wonderful three-bedroom apartment right near us and the girls can go to any of the numerous Jewish schools."

"I can, but Mom is not the same since her heart attack," said May slowly. "I think it would be very hard on her if I moved away."

"You don't have to make any decisions right now," said Ray reassuringly. Turning to Fay, she asked, "Tell us, what do you need from us what are you planning to do?"

"I already consulted an attorney, who said I can file a lawsuit. What I think I need is to see Danny in a court of law, answering to a judge and jury."

"Then that's what you must do," said May. "Nothing is more

important than you reclaiming the part of yourself that he took from you. If I think of how brave you were, keeping that to yourself, to spare us. Oh Fay, the sleepless nights and lonely days you must have had. Moving so far away... all by yourself... How? How did you survive?"

"I was extremely lucky, May. I turned to Chava-Sara and her parents. They are the most wonderful, caring people. They literally were like family to me and they were really there for me, all the time. I also had my therapist and my art. And when I was homesick and missed you guys, I reached out."

"No wonder you missed so many events," said Ray, understanding in that moment what Fay had sacrificed. "I always thought it was because of Jared and here it was because of Danny."

"Come to think of it," said May. "I remember thinking a few times how odd it was that you never once saw Danny each time you came back. But in my wildest imagination, I could never have known why you needed it to be that way."

"Girls," said Fay, "this was the hard part for me. I did everything I could to protect you and the girls, and I hope you forgive me for needing to take this final step."

"Forgive you?" exclaimed May. "I am right there with you. He is not my husband anymore. He is a rapist and I am throwing him and his designer clothes out tonight and changing the locks tomorrow. He won't know why. Maybe he will think I finally had enough of all his cheap affairs. You do know he gave me an STD more than once."

"Fay," said Ray compassionately, "you and May have my complete support. I am glad your parents and Bobby Ava are out of the country. I'd like to discuss with Sammy how to prepare my mother for what's coming. May, we can start with the divorce and then we can decide how to tell her the rest."

"Poor Mom," cried May in earnest. "She doesn't deserve this!"

"You are absolutely right," said Ray. "My brother is a product of his father. This is the result of covering up for him. I am livid that my father's disgusting behavior set an example for his protégé. I am so grateful that the year in Israel post-high school really changed Ralphie and Ikey. They are good men, thank God."

"I am happy to hear that," said Fay. "I can't even begin to express my utter gratitude for the way in which you both received my confession. I was terrified that you would turn against me." She started to cry then. She cried for the night of the rape. She cried for every lonely moment she spent banished in Israel. She cried for her beautiful body that she felt did not belong to her anymore, even when she traveled to Milan for fabrics and slept repeatedly with the charming Ari Halevi, who loved her and wanted to make a life with her.

Ray and May held her for a long time, until she was able to catch her breath.

"All the therapy in the world didn't do as much as those tears and you two being here for me," she said. "I will never forget this."

"Let's be realistic, the road ahead is not going to be easy," said Ray. "But you have us. I just pray to God that there are no other women that come forward. I think that if my brother is a serial rapist, I might kill him myself."

"Well," said May, "unfortunately, there are too many desperate women who will indulge a dog like him, for a meal, a vacation or a bracelet. I am ashamed to tell you both, but I compromised myself the very first time I went out with Danny. I thought I needed to make him happy in order to keep him. Thankfully, I realized on time that this was not what I wanted."

"May Salem!" Ray exclaimed. "All these years and now, today, you come clean? I'm glad you got that off your chest. Don't think about it ever again! Oh my goodness, who would ever have believed this. We were so naive once upon a time! Oh my Fay, my poor, poor Fay. My heart is breaking thinking about this tragedy that befell you. And yet, in spite of this devastation Fay, look what you achieved. I know in my heart of hearts that you will find personal happiness someday. I know you have helped so many people and have a network of friends that May and I don't even know about... but that's not what I'm talking about. I beg you Fay. Please open your mind to the idea of love. You just have to want it and the universe will make it happen. I can tell you both now, that I was once spiritually lost but then I found Reb Shlomo Carlebach. What an incredibly unusual man. He created his

269

own style of teaching through his songs and storytelling. When he died, a piece of me died too, but every day I listen to his music, every single day. The kids know the words to every one of his nigunim. Those songs, that's what made the difference in my life. I know something will change if you want it enough, Fay. You will find happiness that will make your soul song and I know we will all dance at your wedding."

"Thank you, my darling, for your faith and optimism. I've changed quite a lot over the years. I am no longer the same girl I once was. I'd like to believe I can trust someone enough to open my heart to them, but it hasn't happened yet. Lord knows, Rabbi Shanzer, bless his soul, set me up with the most eligible young men from London to Belgium and, of course, in Israel. After a while, I think it became clear that I wasn't ready and the calls, even from America, stopped."

"Please, Fay-Fay," said May. "If you care even a little about me, promise me you will never give up on love. I'll make a deal with you. The day I get my Jewish divorce, my *get*—and you can be sure I will have no trouble obtaining my Jewish divorce—let's go to a real posh singles event on the Upper West Side together! There are so many social gatherings for women our age. And if I, with three kids, am willing to try again, you must join me."

"You know what, May-May?" said Fay, smiling slightly for the first time in two hours. "I love you so much and if that's what you want, I will go for you. And if, by some miracle, a really nice, handsome, eligible man wants to date me, I will."

Ray listened and didn't offer her opinion. She was convinced that Fay was still in love with Jared. Sammy, she thought, being Jared's best friend, would surely know what to do to facilitate a reunion between the two of them. She was cautiously optimistic and hopeful that Jared and Fay would find their own way back.

53

"We must take sides. Neutrality helps the oppressor, never the victim.
Silence encourages the tormentor, never the tormented."
—Elie Wiesel

Sammy was astounded when Ray broke the news to him. The regard he held for May and Fay, which he thought couldn't get higher, quadrupled as Ray told him verbatim what May resolved to do about Danny and what Fay had done all these years to protect her soul sisters. He agreed with Ray that both of them would lend the women all the support they would need in the months ahead. Sammy never got close to Danny, whom he instinctively did not care for. However, he worried how Ralph and Ikey would feel and resolved to tell them personally at the right time.

He texted May that night, offering his support if she was determined to throw Danny out. He was not concerned whatsoever about getting involved. On the contrary, he wanted people to know that he took a stand. All too often, he saw what happened when people said nothing and did nothing.

May was grateful for Sammy's support, but wanted to do it herself. She was ready for this moment. It was a long time coming. On some level, she had already begun acting like a single mom in anticipation of the time when she would have enough of Danny. She remembered the wildly successful vacation to Disneyland last year without him. The girls had never once asked for their dad. And there were the summers in Deal, when he rarely showed up. She was fully competent to take care of the girls by herself. Then too, knowing Victoria, she would be there in whatever capacity May felt was best for the children. All that really concerned May was her daughters and Fay. She didn't know how to begin to make it up to Fay for the evil her husband had perpetrated on her, taking advantage of her and even blaming her! She knew that as long as she lived, she would never forgive Danny for what he did to Fay and hoped that he would be locked up forever. As for the girls, she prayed that she and her support team would be enough to carry them through the hard times: when they would miss their dad, when it was embarrassing not to have a father, and when, as teenagers, it just felt weird.

When May heard his car door, she checked to make sure her precious angels were all sleeping. They were. She brought the four oversized suitcases filled with his clothes downstairs and put them by the door where she waited in the dark.

"Oh, you scared me," he said. "What the hell are you doing here in the dark?"

"Waiting for you," said May. "To say goodbye."

"Are you smoking crack?" asked Danny sarcastically. "I just walked in. Shouldn't you say hello?"

"No," said May pointedly. "I'm saying goodbye, because you are leaving, right now, forever."

"Leaving? Going where? And why?"

"I don't care to explain anything to you, Danny Salem. You are a disgrace to your mother, you don't exist anymore, not to me, not to your children. Take your suitcases and go. And Danny, if you know what's good for you, be at the rabbi's office tomorrow at 4:00 p.m. You will give me a *get*."

"May, wait!" yelled Danny. "I don't know what's gotten into your head or if someone said something to upset you, but we can work this out, baby. Please."

"Not now, not ever, Danny," said May firmly and with no remorse whatsoever. "You have 30 seconds to pick up those suitcases, after which I will throw them out the door and text Sammy, who is around the corner waiting to escort you out of the house."

Danny realized it was really over. His heart started to beat fast. He wondered if Esmeralda Lopez, the home care worker he had met while visiting his great-aunt Marcella, had finally made good on her threat to let May know she had given birth to his son a year ago. If that was the case, he viciously thought to himself as he picked up the first two suitcases, he would reduce the child support payments, not increase them like Esmeralda wanted.

As he walked out the door, Danny looked back at May and suddenly remembered Fay's curse. For 17 years, every single Yom Kippur he needed anti-anxiety medication just to get through the holidays. Her words were emblazoned in his mind and there wasn't a year when he didn't tremble before God, terrified that Fay's curse would destroy him. And now he knew it had finally caught up with him. He didn't know yet to what degree, but he would soon find out.

"May, I swear on my life, I can change," he tried one last time.

But May was looking down at her cell phone. Damn, he had underestimated her, he thought. She had been a docile little girl for a very short time and had evolved into an amazing woman that he had treated like garbage. For the first time in his life, Danny took responsibility for his actions. He knew May deserved better than him. He was so ashamed of his affair with Esmeralda and the son that she had given him that he had stopped sleeping with May two years ago.

When he left, May recited the *shehecheyanu* blessing, thanking God that this very day had arrived. She locked the doors, walked into the kitchen, poured herself a glass of Shiraz wine and texted Ray and Fay: *He is gone. I feel so strong and happy. This day had to come! Now, I will focus on the girls and we will be alright. I have total faith.*

273

54

"There is peace, even in the storm."
—Vincent van Gogh

May was not surprised that Danny complied and met her at the rabbi's office, trying hard to make a good impression by dressing in a conservative suit and tie, desperate to appear like the aggrieved party. When he tried to imply that May was not an attentive wife, neglected him and the girls for her job, the rabbi raised his hand.

"Mr. Salem," he cautioned him sternly, "I urge you to say nothing. I personally have worked with your wife numerous times. She is nothing less than an angel, a true *tzadeket*, the most righteous young woman I have ever met. And that's not just my opinion, there is no one in the community, perhaps besides you, who doesn't revere and idolize your wife. She has given hope to countless unfortunate women and yet you dare to stand here and denigrate her?"

Danny handed May the get, her Jewish divorce and she surrendered her *ketubah* [marriage contract]. He closed his eyes. He knew at that moment that if he looked at her, he would cry. Suddenly, he felt scared and alone. Who would care about him, he wondered? Not his parents, especially his father who would be furious with him for bringing more shame on their family name. Certainly not his mother, who adored May. Esmeralda? He knew she was only after his money and he had no interest in her converting and becoming his wife. He softly said one word as he walked out the door: "shalom."

What compelled Danny to wish May peace, even he didn't know, but she was satisfied. The locks had been changed and she had booked a spontaneous short trip to Cancun with her girls. In the comfort of the Ritz-Carlton hotel, she would explain to them that Daddy wasn't coming back. She had a feeling that Vicky wouldn't care and that Becca and Alison would look to their big sister for their own reaction. She only wanted to be sure that Victoria would be okay. Impulsively, she invited her to join them. Maybe she could tell Victoria at the same time as the girls. May texted Ray again to ask her opinion and was relieved when she was on board. Ray spontaneously offered to join them in the hope that she could somehow be of help to both May and her mother in processing the pain and anguish of Danny's perfidy and loathsome behavior. On hearing Ray's gracious offer, May simply felt glad that Ray was her sister.

Victoria maintained the most incredible attitude in front of the girls, but when they were asleep, she cried copious tears. It was the first time Ray had ever seen her mother cry. As the three of them sat on the hotel balcony, Victoria finally shared her innermost thoughts. "May, my dearest, this is all my fault. I am ashamed of my son and at the same time, I blame myself. How could I have raised a son like Danny?"

"Mom, I beg you," pleaded May. "Please do not ever take responsibility for him. I know for a fact, after all, I practically lived in your house growing up, that if anyone influenced Danny or condoned his behavior, it was his father, not you."

"Mom," said Ray, validating May's words, "we are all adults now. It's time to face the facts. Danny is his father's son. It's exactly why my boys will never have anything to do with their grandfather. Please Mom, let it go, don't worry about anything. We will all be here for May and the girls and in case you haven't noticed, she has become quite the woman."

"I know, girls," said Victoria. "Please forgive me, maybe it's my age. In truth, I wish I had had the guts to do what you did, May."

Ray and May were flabbergasted.

"It's never too late, Mom," said Ray. "Look at Fay's grandmother—she's way older than you, packed her bags and moved to Israel after her husband died. Fay says she is charming the entire city of Jerusalem! She was on a local morning talk show as the Ava behind AvaFay. Everyone wants to hear her story. Even the prime minister called and presented her with a key to the city. Fay tells us that after spending months in a hotel, she recently bought a magnificent house in an area called Rehavia, with a view of the Old City. Fay says that her parents flew to Israel ostensibly to visit Ava, and assure that she was doing well, but instead are getting a glimpse of early retirement for themselves. Fay shared with me that Imre, Ava's husband, was quite generous and left her parents quite a substantial amount of money and real estate—they are reluctant to come back to the States; it's that marvelous! So listen up Mom. All change is good. Please, I beg of you... don't underestimate it or think you can't do it."

"One should never say never," agreed Victoria slowly. "But today, this isn't about me, it's about May and the girls. You are my priorities. I've also sadly made a decision; Danny will not be welcome in my house ever again."

The girls looked at each other thinking that if Victoria cut away from Danny just for his tawdry affairs, how much worse would she feel if and when she found out he was a rapist too? In truth, Victoria knew something May and ray were not yet aware of, that Danny had an illegitimate son. On receiving an anonymous picture of Danny holding his son at his Brit Milah circumcision ceremony, that was the day Victoria had the heart attack that nearly killed her. Knowing that her son had gotten a 17-year-old Mexican girl pregnant was more than she could bear. It was the only time in her life that she had been less than honest with May, terrified of hurting her with the news. Keeping it to herself felt like the right thing to do at the time. The only one she hadn't spared was her husband.

"Now you can die happy, knowing the esteemed Salem name will live on," she had said viciously. "Look at your cell phone, Isaac, the picture I just sent you. Your son finally has his son."

For once in his life Isaac Salem was speechless, but not for long.

He called his son to meet him at a bar on First Avenue and cut off all ties with him. Then, he came home to find Victoria in cardiac arrest. He called Hatzalah, the volunteer ambulance corp the community sponsored, to take her to Lenox Hill Hospital. He pitied himself for the shame his son had brought on him, never once thinking about his wife, May, his granddaughters or even Danny. It was always about him.

When Victoria left him a short while later, she dissolved their business practice and moved in with May and the girls. He never once asked himself if perhaps something he had done had caused his wife and younger sons to disown him, the way he disowned Danny.

55

"Courage is not having the strength to go on, it's going on when you don't have the strength."
—Theodore Roosevelt

Sammy had to call in many favors in order to bury the story of Danny Salem's trial. He knew that Victoria would never survive the headlines. Without even telling Ray, he went to the district attorney's office for help and got it. When Ray found out what Sammy had done for her mother, May and the girls, she was overcome with gratitude.

"Just when I thought there was nothing you could ever do to make me respect and love you even more, you found a way. I am so grateful for you, Sammy BenAdin. I don't know what I ever did to deserve you, but I am grateful to Elokim, to the righteous and merciful God who created all life. Thank you."

Sammy was touched to the core. He too was grateful to God for his life, his wife and his sons. There was nothing he wouldn't do for them or anyone that Ray loved.

As luck would have it, May was well-known in the office and had provided critically needed services to the assistant district attorney's daughter a year ago. He convinced the district attorney that not to spare May Salem, a woman who was an asset to the city, any further humiliation would be tantamount to a criminal act. The DA took his advice seriously and assured that the story would never see the light of day.

Ray was overcome with happiness. Both she and Fay had heard the other shocking disclosure from May that Danny had fathered a child out of wedlock. Danny's attorney knew that with the monthly payments going to Miss Lopez it was bound to come up in discovery and he decided to preempt May's lawyer from using the information as leverage. Ray and Fay were stunned. Once again, it was May who was the voice of reason. "It doesn't matter, because he doesn't exist," she told them. "And now he has his precious son."

Fay worried that May was simply delaying the grieving process in an effort to be fully present for her girls. There was simply no way that this latest bombshell didn't pierce her heart. One day, May would have to deal with the way in which Danny had tormented her. In the meantime, Fay and Ray would have to immediately start a campaign for May to find a new husband, one who would be her true partner.

No one could have predicted the path May's life would take, but it was destined to happen. She would eventually meet a Lubavitcher Hassid named Gabriel, a widower who came to NON one fine day. He was concerned about his oldest daughter, Mushky. They met often in May's office and over the course of time, long after Mushky was no longer a client, he felt compelled to return day after day, offering help to this incredible organization and in doing so, found that he had a lot in common with May. May appreciated his gentle manner and his dedication to raising his seven children after tragically losing his wife in a car accident. She found herself gravitating more and more to him and the fundamental principles of Rabbi Menachem Mendel Schneerson, known as the Lubavitcher Rebbe. She enjoyed the practical wisdom of the Chabad-Lubavitch dynasty, and their mission to embrace all Jews. She also adored the wise sayings of the Rebbe. Gavriel shared many with her, nearly every night, on the phone after all the children were asleep. One of her favorites was this one:

"We live in a state of emergency, where the fires of confusion are raging. When a fire is burning, everyone is responsible for helping his fellow man."

For the moment, it was enough for May that Gavriel was helping her put out her own fire.

The family decided that Victoria and Isaac should not be present at the trial. It was simply too much for them. Further, Ray, along with her outraged brothers, were adamant that their parents should not be there in case Danny thought even for one minute that they were there in support of him. Although, it would be hard for Danny to make that deduction with his mother not talking to him and his father only long enough to curse him in Arabic, using words that Danny knew were reserved strictly for referring to lowlife scumbags.

In the end, the jury found Danny guilty. There was nothing his lawyer could say. The truth about his character came out when every seat in the courthouse was filled with women whom May had helped and their own rabbi who declared Danny to be in exile, no longer welcome ever again in the Sephardic community, not just in Brooklyn, but at large. The Sephardic community collectively was adamant in taking a stand with dozens of well respected members openly condemning some of the archaic ways in which the men conducted themselves. If any good came out of the trial, it was to encourage both the men and the women in the community to make sweeping changes.

When Fay took the stand, 1justice was finally served. As she began to speak, every eye and ear was trained on her.

"Your honor, members of the jury, thank you for this opportunity today to let me speak my truth. It took me a very long time to get here, but here I am today. Let me be clear, for the record, I seek no civil damages or compensation of any kind. I am well aware that the statute of limitations has expired and that is perfectly fine. If you will indulge me, I will draw a parallel to my incredible grandmother, a Holocaust survivor who never opted to receive reparations from the German government for her forced labor, incarceration, mental and physical abuse, torture and starvation. She didn't want their blood money and that's exactly how I feel. I don't want my assailant's money, because on some level that means he paid his debt and there is no amount of money that can wipe the slate clean. Danny Salem is a thief. He stole my youth, my innocence, my hopes and my dreams. I was a teenage girl in love with life. I was cultivating my God-given talent as an artist when he robbed me of my future. I was coming to terms as a third generation Holocaust survivor with all that my grandmother endured, trying hard to make sense of man's innate ability to hate blindly and perpetrate so much evil. The timing could not have been worse. Through his actions, he confirmed and corroborated my worst fear: that in any generation, in any country, women are not safe. Danny did not rape me because I was easy or because I am a Jew. He raped me because he was weak, disappointed that his wife did not give him a son. In his insecurity and narcissism, he believed he would appear like less of a man in the eyes of his community, some of whom are still laboring under archaic prejudices against women. So, what did he do? He got drunk and in that state of inebriation, he restored the power he felt his wife had taken from him by giving him a beautiful healthy baby girl instead of a boy, by overpowering a young, naive girl like me. He tried to convince himself that I secretly wanted him too, but nothing could be further from the truth. My parents raised me as an Orthodox girl. I never had a boyfriend or desired one, trusting that my parents knew what was right for me. The tragedy is that I knew Danny, because he was my best friend's brother. When he offered me a ride home that fatal night, he might as well have been my blood brother. When he assaulted me, I begged him to remember who I was, but he chose to silence me. It was quite effective. I chose to remain silent all these years. Not to protect my assailant, but to protect his wife and sister, both of whom are my soul sisters.

It is with their express approval that I stand before you today. They themselves are well-known tireless advocates for battered, abused and victimized women. In my case, when I revealed what happened to me, both of them championed for me to find my voice and tell my story. If I learned anything in all these years, it is that the world is still good and kindness does exist. I am extremely fortunate to have had the unwavering support from wonderful people, all these many years, without whom I would never have survived.

I also stand here today, because my grandmother never faced her assailants in any court and if she knew that I had the chance to do so and didn't, she would be devastated. A person, she told me countless times, has an obligation to seek justice. In my Jewish heritage, it is mandatory: '*tzedek tzedek tirdof*,' it says in Deuteronomy, the fifth book of the Jewish Torah. A Jew is obligated to pursue justice, literally run after it. I would have preferred to keep this to myself and spare my loved ones, but I know that the time to close this chapter is now. I will look back on this day and believe that in spite of the pain my action may have caused some innocent people whom I love dearly, that I did the right thing. Thank you for allowing me to be here today."

When Fay sat down, she felt euphoric. She was finally free. Was it sacrilegious she wondered to compare how she felt in this moment to how her beloved grandmother Ava must have felt when the allies and American soldiers liberated the concentration camps? She, like Bobby, could get on with her life and never look back! And therein the dilemma arose. She wasn't quite sure yet where she wanted to live, considering and weighing all the ties she had to both Israel and America. She knew that she didn't have to decide just yet, confident that ultimately the universe would steer her in the right direction.

56

"In the end, nothing matters more than love."
—Suri Rosenberg, Holocaust survivor, beloved matriarch of her
family

That night, Fay desperately needed to be alone. Ray and May understood that while this was a victory, at best it was a Pyrrhic victory—a win but with so much loss. Over the course of the next few days, Fay deliberated. She lay low, spending time meditating. With both May and Ray's approval and encouragement, Fay then decided to get on a plane and go back to Israel. It had worked for her the first time around and now her parents and beloved grandmother were there as well.

Twenty-four hours later, Fay deplaned and knew she had made the right decision. For now, she needed to be in Israel. As she walked through the airport towards baggage claim, she saw the sign with her name and smiled. Her secretary had sent her a car. As she approached the tall gentleman, she noted how good looking he was, he actually slightly resembled Jared. She was surprised that a religious man with a kippah on his head and sideburns behind his ears was working as a taxi driver. She laughed at herself; she was being judgmental, exactly like her mother and grandmother.

He took her bags, looked at her and said, "Shalom Fay, my name is Baruch."

Fay looked at him and instantly recognized the voice. She dropped whatever was in her hands, her phone and handbag. She began to tremble and was afraid she was hallucinating or worse, that this was a sick joke. "Who are you?" she whispered.

"I am your future, Fay," said Jared. He had become a *baal teshuva* [literally someone who returned] many years before. He had made *aliyah*, emigrating to Israel, all while pursuing his career goals. He was now an inventor with eight patents pending across chemistry and medicine. He was also a frequent guest lecturer at the renowned Technion–Israel Institute of Technology in Haifa and widely known for his tireless efforts to turn Tel Aviv into a global tech hot spot. There were rumors about him being a candidate for a Nobel Prize for his work on a battery-operated device to help paraplegics walk again. When Ray called him that morning to tell him about the trial and Fay's triumph, he knew this was the turning point for both of them.

Fay stood there in shock, literally incapable of speaking or breathing.

"You are wondering how I got here?" he prompted her gently. "I, too, had my own complicated journey, Fay. I loved my life, but it was barren, devoid of any meaning. And more so when you abruptly cut off any possibility of a relationship with me. At first I didn't think about what was really troubling me, besides losing you. But eventually, it dawned on me. You were absolutely right—my parents and grandparents took away the most beautiful part of our heritage from me, because that was what was right for them. This, though, being *frum*, religious, is what's right for me and I hope you know that you have always been right for me."

Fay smiled at him. Ironically, the last word Danny ever said to May was exactly what Fay said to Baruch at that moment: "shalom."

They left the airport together and never spent another day apart. Their small, intimate wedding took place in Bobby Ava's courtyard. Baruch's family from all over Israel, Florida and California were there, as were Fay's great-aunts Kati and Zita, May and her daughters, Ray and Sammy and their twins, Judy, Magda and her husband, all of

Fay's cousins, Hinda-Baila, Chava-Sara and her entire family, Victoria and the BenAdins. Fay even arranged for Ibu and Mimi to attend briefly, with their home health attendants and a paramedic team on standby if they required medical assistance. Fay never forgot that these two women were her de facto grandmothers when she unbearably missed her own grandmother and she was grateful that they could give her their blessings, however brief.

Rabbi Shanzer married them according to Jewish law and beamed with pride when he handed Fay her *ketubah*, the marriage contract.

"With your kind indulgence, I will say a few words now," he said in perfect English. "I have married many couples in my lifetime, but this one gives me personally a sense of joy I have never felt before. It is customary, when blessing the bride and groom, to reflect on their parentage. I look at you, Suzi and Zak Zweig, and I know enough. I remember the countless phone calls you each made to me, pleading with me to look out for your daughter. I remember the first time I met Fay. Even in her darkest moment, she had an air about her of one who would overcome. I felt a kinship with her, as I, too, am a descendant of Holocaust survivors. Only in my family, we never spoke about any of it. I knew Fay was mature and wise beyond her years from my first encounter with her. She knew exactly what she was going to do, in order to move on with her life. And indeed she did. And eventually, her *joie de vivre,* her zest for life came back. You all know it's contagious, right? And when I praised her countless good deeds and the enormous impact on my community, she repeatedly downplayed who she was and spoke only of her grandmother. That leads me to the matriarch of this beautiful family." He locked eyes for the first time in his life, on a woman other than his wife. As he addressed Ava, he used her full, Hebrew name. "I am in awe of what you, Chava Sarah Kertesz, have achieved. I salute you. I have watched your granddaughter rise to every challenge—big and small—in her life, because you paved the way by setting an example of living a meaningful life, not dwelling on the past and, most importantly, by living a religious life with charity, hope and kindness. If I may be so bold, I will tell you that I am certain that you come from a noble aristocratic family, the likes of which are far and few in between. There is something about you, your daughters and your granddaughters that evokes a sense of camaraderie in my soul. I am so happy to finally make your acquaintance. I am sure I speak for the entire city when I say that we are honored that you have chosen to relocate to Israel. We are blessed by having you in our midst."

Ava's silent tears fell from her face. Rabbi Shanzer was such an eloquent speaker and his words so profound. As she studied his serious face, with the full beard and long *payos* curled neatly behind his ears, it occurred to her that he reminded her of someone. In that instant a thought occurred to her. *What if he was truly family?* She knew she had to find out who his parents were. There had been many cases of sisters and cousins reuniting, not knowing the others had survived the war. *Imagine if he was a relative of a survivor we didn't know existed*, she thought to herself while smiling. The thought chilled her to the bone. She wouldn't rule anything out just yet, life had surely taught her that.

The beautiful bride approached the chuppah with her parents, calm and serene. She was resplendent in her simple but sophisticated white satin gown that her own factory had produced. Every single person in attendance cried tears of happiness when Baruch broke the glass under the chuppah, replicating an ancient tradition. Chava-Sara, lost in thought, vividly recalled the awkward but eager teenage girl who came to help her many years ago to complete her mandatory charity hours. To see her now, happy and whole, was a true miracle.

Every single woman who had ever worked for AvaFay—past and present—was invited to the spectacular *sheva brachot* dinner party the next night, hosted by Ava and her sisters in the King David Hotel. It was a veritable feast, with Hinda-Baila in her element, bullying the Israeli hotel banquet manager into arranging everything to her liking. It was a celebration that would long be remembered by all.

As the guests mingled, sipping champagne and anxiously awaiting the arrival of the newlyweds, Ava, at nearly 90 years of age, dazzling in her beaded gown, triumphantly said to her daughters, "I knew all along that this boy vas Hungarian."

All three started laughing. Age had certainly not changed their mother at all.

"Mamuka," said Magda to her mother while rolling her eyes at Suzi and Judy. "He is not Hungarian, actually, newsflash, he's American."

Ava looked at her daughter in mock horror and shook her head slowly. "Really, Magdushka? Haven't I taught you anything by now? Who else but a romantic Hungarian man vould vait so long for his beloved? A Polish man? An American? Never." She said it with such conviction that Magda let her have the last word. "He reminds me of my Lajos," continued Ava while looking at the newlyweds who had just walked in. She looked at her newest grandson, handsome in his black suit, Borsalino hat and white satin bow tie and was pleased. Only this morning, she had found out quite accidentally from Mrs. BenAdin that Baruch was the president of one of the biggest tech companies in Israel. "Handsome, religious and rich," she chortled to herself. "My favorite combination."

She then scrutinized her beloved Fay in her Ahuva custom-made wig, crafted of the finest human hair, wearing an elegant Alexander McQueen bias-cut silhouette black knit dress with an asymmetric hem that fell below the knee and Louboutin nude high heels that were overnighted by FedEx from New York. Ava smiled in utter delight and approval. This was exactly how a *kallah* was supposed to dress. She hoped Judy was paying close attention, because her girls were such tomboys, wearing jeans and t-shirts all the time. Ava sighed and mentally made a note to have a serious talk with Judy.

Then she cleared her throat and said to her immediate family, "Finally, this day has arrived and I get to see my Fay married. I vas so vorried about her. I used to cry night after night, asking Imre what went wrong with our beautiful Fay. And Imre—he should rest in peace in Gan Eden—he always told me the same thing: 'in the right time, in the right place, she will find true love and happiness.' Now I know why it took this long and I am so glad Imre was spared. This vould have killed him... But girls, today is a *simcha*, a joyous day, one we will long remember. In Auschwitz, for 11 long months, I told myself the same thing every single day: as long as I am alive, I will live to see another day."

She waved off the offer of an arm from her devoted daughters Suzi, Magda and Judy and jauntily walked over, on her own two feet, to greet the newly wedded professor and Mrs. Baruch Natan. Indeed, she had lived to see this day.

ABOUT THE AUTHOR

Born in Brooklyn, New York, Elizabeth Rosenberg acquired a Masters and Doctoral degree researching the ramifications of the transmission of trauma from Holocaust survivor to their offspring.

The author considers herself fortunate to have been raised by Holocaust Survivor parents who — in spite of the horrific trauma they endured — role modeled empathy, compassion, faith and resilience. As such, the author derives enormous happiness amongst her beloved children and grandchildren and extended family of sisters, nieces and nephews and cousins, a commitment and dedication to clients, anticipates new experiences and challenges, and her career as an inspiring author.

Readers are encouraged to share their thoughts and comments with the author by contacting her at:

toliveanotherday1945@gmail.com.

The author is available to speak at forums holding discussions related to epigenetics and the transmission of trauma, post-traumatic growth and resilience, 2nd and 3rd generation survivors of the Holocaust and women's rights.

AMSTERDAM PUBLISHERS
HOLOCAUST LIBRARY

The series **Holocaust Survivor Memoirs World War II** consists of the following autobiographies of survivors:

Outcry. Holocaust Memoirs, by Manny Steinberg

Hank Brodt Holocaust Memoirs. A Candle and a Promise, by Deborah Donnelly

The Dead Years. Holocaust Memoirs, by Joseph Schupack

Rescued from the Ashes. The Diary of Leokadia Schmidt, Survivor of the Warsaw Ghetto, by Leokadia Schmidt

My Lvov. Holocaust Memoir of a twelve-year-old Girl, by Janina Hescheles

Remembering Ravensbrück. From Holocaust to Healing, by Natalie Hess

Wolf. A Story of Hate, by Zeev Scheinwald with Ella Scheinwald

Save my Children. An Astonishing Tale of Survival and its Unlikely Hero, by Leon Kleiner with Edwin Stepp

Holocaust Memoirs of a Bergen-Belsen Survivor & Classmate of Anne Frank, by Nanette Blitz Konig

Defiant German - Defiant Jew. A Holocaust Memoir from inside the Third Reich, by Walter Leopold with Les Leopold

In a Land of Forest and Darkness. The Holocaust Story of two Jewish Partisans, by Sara Lustigman Omelinski

Holocaust Memories. Annihilation and Survival in Slovakia, by Paul Davidovits

From Auschwitz with Love. The Inspiring Memoir of Two Sisters' Survival, Devotion and Triumph Told by Manci Grunberger Beran & Ruth Grunberger Mermelstein, by Daniel Seymour

Remetz. Resistance Fighter and Survivor of the Warsaw Ghetto, by Jan Yohay Remetz

My March Through Hell. A Young Girl's Terrifying Journey to Survival, by Halina Kleiner with Edwin Stepp

Roman's Journey, by Roman Halter

Memoirs by Elmar Rivosh, Sculptor (1906-1967). Riga Ghetto and Beyond, by Elmar Rivosh

---

The series **Holocaust Survivor True Stories WWII** consists of the following biographies:

Among the Reeds. The true story of how a family survived the Holocaust, by Tammy Bottner

A Holocaust Memoir of Love & Resilience. Mama's Survival from Lithuania to America, by Ettie Zilber

Living among the Dead. My Grandmother's Holocaust Survival Story of Love and Strength, by Adena Bernstein Astrowsky

Heart Songs. A Holocaust Memoir, by Barbara Gilford

Shoes of the Shoah. The Tomorrow of Yesterday, by Dorothy Pierce

Hidden in Berlin. A Holocaust Memoir, by Evelyn Joseph Grossman

Separated Together. The Incredible True WWII Story of Soulmates Stranded an Ocean Apart, by Kenneth P. Price, Ph.D.

The Man Across the River. The incredible story of one man's will to survive the Holocaust, by Zvi Wiesenfeld

If Anyone Calls, Tell Them I Died. A Memoir, by Emanuel (Manu) Rosen

The House on Thrömerstrasse. A Story of Rebirth and Renewal in the Wake of the Holocaust, by Ron Vincent

Dancing with my Father. His hidden past. Her quest for truth. How Nazi Vienna shaped a family's identity, by Jo Sorochinsky

The Story Keeper. Weaving the Threads of Time and Memory - A Memoir, by Fred Feldman

Krisia's Silence. The Girl who was not on Schindler's List, by Ronny Hein

Defying Death on the Danube. A Holocaust Survival Story, by Debbie J. Callahan with Henry Stern

A Doorway to Heroism. A decorated German-Jewish Soldier who became an American Hero, by Rabbi W. Jack Romberg

The Shoemaker's Son. The Life of a Holocaust Resister, by Laura Beth Bakst

The Redhead of Auschwitz. A True Story, by Nechama Birnbaum

Land of Many Bridges. My Father's Story, by Bela Ruth Samuel Tenenholtz

Creating Beauty from the Abyss. The Amazing Story of Sam Herciger, Auschwitz Survivor and Artist, by Lesley Ann Richardson

On Sunny Days We Sang. A Holocaust Story of Survival and Resilience, by Jeannette Grunhaus de Gelman

Painful Joy. A Holocaust Family Memoir, by Max J. Friedman

I Give You My Heart. A True Story of Courage and Survival, by Wendy Holden

In the Time of Madmen, by Mark A. Prelas

Monsters and Miracles. Horror, Heroes and the Holocaust, by Ira Wesley Kitmacher

Flower of Vlora. Growing up Jewish in Communist Albania, by Anna Kohen

Aftermath: Coming of Age on Three Continents. A Memoir, by Annette Libeskind Berkovits

Not a real Enemy. The True Story of a Hungarian Jewish Man's Fight for Freedom, by Robert Wolf

Zaidy's War. Four Armies, Three Continents, Two Brothers. One Man's Impossible Story of Endurance, by Martin Bodek

The Glassmaker's Son. Looking for the World my Father left behind in Nazi Germany, by Peter Kupfer

The Apprentice of Buchenwald. The True Story of the Teenage Boy Who Sabotaged Hitler's War Machine, by Oren Schneider

Good for a Single Journey, by Helen Joyce

Burying the Ghosts, by Sonia Case

American Wolf. From Nazi Refugee to American Spy. A True Story, by Audrey Birnbaum

Bipolar Refugee. A Saga of Survival and Resilience, by Peter Wiesner

---

The series **Jewish Children in the Holocaust** consists of the following autobiographies of Jewish children hidden during WWII in the Netherlands:

Searching for Home. The Impact of WWII on a Hidden Child, by Joseph Gosler

See You Tonight and Promise to be a Good Boy! War memories, by Salo Muller

Sounds from Silence. Reflections of a Child Holocaust Survivor, Psychiatrist and Teacher, by Robert Krell

Sabine's Odyssey. A Hidden Child and her Dutch Rescuers, by Agnes Schipper

The Journey of a Hidden Child, by Harry Pila and Robin Black

The series **New Jewish Fiction** consists of the following novels, written by Jewish authors. All novels are set in the time during or after the Holocaust.

The Corset Maker. A Novel, by Annette Libeskind Berkovits

Escaping the Whale. The Holocaust is over. But is it ever over for the next generation? by Ruth Rotkowitz

When the Music Stopped. Willy Rosen's Holocaust, by Casey Hayes

Hands of Gold. One Man's Quest to Find the Silver Lining in Misfortune, by Roni Robbins

The Girl Who Counted Numbers. A Novel, by Roslyn Bernstein

There was a garden in Nuremberg. A Novel, by Navina Michal Clemerson

The Butterfly and the Axe, by Omer Bartov

To Live Another Day. A Novel, Elizabeth Rosenberg

A Worthy Life. A Novel, by Dahlia Moore

The series **Holocaust Heritage** consists of the following memoirs by 2G:

The Cello Still Sings. A Generational Story of the Holocaust and of the Transformative Power of Music, by Janet Horvath

The Fire and the Bonfire. A Journey into Memory, by Ardyn Halter

The Silk Factory: Finding Threads of My Family's True Holocaust Story, by Michael Hickins

———

The series **Holocaust Books for Young Adults** consists of the following novels, based on true stories:

The Boy behind the Door. How Salomon Kool Escaped the Nazis. Inspired by a True Story, by David Tabatsky

Running for Shelter. A True Story, by Suzette Sheft

The Precious Few. An Inspirational Saga of Courage based on True Stories, by David Twain with Art Twain

———

The series **WW2 Historical Fiction** consists of the following novels, some of which are based on true stories:

Mendelevski's Box. A Heartwarming and Heartbreaking Jewish Survivor's Story, by Roger Swindells

A Quiet Genocide. The Untold Holocaust of Disabled Children WW2 Germany, by Glenn Bryant

The Knife-Edge Path, by Patrick T. Leahy

Brave Face. The Inspiring WWII Memoir of a Dutch/German Child, by I. Caroline Crocker and Meta A. Evenbly

When We Had Wings. The Gripping Story of an Orphan in Janusz Korczak's Orphanage. A Historical Novel, by Tami Shem-Tov

Jacob's Courage: A Holocaust Love Story, by Charles S. Weinblatt

Want to be an AP book reviewer?

Reviews are very important in a world dominated by the social media and social proof. Please drop us a line if you want to join the *AP review team* and show us at least one review already posted on Amazon for one of our books. info@amsterdampublishers.com

Ingram Content Group UK Ltd.
Milton Keynes UK
UKHW040639190323
418778UK00014B/233/J

9 789493 322059